EDMUND L. PALMER

Monk and Me

*a story of the
Golden Twenties*

The General Store Press
Ann Arbor, MI

ISBN-13: 978-0-615-34844-5

Credits:
The poem "Richard Cory" on page 48 is by Edwin Arlington Robinson (1869-1935). It was published in 1922 by Jessie B. Rittenhouse, in *The Second Book of Modern Verse*.

The song "My Buddy" on page 237 was published in 1922 in the *Walter Donaldson Songbook* by Hal Leonard. The lyrics were written by Gus Kahn.

The poem "Abou Ben Adhem" on page 253-4 was first published for the public in 1838. It was written by James Henry Leigh Hunt (1784-1859).

The illustrations in this book were drawn by the author, with these exceptions: Stephen Brown created the illustrations on pages 42 and 100, and contributed to that on page 41. Nico Curtis created the section-opening illustrations on pages 1, 25, 165, 177, 187, and 239.

ACKNOWLEDGMENTS

T he concept of *Monk and Me* began with a few random thoughts on a yellow pad, progressed to a possible short story, and then insisted on becoming a novel. I had great fun writing the story, but that was the easy part. My wife Elaine not only offered me encouragement, but labored countless hours transforming my scribblings into crisp computer pages.

Our wonderful friends, Gail Ryan and her multi-talented daughter, Erin Lichtenstein, then made valued suggestions, edited, formatted, and made the story ready for publication.

Without these three persistent, dedicated, and supportive women, *Monk and Me* would be just a figment of my imagination.

Edmund L. Palmer
Ann Arbor, Michigan

Monk and Me

PADDY

1935

CHAPTER ONE

I t was one of those deceitful July midwestern mornings in 1935. The dewy coolness suggesting promise of relief was just a sham and would soon be replaced by the energy-sapping heat that curled leaves and set tempers on edge. By eleven o'clock each morning the slightest exertion sent droplets of perspiration trickling down the twin avenues along the spine.

I backed my two-year-old Ford company sedan onto 23rd Street, joined the intermittent traffic on Cermak Road and picked up Indianapolis Boulevard to U.S. Route 12. The highway, once the meandering trail of the Sauk Indians, was now the main link between Chicago and Detroit.

On the back seat rested two leather cases. The worn brown Samsonite held toiletry items, a seersucker suit, extra pants, shirts, socks and changes of underwear for seven days on the road. The second, a business briefcase, opened to organized files of brochures, pictures and price lists depicting the offerings of the Gold Bond Tool and Pneumatic Lift Company of East Chicago, Indiana. I was starting my tenth year as business rep for the company's northern Indiana and southern Michigan districts. A small black box-like leather case resembling a woman's vanity occupied the right front seat. Only those with specialized skills would immediately recognize the purpose of the tools within. Wrapped in heavy black velvet beneath the tools lay a blue steel Smith & Wesson revolver, $5,000 in bills of large denominations and a short list of names and addresses.

Earlier that morning I had awakened in the narrow two-story wood frame of my birthplace on the south side of Cicero – an enclave of Chicago long favored by gangster Alphonse Capone until he was convicted and imprisoned four years before for income tax evasion. Now the pleasant city of trees was a haven for the illicit business operations of Frank Nitti, Capone's one-time protégé and "enforcer."

I had showered and dressed, then joined my mother for my usual breakfast of fruit, toast, milk, and wheat cereal, a healthy habit formed during my days as Roosevelt High's starting quarterback a decade and a half earlier. My younger brother and my baby sister had long since departed from home and established families of their own. It wasn't how I planned to live my life, but after my father died unexpectedly in 1921, the obligation to care for my mother grew stronger and was now a way of life.

The droning of the V-8 motor, the endless miles of field corn in regimented rows and the monotony of the white ribbon of dancing concrete induced a feeling of relaxation and introspection. I allowed my mind to drift back to the days of my youth. As usual, my first thoughts were of Monk Harpinski, a boyhood pal and constant companion. We first became close buddies when we were twelve or thirteen and altar boys at St. Francis of Assisi on Central Avenue and 23rd Street. Monk, me and a kid named Gussie Montrono, who had moved to Cicero from Detroit in the fifth grade, shared the honor each Sunday of transferring the consecrated communion hosts, wine, incense, candles, gold chalices and altar cloth from the sacristy to the altar. We also helped Father Gambarelli with his vestments and later passed the collection plates. I remember at that time some of the boys admired Monk for having a fast hand and an innocent face. After church Monk was always good for a bag of chocolate eclairs at Kessler's Bakery on Laramie Avenue.

A couple of Sundays before Christmas, Father Gambarelli became suspicious and gave old man Gus Perishino a five spot and told him to drop it in Monk's collection plate. As Monk was delivering the take, Father Gambarelli gave Brother O'Hanlon the high sign and he took Monk into the vestry and strip-searched him. Of course Brother O'Hanlon didn't find the fiver because Monk always seemed to be one jump ahead of his adversaries. As it turned out, Monk had slapped the fin on the bottom of his tennis shoe with a wad of Blackjack chewing gum. On Monday morning, Monk's ma came storming into the church with blood in her eye, dragging her son by the arm. She demanded, in that high shrill voice of hers, that both Father Gambarelli and Brother O'Hanlon apologize and tell her and Monk they made a terrible mistake. She said, "Just look at him – a innocent little kid who would never steal no money from the church he serves an' loves." The Padre knew he was beaten, but he must have been sure he was right because from then on Monk passed the plate in the row next to the altar, and you could see Father Gambarelli keeping a close eye on him. I remember we didn't stop at Kessler's Bakery after church for a month or two until things quieted down.

Monk loved to tell that story. He would always end by saying "I bet Brother O'Hanlon and the Padre still wonder what happened to that fiver. I hope they don't think ol' Gus Perishino kept it!"

I chuckled at the memory and refocused on the road in front of me. My attention was soon drawn away again by a couple of kids tossing a football in a field beside the road. That made my thoughts drift back in time again, to what might have been – to the fall football season of my senior year at Roosevelt High and the expectations of possible scholarship offers.

Free time that summer was spent working out with weights, completing rigorous mobility calisthenics, and sharpening my passing skills. Monk centered the ball and ran passing patterns in the weedy lot adjacent to my house. We both yelled praise for each other's athleticism and proffered good-humored taunts for overthrown or misjudged passes. Three mornings a week Monk drove his Ford runabout to the Hawthorne Race Course on South Laramie Street where track steward Tony Lazeroni permitted me to run the half-mile oval while Monk used Tony's official stop-watch. One morning in his office Tony said, "Kid, I made $1,200 bucks on them eight wins you had last season, and I expect to double my take this year. You keep in shape, let me know how you feel each week before the game and if there are any key team injuries." That didn't seem like an unreasonable request and I promised to keep in touch.

The season began as expected with wins over Berwyn, Brookfield and River Forest. My dad, Tipper O'Brian, made every game and kept detailed records of my passes attempted and completed, yardage gained in the air and on the ground and, of course, my points scored. By the first week of November, everyone was saying that I would smash all existing Chicago area school-boy records before the season ended. Late on a Sunday morning after the 49-12 win over a powerful Skokie team, the legendary University of Chicago football coach Amos Alonzo Stagg knocked on my front door in Cicero. After presenting his credentials and apologizing for calling on a Sunday, Coach Stagg praised my athletic skills, academic excellence and community service. He said my many-faceted achievements and character would qualify me for admission to the University of Chicago – and to a full football scholarship. Then with a wink to my dad, Coach Stagg said, "I must admit, I have a personal reason for wanting your boy Paddy in our program. I believe your son has the ability to make the first team in his freshman year and would help us wrestle the Big Ten Conference title from my old nemesis, Coach Fielding Yost and the great University of Michigan team."

After enjoying a large mug of Irish "coffee" and indulging in pleasant small talk, Coach Stagg pulled out his vest pocket watch and said, "Mr. and Mrs. O'Brian, at this point all I need is a signed letter of intent from you and a gentleman's agreement from Paddy and I can start the scholarship paperwork moving. I can't offer any remuneration as that would be against the Big Ten Conference rules, but I can offer Paddy an opportunity for an education at a world-class school. The scholarship includes all university fees, books, and housing. Paddy can cover his food expenses bussing tables in the team dining room, and I have friends who will help him obtain a part-time job as night watchman from eight to eleven p.m. weekdays in the University Museum – an excellent quiet place for study. Please take your time and talk my offer over among yourselves, and whether you accept or not, I want to congratulate you as a family for Paddy's achievements. I know parenting isn't an easy task, Mr. and Mrs. O'Brian, but you two have done admirably well." With those happy thoughts, Coach Stagg said he looked forward to the possibility of working with me during the upcoming summer's practice sessions. Within moments, the black, chauffeur-driven Studebaker sedan left the curbside of middle class Cicero for the other world of Hyde Park on the lake.

I was brought back to reality by a hissing radiator and a rapidly rising dashboard temperature gauge. Within a mile or two, the familiar blue-and-white sign of a Double D two-pump gasoline station came into view.

As my little Ford V-8 came to a stop, the knocking, steaming, overburdened engine continued to run, even with the ignition turned off. A stooped middle-aged man rubbing grease-stained hands on his dirty Oshkosh overalls ambled out and appraised the situation. In a slight drawl, sounding more northern Kentucky than Michiganese, he said, "It peers like you all is another victum of the Michigan mid-day

The familiar blue-and-white sign of a Double D two-pump gasoline station came into view.

heebie-geebies. Keep her runnin' and pull over to thet there water hose an' I'll cool yer monster down 'fore I yank off the raadeator cap. I got some green five-gallon army surplus water cans inside fer 85 cents each, an' you'd do well ta stash one in yer trunk if'in yer goin' any distance."

Before I could respond the old gent had begun spraying the radiator with cool water and said, "How do ya like ol' Henry's V-8? It goes like a scalded rooster, but I bet ya add a quart a' oil fer ever' tank or two a' gas. It's them damn Hollner piston rings that let the oil blow back inta the exhaust manifold. 'Course the bank robbers Bonnie an' Clyde an' John Dillinger kinda liked it 'cause they could lay down a black smoke screen by rammin' her in second gear an' floorin' the accelerator durin' their getaways. They's one thing I 'specially like 'bout the '33 an' '34 V-8's, though. It's them suicide front doors that open from the front. When ladies come in fer service an' get out ya kin see almost clear up to their bellybuttons. 'Course I ain't much interested when my misses is keepin' an eye on me. By the way, speakin' 'bout that Mr. Dillinger, he was a fine upstandin' gent. He was in here 'bout a year ago an' standin' almost zackly where you is now. We jawed a while an' he said he was headin' back to Indiana ta see his daddy on the family farm. After I checked his oil an' tires an' filled his tank with ethyl he give me a twenty an' says ta keep the change. He couldn't hardly believe it when I said, 'Mr. Dillinger, I'd rather have a ten spot if you'd sign yer name on it.' He laughed when I tol' him I couldn't afford keepin' a twenty outta circulation. That tenner is pinned on the wall in back a' the cash register, if ya got time ta have a gander at it. I was plumb upset when I heared them Feds gunned him down in Chicago last summer. He never took nothin' from people like me – just from them rich sons-a-bitches in banks. He was a nice gent," the old man said, his voice trailing off.

I walked over to the red Coca Cola soda pop cooler. It sat no higher than my waist and was flanked on either side by eight quarts of green motor oil in wire carriers. I lifted one side of the double-hinged cooler lid and swished my hand and arm into the cold ice water until coming up with a familiar glass bottle of Nehi grape soda. Popping off the steel cap, I tipped the bottle up and enjoyed a long refreshing drink. The old man had finished cooling the radiator and followed me into the rectangular room attached to the outside grease pit. He said, "That grape is my favorite too. I bet we sell ten a' them to ever' orange an' strawberry."

The pleasant masculine odor of the room was a mixture of new tires on overhead racks, twenty or thirty Firestone and Goodyear fanbelts hanging on the side wall, an open 30-gallon drum of grease, and a Lucky Strike cigarette smoldering in a "See Niagara Falls" glass ashtray. A large orange tabby cat with white chest and paws lay contentedly asleep on the back counter. The three-sided glass display case to the right of the register contained two boxes of cigars – King Edwards priced at two for a nickel and dark rum crooks with twisted shanks at five cents each. Green-packaged Lucky Strikes, as well as Camels and Kool cigarettes sold for fifteen cents, while Spuds and Twenty Grand were a bargain at ten cents. Baby Ruth and Butterfinger candy bars competed with Beeman's Pepsin, Clark's Teaberry and Wrigley Juicy Fruit gum. Valve caps, pressure valves, ignition feeler gauges, innertube patching kits and Delco Ramy spark plugs partially hid small square packages of Trojan prophylactics.

I was impressed with the ten-dollar bill pinned to the back wall. The inked handwriting across Alexander Hamilton's face and body clearly read,

> "To my good friend, Opie Cantrill, with best wishes,
> John Dillinger"

As I drained the last drop of grape soda, I said, "Mr. Cantrill…" The old man stopped me in mid-sentence. "Folks 'round these parts jus' call me Opie an' that suits me jus' fine. 'Mr. Cantrill' makes me sound more like a' undertaker or bank president. What's yer moniker?" "My given name is Patrick O'Brian, but people have called me Paddy for as long as I can remember." "Paddy it is then. What kind a' business you in Paddy, if you don't mind my askin'?" "I've been a sales rep with the Gold Bond Tool and Pneumatic Lift Company in East Chicago, Indiana for about ten years. Have you ever heard of us?"

"Oh, hell yes," Opie replied. "As a matter of fact, I got a set a Gold Bond end wrenches nobody could pry away from me. Say, Paddy, you bein' in the auto tool business, in a manner of speakin', I got somethin' out back I think you might be interested in, if you got a few minutes to spare." I confirmed that I did have time and followed Opie into a surprisingly well-equipped room adjacent to his "office." A drill press rested on a seven-foot long workbench with an array of hand tools hanging on the wall behind it. A metal-turning lathe occupied a space in front of the bench, but the object of interest was a six- cylinder engine on a motor mount frame perpendicular to the rear outside wall. A flexible metal pipe extended from the exhaust headers through the exterior wall. Opie's eyes brightened when he saw the expression on my face. "Thet's a '33 Dodge six I got from Skip Richter's junk yard over in White Pigeon. It come from a car that was totaled 'bout six months ago. The ol' man pulled in front of a gravel truck an' he an' his missus was killed instantly. Skip give it to me for $35 an' all I had to do was put in a new raadeator, fan assembly an' water pump. 'Course everythin' from the transmission back was ripped off, but I didn't have no need fer that stuff anyways. I'm gonna rev her up an' I want you to check her over an' tell me if ya see anythin' at all thet's different."

Opie opened a petcock on a brass line extending from a 15-gallon gas tank to the carburetor of the mounted engine. With an almost effortless turn of the crank, the engine burst into life. Opie let it run for about five minutes at a simulated speed of 35 miles an hour and then shut it down. I checked the engine over carefully and said, "Well, Opie, the only thing I can see that's different is the ten-inch steel cylinder attached to the right side of the motor and tied into the oil return pipe. Is it some kind of a filter?"

Opie fairly hopped up and down and said, "Paddy, you is one smart guy." He then turned a wing nut off the cylinder top, popped off the rubber gasket-protected cap and pulled out a black gooey mess.

"What in the hell is that, Opie?" Opie grinned, put the mess on a folded *Kalamazoo Gazette* and said, "Thet, my friend, is two five-cent rolls a' Woolworth's best toilet paper." He then checked in a notebook and said, "Thet Dodge 6 has run fer thirty hours at 35 miles a' hour an' the oil has what would amount to 1,050 miles on it. Now I want ya to pull the dip stick, rub some oil between yer fingers, and smell it." I followed Opie's directions and said with amazement, "Opie, that oil is a beautiful honey color, as slick as warm butter, and smells like it just came out of a new barrel. Unbelievable! Have you tried to market your idea?"

"I'm afraid to do it, Paddy; bein' in the gasoline an' garage business I know outfits like Delco, Autolite, O. T. Stevens – companies like them thets in the oil filter business, an' people like Standard Oil, Mobil an' Texaco who supply oil would put me outta business – or worse. Them gasoline companies try to convince people they got ta change filters an' oil ever' 1,000 miles. With my filter you could drive 1,500-2,000 miles an' jus' pop in a coupla five-cent rolls a' toilet paper. Not only thet, but ya don't never have to put new oil in. Them oil an' filter fellas would be as sore at me as a dog which cornered a' upset porcupine."

I shook my head in amazement and said, "Opie, you are one ingenious fellow and I'm mighty happy my motor overheated so I could get to know you. I'll tell you what, if it suits you I'll tell my company executives about your filter and if they are interested you won't have to worry about the big gasoline or filter companies. You and your missus will be able to retire in Kentucky; you could just sit back, hunt 'coon and drink white lightning." "I think I could get used ta thet, Paddy, but how'd ya know I was from Kentucky?"

"Just a guess by your accent, Opie. What part of the state are you from?"

"I was born and raised on a farm a few miles east a' the little village of Milton on the Ohio River. Me and the missus hope to go back someday an' raise a few chickens, have a little garden and a coupla milk cows. You go ahead an' tell your people what I got. Maybe somethin' good will come of it."

Opie flicked off the lights in the workroom and motioned me into the office. "I've been meanin' to ask ya, Paddy, livin' an' workin' all them years in Chicago, did ya ever chanct ta see or meet Mr. Dillinger, Baby Face Nelson, or fellas like that?" I gave him a serious look and said, "Opie, I know you thought highly of John Dillinger and if you'd like, I'll tell you all I know about Dillinger, his gang and those involved in his untimely death." Opie said, "I'd be obliged ta know the truth about it, Paddy, but first let me call the missus and have her bring over some cold chicken sandwiches and ice lemonade." Opie cranked two long and three short rings on the wall phone and talked with Mrs. Cantrill.

A few moments later a Hudson Terraplane sedan pulled up to the ethyl pump and the driver honked his horn impatiently. Opie, mumbling under his breath, took his time ambling out to the pump. In short order, a sixtyish looking woman entered the room carrying a tray against her chest. She bent slightly and bumped the door closed with her hip. Mrs. Cantrill was of medium height, slender, with gray-streaked black hair pulled back into a bun and a complexion probably darkened more by genetics than by the sun. Her high cheekbones and black eyes suggested an Indian heritage. When I thanked her for bringing the lunch, she gave an embarrassed little smile, said she was pleased and slipped silently out the door.

Opie was followed into the office by a perspiring, fat, baldheaded man mopping his face and grumbling about the heat. He asked for two rum crook cigars, a package of Beeman's gum and a three-count package of Trojan rubbers. With a self-conscious laugh he said, "I ain't no boy scout, but I'm always prepared. How much do I owe ya?" Opie answered in a businesslike voice without a trace of humor, "Thet comes to a total a' two dollars and forty cents, includin' 9½ gallons a' ethyl." As the man left, Opie turned the cardboard "Open" sign to "Closed" and hooked the screen door. He wiped the beads of moisture off his cold lemonade glass with an orange grease cloth and settled back in his ancient rocker.

I began, "Opie, what I'm about to tell you is 90% personal knowledge and 10% fact or fiction reported in the Chicago papers. You'll hear the good and the bad – warts and all. You asked if I had seen or knew John Dillinger. The answer is yes. I not only knew him, I personally knew the three people most responsible for his death. Before I begin though, it's rather ironic, but the very model Terraplane you just serviced was the one Dillinger preferred as a getaway car. He began his bank robbing spree using a '31 Ford Model A, but switched because the Terraplane had a faster pickup and could go about four miles an hour faster." I went on. "In May, 1933 Dillinger was paroled from the Indiana State Prison in Michigan City, Indiana after serving nine years for the brutal assault and robbery of a local grocery store owner. At that time he was a twenty-seven-year-old, small-time hood. I first saw him that summer in some of the honky-tonk saloons in East Chicago favored by Chicago gangsters and lesser hangers-on. I'd stop in for a drink and just fade into the background and watch the action. As their reputations grew, Dillinger and gang members Homer Van Meter, Baby Face Nelson, Eddie Green and Tommy Carroll, would show up about 11 p.m. Sometimes East Chicago police officer

Martin Zarkovich, in street clothes, would be a part of the group. They weren't an unruly bunch – a stranger might think they were businessmen letting off steam. They were all pretty good drinkers – all, that is, except Dillinger. He sat with his back to the wall and nursed a gin fizz while the gang members laughed, joked and bought rounds for the house. Homer Van Meter loved to needle Dillinger and in that loud whiny voice of his reminded him that his favorite Cubbies had just lost three in a row to the Cincinnati Reds – and Leon Warneke got chased in the seventh inning. Dillinger smiled, but I could see he was annoyed.

"I was very impressed with John Dillinger. As you know, he was a good looking guy about 5'9", well-dressed, broad shoulders and slim waist. There was a calmness about him, but his steely blue eyes left no doubt as to who was in charge of the gang. I couldn't help but notice his overall cleanliness and well-groomed hands – in such stark contrast to his companions. If you saw him in a different setting, you might think he was a bank executive rather than a bank robber. Anyway, it wasn't unusual for the East Chicago mayor, city councilmen, and even the police chief to join the fun."

I continued my story as Opie slowly rocked in his chair. "About mid June every summer, the Paradise Pavilion on Lake Michigan in East Chicago opened for the season. The management put on a talent show each Sunday night and a small crowd danced to jukebox music Monday through Thursday. Every Friday and Saturday night, the best dance bands in the country performed – Shep Fields, Ben Bernie, Benny Goodman, Jan Garber and a host of others. The band season lasted until just after Labor Day, and because I loved to dance, and sometimes just listen to great music, I rarely missed a performance. Since my company was only about four blocks from the pavilion, I could finish my paperwork for the week, grab a sandwich and make the opening number by 9 o'clock. About the first week in July two years ago I noticed a pretty little blonde girl who had been showing up each Friday and Saturday night. It was strange though, she was never with a guy and she always left alone at exactly midnight. She loved to dance and drank only one or two Manhattans the entire evening. Even though I knew I was a few years older, I asked her to dance. For the rest of the summer of 1933 I held Polly Hamilton in my arms every Friday and Saturday night, but only until midnight. She insisted on leaving alone, and it wasn't until after Labor Day when the pavilion was converted into a roller skating rink did I meet her during the daytime. Even then I had to content myself by holding her close while we skated. We never had what would be called a regular date. When the pavilion closed for the year at the end of October, Polly and I drifted apart. I was given the southern Michigan territory so stayed pretty busy throughout the winter and spring. But, in May of last year I got a real shocker."

Opie was now on the edge of his chair. "What happened, Paddy? Did you get in the middle of a gun fight?" "No, Opie, nothing that exciting. During the spring of last year, the East Chicago, Indiana City Council was forced to pass an ordinance banning houses of prostitution and gambling dens, but the politicians and police were much too busy dealing with the needs of the Chicago gangsters to attack so small a mischief. Oh, they closed a few for appearances, but that was about it. The very popular and lucrative bawdy house on the edge of town was run by a 40-year-old woman, Anna Sage. She was born in Rumania and entered the United States illegally when in her teens. Like many immigrants, she didn't apply for American citizenship. She didn't see the need. Within a few years Anna, with the help and protection of East Chicago policeman Martin Zarkovich, established whorehouses in Gary as well as East Chicago. Her undoing, however, began when she crossed the state line and opened a brothel in North Chicago. Now she was dealing in illegal interstate commerce and flaunting the Mann Act – both actions that came under the scrutiny of federal agents. During this time officer Zarkovich became Anna's lover as well as business partner. While I'm not proud of it, I, on occasion, stopped at Anna's during the lunch hour for a beer and one of her famous hamburgers. Whatever else Anna was, she was renowned as a great cook and insisted on preparing the lunch menu as well as baking delicious cream pies. On many occasions I sat at the bar and chatted with patrolman Zarkovich. It was not unusual to also see the city's movers and shakers enjoying lunch and a few drinks. On the day I mentioned that I was shocked – perhaps the word revulsion better describes my feelings – I looked up and saw Polly Hamilton coming down from an upstairs room with Baby Face Nelson. Now I knew why Polly attended dances alone at the pavilion, left at midnight and refused my pleadings for a date. I didn't return to Anna's place of business mainly because I didn't want to run into Polly.

"When the 1934 dance season began again at the pavilion in mid June I found myself watching for Polly, half hoping she wouldn't be there. When she didn't arrive by eleven p.m., I called it a night and drove home. Business kept me out of town for the next two weekends, but on Friday night, July 6, I took in the dance at the pavilion. To my surprise, there was Polly sitting at our special table near the lakeside deck. She looked as bright and beautiful as ever, but as we danced to the Duke Ellington orchestra playing *For All We Know*, I could feel the tenseness in her body. I had already decided to accept her on her terms, knowing we had no future together, when she led me to the outside deck. I thought she was shaking because of the coolness of the evening, but she took both my hands in hers, looked up into my eyes and said, 'Paddy, I've got to tell you something that I know will hurt you. I've fallen in love with a younger man by the name of Jimmy Lawrence. He's a stockbroker's clerk over on La Salle Street by the Loop. I've dreaded this moment, but I knew I had to tell you.' I was filled with mixed emotion – strangely relieved, but saddened by the loss of someone I had come to care for. Polly said it was important to her that I understand, so I bravely wished her well and kissed her lightly on the forehead. She made me promise that I would be at the pavilion the following Friday so I could meet her Jimmy Lawrence. She seemed almost a stranger in my arms as we danced for the last time to the Duke and his beautiful *Solitude*. As the last lingering notes died away Polly Hamilton slipped out the door and I knew my feelings for her would never be the same again.

"Events now began to move very rapidly. Much of what I'm about to tell you, Opie, still comes from my personal knowledge, but I must also rely on stories that appeared daily in the Chicago papers. Dillinger was front-page news and each paper kept a history and running account of his exploits. A lead story in the *Herald Examiner* didn't calm any nerves when it reported that Dillinger and Homer Van Meter had plastic surgery performed by a German doctor – a William Loeser – in late May. The doctor admitted removing forehead moles, burning fingerprints away with hydrochloric acid and altering Dillinger's nose, eyes, cheeks and chin. The doctor bragged that after the job he had done on Van Meter and Dillinger, even their mothers wouldn't recognize them. The *Trib* ran a story stating that from July 17,1933 to June 30, 1934, 26 people were killed, 19 wounded and 23 sentenced to prison during the Dillinger gang spree. It was estimated approximately $300,000 was taken from banks; scores of pistols, rifles, Tommy guns, bullet-proof vests, and thousands of rounds of ammunition were hijacked from police stations. At least one million dollars was spent by the federal and local governments hunting the gang."

Opie, shaking his head slowly from side to side, said, "I had no idear,

Paddy. Me an' the people 'round here thought Dillinger was a kinda hero – a guy which took from the rich and give to the poor, an' mebby jus' kep' a little for hisself."

"You and half the country, Opie." I continued, "I wasn't too keen on meeting Polly's Jimmy Lawrence the next week, but I showed up about 9:30. The place was jumping to Johnny Long's orchestra when I saw Polly and her guy sitting at a table against a far wall. Polly introduced us and Jimmy, half rising, gave me a firm handshake. A pretty waitress came over and I ordered a beer; Jimmy and Polly waved off a refill. I was surprised at how easily and naturally the conversation flowed. Polly and Jimmy were holding hands and when Jimmy learned I was a White Sox fan he kidded me good naturedly about the Sox being a farm team for the Cubs. I countered by saying it was still early in the season, and with Al Simmons batting .344 and George Earnshaw posting eight wins already, it might be a 'streetcar series' between the two Chicago teams. At that moment a young guy came up to the table and asked Jimmy if he might have the next dance with his girlfriend. Jimmy smiled and said, 'Of course, if Polly is agreeable.' Polly hesitated, but Jimmy encouraged her to have some fun.

"When Polly and the young man left, Jimmy said he still felt a little unsteady on his feet since a rather serious auto accident a few weeks back and didn't feel up to dancing. After listening to a few bars of *Love Letters In the Sand*, Jimmy turned to me and said, 'Paddy, I know it was hard for you to come here tonight. Polly has told me what a great friend you have been. I just want to thank you for looking out for her.' What could I say? I'm sure he knew I had had deep feelings for Polly, but he was such a gentleman about it, I just mumbled something like it had been my pleasure and I wished them both every happiness. I drained the last of my beer and said I thought I should be going. As I started to rise, Jimmy put his hand on my arm and said, 'Please stay, Paddy. Polly would be upset if you left without saying good-bye. Let me get you another beer.' I stared dumbly at his carefully groomed hand and sat down.

"As Jimmy walked over to the bar, my mind began to race – about 5'9", broad shoulders, small waist, Chicago Cubs, pink scars on cheeks and nose. My God, I thought, Jimmy Lawrence is the killer, John Dillinger! When 'Jimmy' returned with a beer and a gin fizz my blood ran cold. What should I do? The terror in my voice would be a dead giveaway and running could be fatal. I took a long pull on my beer; at that moment, a rumble broke out near the bandstand. Fists began to fly and a few dancers were caught in the scuffle. I got up to see if Polly was safe just as several special duty East Chicago policemen waded in and attempted to restore order. Polly's dance partner returned her to our table and quickly disappeared. Clearly upset, Polly straightened her dress, patted her hair and asked, 'Where's Jimmy?' The exit door just to our left was open. Multicolored balloons hanging from their silver ceiling cords swayed gently in the cool night breeze. By then Jimmy was long gone, so I walked Polly to the streetcar stop and wished her a good night.

"You know, Opie, the brutal killing of John Dillinger on a steamy Sunday night in Chicago not long after my introduction to 'Jimmy Lawrence' is still surrounded by controversy. I don't suppose we'll ever know the full story. Testimony taken by Chicago police after the night of July 22 in '34 gives us some insight. Polly Hamilton had known Anna Sage for a number of years, both as a friend and prostitute in Anna's brothels. Polly met John Dillinger in a cabaret in mid June, and a whirlwind romance developed. As we know, Dillinger passed himself off as Jimmy Lawrence, a clerk in the brokerage firm of Benson and Shields on La Salle Street. Polly was easily convinced that Jimmy was a farm boy from Indiana who longed to return to the country. He said that as soon as he saved enough money he wanted to return home, buy a chicken ranch, and begin a family. Polly immediately saw a chance to leave her current life and start a new one.

"From what I now understand she scoffed when her girl friends suggested that Jimmy resembled John Dillinger. When she asked about his fresh facial scars and burned fingers Jimmy said he had been in a serious auto accident in early May. When he changed the subject and talked of church suppers back home piled high with fried chicken, creamy mashed potatoes, fresh vegetables and three kinds of pie, Polly was reminded of the great food prepared by her friend, Anna Sage. Anna had recently invited them both to a Sunday dinner at her house on Chicago's north side. The invitation had been eagerly accepted by Jimmy and Polly. After an elaborate meal, topped off with homemade cream pie, the conversation turned to Jimmy's inadequate living quarters. Anna was captivated by Jimmy's outgoing personality. When she suggested Polly and Jimmy move in with her, the offer was immediately accepted. Dillinger, of course, desperately needed a safe hideout.

"Anna became alarmed one day when Jimmy was out and she discovered several weapons, ammunition, and bulletproof vests in a large trunk in his closet. Pictures of Dillinger on the front page of the *Chicago*

Tribune convinced Anna that Jimmy was really John Dillinger. When she confronted him, he admitted he was Dillinger and would move out as soon as he found another location. Anna knew the federal government was planning to deport her on moral turpitude charges and the state of Indiana was investigating corruption in East Chicago which would likely expose her lover and business partner, Sergeant Martin Zarkovich." At this point in the story Opie had a quizzical look on his face and said, "I don't understand thet moral terpertude or whatever it was you said the feds had on Anna." I replied, "Oh, that was a high-sounding word that meant Anna was a whore, and an undesirable person. She was also an illegal from a foreign country. There were two strikes against her and she was becoming desperate.

"When Anna called Sergeant Zarkovich and told him John Dillinger was staying at her place, the two of them hatched a plan to save their skins. Zarkovich contacted federal agent Melvin Purvis and arranged a meeting on Thursday night, July 19. With Zarkovich driving the car, Anna and Purvis conversed in the back seat. Anna said she could deliver John Dillinger if deportation charges against her were dropped and if Sergeant Zarkovich was no longer a target of the Indiana officials. Purvis, while not making any promises, said he would intervene on their behalf with his superiors. He also said they would both receive a portion of the $15,000 reward if Dillinger was apprehended.

"The plan was put into motion. Dillinger particularly enjoyed gangster movies, so when Anna suggested they see *Manhattan Melodrama*, starring Clark Gable, Myrna Loy and young Mickey Rooney, Dillinger eagerly agreed. Perhaps most important to Dillinger, the Biograph Theatre on Lincoln Avenue was just around the corner from Anna's house and boasted that new innovation, refrigerated air. Anna called agent Purvis on Sunday afternoon, July 22, and said the plan was on for that night. She would be wearing an orange skirt and white blouse; her friend, Polly Hamilton, would wear a tan skirt and white blouse. When they came out of the theater after the show, she and her friend would position themselves on either side of Dillinger. Agent Purvis warned Anna to alert her friend and jump aside when he identified himself to Dillinger. His agents and several East Chicago policemen would then quickly move in. Well, it almost worked as they had planned, but as Dillinger and the movie crowd emerged from the theatre, the glint of a revolver caught the killer's eye. He dashed into an adjacent alley and desperately attempted to draw a pistol from his trouser pocket. Five shots were fired – three bullets tore into Dillinger's body. The fatal slug entered the back of his neck and emerged under his right eye. Anna Sage and Polly Hamilton were pushed safely out of harm's way, but two bystanders collapsed with bullet wounds to the legs."

Opie, his left hand over his eyes and shaking his head from side to side, said, "My God, Paddy, they shot him runnin' away. Couldn't them agents a' wrestled him down? It don't seem like they had to kill him."

"You may be right, Opie. It has been speculated that an East Chicago policeman, maybe Sergeant Zarkovich, fired the fatal shot. It would be to his advantage to silence Dillinger so he couldn't talk." Opie rummaged in the top left pocket of his overalls and pulled out a rumpled Camel pack only to find it empty. He arched the spent pack into an empty 5-gallon oil container. Walking stiffly over to the merchandise case next to the cash register, he pulled down the hinged door, reached in, and plucked out a fresh pack of Camels. I watched as Opie carefully tore away a small portion of the silver foil. Three cigarettes emerged as he tapped the pack against his left thumb. He offered a cigarette to me, took one for himself and expertly flicked off the top of a kitchen match with his thumbnail. I leaned forward for a light and Opie tipped his head sideways to protect himself from the flame as he torched his cigarette. Opie inhaled deeply and said, "From what you tol' me Paddy, I know I can't keep thinkin' a' John Dillinger as no hero an' I sure ain't gonna brag him up no more. I guess I'll jus' take thet $10 bill down an' put it away some place in the house. It won't do no harm though if I jus' remember him as a guy who stopped in fer gas an' was real friendly. I suppose gettin' shot an' dyin' fast was better then gettin' put in a' electric chair with people gawkin' at ya. Do you know whatever happened to Anna Sage, Polly Hamilton, an' that Zarkovich fella?"

"Polly disappeared after testifying that she had no knowledge of the Biograph plan, Opie. I believe Sergeant Zarkovich is still on the East Chicago police force. Anna Sage, because her orange skirt glowed red under the marquee lights, became known and hated across the nation as 'The Woman in Red.' She and Zarkovich each received $5,000 reward money. The last I heard she had filed her last appeal and will probably be deported to Rumania.

"Well Opie, I'd better get back on the road if I expect to be in Detroit before dark. It's been a pleasure to get to know you. Thank Mrs. Cantrill for me; the chicken sandwich and cold lemonade really hit the spot. My next time through I'll let you know if my company is interested in your oil filter."

Opie accepted $1.32 for seven gallons of gas, 85 cents for the five-gallon army surplus water can, 60 cents for four quarts of reclaimed motor oil, and 5 cents for two King Edward cigars. He refused payment for cooling down the boiling radiator, the chicken sandwich and lemonade, and the bottle of Nehi grape, saying he'd just charge it off to overhead. Opie leaned down, grasped the window ledge of the Ford and said, "I ment ta tell ya earlier Paddy, I developed a piston ring thet expands with heat. It swipes down the oil on the cylinder wall so it don't escape inta the chamber an' blow out the exhaust. I figger it'l last 20 or 30 thousand miles an' the oil you'll save will pay fer the ring job in the first few hundred miles. If yer interested, give me two or three hours next time yer through. I'll only charge ya time an' parts." "That sounds great, Opie; I'll drop you a postcard before my next swing and look forward to seeing you. Stay well." As the V-8 nosed onto U.S.12, I checked my rearview mirror and saw a bent old man in overalls and railroad engineer's hat waving a dirty orange grease rag and fading in the distance.

T raffic on U.S 12 was moderate at mid-afternoon, and the stifling heat seemed less oppressive with the Ford's wind wings fully opened. Inrushing air helped dry perspiration and blow out the foul odor of the cheap King Edward cigar. The familiar Elkhart-Goshen, Indiana sign pointing south on Route 19 reminded me that Detroit was roughly four hours away. I made a 30-minute stop a few miles east in the tiny village of White Pigeon, lunched at Mom's Family Restaurant and tucked $5,000 in my rented lock box in the Farmers and Mechanics Bank. No one at the bank knew or cared who I was.

Settling in for the not unpleasant drive ahead gave me an opportunity to once again allow my mind to wander back to my earlier years. How different my life might be today if not for those seconds in November of 1921 during the championship game between Roosevelt High and Oak Lawn. The score tied 14-14 late in the fourth quarter; third down, a routine draw play, only three yards for a first down. Del Packard made a perfect snap, and then the guards missed an assignment up front. Two Oak Lawn tackles hit simultaneously. The contact could be heard in the stands. Doctor Turner said he had never seen as severe a knee and leg injury. The right tibia was broken – no, smashed in three places; the patella broken; tendon and ligaments torn and stretched. The prognosis: with surgery and a long rehabilitation, I would walk again, but my football career was over – all in a matter of a second or two on a cold November night.

Coach Stagg was visually upset and deeply concerned. He explained that the Athletic Department was allowed 15 football scholarships. Each scholarship was contingent upon the recipient being physically able to participate in the varsity program. He would request an academic scholarship, but the competition was great and the probability low for the following academic year.

By February, I was walking with a cane, but with missed school time I could not graduate with my class. Dad O'Brian plied his connections and obtained a part-time job for me in Abe Schulenberg's lock and vault shop on Kostner Avenue. Abe was a kindly man in his middle fifties with slightly stooped and round shoulders, wispy hair and a persistent cough. He was an excellent locksmith and commercial bank vault repairman, and had more business than he could handle alone.

I remember with apprehension that first day. Abe said, "Paddy, I've followed your football career the last couple of years. I'm sorry as hell about the leg injury, but I guess it's time to start looking ahead instead of thinking about what might have been. Let's give it a try and see how things work out, if that suits you." I was eager to learn a trade so working afternoons and attending morning classes at Roosevelt High seemed like a perfect combination. At first I waited on customers, but as my rehabilitation at Loyola University Hospital progressed, Abe gave me more responsibility. I became adept at turning a key blank into a finished product as well as using wax impressions to create duplicate keys. I even learned to employ probes to explore the interior of a lock and fabricate a workable key. One afternoon in late May, Abe said I was ready to examine the intricacies of wall safes and bank vaults. I studied numerous books and pamphlets, but the best training by far was on-the-job experience under Abe's guidance and patience. I became familiar with tumbler and bolt action as well as time-release mechanisms.

On August 15, 1922, at 4:15 in the afternoon – I'll never forget the date or time – I received a call at the shop from Mother. Her voice was calm but somewhat higher in pitch. I knew instinctively something was wrong. She asked me to return home as quickly as possible. When I entered the front door, Mother ran to my arms and cried, "Your father's gone, he's gone!" I tried to calm her and at the same time said, "Gone, what do you mean, gone, where?" She lifted her face from my chest and sobbed, "He suffered a massive heart attack in his office shortly before I called you – and now he's gone!"

I vowed after my father's funeral that I would remain with mother for the rest of her days and provide for her every need.

B etween Coldwater and Jonesville I was hailed down by a nervous family standing alongside a 1930 Buick sedan. As I pulled up on the shoulder I asked, "What's the trouble?" An older man, probably the father, said, "Thanks for stopping. We've been stranded for almost an hour. This is not a good start to our beach vacation. I've managed to cool the engine down, but the old girl just won't start. Could I hitch a ride with you to the next town?"

I replied, "Of course, but first, let me make a suggestion. Drench a couple of your beach towels in my 5-gallon water container and wrap them snugly around the carburetor." I explained that I suspected his problem was vapor lock. Within ten minutes, the father hit the starter and grinned broadly as the engine caught and purred contentedly. "Dump the remaining water from my container in your radiator and I think you'll get to the beach without further trouble."

As the relieved family piled into the car the father pulled three rumpled bills from his pocket. I waved him off and said, "I was more than happy to help. Your slight obligation to me can be paid in full when you offer your help to someone down the line. It's just a simple process of giving a little part of yourself away."

T he late daytime gloom of Detroit City was slowly transcending into bright neon as I drove east on Michigan Avenue. Boarded storefronts and alleys piled high with trash gave way to the glimmer of supper clubs, theatre marquees and the throbbing excitement of Cadillac Square. Parking a couple of car lengths from the front of the Milner Hotel on Bagley, I locked my business briefcase in the trunk and carried my suitcase and "specialty" case into the hotel lobby.

Punching the bell on the registration desk brought a stiff-jointed, elderly man from the small adjacent office. I recognized him as Billy G. After I signed in he swung the register around and said, "Paddy O'Brian, – ain't you been here before?" I assured him that I had and we negotiated for a room on the 5th floor at $2.50 a night, with a toilet and bath at the end of the hall. Making small talk until the porter appeared I said, "My company headquarters is in East Chicago, Billy, but I stop here every month or two. Being close to Navin Field, the Gayety and Avenue burlesque houses and Lefty O'Doul's bar is very convenient." Billy G. screwed up his face and said, "I knew I recognized you, Paddy. I never forget a face. I ain't so good at names no more, but I never forget a face." He continued, "I don't mean no disrespect, Paddy, but since you is a kind of regular, I got a niece who is stayin' with us for a couple a weeks an' she is a very obligin' girl – if you get my drift. She don't need a whole lot to keep her happy an' I could put her in touch with you." I knew it would be about 110 degrees in my room so I thanked Billy G. and said I'd get back to him when the weather cooled.

Parking a couple of car lengths from the front of the Milner Hotel on Bagley, I locked my business briefcase in the trunk and carried my suitcase... into the hotel lobby.

I made a couple of business courtesy calls the following morning and landed an $800 tool order with the Detroit Garage and Storage Company on East Jefferson. The Detroit Tigers were scheduled to play an exhibition game with the St. Louis Cardinals at 2 o'clock, so I drove the V-8 down by the Detroit River and killed some time watching the ore boats go by and skipping a few flat stones on the south-flowing water. The Tigers had a three game lead over the Yankees, and with half the season to go, first baseman Hank Greenberg was leading the league with 32 homers. Frank

Navin's trade with Connie Mack for "Black" Mike Cochrane at the end of the '33 season was a stroke of genius. As a player-manager, Mickey was batting over .300 and inspiring last year's 5th place Tigers to new heights. Young "Schoolboy" Rowe was scheduled to pitch against the great Dizzy Dean. Diz had 18 wins to date and the scribes predicted he'd have 30 by October. Dean was such a showboat. Before a game with Pittsburgh a couple of weeks before, he walked in the Pirates' dugout and said, "Ain't no use a you guys bringin' a bat up to the plate. You couldn't get a hit offin me today with a leaf from your momma's dining room table." Then he went on to retire 17 batters in a row and won a two-hitter four to zip. I was hoping to get a 50-cent ticket in back of 3rd so I could needle Detroit's cocky little shortstop Billy Rogell.

I got tired of skipping stones so I sat on the running board and looked across the water to Canada. Seeing the shoreline of Windsor reminded me of a story my pal Monk had once told me. From his description and those of some of the others involved, I managed to put together a pretty good account of what had happened that freezing winter nine years before.

1926

CHAPTER TWO

December of 1925 had been the coldest month in Chicago since they started keeping records. There were ten days in a row where the temperature never went above zero, and some nights dropped down to minus twenty. Monk was hustling drinks and a couple bucks a game on 8-ball in Mulrooney's one night when Freddie Prostak said the word on the street was Al Capone would pay twelve bucks a fifth for premium imported booze. While nursing his third or fourth alky beer a brainstorm hit him smack between the eyes: if it's this damn cold in Chi-Town then it's just about got to be this cold in Detroit City. He had no real folding money, but this great idea kept hopping around in his head, so Monk called Gussie Montrono in Detroit.

Monk had fond memories of Gussie and hated to lose him as a pal. When Gussie's parents died in the flu epidemic of 1918 he moved to Detroit and lived with his aunt for a couple of years. He got to traveling with a bad bunch and spent a year in juvenile hall for stealing a car. Gussie called it joy riding, but the judge disagreed. After that he was in and out of trouble and finally hooked up with Abe Bernstein and his Purple Gang.

When Monk asked about the weather in Detroit, Gussie confirmed his hope that the Detroit River was frozen all the way to Canada, and said yes, he had been bringing booze in by boat before the big freeze. Recently a few dummies had pushed their luck and tried running light

27

cars across the ice and ended up fish bait. Gussie said he had a middleman in Windsor, a Reggie McKenzie, whose supplier was the night foreman in the Hiram Walker warehouse. The guy specialized in premium imports and had "requisitioned" a barnful of Johnnie Walker Black Label scotch, Old Bushmills, Connemara, Redbreast Irish whiskey, and Gold Label Ron Rico Puerto Rican rum.

Monk let out a low whistle and said that was the kind of cheer Marshall Field and Colonel McCormick of the *Trib* would probably serve at their high-class dinner parties. He asked what kind of ransom McKenzie was getting. Gussie took a deep drag on his Camel and said, "A ton, Monk, a ton – seventy-two bucks a case with a 10-case minimum, cash on the barrelhead." Monk asked how wide the river was where he made his run and Gussie said about a half a mile from the old Detroit Ferry Building near East Jefferson over to the Windsor shore, but it might be a month before he could start his operation again. Monk said, "Just for the hell of it, supposing I could somehow move a shipment across in the next couple of weeks, could you arrange for me to pick up 25 cases of Johnnie Walker, C.O.D. in Windsor?" Gussie said there would be no problem getting the booze, but other than carrying three or four bottles at a time and walking across at night, the revenuers would nail his ass for sure. Monk told him that he was mulling over a plan and would call him again in a couple days.

He knew he would need someone with experience and connections, so his thoughts of course turned to Uncle Izzy. When Monk was a kid, Uncle Izz told interesting and amusing stories on the front porch while Izz's sister, Zeta Harpinski, was doing the Sunday dishes. Izzy didn't brag about his past, but just told it like it was – working in whorehouses, pool halls, and getting to know the small-time hoods and maybe picking up a few bucks running the numbers or delivering questionable packages. One time he had mentioned doing a job for Al Capone, but didn't say what it was. That's because when Monk's Ma came out on the porch for some fresh air, Izz quickly changed the subject.

He started telling how, as a young guy, he made a couple bucks a game selling peanuts, popcorn and Moxie to the Cub fans in Wrigley Field. The peanuts were delivered in 50-pound gunny sacks, so before game time he and a couple of other hawkers filled small brown paper sacks, folded the tops and twirled little ears on each bag. That way, the bags could be tossed to a customer sitting four or five seats from the aisle without spilling. After the fans filled up on peanuts and salty popcorn, they were ready for an ice-cold bottle of Moxie. That was the hardest part of the job – lugging eight glass bottles up twenty or thirty rows of seats on 90-degree days.

Uncle Izzy pulled a dime out of his pocket, walked ten feet down the front sidewalk and said for Monk to toss him the coin – high, low, or on either side. Uncle Izzy chuckled as he snagged each toss like one of the Cubby infielders. Ma wasn't impressed and said he should have gotten a real job in one of the packing plants. Izz ignored Ma's sharp tongue and said the hard work was worth it just to see part of the ballgame for free, especially the great double-play combination of Tinker to Evers to Chance. Before leaving for Detroit in 1914 Izzy said he saw the last game the great Giants' pitcher, Christy Mathewson, tossed against Chicago.

It was easy for anyone to see that Monk looked up to Izzy, but his mother thought her brother was a bad influence and cut him down every chance she got. Monk, needing some guidance and hoping his uncle Izzy still might have some solid contacts in the Pershing-Halsted neighborhood, called him up one Sunday morning. He knew Izz was generally an early riser, but on occasion, when he'd had an all-nighter, slept in. A fuzzy voice finally answered after about twelve rings.

"Izz? Monk here. I probably shouldn't have bothered you this late on a Sunday morning, but I was afraid you'd get bedsores."

"Very funny, you damn nephew. I been awake for hours, just layin' here restin' my eyes and thinkin' about givin' up booze and broads. What the hell do you want at this hour of the day – it's not even noon."

Monk told Izz about his pal Gussie Montrono who had contacts in Windsor, and that he could get Johnnie Walker Black for six bucks a fifth. Word on the street was Al Capone would pay twelve bucks a fifth in case lots and that the Detroit River was only a half-mile wide. Izz said, "Hold it, Monk. Hold it just a damn minute. I can tell you for sure the revenue guys will be patrolin' the river in their cutters. You ain't got no chance of dodgin' them sharpies."

"That's just it, Izz. They're not patrolling. The river is frozen clear across to Windsor. Gussie says there hasn't been any river activity for two or three weeks. I've got a plan I'd like to run past you concerning maybe twenty-five cases of Johnnie Walker." Monk could tell by Izz's voice that he was wide awake and beginning to show some interest. He could just imagine Uncle Izzy licking a pencil stub and jotting down figures on the back of a racing form.

"Let's see, Monk, twenty-five cases of Johnnie Walker wholesale times six bucks a fifth comes to $1,800 gross profit – and that's just for one delivery. What kind of a plan are you thinkin' about?"

Monk nervously cleared his throat and said, "Well, it's not exactly a finished plan Izz, it's really more of an idea. I was thinking of renting a couple of those horse-drawn delivery sleighs in Windsor. We could make the half-mile run across the ice at night in less than twenty or thirty minutes."

There was a long silence on the line and Izzy finally said, "Monk, your idea might work, but it would only be good for one crossin.' The sleighs and horses would make deep ruts in the snow, and the piled-up horse shit would be a dead giveaway. Not only that, but you'd be makin' a lot of noise and the revenuers would be watchin' from then on. Another problem would be storage and peddlin' the product. Nope, we gotta think of a long-range plan that wouldn't cause no suspicion. Lemme think on it, and in the meantime I'll ring up Frank Nitti and see if he thinks Mr. Capone might be interested. We gotta have a wad of dough up front. I still got a couple of chits due me for the special job I done for Mr. Capone early in the spring of 1920."

After he hung up with Monk, Izzy called Mr. Nitti at Al Capone's Chicago headquarters in the Metropole Hotel and, after a couple of long-time no sees and some small talk, told him he and his sister's kid could deliver twenty-five cases of Johnnie Walker Black a week for 144 bucks a case, for pick-up in Detroit – and maybe up to seventy-five cases a week if the cold weather held. The only problem was the start-up money for the operation and the cost of the booze. Izz said they'd need four grand but they could pay back the entire loan in two or three weeks. Uncle Izzy said he'd personally guarantee the advance, and if anything went wrong Mr. Capone wouldn't be out a cent. He and his nephew would work for any wage Mr. Capone wanted to pay for one year, or as long as it took for him to recoup his investment.

Mr. Nitti didn't even ask any questions. He just said, "Al thinks you're a square shooter, Izz, and he don't forget what you done for him a few years back. In fact, a couple days ago he was talkin' about havin' me look you up for another job he's got in mind. I'll be seein' him this afternoon and will lay out your proposition. I know he's always on the lookout for premium stock for his fancy clubs. Be at the Four Deuces tonight at 10 o'clock an' I might have a' answer for ya."

Uncle Izzy called Monk back and told him about the plan to meet at the Four Deuces. Not wanting to miss anything, Monk showed up early, about 9 o'clock, and Izzy was already there with half a bag on. Sparky Vaughn's band was beginning to warm up with *I Found a Million Dollar Baby in a Five and Ten Cent Store*. Francine and her girls were mingling with the customers and singling out the butter-and-egg men. Monk took this opportunity to ask Izzy something that he had been curious about. "Izz, what kind of profit is Capone gonna make on twenty-five cases of Johnnie Walker?"

Izzy snorted. "One hell of a lot more than us, Monk. I'm sure Al's bartenders can squeeze twenty or more shots from a fifth by adding caramel and a little water. If Al pays $12 a fifth and gets $2 a shot from his rich Gold Coast customers, he stands to make $40 a fifth less the $12 he pays up front. On twenty-five cases, he nets $8,400, less maybe a grand for overhead which includes transportin' the booze and greasin' the palms of the boys in blue. When Capone and Lucky Luciano were partners in New York and runnin' the numbers in Five Points, they probably would have been happy to clear $5 or $6 bucks a day."

About the time Monk was on his second double, there was a commotion out front and Oddie D'Angelo came in. He walked calmly over to where Pinky Moretti was sitting hunched over his drink at the bar and nailed Pinky behind the left ear with a .38 slug. A couple more slugs smashed the big mirror and shattered eight or nine bottles lined up on the back of the bar. Those who were close to Pinky moved down a seat or two and the band started playing *Who's Sorry Now?* Oddie apologized to nightman Petro Gardella and said he'd pay for any glass breakage. Gardella shrugged his shoulders and said not to worry and bought Oddie a drink. Nobody in the Deuces was too surprised because it was common knowledge Pinky had been shacking with Oddie's whore.

By the time Frank Nitti showed, Pinky had been dragged out back and things were back to normal. Mr. Nitti sat down with his back to the wall, ordered his usual and asked Antonia to freshen the table's drinks. He looked around and asked, "What the hell happened to the mirror?" Izz said Oddie D'Angelo and Pinky Moretti had a little falling out and one of Oddie's slugs must a' busted it. Izz pointed to Monk with his fresh glass and said, "This here's Monk, my sister's kid I told you about." Mr. Nitti reached across the table, shook Monk's hand and said, "I understand you got a scheme to furnish Mr. Capone with first-class booze, Monk. You come through an' Mr. Capone will want to thank you in person."

Monk mumbled that he'd be honored to meet Mr. Capone, and Frank Nitti said something about winning the Trifecta at the Hialeah track as the results came over the wire at the Hawthorne Inn that afternoon. After another round and more small talk, Mr. Nitti lost his smile. He leaned forward, narrowed his eyes and in a cold, controlled voice said Mr. Capone had decided to finance our plan. If we were successful there'd be more orders, but if we screwed up, the best we could hope for was twenty or thirty bucks a week until we worked off our obligation, if Mr. Capone happened to be in a good mood. Mr. Nitti pushed a brown leather satchel under Izzy's chair and nodded to a couple of his gorillas at the bar that he was ready to leave.

Monk and Izz took the bag into the john and gleefully counted out $4,000 in 100s, 50s and 20s. They had their grubstake, but now they knew they had to produce – or else. One thing was certain: there were no dummies still walking around Cicero who had crossed Mr. Capone!

CHAPTER THREE

On January 10, 1926, Monk and his Uncle Izzy met at the La Salle Street station about 12 noon and jumped on the 1:15 Michigan Central *Wolverine* bound for Detroit City. Monk's mother had packed pepperoni and cheese sandwiches, hard-boiled eggs, five-inch dill pickles, apple pie and a huge thermos of black coffee. About the time the *Wolverine* was passing through Michigan City Monk said to Izzy, "You mentioned Mr. Capone owed you a couple of chits for a job you had done one time. What was that all about?" Just then the conductor came by, and Izzy slipped him a couple of bills so's he'd look the other way, pulled a pint of Old Log Cabin out of his overcoat pocket and took a long pull.

"Kid, they's things you'd be better off not knowin', but I guess since we're in this caper on an equal basis, so's to speak, maybe you should know some of the kind a' guys we're gonna run into." He paused, and when Monk sat expectantly waiting, Izz went on. "Remember when I come back from Detroit City for a few days and stayed at your folks' place? You was fifteen or sixteen and already talkin' about quittin' school and gettin' a job at the meat packin' plant on Austin Ave? I said quittin' school after sixth grade was the dumbest damn thing I ever done, and if you stayed in school until you graduated, I'd buy you a Ford runabout on your eighteenth birthday?"

Monk's eyes lit up and he exclaimed, "Damn, Izz, do I remember! When I graduated, I was the only guy south of Roosevelt Road to have wheels. Matter of fact, I got my first lay in that buggy." Izzy's neck started getting red like it does when he gets mad and he growled, "Damn it Monk, I don't need to know that kind of shit. Besides, your mom would probably blame me for what you done. She said more than once I was a bad influence on her when we was kids, and if she thought I'd had anythin' to do with you gettin' some nooky, she'd kick my ass to Archer Ave. and back."

"O.K., Izz, I'll keep my mouth shut about personal stuff, but what about Frank Nitti, wasn't he Big Al's enforcer?" Izzy was surprised Monk even knew about Nitti, but went on.

"Nitti knew I'd worked for old Henry Ford on the truck line at the Highland Park factory in Detroit City. I done weldin' and quite a bit of hydraulic work on the T Model truck the government was sendin' to France in 1917 and '18. Those babies had a high wheelbase with 30 x 3½ inch tires, a 25-horse motor and a planetary gear system. They could go anywhere a damn mule could go and didn't eat no oats. A few of them was even outfitted for ambulance work. When the Volstead Act become law in January of 1920 and you couldn't get no legal booze anymore, I decided to pack it in and come back to Chi-Town. By that time I'd had enough factory work and besides I'd saved up a chunk a' dough over the years. When I come back home, I used to hang around Colosimo's Cafe on South Wabash during the winter and early spring of 1920 – just before "Big Jim," the cafe owner, got nailed behind the right ear with a .38 slug.

"About noon everyday, the regulars started comin' in for a corned beef on rye or maybe one of them good Dago provolone and salamis. After a few beers, the guys would start raggin' each other about who got laid or whose guy took a dive in the fights – fun stuff like that. One time Vinnie Lazari come in – you know, the guy what does them double books for Carman Vaschetti's Hi-De-Ho Club over on Cottage Grove. He sits down at our table and starts braggin' about the new hearin' aid he just bought. He said it set him back 200 bucks, but worth every nickel. He's got a battery the size of a large sardine can hooked onto his belt with a wire runnin' up inside his shirt and fastened on a large button stuck in his ear. Willie Ferrero is sittin' next to him and says, 'What kind is it, Vinnie?' Vinnie pulls out his watch and says, 'Just a little past 3:30, Will.' We all got a big laugh outta that.

"Monk, you'd have to just saw Colosimo's Cafe to believe it. First of all, it weren't no cafe at all, but a high-class cabaret joint. The bar itself was maybe thirty or forty feet long, with a half-dozen full-time bar men. Big Jim Colosimo wouldn't put out no rotgut booze neither; all the stuff was premium, includin' the prices.

"I used to hang around Colosimo's Cafe on South Wabash"

"After 4 o'clock, Big Jim put out free food on the bar, and you shoulda seen the spread – roast beef, boiled ham, chicken, turkey, maybe five different kinds of cheese. As long as you was buyin' drinks, everythin' was on the house, but if a guy nursed his drink too long, Big Jim's goons would grab him by the ass and nape of the neck and help him outside.

"Everywhere you looked you seen the best that dirty money could buy – like gold and silver crystal chandeliers, walls covered with green velvet, and silver-framed mirrors. Big Jim could just touch a switch and raise and lower the dance floor. The best jazz bands in Chi-Town, guys the likes of Mezz Mezzrow and Austin Mack and his Century Serenaders was knockin' out tunes like *Tiger Rag, Ja Da*, and *Dardanella*. After all the dancin' and squirmin' to the *Turkey Trot*, the *Grizzly Bear*, and the *Bunny Hug*, you wouldn't think the crowd would sit still for some serious singin,' but when Dale Winter come on and sung *Alice Blue Gown*, or *Every Little Movement Has a Meanin' All Its Own*, she got a standin' ovation, and they wouldn't let her quit 'til she sung another tune or two."

Izzy went on. "The big shots you seen there was maybe the best part of the show. There'd be hoods like Dion O'Banion, Bugs Moran, 'Greasy Thumb' Guzik and the Genna brothers mixin' in with rich business guys like Marshall Field and Potter Palmer. You might even see Big Bill Thompson, the crooked mayor hisself whisperin' in Alderman 'Bathhouse' Coughlin's ear.

"A couple times each month 'Umbrella Mike' Boyle would show up late in the afternoon and set up shop in a far corner of the bar."

"What the hell would an umbrella salesman be doing in a class joint like Colosimo's, Izz? I wouldn't think he could make much money pushing his product to a bunch of serious daytime drinkers – especially if it wasn't raining."

"Oh, he weren't sellin' no umbrellas, nephew. And you'd be surprised at the amount of cash he pulled in. Mike is the steward for the electrical union and he's got very sticky fingers. He always ordered six double whiskeys straight, lined up the glasses on his table, opened his big black umbrella by his side and waited for the action.

"Around 6 o'clock the contractors – guys who don't want no labor slowdowns – started stragglin' in. There wasn't no words spoke, but every few minutes a contractor walked by on his way to the john and dropped a 'donation' into the umbrella. Mike studied each guy, took a sip of whiskey, touched a pencil stub to his tongue and wrote down somethin' in a little red book. By the time Mike finished his last drink and the band begin tunin' up, he folded and buttoned his umbrella, dropped Estelle a fat tip, and staggered out the back door.

"One night I seen the great Caruso sittin' at a table with Georgie Jessel, Al Jolson and Eddie Cantor. After a few drinks, Caruso had little Eddie sittin' on his knee and singin' Jolson's show stoppin' song *Sonny Boy* to him. Every time Caruso sung the line, 'Climb upon my knee, Sonny Boy', an' Eddie blinked them big banjo eyes, Jolson and Jessel near fell off their chairs laughin'.

"When the Yankees come to town and played the White Sox in Comiskey Park, Babe Ruth would show up for a couple of sirloins and drinks. He couldn't remember no names so called everybody 'Keed' – even the mayor and Caruso. After Ruth slammed 54 homers in 1920 he couldn't pay for nothin' at Colosimo's. Some guy asked the Babe one night if he ever played snockered. He smiled and said, 'Hell yes; sometimes I'm standin' at the plate and I see a couple fuzzy balls comin' at me. I just sorta swing in the middle of them bastards and one of 'em usually obliges by goin' over the wall.'

"One of the funniest nights was when Jack Dempsey showed up. He had just beat Jess Willard for the world heavyweight crown. He and Big Bill Tilden, the amateur tennis champ, got to sparrin' on the dance floor— you know, like they was in a regular boxin' ring. Jack come at him in that crouch of his with his head tucked into his left shoulder. Big Bill started jabbin' the champ with his tennis racket and runnin' to a neutral corner. The crowd was yellin' and stompin' like they was in Madison Square Garden.

"Sometimes Big Al was sittin' quietly with his wife, Mae, at a table, but more than likely he was at the bar tellin' jokes and buyin' drinks for his pals. There was always three or four guys sittin' with their backs to Al, drinkin' coffee while watchin' all the doors. Al had come to Chi-Town early in 1919 from New York City. By 1920 Johnny Torrio, Colosimo's nephew, had made the tough lookin', barrel-chested Dago the boss and part owner of the Four Deuces over on South Wabash. He also cut Capone in on the take from his cathouses in Little Italy and the two-bit shacks over in the Levee district. All Al had to do was keep the booze and alky beer flowing in Big Jim's clubs and whorehouses – that and paying off the cops and political hacks downtown. Of course, Al was also on call to stiff some wiseguy who was tryin' to muscle in on the rackets."

By this time Monk was sitting on the edge of his seat. Izz took another drag from his pint, glared back at a couple of nosey bastards across the aisle, and went on.

"Monk, I'm gettin' ahead of my story. Let me back up a little. In 1913, I was a twenty-three year old punk tryin' to make a score by runnin' the numbers, dealin' blackjack and sometimes deliverin' packages late at night to tough-looking bastards in back rooms. They seemed to like me because I never asked no questions – just did what I was told. Towards the end of the year I seen an ad in the *Trib* for a janitor and handyman at the South Park Avenue Methodist Church. It kinda caught my eye and besides, I thought workin' for a church might straighten me out a little.

"After workin' there for a month or two, I met this beautiful nineteen-year-old girl by the name of Dale Winter. Now don't start gettin' some dumb ideas, Monk. I can tell by the look on your face you figured I probably laid her." Monk got a hurt look on his face and told Izzy he wasn't even thinking of such a thing. Not from his mother's younger brother and his favorite uncle. Izz said, "You little prick, you know I'm the *only* uncle you got. Anyway, Dale had a beautiful voice and had sang in some musicals in New York City and even San Francisco before comin' to Chicago and joinin' the church choir. She was so good the minister even let her sing by herself some Sundays. Dale always treated me right and her and her mother even had me over to their flat on Cottage Grove for supper a few times.

"One Sunday, a reporter from the *Chicago News* heard Dale sing in church, which surprised me because I never woulda thought they'd let a bum like that in the front door. This guy, Jack Lait, was tippin' a few in Colosimo's Cafe one night and tells Big Jim about this beautiful girl with the golden voice and that he ought ta' give her an audition. Well, she wowed Big Jim, and Dale not only come to be his outstanding act, a few years later she even become his wife – something I could hardly believe because Big Jim was not only fifteen or so years older than her, but was a whoremonger and as bad an apple as Chicago ever turned out.

"The reason I'm tellin' you all this is because of Dale. Even when she got rich and famous, she always had time and a good word for me. I'd go into Colosimo's and the first drink would always be on the house with a wave and smile from Dale. Big Jim and Dale was married only a couple of months before Big Jim got whacked. You'd think Dale would've been set for life, and I bet Big Jim would a' thought so too, but a judge ruled that because they was married less than a year after Big Jim divorced Victoria, the marriage wasn't legit and Dale was gettin' nothin.' Oh, Big Jim's kids tried to treat her right. They give her four or five grand, but that didn't go far. Dale tried to run the club for a while, but a business like that needs a guy who'll stiff any punks who get in the way, and you gotta jump in bed, so to speak, with the police commissioner and keep the precinct captain and his guys happy. Dale hung on for a few months, then her and her mother scrammed back to New York. I got a card once on my birthday. She remembered the date because that's the day her Jim bought the farm. I ain't heard from her since."

Monk looked out the window of the rocking train and saw a sign for Jackson, Michigan go whizzing by. Izzy was just catching his second wind. After a trip to the john, Izzy continued his story.

"It's now early spring 1920, and I'm sittin' in Colosimo's Cafe when Frank Nitti comes over and introduces hisself. He asks if he can buy me a drink and I say 'Hell yes.' I sure ain't dumb enough to irritate Big Al's top gun. After a couple, Nitti says he hears I got some special skills his boss, Al Capone, might be interested in. He says Al has been havin' some trouble gettin' his product to his customers on the North Side. This bum Dion O'Banion's got the territory sewed up north of Madison Street, and his goons has been hijackin' Al's trucks when they take the back streets at night. What they do is park a junk car crossways in a narrow street and when Al's lead truck has to stop, O'Banion's guys open fire with their new Tommy guns they call 'Chicago typewriters.' They're careful not to nick any of Al's boys because O'Banion knows that would lead to outright gang warfare. Al's guys figger they're sittin' ducks so have to scram outta there quick. O'Banion's goons take over the convoy and head north like nothin' happened. Of course O'Banion has already bought and paid for the boys in blue in his territory, so he's got all the bases covered.

"Nitti put two fingers in the air and before Meg come back with the drinks, I said, 'Mr. Nitti, give me a few days, and I believe I can come up with somethin' that will help solve your problem.' Nitti finished his drink, got up to leave, put his hand on my shoulder and said, 'Izz, you'll be doin' Al a great favor, an' he don't forget his friends. One more thing, drop the 'Mr.' shit. The guys I trust call me Frankie.'"

There was a lull when the *Wolverine* stopped in Ann Arbor. Izz had just about talked himself out, so it gave Monk a chance to eye some of those University of Michigan coeds sashaying their cute asses down the aisle. With about forty-five minutes left until Detroit City, Monk asked Izz if he ever came up with a solution to Capone's hijacking problems. Izzy's face lit up and he half shouted, "Hell yes, and after thinkin' on it and losin' a few nights sleep, a simple answer just popped into my head. I found Frankie in Colosimo's at his private table a few nights later and laid out my plan. Halfway through I figured he was interested because he motioned to Meg to bring two more double scotches, straight up. Frankie slowly sipped his drink while I finished my spiel. He was quiet for maybe a minute, just kinda staring at the ceiling. Then he looked me straight in the eye and said, 'Izz, your plan is just nutty enough that it might work. I'll run it past Al and you meet me here about 10 tomorrow night.'

"Well, Mr. Capone went for it and told Frankie to give me all the dough I needed. Of course, he put a time limit on the job and I understood what he meant when Frankie said Al don't like a guy who ain't as good as his word.

"The first thing I done was contact Mike Donnelly in Detroit at the Mack Truck Company. Mike and me worked together for years on the line at the Highland Park Ford factory and was good friends. I told Mike I wanted the biggest truck the Mack Company made and two regular-sized trucks, but they all had to have hard rubber tires. Mike said I was nuts because balloon tires was far superior and rode a lot smoother. Besides, he said, hard rubber tires hadn't been made for years. Without goin' into any detail I told him the trucks was for Al Capone and I had to have hard rubber tires. Mike got the picture and promised he'd see what he could do. After rummaging around he come up with the tires and wheels I needed. The trucks was delivered in about three weeks and Nitti give me eight grand in hard cash to pay for them in my own name. I found out later that Al never had a checkin' account and never even owned any property with his moniker on it.

"Frankie rented me a shop over on Halsted with all the tools, jacks, torches and iron I'd need. The first thing I done was weld two five-foot moveable steel arms on a four-foot high curved steel blade that was a few inches wider than the truck front wheels. Nitti give me two helpers, Dink Silvani and Joe Mangano, who was pretty good journeymen mechanics. In fact, Joey told me he worked on the British Mark IV and the French Renault FT tanks we used in France towards the end of the Big War.

"Our next step was drillin' holes clear through the undercarriage frame and addin' I-beam reinforcements just in front of the cab doors. Two round steel bars with tungsten-hardened gears and bushings on each end was shoved through the drill holes clear through the frame from side to side and attached with swivels that was fastened to the arms raisin' and lowerin' the steel blade. I mounted a Continental engine – the kind Mr. Ford had put in them Eagle power boats he built for the government in '17 – in the big truck bed right up against the cab. Above the engine two or three feet we mounted a reinforced barrel cylinder about a foot-and-a-half in diameter and five-foot-long on an axle. A strong chain that we wrapped around the cylinder came out through an opening above the cab and extended down to a yoke onto the arms attached to the steel scraper blade. All the driver had to do was give the guy in the truck bed a holler and he would crank up the Continental, throw her into low-range reverse, and lower the blade to street level. We tried her several times on junk cars and she worked like a charm. That big Mack picked up them junks and pushed them outta the way without hardly slowin' down.

"Nitti was still worried about the drivers and guys ridin' in the followin' trucks so that's where Joe's tank experience come in handy. We mounted inch-thick glass in the windshield and side windows. I got half-inch boilerplate from Inland Steel and Joe welded them protective strips on the sides of the engines and along both sides of all three truck bodies.

Me and Franco Battiato drove the lead Mack on the first two or three loads and got through with hardly no trouble – maybe one or two of the beer barrels might have got nicked a little. I'd like to have saw the look on O'Banion's face when his goons told him how we plowed through them junk cars, and how their 100-shots-a-minute Chicago typewriters hardly made a dent in our trucks and hard rubber tires.

"That big Mack picked up them junks and pushed them outta the way without hardly slowin' down."

"Just in case O'Banion's dummies tried to follow us, I mounted an injection pump and a 5-gallon oil reservoir on the left side of the engine on the last truck. All the driver had to do was pull out a knob on the dashboard and oil was forced into the intake manifold. When the oil hit that hot metal, black smoke come pourin' outta the tail pipe which covered the street for two or three blocks. It took ten or fifteen minutes for the smoke to clear enough before O'Banion's monkeys could start after us, and by that time we was long gone.

"Big Al was so pleased he told Nitti to give me ten C notes and one of them diamond belt buckles he gives to his close friends. And that's another reason, Monk, Frank Nitti jumped on the bandwagon when I told him we could deliver Johnnie Walker Black for 144 bucks a case, gross. He knew Izzy Brodsky's word was his bond – and here you thought your old unk was a dumb ass."

Monk assured his Uncle Izzy that he had never, for one second, thought he was dumb – just a little bit goofy at times. Izz laughed, roughed up his nephew's hair, and settled back in his seat. Before the *Wolverine* pulled into Michigan Central depot at 5:45 p.m. the two men had finished the supper Mrs. Harpinski had prepared.

I t was snowing hard when Monk and Izz walked out of the Michigan Central depot, so they hailed a Checker for downtown Detroit City instead of taking the trolley. Izz told Monk it was important for them to arrive in style. The cabbie answered Monk's question about findin' a reasonable room and said, "Youse tourists look like big spenders so I'm droppin' ya at the Embassy Hotel on Howard Street. They's plenty a' joints in the area where a guy can tip a few an' yer only a couple blocks from the Avenue and Gayety burlesque houses. If ya catch tonight's show at the Avenue, go backstage durin' the intermission an' tell top banana Scurvy Miller Vito D'Amato sent ya. If yer lucky, ya might even get a close-up peek at that new young broad from New York City with the big titties they call "Ann Howe and Her Million Dollar Treasure Chest". Some English outfit they call Lloyds of London carries a policy worth $400,000 on her left tittie, and $500,000 on her right tittie 'cause it's a little bigger." Monk give Vito a thanks for both the ride and the info', and flipped him a two-bit tip. The boys settled into the fleabag hotel for a buck twenty-five each with the can and tub located conveniently at the end of the hall, down one flight.

That evening, after a quick meal at the Oriental Palms next to the Blue Goose Bus Station on Second Avenue, they took in the 9 o'clock show at the Avenue.

They took in the 9 o'clock show at the Avenue.

The first two strippers looked a little worse for wear, and the third girl, a blonde, didn't even raise much excitement when she showed a few dark hairs. Scurvy Miller, though, was in great form. In one skit, Scurv was standing on a corner dressed in baggy pants with his hands jammed in his pockets. One of the strippers came mincing along in a skimpy dress, four-inch heels, a naughty twinkle in her eye and asked, "Why Mr. Miller, what are you doing?" Scurvy looked at her with his goofy grin and said, "Oh, I'm just shakin' hands with the unemployed."

During Intermission the candy butchers came down the aisles selling ten-cent boxes of stale caramels for thirty-five cents and special "Frenchy" pictures for two bits. Monk and Izz went back-stage and Monk told Scurvy they had just come in from Chi-Town on the *Wolverine* and that Vito D'Amato had said to look him up. Well, Scurvy couldn't have been nicer. He gave them two free matinee passes and said for them to sit in the front row during the second half of the show.

When the lights came on to start the second half of the show, Scurvy shuffled out to a drum beat, tripped on an imaginary crack in the floor, and turned a complete flip. As the laughing died down, Scurv said, "I want you to meet a couple of my good pals, Monk Harpinski and Isadore Brodsky, who just blew in on the *Wolverine* from Chicago. Give the boys a big hand." The operator in the left half balcony turned the green and red spotlights on the two men in the front row and the drummer did a dot-dotta-dot-dot-dot-dot. Monk was embarrassed but Izz, never one to be called shy or retiring, clapped his hands over his head and pumped his arms like he had just won the heavy-weight crown in Madison Square Garden. Monk threw his uncle a look of disbelief, but Izz replied, "What the hell, there ain't no use in hidin' your light under a bushel basket, nephew."

Everybody was waiting and watching for Ann Howe to break loose – especially Uncle Izz. After a couple more tired strippers went through their routines, Ann busted out of the curtains. She started kind of slow, but after the five-piece band jumped on *Hold That Tiger* she commenced moving and gyrating in four different directions at the same time. By the third chorus Ann had one tassel going left and one going right. All the guys were yelling and stomping, and just a split second later she grabbed the curtain and gave it a working over. The dark blue spotlight hit her as she whipped off her G-string and tassels and tossed them to the boys in the front row. The guys weren't really sure of what they had just seen. Izz smiled and said that taking out that million dollar insurance policy was a damn smart idea!

Monk and Uncle Izzy finished a very successful first evening in Detroit by sampling the booze in every illegal gin mill around Cadillac Square and returned to the Embassy about 2 a.m.

The intermittent flashing of light from a neon sign across the street from the Embassy pierced the darkness of room 223 and made sleep difficult for Monk – that and the exciting plan to bring twenty-five cases of illegal Canadian whiskey across the frozen Detroit River. Izzy had also been sleeping fitfully in the stifling room. Their night of drinking had a calming effect at first, but now he too was wide awake. After returning from an urgent trip down the hall, Izzy propped his pillow against the wall, lit a cigarette and said, "There's somethin' I've been meanin' to talk to you about for a long time, Monk. As long as we both can't sleep, this is probably as good a time as any.

"You know your Ma and me ain't been on the best of terms for a long time, and I take full responsibility for that. Since your Dad up and left when you was just a little kid, your Ma has had a pretty rough time. Workin' in the packin' plant ten hours a day didn't give her much time to be a mom and dad to you. Whenever I could, which wasn't often enough, I'd try to fill in a little bit. Then, in your middle years, when I was workin' in Detroit, I only got back to Chi-Town once or twice a year. Now that you're growed up I don't want you to think I'm tryin' to run your life."

"I'd never think that, Izz. And I want you to know how much I always looked forward to seeing you. You most always seemed to make it home on my birthday or at Christmastime. I'll never forget the thrill of playing 'left pocket.' If I yelled it first when you walked in the door, you gave me whatever was in your left pocket. When I was little, it was always a shiny dime or maybe a toy soldier. On my twelfth birthday it was a 1916 silver dollar – I still have it in my bedroom drawer at home. I remember when I made the baseball second team at Roosevelt and you came home for a few days that spring. I was too old for 'left pocket,' but you left me something I'll keep the rest of my life. When I woke up after you caught the train for Detroit, the first thing I saw by my bed was a baseball signed 'Ty Cobb.'

"There's something else I'd like you to know," Monk added. "Mother, in her own way, really loves you. When I was growing up she'd say, 'Now, I don't want you making your uncle Izzy a hero, but you'd do well to remember he's as honest as the day is long, and he never hurt nobody on purpose.'"

Izzy pulled out a handkerchief, looked away and said he thought he must have a hair in his eye. When he composed himself, he said, "The big reason your ma has been upset with me is because of the way I've lived my life. It probably started when she was sixteen and I was fourteen. I embarrassed her in the eyes of her friends by workin' in Maudie's whorehouse in Canaryville over by the Union Stockyards. Maudie's was a few miles from home so most nights I just slept on a cot in the backroom. It wasn't long after that I left home for good, and I've been on my own ever since, hustlin' pool, gamblin' and pickin' up a buck here and there.

"Workin' in a whorehouse don't sound like much, but with tips and all I was makin' a lot more than settin' duck pins or haulin' groceries and coal for old man Polanski. I remember after about a month I saved up enough to buy a small box of Frango mints at Marshall Field's. I had the box wrapped special in gold paper and put it on your ma's bed. When she found out who give it to her she dumped all the mints down the toilet and said they was bought with dirty money. I can see now how she must have felt, but I thought I was doin' somethin' nice for her.

"Workin' at Maudie's was probably the best education I ever got. Most of the girls was kinda pretty and they treated me great, incudin' Maudie. I guess I was like a pet or a little brother. If I got caught swearin' or smokin' they raised holy hell. One time I kept a two-dollar bill I found on the foor. Maudie found out and docked my pay for five weeks. I sure learned a lesson that time! I didn't have to do any heavy liftin'. I'd sweep out, put away groceries, clean oil lamp chimneys, and run errands for the girls.

"Felix Rikenberger, the cocky piano player, come in about eight at night, put on a derby hat and played until two in the mornin' – or longer if some drunk offered him a couple two-dollar bills. Felix was rough on me at first, but turned out to be a good guy. Some nights he'd give me a nickel or dime to run out and pick up a pint of gin and cigarettes. One night durin' his break he said, 'Kid, how'd you like to become a piano player in a whorehouse – or maybe even in a legit band?' I thought that would be great so Felix came in early a couple nights a week and learned me the keys. I can still play *In the Good Old Summertime, Sweet Rosie*

O'Grady and a couple other tunes by ear.

"Maudie's was different from most houses. She closed at 3 a.m. so her girls could get the sleep they needed, and she let them have time off in the early afternoon. Also, she split the take with them 60-30, with 10% goin' for police protection.

"Maudie's nephew, Albert, a big, slow-witted kid about four or five years older than me, was sorta the man of the house. He was a jack-of-all-trades and acted as Maudie's and the girls' protector. He was what you might call a quart or two low, but always happy and willin' to help. One night a drunk started raisin' hell – claimin' one of the girls rolled him. Maudie tried to calm the guy down – even said she'd give him his two dollars back, but he backhanded her and smashed her nose. Albert seen him do it so he rushed the bastard and began poundin' the piss outta him. As Albert leaned down to pick him up, the guy jammed a 6-inch switchblade into Albert's gut. I can still see the whole thing like it was in slow motion.

"Albert tried to stand up while holdin' both hands over his belly. He had a surprised look on his face and tried to say somethin', but just crumpled to his knees and fell face forward on the carpet. We all stood there dumb for a minute or two while the john staggered out the door. I finally had enough sense to run the three blocks to the precinct station. The cops really tried, but they never found the guy. After that, Sergeant Shanahan told Maudie, me, and the girls if there was ever even a hint of trouble we should call the station.

"Maudie paid for Albert's wake and funeral. All the girls and me, and even some of the johns, chipped in and sent a card and some money to Albert's mother in Galena. I think that was the worst time of my young life."

"What a terrible thing for a kid to go through. Did you ever tell ma about it?"

"No, there was no point. It probably woulda just made things worse. You'd be surprised at some of the guys who come in Maudie's. I ain't what some people call religious, and I suppose that's because of things I've seen. A couple times a week – sometimes in mid-morning or even ten or eleven at night, Maudie would tell me to unlock the back door and wait for a special customer.

"Maudie had a soft spot for kids and down and outers. She always had a box in the front room for donations. One day she put the money in a yellow envelope and told me to take it to the reverend at the church on 41st Street and Morgan. I run over and asked for the reverend. He come out of his office and who should it be but the special customer I'd been lettin' in the back door for months. Here was a guy with a wife and kids who'd probably been tellin' his flock that God watches every move they make and he thinks he's got a special pass. I made sure he knew who I was and told him I'd see him at the back door at Maudie's, and maybe I'd be interested in joinin' his church. Each coupla weeks I'd deliver the envelope and I'd always insist on handing it to the reverend hisself. Before long he stopped coming and I never saw him at the back door of Maudie's again.

"There was a pretty little girl about eighteen or nineteen named Ardis workin' at Maudie's. She come from a little farmin' village down state and had answered a help-wanted ad for general housekeepin' work – a trick the whoremongers would pull to get new unsuspectin' young girls. They'd make the girls slaves and just give them enough food so they looked healthy. The madam she worked for, afore comin' to Maudie's, was a broken down old whore who kept an eye on the young ones and never even let them out of the house.

"At first Ardis looked down at the floor every time I talked to her, but after a few weeks of being polite and friendly I got her to smile at some of my dumb jokes. Once she knew all I wanted was to be her friend, she really opened up. One afternoon when Ardis was gettin' some sun in the backyard we talked for about a hour. She told me how much she hated the farm and her father. Her mother died when she was thirteen and her father forced her to do all the cookin', house cleaning,' and lookin' after her four brothers and sisters. She said she still felt guilty, but just after her sixteenth birthday she stole the egg money and caught the Red Dot bus to Chicago. The ad she answered was supposed to set her free, but it just about ruined her life. After they near broke her spirit in the whorehouse she got in trouble with the madam. She sassed her and refused to do certain horrible things. The daily pick-up man told the syndicate and after being beaten and locked in the rat-infested basement for several days, she was thrown out on the street.

"Ardis broke down sobbin.' She said she begged, slept in alleys under cardboard boxes and fought off drunks. Finally, just to stay alive, she did two-bit tricks for pimps. One cold night Maudie saw her on the street and brought her home. She cleaned her up, gave her clothes and a bed of her own on the third floor. As our friendship and her trust grew, Ardis told me she had always wanted to be a teacher some day.

"Once a month I'd pick up a couple magazines for Maudie at Zonie's newsstand. After she was done with them she'd put them out for the girls. Ardis liked the one called *Ev'ry Month* the best. It had poems, songs, health ideas and interestin' stories. Ardis not only read the whole magazine, she even heped me with my sorry readin'. I remember one story I really liked was about Teddy Roosevelt takin' his horse soldiers to Cuba and fightin' the Spanish army.

"Ardis especially liked poems. There was one we both liked but I didn't understand it. She read it to me a few times and then give me a pad and pencil and said for me to write the words ten times and then tell her what I thought it was about. I can still remember some of it, Monk – 'Whenever Richard Cory went down town, we people on the pavement looked at him; he was a gentleman from sole to crown' – I kinda forget the next part, but at the end, the guy one summer night went home and shot hisself in the head.

"When Ardis asked me what I thought, I said I guessed it showed it don't matter how a guy looks or how rich he is, he might have troubles we don't know nothin' about. Ardis give me a pat on the arm, a little peck on the forehead, and said I'd done good.

"Over the months it almost seemed like a miracle was takin' place. Ardis walked different, acted different, and even looked you right in the eyes when she talked to you.

"A couple times a week I'd go over to the settlement house on Halstead. I'd play checkers, talk to people from far off places, and maybe have a hot bowl of soup. Everythin' was free, and you could even take a bath if you wanted. Sometimes I'd help out in the kitchen, do a little paintin', or maybe run over to Maxwell Street and pick up bruised fruit and vegetables. One night Miss Jane Addams, the lady who started the Hull House, as the settlement was called, put a white sheet on the wall and showed a bunch of us roughnecks pictures of faraway places like Japan and India. The machine she used was somethin' new called a Magic Lantern. When the show was over and I was puttin' the chairs away, I had a chance to tell Miss Addams about Ardis and her dream of becomin' a teacher. She didn't even care what Ardis was doin'. She said she'd like to meet her so I brought Ardis over and the two of them hit it off right away. To end this long story, Monk, after twenty years Ardis is still livin' at Hull House and helpin' young girls, and anybody else who needs straightenin' out."

"That was a swell story, Izz. I always like a happy ending. No matter what you say, I'm going to tell Ma about it someday. I think I can get some sleep now and even have a pleasant dream."

CHAPTER FOUR

M onday morning, January 11, 1926 was perfect, maybe ten degrees with a light dusting of snow. It would be just right for the planned caper. Uncle Izzy, an early riser from his swing-shift days at the Highland Park Ford factory, was up and enjoying a cup of java and a sinker by 7 a.m. in Pete Consani's Early Bird Cafe. When Izz had left the fleabag, Monk was still passed out, face down with his head between two pillows, probably dreaming of Ann Howe and her million-dollar treasure chest.

A kid came into the Early Bird with a shoulder sack full of three-cent *Detroit Free Press* papers. Izz gave the boy a five-cent buffalo and spread the sports page on the counter, barely noticing the front page, which had an above-the-fold story that the Democrats were keeping alive about President Harding and the Teapot Dome oil scandal in Wyoming. President Coolidge said he had no knowledge of wrong-doing while Vice President. Another story rehashed the details of the 1925 court-martial of General Billy Mitchell, in which many experts agreed that top army and navy brass were out to get Mitchell for his belief that air power could win or shorten future conflicts. Izzy skipped the hard news and was more concerned that the Chicago Black Hawks lost to the Boston Bruins 3-2. Baseball was still a hot topic. O. B. Osborne wrote a great piece on thirty-eight-year-old Grover Cleveland Alexander who planned to open the '26 season for the Cubs. The Yankees were expecting great things at first base from a 22 year-old Columbia College kid named Lou Gehrig. Ty Cobb, the Tiger manager and still a full-time player, got most of the ink, though. Cobb, at 39, continued to be the most feared base runner in the game and had compiled a .378 batting average in '25. Sports writers still liked to talk about how the "Georgia Peach," in his heyday, sat on the top step of the dugout sharpening his spikes with a file. If he wasn't the meanest son-of-a-bitch in baseball, he sure was an awful close second.

When he finished his coffee and donuts, Izzy asked Betty Lou, the pretty girl on the cash register from the Upper Peninsula of Michigan, to wrap up a couple Danish and fill an empty Old Log Cabin bottle with black coffee for his nephew. Back at the Embassy, Monk had already shaved and taken a tub bath, and almost looked human. When Izz returned, Monk drank the coffee with both hands steadying the bottle, but passed on the Danish. After downing the hot java, Monk's color started to come back a little, so Izzy said, "Monk, it's time we done some serious thinkin' on this here idea of yours and make a list of what we're gonna need. But first, ring up Gussie Montrono and see if he's got things progressin' on the Canada side."

Monk called the number Gussie had given him, and a sleepy sounding broad answered. When Monk asked if Gussie was there, the dame said, "Who the shit wants ta know?" Gussie grabbed the phone and recognized Monk's voice right away. Gussie said, "Damn, Monk, I've been waitin' for your call. I got twenty-five cases a' Johnnie Walker Black lined up in Windsor. My guys is just waitin' for the high sign to start stashin' the booze in a' empty garage down by the river. I got six Cannucks from the McElvery gang who'll help in any way you want."

"I think it'll be a go come this Sunday night, Gussie. We just got a few loose ends to tie up here. Uncle Izzy and I are at the Embassy on Howard Street. If you want, you could meet us about ten tonight and we'll hand over the cash for the Johnnie Walker and half payment for the Cannucks. Thanks for getting the booze and lining up the boys in Windsor."

"Think nothin' of it, Monk. I got a' A-1 credit rating with the handlers across the river. I'll see ya 'bout ten tonight."

Izzy, satisfied with the report, touched a pencil stub to his tongue and scratched out some figures. "Gussie said it was a half mile across the river. There's 5,280 feet in a mile, so half of that is, lessee – about 2,600 feet plus a little more. That gives me a good idea about how much rope we need."

Monk looked at Izz with astonishment and sarcastically said, "Damn, Izz, I sure didn't know you were a student of that Einstein fella."

Izz, ignoring the crack, popped open a pint of Old Log Cabin, and after a long pull offered the bottle to his nephew saying, "Monk, you better have a little hair of the dog which bit you last night." Monk, with a shudder, waved the bottle away and groaned, "If you don't mind, Izz, I'll just sit here a minute or two until my eyes stop bleeding – and after I drain that water pitcher I'll be ready to get this damn show on the road."

Monk and Izzy walked a couple of blocks to the saddle and harness district on Fort Street and talked with the old Sicilian leather shop owner, Giuseppe Scalese. Izzy made a sketch of what he had in mind – a stout leather pouch with reinforced drawstring top and a one-inch-steel breeching ring sewn securely on the neck of the pouch about three inches from the top. The pouch had to hold and protect a whiskey bottle from rough handling. Izzy gave Scalese an empty slab-sided Johnnie Walker bottle to use as a pattern.

Izzy told Scalese he needed three-hundred pouches and three-hundred breeching rings sewn fifteen inches apart on four hundred-foot lengths of rope – and he needed them in five days. The old man rubbed his grizzled chin and said for an order that large he'd have to have hides sent over from his shop and warehouse in Windsor, but no ferries were running because the river was frozen solid. When Izz asked if his people in Canada could do a job that big, Scalese replied, "Hella yes, an' I canna have four or five a' my besta people walk over an' helpa out. Youa say the pouches they donna need no finish look, justa strong? I maka sample an' you comma back in a coupla hours." When Izz asked what the job would cost, Scalese said, "Maybe a buck a pouch, maybe a little more to sew rings onna pouches and ropes. You gotta furnish the rings ana ropes. I don't wanna even know watta you gonna do with three-hundred leather pouches."

Izzy heard from the cabbie Vito D'Amato that the Acme Ice and Cold Storage Company on Brush Street had some used delivery wagons for sale cheap, so he bought a five-year-old T model Ford truck with a closed bed and a pull-down canvas cover for $75.

Stopping at Sharky's pool hall for drinks about 11 a.m., Izzy started thinking out loud and said, "We'll need 5/8-inch manila rope, 3,500-pound-test. It comes in three-hundred-foot lengths wound on wood reels. Make sure the center holes in the reels measure two inches across. Damn it Monk, start writin' this shit down! Get five of them reels plus an extra hundred feet of rope and eight empty reels."

Monk looked up and said, "Hell Izz, that ain't near enough rope to stretch clear across to Windsor – and what do we need eight empties for?" Izzy looked irritated and said, "Close down your damn trap, Monk. I'll tell you my way of thinkin' later. The copper wire we need comes five-hundred feet to the spool. Get six spools of eighteen-gauge double-strand cotton wrapped and paraffined. The six wood spools and wire will weigh about twenty-five or thirty pounds. The spools come with one- and two-inch center holes. Make sure you get the one-inch. Oh, and get two of them army surplus crank telephones and six Rock Island 1½-volt dry-cell batteries. Go to the sports department and pick up thirteen dozen #7 split shot lead sinkers – the ones used by guys which fish. While you're at H. L. Liscomb over on Griswold pick up one of them six-foot Flexible Flyer sleds, you know, the kind kids like to get at Christmas. I think they got hundred-pound gunny sacks of sand out back. Pay for five bags and get a couple long-handled coal shovels and rakes. Oh yeah, and a five-gallon can of kerosene. I'll walk over to Harris Brothers lumber yard on West Jefferson and have them hold a bunch of things I'll need like three 2 x 6 x 12 foot planks, tools, nails and lag bolts. We'll pick the stuff up later today. On second thought, maybe you'd better go to three or four hardware stores so we don't raise no suspicions."

Monk stopped writing, bent his fingers backwards, cracked his knuckles and said, "How about warm duds, Izz – stuff like hats, gloves, scarfs, galoshes, long underwear and mackinaws?"

"Your department, Monk. Find an army surplus and get everything you think we'll need for us and six or seven guys. I put in a call to Bob Beason, a guy I knowed for years who works over at the Stroh Brewery. He said he'd round up thirty old wood booze crates. He still can't get used to a brewery just makin' ice cream and chicken feed. That damn Volstead Act those dummies thought up sure raised hell with the legit beer outfits. O.K. Monk, I can't think of no other stuff we'll need. If anything else comes to you, write it down. Let's meet about 4 o'clock over at Lefty O'Doul's on Howard Street. We'll make our pick-ups and then drop off the three-hundred breeching rings at Scalese's.

"But first, let's grab some lunch. It might help settle that stomach of yours."

The Early Bird Cafe was bustling with the lunch-hour crowd. When Betty Lou saw Monk and Izzy come in she diplomatically encouraged two regulars to finish their coffee. Clearing and wiping the table, she waved the boys over. Izzy introduced his nephew and Monk exchanged a little innocent banter with Betty Lou, then ordered a bowl of navy bean soup, coffee and apple pie. On Betty Lou's recommendation, Izz ordered the blue plate special. While enjoying lunch, Izz marveled at the dexterity of an attractive older waitress who also caught the eyes of several other male diners. Monk approached the cash register, winked at Betty Lou and pressed a fifteen-cent tip into her hand. He said, "Monk Harpinski has been called a lot of things, but being a tightwad sure ain't one of them. Keep that pretty smile on your face and I'll see you later." Betty Lou beamed and said, "I'll be looking for you, Monk. Don't do anything I wouldn't do."

Outside, while picking his teeth, Izz said, "I think that young lady has the hots for you, nephew. What did she mean, don't do anything she wouldn't do?" Monk stammered "She probably meant I – we – shouldn't do – oh hell, Izz, Betty Lou's just a lonely kid from the boondocks of Northern Michigan. She's just trying to be friendly." Izzy had a knowing smile on his face when they split up to make the necessary purchases.

Around 4:15 p.m. Monk found Izzy in Lefty O'Doul's yelling and arguing with Lefty about the so-called Black Sox baseball scandal of 1919. Lefty was shouting that the White Sox players were money hungry and had no character. Izz replied angrily, "Damn it, if Comiskey had paid the guys a decent wage none of that shit woulda took place." When Lefty accused Shoeless Joe Jackson of causing the mess and throwing the Series, Izzy's neck started getting a deep red and he shouted, "How in hell can a guy hit .375 and throw the Series? And what about Buck Weaver hittin' .324? And little Dickie Kerr winnin' two complete games against Cinci?" Lefty lit up a cigarette and growled, "What about them other clowns, the guys the commissioner throwed outta baseball for life, like Chick Gandil, Swede Risberg an' Eddie Cicotte?" Izzy looked a little stunned but recovered enough to say, "Commissioner Kenesaw Mountain Landis was to blame, and how in hell could a guy with a name like that know anythin' about baseball? He sounds more like one of them crooked wrasslers." Monk finally got Izz calmed down and out to the truck without any blood getting spilled. Izzy was still fuming when they picked up all the equipment at the supply houses and lumber yard and hauled it to an empty warehouse Gussie had found down by the river off

St. Aubin Street.

After a couple of blue plate specials at the Oriental Palms, the boys headed back to the Embassy for a few hands of gin rummy, playing for matches and toothpicks they had lifted from the Palms. About 10:15 Gussie showed up a little snockered along with the dame Monk talked to in the morning. Izz was polite but wasn't in any mood for entertaining. He gave the broad a couple bucks and told her to come back at midnight. She grumbled a little bit, kissed Gussie and staggered out the door. Monk, with a deep frown, said, "Gussie, there's one thing bothering the hell out of me. I know things are going smooth, but what if some copper comes nosing around in the middle of the job?" Gussie took a long drag on his cigarette, ground the butt out in a snuff can and said, "You got nuthin' to worry about, Monk. I gave Corporal Jack Carmichael a couple of twenties so's we ain't interrupted, an' jus' to make sure he unnerstands, I told him Abe Bernstein an' his Purple Gang sure thanks him for his cooperation."

Izzy asked Gussie if he could pick up six wiseguys who weren't afraid of hard work and had tight lips. Gussie said that wouldn't be a problem and he'd have them by noon the next day. Gussie was filled in on the entire plan and about 12:30 a.m. Gussie's whore showed up pie-eyed, hanging on some creep's arm and said, "At least some people appreciate me for my lovin' ways." Gussie chased the pair down the hallway cursing a blue streak and threatening to cut the jerk's balls off. Monk and Izzy had a good laugh, grabbed one last belt and hit the sheets.

With the steam radiator clanking and hissing and the two windows nailed shut, Monk sat on the side of the bed rubbing his head and eyes. Izz, raised up on one elbow, saw the Little Ben pointing to 1:30 a.m., and asked, "What's the matter, Monk, ain't you been asleep yet?"

"Not only ain't I been asleep, I feel like I've been on a coffee jag. You want to talk a little while?" Izz climbed out of bed in his long underwear and mixed a little warm Vernors ginger ale and Old Log Cabin in a yellowed coffee mug. "What do you want to talk about, Monk?" Monk stifled a yawn with the back of his hand, "Oh hell, I dunno Izz. You started telling me once how you went back and forth all over the country on practically no dough. How did you do that?"

Izz took a gulp of booze, narrowed his eyes, shook his head from side to side and said, "Damn, that Vernors tastes like the bottom of a chicken coop – wonder what the hell they're puttin' in it these days." He sat on the floor, his back against the wall and his knees drawn up with the Old Log Cabin bottle between his feet. He belched, took a deep breath and said, "Well Monk, when you're travelin' light, in order to stay alive you gotta have a lot of common sense, a bit of luck, a strong jack knife, some savvy, and it don't hurt none to be a little stupid." Monk laughed and said, "Four out of five ain't bad, unk."

Izz continued, "Before I jumped on Henry Ford's gravy train payin' five bucks a day in '14, I was footloose, without no cares, but gettin' street smart don't come all at once. Sometimes you get some hard knocks and the best thing is to go slow and learn from guys what's been there. I remember the first freight I hopped. It was goin' west out of the Cicero yards. A bunch of guys pried open the slidin' door of a boxcar and we all piled in. One guy had a little wire contraption he made what would hold a soup can on top. Underneath he opened somethin' they called 'canned heat'. When he touched a match to it, he had hisself a little cook stove. Most of the guys had somethin' to share – some bread, a can of beans, stale doughnuts – stuff like that. After eatin', a couple guys drank what was left of the canned heat cuz they didn't have nuthin' better to drink. They got to yellin' and shakin' so bad we had to put them off when the train slowed down so's they wouldn't give us away.

"By the time we pulled into the Peoria freight yards I learned my first lesson. The railroad dicks pulled open the slidin' door and started using them lead-tipped blackjacks on any guy they could grab. I was lucky, I only got a couple walnut size knots on my head. The trick in dodging them yard dicks is to jump outta the boxcar and start runnin' in the same direction the train is goin' before you hit the ground, maybe a half mile from the train yard. Of course you got to be careful. I seen guys bust up ankles and knees, and one guy hit the handle of a switch head and rolled under the wheels. We never knew if he lived or not.

"The best way to travel by train in warm weather is to ride the rods. You get yourself a sturdy piece of cardboard about six feet long and a couple feet wide. It's a good idea to fold it up while you're walkin' so's not to look so noticeable. Go into the crapper in a train station, or some public place that's got one of them rollers with a cloth towel which winds itself up. You cut about six feet of towel off and wrap it around your waist. Then you hang out in the switchin' yard. When the train starts to pull out you slide the cardboard in on top of the rods which most all boxcars got for reinforcement. You then squeeze yourself in on top of the cardboard and you got a cozy place to ride. After a spell you can unwind the towel and use it for a pillow, or even a light blanket. Of course you're ridin' at forty or fifty miles per, only eighteen inches from the ties wizzin' by, but the price is sure right."

Monk was now wide awake and eager to hear more. He asked, "What about regular meals, Izz? How did you eat without much money?"

Izz said, "Eatin' regular is one thing you gotta learn to do without, Monk, but they's plenty a ways to get grub. Take for example when it's real cold, like these last coupla nights. You seen milk bottles on front porches what the milkman delivered a few hours before, and the frozen cream pops the caps and sticks up about an inch or two?"

Monk said, "Sure, I saw that plenty of times on my way to school on a winter morning."

"Well," Izz explained, "you keep an empty pint milk bottle in your pocket – they got the same size openin' as a quart bottle, and a pint whiskey bottle of warm water in another pocket. About 5:00 in the mornin' when nobody's lookin', you slip up and slice that frozen cream off the top with your jackknife and pop it in your pint milk bottle. You then poke a hole in the frozen cream that's left in the quart bottle on the porch. You pour a couple ounces of warm water in, shake it up and press the cardboard cap back in place. Nobody knows you been there and the milk don't taste much different. You do that until you get your pint bottle filled with frozen cream."

Monk said, "What I don't get, Izz, why don't you just take the whole damn bottle of milk?"

"Hell, Monk, that'd be stealing. This way you is only borrowin' a little cream that won't never be missed."

"What do you do with the cream, Izz?"

"Well, you keep the bottle of frozen cream under your arm pit, and find yourself an all-night cafe. Order up two of them Niagara Falls shredded wheat biscuits and a piece of hot buttered toast. You put the toast in the bottom of a bowl, with the biscuits on top, and pour the warmed up cream over the whole mess. You got yourself a healthy breakfast for about 8 cents. Another way to get a good meal is to find a joint that's kinda crowded and busy. Watch for a young waitress or an old one. The kid is probably green and don't know what you're up to, and the old dame don't give a damn. You ask for a pot of hot water and a package of tea which costs four or five cents. Find a booth or a table where nobody notices you. They's most always a bowl of crackers and a ketchup bottle handy. Crunch up the crackers in the bowl, dump in plenty of ketchup and pour hot water on top. Sprinkle on a little salt and pepper and you got yourself a dandy bowl of tomato soup."

"That's pretty nifty, Izz, but you can't live on a little soup and shredded wheat forever."

"Oh, I ain't sayin' you do that stuff ever' day, Monk. They's lots of times you can work a little for a home-cooked meal. You can chop wood, make some repairs, lots a' things. I remember I was hoe'n in this here lady's vegetable garden one time. She says, 'Izzy, you mightin' believe it, but when I was a young girl about 18, I won a prize for being the best hoe'er in Clinton County.' I didn't say nuthin', but I sure had to smile to myself. They's other ways you can get a meal and sometimes extra duds and a bed for the night, too. Keep your eyes open for revival meetin's and baptisms. They usually got plenty of grub at them things. Sal O'Donnell once told me he got baptized and saved eight times in a month and gained 8 pounds, not countin' all the water he swallowed! Well, Monk, that's enough stories for one night. We gotta get some shut-eye – we got a big day comin' up."

The bunch Gussie rounded up on Tuesday weren't the kind of guys you'd take home for a beer and sandwich, especially with your sister in the house, but as soon as they were told it was Al Capone's caper and that Izzy would put in a good word with Frank Nitti, they were all business and ready to work. Izzy asked if they were carrying and five of the wiseguys pulled out .38 snubs. The sixth wiseguy smiled and took a ten-inch ice pick out of a steel-tipped leather holster strapped to his belt. They all came with good reps: three of the boys, Angie Zambelli, Petro Manelli, and Joseph Aiello, had done jobs with the Purple Gang in Detroit. Victor Ciambi and Geno Evola were out of Toledo, and the Kraut called Gunter, with the lethal ice pick, had been in the Communications Corps of the German Army during the Great War. Monk O.K.'d the guys and told them to be at the river warehouse by 11 o'clock that night. They would get half a C note when the work started and the other half when the job was done.

After the wiseguys left, Monk said, "Did you get a whiff of the two birds from Toledo, Ciambi and Evola? They could stink up a whole room with their garlic breath. They must eat the damn stuff three times a day."

"I ain't too sure of that, Monk. I heard that the Genna brothers in Little Italy rub a garlic paste on their .38 slugs. They claim that if the slugs don't waste a guy, the garlic causes what they call gangrene to finish the bum off. But we better keep an eye on them two."

Late Tuesday afternoon the boys went over to the warehouse. Monk unloaded the truck and organized the equipment and supplies on the wooden floor while Izzy began working on his project that would make possible the pulling of 1,320 feet of rope half way across the frozen Detroit River.

Wooden reels containing three-hundred feet of rope would have to be unwound quickly, quietly and easily. As each reel was emptied, the rope would be tied securely to the rope on each succeeding reel until the midpoint of the frozen river was reached; 1,320 feet of rope was to be simultaneously unwound from Windsor and tied to the Detroit rope. This procedure would be completed just before 1 a.m. on the night of the job. Darkness was essential and a cover of falling snow would be helpful.

Izzy clamped two twelve-foot 2x6-inch planks on the warehouse roof rafters thirty-six inches apart. One thirty-six-inch 2x6 brace was nailed between the vertical planks twelve inches below the ceiling. The planks were nailed to the floor and rafters. Next, Izz drilled two-inch holes through each of the vertical planks four feet up from the floor and pounded a round two-inch diameter steel bar, or axle, through the holes extending out sixteen inches on the left side and six inches on the right. He placed a three-hundred-foot rope reel on the left axle extension and secured it with a quarter-inch cotter pin. A fifteen-inch removable crank was

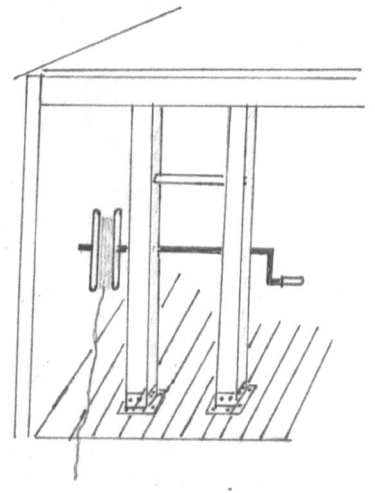

then placed on the right axle and secured. With Monk turning the crank and Izzy oiling the axle as it turned in the wood, the friction lessened until the rope reel could be easily rotated by one hand.

With the project completed, Monk sat on a box, opened a fifth of Old Log Cabin, passed it to Izz and said, "Izzy, you are a genuine genius!" Izz took a long pull and said, "Nephew, I'm glad you finally realized it, but what took you so damn long?"

There was still the problem of pulling the three-hundred bottles of Johnnie Walker from Windsor to Detroit. Izz calculated the total weight of a half-mile of rope, hardware, pouches and Johnnie Walker, to be about one-thousand pounds – far too much for one man using the crank on his wind-up mechanism in the warehouse, even though the pouches would be sliding across ice. A solution was forming in Izzy's mind, but he put it aside for more pressing needs.

By 11 o'clock Tuesday night, all six of the wiseguys had arrived at the river warehouse. Monk asked if anyone had seen them and Petro Manelli said, "Jus' some damn copper who smiled and give us a salute as we walked by." "Good," said Izz. "That was Corporal Carmichael keepin' an eye on things for us."

Monk had covered the windows earlier with blankets so the kerosene stove was beginning to warm the large room. After the boys eagerly finished ham sandwiches and downed several alky beers, Izzy sharply rapped his empty beer bottle on the stove and said, "I want to thank you all for comin' tonight. Every one of ya has been picked because of your special skills and tight lips – that and because you're all handsome, upstanding citizens." The wiseguys nudged each other and made appropriate humorous, degrading remarks.

Izz went on, "You know Mr. Capone and Mr. Bernstein is supportin' this caper. Do your job and the big boys will look kindly on you. Screw up and there ain't nowhere you can hide. The success of this entire operation is gonna come down to one little thing – your learnin' to tie ropes together that don't pull apart – learnin' to tie a damn little knot. Awright, Monk, take over."

Monk gave each man twelve pieces of rope about ten inches long. He slowly demonstrated the technique of tying two ropes together in a square knot. He did this over and over as if his audience was a group of twelve-year-old boys. He then directed two wiseguys to pull the ropes apart. The harder they pulled, the tighter the knot became. He then tied what appeared to be a square knot, but made a reverse loop. The same two wiseguys pulled the rope ends and the knot gave way without resistance.

Monk said, "The second knot is called a granny, and, as you can see, is entirely useless. You will be unwinding and tying together three-hundred-foot reels of rope. If one knot fails, the entire operation fails and we won't be able to pull three-hundred bottles of premium booze across the ice from Canada." There was a murmur among the men. "If that happens, Izzy and I will be upset, Mr. Capone and Mr. Bernstein will be furious and you would be well advised to catch a fast freight to somewhere very far away. Let's get busy learnin' to tie a square knot!"

Each man was told to tie ten knots that would be carefully inspected. If only one granny out of ten was tied, the man had to tie ten square knots in front of Monk. After Gunter had mis-tied his third square knot, Angie Zambelli said loudly, "That dumb Kraut don't know his ass from his elbow, Izz. You oughta send the bastard packin' back to the Kaiser." All the guys laughed except Gunter. He held his temper, but Monk could see the hate boiling in his dark eyes. Forty-five minutes later Izz said, "Awright you Boy Scouts, listen up. There's a few more things you gotta know. Number 1: Only me, Monk and Gussie is in charge; whatever we say, goes. Number 2: While you're workin' outside here in Detroit, no talkin', smokin' or makin' any other noise. Number 3: It's just like the army, each guy does his job and helps the other guy if needed. If you got a question about sumpthin' – you whisper. Any guy breaks them rules, he takes a walk and don't get paid. Any questions?" All six wiseguys were silent, so Izzy went on, "O.K., finish the alky and get some sleep. Angie, Petro, and Gunter be here Wednesday night at 11 o'clock. You'll get a bonus for doin' some extra work. Gussie will contact you other guys when we need you."

Izzy's next project on Wednesday afternoon was to fashion a small platform on the back of the Flexible Flyer sled with a one-inch diameter axle running parallel through two supports and extending out twelve inches on either side of the sled. Two five-hundred-foot reels of coated copper wire would be placed on either side of the axle. A wooden box bolted to the middle of the sled was large enough to hold three extra reels and a crank telephone. The five reels, when spliced together, would easily reach from the Detroit warehouse to the garage in Windsor. The sled conversion was completed a little after 6 o'clock.

After enjoying the blue plate special at the Palms, Monk and Izzy returned to the warehouse. The final job was to silence the T truck motor so it wouldn't attract attention. Izz solved the problem by installing a three-baffle muffler and attaching a can filled with coarse steel wool and shredded asbestos over the end of the tailpipe. When he revved her up, the old engine whispered, "chunk-a chunk, chunk-a-chunk, chunk-a-chunk," and wouldn't have awakened a sleeping baby.

By 10:30 Wednesday night a light snow began to fall. A half hour later Angie, Petro, and Gunter "The Iceman" arrived at the warehouse as ordered. Izz instructed the Iceman to position two spools of copper wire on the sled axle and stash three extra spools and a crank telephone in the sled box. He was to connect the wires to the telephone in the Detroit warehouse, then begin pulling the sled to Canada. When the Windsor telephone was wired he was instructed to make a test call to Detroit. During the crossing, Angie and Petro were to follow a few paces behind the Iceman – Petro pulling the wires from each spool and keeping them two feet apart, Angie attaching lead sinkers on the wires and anchoring them in the snow cover.

When Angie heard the plan he blew his top. "Why the shit should the Kraut have the easy job pullin' the sled 'cross slick ice while I got to break my ass bendin' over every twenty feet pressing them damn sinkers in the snow?"

Izzy growled, "That's because the Iceman ain't a dumb peckerhead like you, Angie. He's not only gonna pull the sled, but hook up both telephones together and that takes some brains, somethin' you ain't got. If you want out I'd be happy to tell Frank Nitti and Abe Bernstein how you queered this deal."

Angie quieted down, but he was steaming mad. Before starting for Windsor Izzy reminded the wiseguys to return to Detroit before sun-up so they wouldn't be seen.

The sled slipped easily across the ice as the temperature hovered in the low 20's. The swirling action of the wind and snow covered the wires, footprints and sled tracks.

Izz grabbed the warehouse phone about 2:30 a.m. and Gunter's voice came across loud and clear. When asked if he'd had any problems, the Iceman said, "Only that got-damn Angie riding my ass all the vey to Kenida. If he keeps it up I'm gonna–" "Hold it, Gunter," Izzy said, "let me take care of the no-good bastard. Don't tell him, but he's workin' his last job for Monk and me."

Izz hung up the line and said, "Let's get the hell back to the Embassy, Monk, have a nightcap and a catch few snores."

When Izz awoke Thursday morning he had an answer to the perplexing problem of how best to pull a half-ton load across the ice from Windsor to Detroit. Ford T model cars and trucks had long been used to power everything from farm equipment to water pumps and even sawmills. Why not harness truck power for Monk's project? After lighting the kerosene stove in the warehouse and putting the twelve-cup coffee pot on the hot plate in the office, the boys walked to the Early Bird Cafe for breakfast. (Monk was disappointed Betty Lou's shift didn't begin until 11:30 a.m.)

Returning to the warehouse, the boys found the stove had warmed the room to a comfortable sixty degrees and the truck motor started after only two or three turns of the crank. Izz gave Monk a lengthy list of items to pick up at H. L. Liscomb Hardware. The list included welding equipment, a vice, assorted tools, three five-foot lengths of flat steel, axle grease, an eight-foot round tempered rod two inches in diameter, a six-foot cast iron pipe two-and-a-half inches in diameter, pulleys, belts and assorted bolts, nuts and washers.

After a successful trip to Liscomb's, Monk stopped at Harris Brothers' lumberyard and picked up five pounds of fine sawdust. The two hours Monk was gone gave Izz a chance to sketch his plan on a discarded piece of cardboard. After a few measurement changes and weight calculations, he was certain his scheme would work.

Hearing the approaching truck, Izz swung open the garage door and Monk drove into the warm enclosure. "Did you get all the stuff?" Izz yelled over the noise of the motor. "You bet your ass, unk – and a fresh bottle of Old Log Cabin from Lefty O'Doul's, too." Monk busied himself laying out the supplies on the floor while Izz energetically began to work. He cut the tempered steel axle and cast iron pipe to the approximate finished size. Monk brought the metal cream pitcher from the office and filled it with axle grease. As Izz converted the heavy grease into a liquid with the acetylene torch, Monk dumped in handfuls of sawdust and stirred the mixture into a gruel-like consistency. The two-inch diameter axle was placed inside the cast iron pipe. As the grease mixture was poured around the axle, Izzy used a thin piece of steel to tamp and force the grease in place. When about two-and-a-half feet of the pipe had been packed, it was upended and the procedure repeated. Washers were slipped over the axle and secured against the cast iron pipe so grease would not seep out. Izz then buried the pipe in a snow bank until the grease hardened. Now the assembly was ready to be installed on the oak deck boards of the truck bed. Izzy fashioned two steel brackets and bolted the cast iron pipe to the deck. The axle was recut leaving a twelve-inch extension over the left rear wheel and a fourteen-inch extension over the right. Monk slipped a three-hundred-foot rope reel on the right axle and locked it in place. Izz secured a three-inch pulley on the left extension and welded a three-inch wide pulley on the left rear truck wheel.

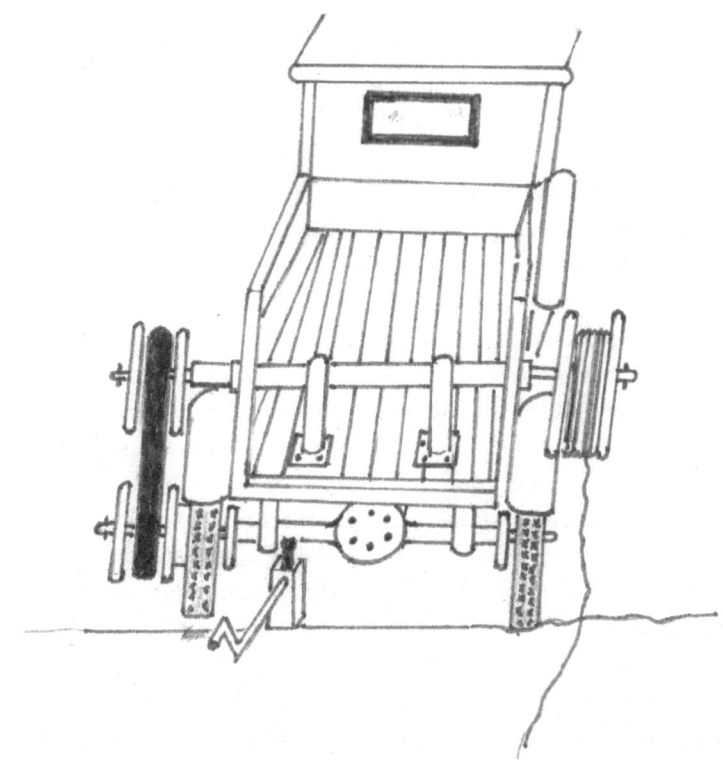

The master plan was almost ready for trial. Monk held a measuring tape to the rear wheel while Izz walked fifty feet and dropped a stick as a marker. He walked another fifty feet to the edge of the river. Returning to the truck he counted his steps. "There's exactly forty steps in one-hundred feet, Monk." Finding a scrap of paper and a pencil stub in a pocket, he scribbled some figures. "That'd make 120 steps to each 300-foot of rope, give or take a couple. The guys will need to count 120 steps, then stop until we put on another 300-foot reel. They'll have to step off that distance 4 times plus 48 more steps to reach the middle of the river."

Monk blocked three of the truck wheels as Izz jacked up the left rear about two inches. A two-and-a-half-inch wide leather belt joined the two pulleys. The jack was adjusted up slightly to put proper tension on the drive belt. At about 7 o'clock Izz said, "O.K. Monk, let's give her a test run. I'll put the transmission in low reverse while you pull the rope off the reel and walk to the river."

Reaching the water's edge, Monk gave the rope a jerk and Izz slammed the clutch into slow forward. The belt on the pulleys transferred power from the turning left wheel to the axle encased in the cast iron pipe. The packed grease and sawdust lubricated the axle as it turned the reel and rewound the one hundred-feet of rope. "You did it again, Izz," Monk enthused, "she works like a charm!"

About midnight Thursday Izzy walked across the ice to Canada and rented a room at the King Edward Hotel on the corner of Glengarry Ave. and Assumption St. The next morning he contacted the boss of the Cannucks, Reggie McKenzie, and filled him in on only as much as he needed to know. Reggie directed Izz to a cousin's used car lot where he bought a six-year-old T model Ford truck and a forged registration. Izzy picked up the truck for $60 American and $25 for the "creative" document. He then called on two hardware supply houses and the MacGregor Lumber Yard. He purchased six reels of manila rope, tools, two-and-a-half gross one-inch steel rings, and two-and-a-half gross double end harness snaps. Izzy drove over to Scalese's Canadian shop on Tecumseh Road to check on the progress of the promised pouches. Scalese's brother-in-law, Mario Sillari, told Izz that Giuseppe had sent over five of his best men the night before to help his people, and they had already completed one-hundred-and-sixty pouches. He could guarantee the remaining one-hundred and forty, with rings attached, no later than 5 o'clock Saturday. When Izz said he also needed three-hundred steel rings sewn on four hundred-foot lengths of rope fifteen-inches apart, Mario said, "Giuseppe, he told a me about the job an iffa you bring the ropes and a rings by 3 o'clock today, they willa be ready with the pouches onna Saturday."

After a fish and chips lunch at the King Edward, Izz stopped in the Maple Leaf Room for a couple whiskeys. Proceeding to the garage by the river, Izzy then constructed a wooden wind-up reel mechanism as he had done in Detroit, and secured it to the floor and rafters. Reggie's men practiced tying square knots until no mistakes were made. Izzy cut four ropes into hundred-foot lengths and delivered them, along with three hundred rings, to Mario thirty minutes before the 3 o'clock deadline.

Izzy said later it felt like he had spent a week in Windsor that Friday night.

It was so cold when Izz left the King Edward only one or two bars and a sleazy burlesque were open. Izz hustled a couple of drunks at English billiards on a huge snooker table with pocket inserts at the Hound and Fox Pub, enjoyed several Connemara Irish whiskeys, and made his way through a blinding snowstorm back to the hotel.

Most of Saturday was uneventful. Izzy briefed Reggie and his men again on that night's work. He cautioned them to double check all the square knots. By 5 p.m. Mario Sillari had the four ropes and three-hundred pouches completed as promised. After tucking $350 in his inside pocket, Mario said, "I don'ta suppose it'sa anya my business whatta youa gonna do with three-hundreda pouches." Izzy said, "You suppose right, Mario."

When Izz returned to the garage, the plan was set in motion. Ernest and George began attaching pouches on the rope rings with double-ended harness snaps while the other four Cannucks slid the Johnnie Walker into the pouches, cinched up the drawstrings and tied a double bowknot. At 11 o'clock Izzy rang up Monk and told him to have Gussie, Angie, the Iceman and two wiseguys begin pulling the Detroit rope across the ice. He would meet them half way with the rope from Canada and connect the two lines. Within forty minutes there was not only a telephone line, but a stout rope connecting Detroit and Windsor.

Gussie, Angie and the Iceman continued on to Windsor so Gussie could pay Reggie the $1,800 for the Johnnie Walker and half the Cannucks' wages. The two wiseguys were instructed to help fill the pouches and pull the pouch lines to the edge of the ice. As Izzy, Petro and Geno Evola walked back to Detroit, the weather was very cooperative – about five degrees with enough snow to make the ice slick, and best of all, no moon.

Back at the warehouse, Izz lit a Camel and said, "Damn it, Monk, stop fidgitin' around. You look like some whore gettin' ready for confession. Everythin' is goin' great, just like we planned. Here, have a gulp of Old

Log Cabin, it'll settle you down." At 1:30 a.m. Izz grabbed the phone. Gussie shouted in an excited voice, "We're close to ready here, Izz. Start pullin' slow in 'bout ten minutes when ya hear three rings. From then on, three longs mean 'pull' and two shorts mean 'stop'."

Izz yelled, "This is it, Monk. Let's get the T model fired up!" Monk hopped in the cab, pushed up the spark lever, pulled down the accelerator lever about an inch and turned on the ignition key and gas line. He then jumped out and attempted to crank her up. The oil was so cold and thick Monk could barely turn the motor over, much less get it started. Monk frantically yelled to Izz, "The damn thing won't hardly turn over, Izz. What the shit should I do?"

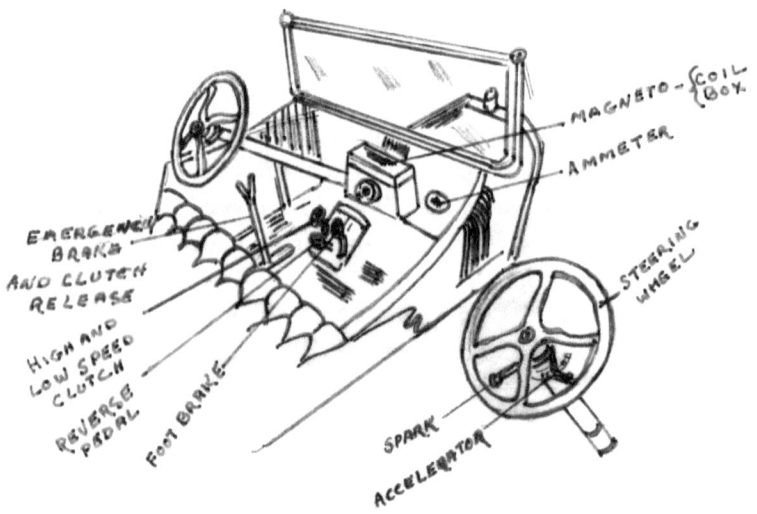

Izz said, "Calm down a damn New York minute, Monk, and let me think... Awright, go into the warehouse and get that twelve-cup coffee pot off the stove." While Monk was gone, Izz calmly jacked up the left rear wheel. When Monk came running back with the boiling coffee, Izz grabbed the pot, opened the hood and poured the hot java on the carburetor, gas line and manifold. Monk climbed into the cab as Izz ordered, pulled the emergency brake lever to neutral position and was ready to operate the spark and accelerator levers. Izz spun the crank while activating the choke wire protruding through the radiator. Being in neutral, with the back wheel jacked up, there was very little friction and with the carburetor, manifold and gas line hot, the old T model backfired a couple of times and began purring like a contented cat.

Izzy let the back wheel down, and even with the transmission in neutral, the continuing rotation of the planetary band system peculiar to Ford vehicles caused the truck to slowly inch forward. Izz ran to the front, leaned on the radiator and easily stopped the motion while Monk blocked the front wheels. Izz laughed and said it reminded him of his old milk-route horse, Dolly, gently pushing and nudging him for a bite of apple.

Hearing three telephone rings, Izz jacked the left rear up again and attached the flat belt to both the wheel and wind-up pulley. Monk jammed the clutch pedal into slow forward and the towrope began to rewind. The boys in Windsor cheered loudly as the pouches began to slide toward Detroit. Monk kept the motor speed at about three miles an hour, and as one three-hundred-foot reel filled, a "pigtail" was tied to the next towrope and a second reel rewound. Just before the eighth reel filled, the first Johnnie Walker pouches reached the Detroit shoreline.

Monk put the motor into neutral, removed the belt from the truck and axle pulleys, and lowered the tire to the warehouse floor. He backed to the river ice and Izzy hooked the pouch towline to the rear of the truck frame. As Monk slowly pulled the pouches toward the warehouse, Izzy and four wiseguys emptied the pouches and carefully put the Johnnie Walker bottles into crates. Within minutes, two Cannucks arrived and helped unload the incoming line, pushed the empty pouch line to one side, and carried the full crates to the warehouse. After the second run, Izzy shoveled sand on Monk's path for better traction. As the last pouch line approached the warehouse, Izz yelled, "Boys, it's just like the assembly line at old Henry's Highland Park factory. Keep case'n them bottles like you're doin'."

By the time the last pouch line was emptied, Gussie and his guys showed up almost frozen stiff. Monk hustled them into the warehouse. While thawing out around the stove, Gussie, stomping his feet and briskly rubbing his hands, growled, "Where in hell is the hot coffee, Monk?" Monk said, "You wouldn't believe it if I told you, Gussie."

Izz rang up Reggie while the boys continued carrying the full whiskey cases to the warehouse. Reg enthused, "You blokes done the smoothest job I ever seen and we're ready to work with you Yanks whenever you say. I wanna apologize to you an' Gussie for my abruptness over the money."

"Don't let it bother you none, Reg, I'd a' done the same thing in your shoes. There is one last thing what will clean up all the loose ends. In ten minutes three of my guys will start helpin' your two guys pull your towrope an' pouches to the middle of the river. If you could send a couple of your boys to meet them, my men wouldn't have to go all the way to Windsor, and it would save us a lot of time. That way we'll be ready to join our ropes again if Mr. Capone wants another order. I think we can leave the telephone line in place because it ain't hardly noticeable."

Reg replied, "Consider the job done, Izz, my guys are startin' now."

"Thanks, Reg. I'm sendin' a bonus of six tenners to be split among your guys for working so hard. I'll put in a call to Frank Nitti in Chicago to send a truck to pick up the booze. I got a feelin' Mr. Capone is gonna be real happy. I wouldn't be surprised none if he don't want another, and maybe twice as big an order, in a few days. Are you and your guys interested?"

"We are eager and waitin', Izz. Please convey my best wishes to Mr. Capone an' tell him we admire him greatly here in Canada."

"All right Reg, I'll ring you at the garage at midnight Tuesday and tell you if Mr. Capone wants another order."

Gussie and the two wiseguys, still blowing on their hands, carried the last of the cases into the warehouse and raked over the footprints and tire tracks. Izzy gave the Iceman, Angie, and Vincent an extra ten spot each for their good work and told them to be on call for another job in three or four days. As Monk pulled the truck into the warehouse, a gentle snowfall covered all evidence of the night's work. By 4:30 Sunday morning Monk, Izz and Gussie began walking back to the Embassy. As they approached Corporal Carmichael on East Atwater Street, Izzy pressed a twenty into the corporal's hand. Carmichael gave a smart salute and said, "Nice night for a walk. Good night, gentlemen."

When they reached their room, Monk poured them each a half tumbler of Old Log Cabin. A short time later, as he refreshed their drinks, Gussie leaned against the wall and said, "A funny damn thing happened comin' back acrost the river. The Iceman seen one of them big white birds they calls seagauls layin' real still on the ice. The thing starts flutterin' when he picks it up in them big mitts a' his, but he handles it real tender like. Angie, who's been on the Iceman's ass real hard for a coupla days asks him if he's plannin' to have the bird for supper. I thought the Kraut was gonna kill the bastard; he glares at him but don't say nothin.' He jus' slips the bird in the pocket of his great coat ever so careful and finally says maybe he can save its life. Who'd ever thought the Kraut would have a soft spot fer a damn bird?"

CHAPTER FIVE

Monday morning about 9 a.m. Izzy made a toll call to Frank Nitti in Chi-Town and told him he had twenty-five cases of Johnnie Walker Black and could he send a truck? Frankie, in an excited voice said, "You bet your ass, Izz. What time can we make the pick-up?" Izzy said to have his guys meet him and Monk about midnight at the Michigan Central railroad station and he'd take them to where the booze was stashed. Izz said, "Mr. Nitti, – Frankie, we got a little problem. The cost of the Johnnie Walker which Al give us, plus the start-up money for the equipment, wages for fourteen guys, plus payoff money, has left us with no profit and just enough dough for eats and a couple more nights at the flop house."

After a long pause Frankie said, "I understand what you guys is up against, Izz, and I'll talk with Al. I know he's satisfied with the job you boys done, so don't worry none 'cause Al always takes care a' guys who treat him right. Call me back at the Metropole, Oakview 5580 'bout 4 o'clock this afternoon and I'll have some answers for ya."

Once Izzy filled Monk in on his gab with Nitti, the boys went down to the Early Bird for some java and sinkers. Betty Lou greeted them with a big smile and hello. When she returned with their order Monk said, "Betty Lou, I never knew Yooper girls were so pretty and accommodating. It must be that cold Northern Michigan weather that puts roses in your cheeks."

Betty Lou blushed and said "Monk, Upper Peninsula girls aren't no different than those Chicago girls you're used to. You've just been away from home too long." After finishing their java and engaging in some mildly suggestive chit-chat, Izz said, "Don't take no wooden nickels, Betty Lou. We've got to scram now because me and Monk have a big day comin' up." Monk gave Betty Lou a wink and awkwardly squeezed her hand as she reached for the empty coffee mugs.

After returning to the Embassy Izz bought the morning *Detroit Free Press* and chatted with old Fred on the desk. Fred was upset about working a double shift because the new night man staggered in falling-down drunk, pissed in the artificial palm tree in the lobby, mumbled his regrets and was last seen wobbling toward West Lafayette Boulevard. With Fred threatening to quit his job, Izz bolstered his spirits by assuring him he was the best damn deskman the Embassy ever had.

Room 223 was the usual steam-heated eighty-five or ninety degrees. Monk asked Izz to remind him to bring a hammer and screwdriver from the warehouse so he could pry open one of the nailed windows. Monk smoked and relaxed on his cot while Izz read the skimpy January sports pages. The Chicago Black Hawks defeated the Rangers 4-1. Montreal defeated Toronto 2-1 in overtime and O. B. Osborne had an article on the Detroit Tigers looking forward to spring training in Arizona on March 1.

Izz began to chuckle and said, "Monk, here's some news I know you been waitin' for. Windsor defeated Chatham in the first game of the curling championship. I seen one of them games once in about 1916. You ever seen one?" When Monk replied in the negative, Izzy proceeded to explain what he remembered of the sport. "It's kinda like shuffleboard but played on a strip of ice about as long and wide as a bowling alley. At each end of the ice is circles with blue dots in the middle. One team tries to slide a goofy looking thing they call a stone, which weighs thirty-five or forty pounds, closest to the dot in one of the circles. The stone looks somethin' like a large round teakettle with a big handle stickin' out the back. The second team then tries to knock the other guy's stone off the ice with his stone. But here's the funny part. While the stone is slidin' down the ice at about one mile an hour, two team-mates in suits and ties with little whisk brooms is sweepin' the ice in front to make it go faster or slower. You can bet them boys with the brooms wouldn't lift a hand to help their missus sweep out the kitchen. The game I saw was so excitin' my blood pressure musta topped out at about 85/50. I woulda had more fun watchin' paint dry in the men's room at the bus station."

"If you think curling is boring, Izz, you should see a cricket match. There's two teams of eleven players each on a grass field about the size of a baseball field. The bowler or pitcher has to throw a ball without bending his elbow to an opposing batter who is standing in front of a three-pronged wicket about two-and-a-half feet tall. The batter's partner stands by the wicket next to the bowler about sixty feet away. If the bowler hits the wicket, the batter is out, but if the batter hits the ball to any place in the field, both batter and partner start running back and forth to each wicket as long as the ball is in play. If any player – and they've got some strange names like 'square leg,' 'fine leg,' and 'silly mid-on' – can field the ball and hit the batter's wicket with his throw, the batter is out. A game can last anywhere from a few hours to several days. Some of the best hitters, using a flat paddle-like bat, can score more than a hundred runs in one inning. I can tell you, Izz, the game looks like a Chinese fire drill and they need a public accountant to keep score."

"Damn, Monk, I'm tired just listenin' to your explainin' a cricket game. If you don't mind, I'd just as soon get my kicks watchin' the girls at the Gayety and Avenue burlesques. Them Cannucks is sure hard to unnerstand sometimes."

By late Monday morning Izz, lying on his back, dropped off into an easy sleep, oblivious to Monk's growing apprehension. What would Nitti say at 4 o'clock? Would Capone carry them a little longer? What if Capone took the Johnnie Walker and left them high and dry? Or worse, what if his pick-up men were instructed to waste them in the warehouse? Who would know – or care?

By the time Izz snorted himself awake, Monk had downed two tumblers of Old Log Cabin and half finished a pack of Camels. With his nervousness somewhat calmed, but still feeling uneasy, Monk said, "You wanna play some cards Izz, just to pass the time? I found a cribbage board in the closet some overnighter must of left."

Izz stretched and said, "Sure, but I ain't gonna play no sissy game like cribbage. That's for a coupla little old ladies drinkin' gin and eatin' fancy cookies. Besides, I can't keep track of them 15-2's and 15-4's. Let's just play a man's game – five-card stud poker. Each half-match stick is worth a penny and a whole stick, five cents. You can pay off when you get your share of the next job."

Monk pretended he was insulted and replied, "You sure know how to hurt a guy, unk. Just for that last crack, I'm gonna whip your ass. Gimme them bicycles."

After an hour or so, Monk, tired of losing, said, "I'm getting bored as hell. Why don't we pool what we got left on eggs and bacon, and use the matinee tickets Scurvy Miller gave us?" Izzy stuffed the dirty bicycles in his pocket while scooping up his winnings.

"You know, Monk, for a little prick, you come up with some pretty adult ideas, and thanks for lettin' your old unk win again." Monk made a face but didn't reply.

The 2 p.m. matinee at The Avenue was pretty raggy. Of course they didn't expect the headliner, Ann Howe, to be displaying her charms to fifteen or twenty stumble-bums in overcoats trying to keep warm at 2:00 in the afternoon. Watching three or four willing but inexperienced strippers strut their stuff was somewhat entertaining, but all in all, Monk was right when he said, "Izz, I've had just about as much fun sitting in the bus station waiting room watching the broads come and go. Let's mosey back to the Embassy."

At 4 o'clock sharp, Izz used his last bit of change to call Frank Nitti. Matter of fact, he had to ask Frank to call him back when the operator said his three minutes were up. Frankie returned the call and reported he had some good news and some not so good. Izz said, "I think the good news would make me feel a whole lot better, Frankie."

"Awright, Izz, Al is sendin' a truck an' two of his best boys to pick up the Johnnie Walker at midnight. He sends his congratulations to both you guys for your first-rate work." So far so good, thought Izz.

"Next, Al wants fifty cases on the next order. I told him you was broke an' he said he'd send a grand for added expenses so you and Monk could have a little fun. He'll send the dough with Rico Profacini an' Ciro Cataldo on the truck tonight. The grand will come outta your profit when the next order is delivered. Al will contact Abe Bernstein in Detroit an' make arrangements for him to give you the $3,600 to cover the wholesale cost of the next fifty cases of Johnnie Walker. Al an' the Purple Gang work together on deals like this."

"What's the bad news, Frankie?" Izz asked.

"Al sez to tell ya he ain't runnin' no charity an' you guys'll get paid in full when the next fifty cases is delivered to the Hawthorne. Can you and Monk live with them arrangements?"

"It don't look like we got no other choice, Frankie. I'll ring you up when the next order is ready, probably next Saturday or Sunday. Thanks for goin' to bat for us."

When Izz hung up, Fred motioned him over to the Embassy desk. He had a bottle of Three Feathers in a brown paper bag and offered Izz a snort. Izzy took a gulp and said, "Where the hell did you get this premium stuff, Fred?" Fred smiled, took a nip and replied, "You ain't the onlyest guy wit' connections, Izz."

Izzy returned to the room, sat on the bed and said, "Al's got us over a barrel with our asses showin', Monk, but he's sendin' us an extra grand tonight. That'll tide us over and in a week we'll have more dough than you ever seen."

Monk turned on his charm and got Betty Lou at the Early Bird to stake him and Izz to the blue-plate special – meat loaf, peas and mashed potatoes, a wedge of apple pie and a couple mugs of coffee. Monk told her if she wanted, he'd talk to Scurvy Miller at The Avenue burlesque and get her an audition. Betty Lou giggled, gave him a little peck on the check, and said, "Monk, you are somethin' else! Here you and Izz haven't the price of a blue-plate special and you're gonna set me up with an audition for a stage career."

Once outside, Izz asked, "Monk, don't you think Betty Lou is a little broad in the beam for that kind of work?"

Monk winked and replied, "There's no harm in making a pretty girl feel good, Izz. Besides, lots of guys are large-ass men."

Izzy pulled up his skimpy collar, lit a Camel and said they'd better get back to the hotel. There was a pile of figuring to be done before the start of the next job. On the way to the Embassy they stopped at O'Doul's for a couple of drinks. Izz apologized to Lefty for having such a loud mouth when he was last in the joint. Lefty said, "Forget it, Izz, we both got kinda nuts," and gave Izz a fifth of Old Log Cabin on credit.

When they got back to the Embassy hotel Fred was behind the desk, about to start his 10 p.m. to 6 a.m. shift. He had been after Izz for a week to show him how the missing ace card trick worked, so Izz complied and got six Vernors and a chunk of ice for revealing his sleight-of-hand secret.

When Monk and Izz walked into their room, it was hot and fragrant, as usual. The steam radiator was hissing and the place smelled of stale beer, snuffed-out cigarettes and dirty sheets. Izz pulled the night table up to the bed, took out a pad, and licked the end of a pencil stub.

"Monk, I know you think a grand is a whole lot of money, and usually it is, but I'm gonna write down what we need up front to make this second job work. We got no problem payin' for the booze – Al's takin' care of that, but we need three-hundred more pouches and hardware. That's about three-hundred-fifty to four-hundred bucks. Six wiseguys and six Cannucks in Windsor will run us a hunnert each – even if we do like last time and hold out fifty bucks each until the job's done – that's six-hundred bucks right there. Now we're up to $950 and that don't count Gussie or anythin' for us."

"Damn Izz, I never thought of it that way. What the hell are we gonna do?"

Izz continued, "O.K., here's my plan. I'll see Scalese and offer him a hunnert now and a bonus of maybe a hunnert when the job's done. I think he'll go for it because we was money on the barrel-head last time. Gussie's your pal, so don't keep no secrets from him. Tell him we is on our uppers just now, but we'll take care of him later. Give him a hunnert now and maybe cut him in for ten per cent on jobs comin' up. He's also got to sell the wiseguys and the Cannucks. He could offer them twenty bucks when the job starts and a bonus of say another fifty bucks on top of the $80 they got comin.' Make sure they know Al Capone is backin' us, and it won't hurt none to again mention Abe Bernstein and his Purple Gang. Lemme add this up. I got 440 bucks we pay out, and $560 for us."

"That sounds great, Izz. We can have us one hell of a time for that kind of dough and, in another few days, we'll be rollin' in loot."

"Just one problem, Monk. You gotta sell the deal to Gussie, he's gotta sell the wiseguys and the Cannucks, and I gotta sell ol' man Scalese. This here job comin' up is the one that'll get us over the hump. Right now, we is workin' for peanuts. I figure we got three or maybe four more weeks of solid ice. Now that we know what we're doin,' we could easy pull two jobs a week. Frankie said Al would take all the Johnnie Walker we could get, and expenses for two hauls ain't much more than for one. Two hauls a week of fifty cases on each run would be, lessee – $72 times 25, and 25 more equals $3,600 times 4 – no, by 2, equals $7,200 gross. Outta that we should clear five grand, easy. And, I've been thinkin', what if we put in a second line next to the one we got now, maybe twenty-five feet or so away. We could get a couple more dirty cops for protection and before the ice goes out we stand to make ten grand!"

Monk sat there dumbfounded. He took a big gulp of Log Cabin and said, "Izz, I can hardly believe what you're telling me. Hot damn, we'll be as rich as that Rockerfeller guy. We could buy us a new Packard and all the pussy you'd ever want – or can't you just see us rolling up in front of Mahoney's pool hall in one of those new Stutz Bearcats!"

"There ain't no reason not to think big, Monk, which reminds me, there's somethin' I've been meanin' to talk over with you. I won't go into any details now, but we gotta start thinkin' of how we're gonna supply Al with booze when the weather warms up and the river ain't froze over."

"I've been giving that some thought too, Izz, but can't come up with any brilliant ideas."

"Have you ever heard of Gar Wood?"

Monk thought on it and said, "Give me a little hint, was he in sports?"

"You're in the general area, nephew. Gar is the fastest man in the world on water. He recently built a speed boat that'll do better than 70 miles an hour."

"Oh yeah, I remember now; there was a big spread in the *Trib* about him racing the band leader Guy Lombardo on the Detroit River."

"Does bein' able to go 70 miles an hour on water give you any ideas?"

Monk's eyes widened. "Damn, unk, that opens up some very interesting possibilities. I think you might be on to something."

Izzy put his arm around his favorite nephew's shoulder. "I don't want you to lose any sleep over it, but Gar has been a good friend since he come to Detroit in 1915 and started foolin' with motors. But it's gettin' late. We better catch a trolley to the Michigan Central and meet Al's two goons.

The boys rode in the truck with Rico Profacini and Ciro Cataldo to the warehouse down by the Detroit River. Izz felt the warm comfort of the .38 snub in his right pocket. Monk had gotten over his apprehension and asked Rico if the Mack still had the injection pump hooked to the intake manifold which sent up a black cloud of smoke if any dummies were following. Rico exclaimed, "Hell yes, Monk. How the shit did you know 'bout that?"

Monk swelled up and said, "Izzy's the guy who first thought up the idea."

Rico looked surprised. "Damn, you is Izzy Brodsky, ain't ya? Lemme shake your hand. That invention a' yours saved my ass more 'n once. If we had time, I'd like ta buy ya both a drink."

Monk and Izz helped the boys load the Mack truck and before

pulling out Rico gave Izzy a sealed envelope. Back at the Embassy, Izz poured a couple of nightcaps, opened the envelope and ten crisp Ben Franklins dropped out. Monk scooped up the century notes and held them like he had just been dealt a hand of gin rummy. As he fondled the bills he said, "Izz, these babies feel almost as good as an eighteen-year-old girl's titties."

Izzy slit open a three-inch gash in the underside of his mattress and pushed five C notes into the padding. "That's our grub steak, Monk. We'll add sixty bucks more after we pay off our obligations to Scalese, Gussie, the wiseguys and the Cannucks."

By 9 o'clock Tuesday morning, Izz had presented his proposition to Scalese, and after some fast talking by Izzy, Scalese had agreed to the deal provided Izz would sweeten the bonus to $150. Scalese promised that his people in Windsor would have three-hundred more pouches made, and rings sewn on the extra ropes, by noon on Saturday. Gussie met Monk at the warehouse and said that, after some minor grumbling, the wiseguys agreed to fall in line for an extra $50 on top of their bonus money. Gussie said he thought ten per cent of all new shipments coming across from Windsor seemed fair. He didn't have trouble convincing Reggie McKenzie and his boys. They thought so much of Capone and the way Izzy treated them on the last job that they were eager to go. Reggie said fifty cases of Johnnie Walker could be easily had, but his sources would need $3,600 up front for that large an order. The money would have to be in hand by Friday afternoon.

When Monk and Izzy returned to the Embassy at midday just about everything seemed set. There was plenty of time to get the pouches and hardware ready by late Saturday. Izz asked Monk to run down to the desk and get a couple of fresh Vernors and a piece of ice. He said to give Fred an extra buck and when he returned they would finish off the pint and start figuring how best to spend their advance money.

The first thing they did was go down to Conn's Clothes on LaFayette Boulevard. Izz bought a black double-breasted pinstripe suit, a purple shirt, black tie, black socks, and black shoes with white tips. He couldn't resist pearl gray spats, several changes of silk underwear, and a gray fedora just like the one Big Al always wore. Monk bought a dark blue pinstripe, black shirt, white tie, black socks, and black shoes with white tips. He also bought gray spats, silk underwear, and a black fedora. Both men settled for black Chesterfield topcoats with black velvet lapels, and black pigskin gloves. They were lucky to find two nearly new brown suitcases with leather straps. After changing into their new clothes in the back room of Conn's they crossed the street to Abe Goldstein's reclaimed jewelry shop. There they found diamond tie pins and silver cuff links that looked almost real. Monk said they looked like two studs on the make and he never felt better in his life.

CHAPTER SIX

Being in the bucks, Monk and Izz grabbed a Checker to the ritzy Book Cadillac on Washington Street. They plunked down fourteen bucks for a double room and Uncle Izzy slipped the bell captain two Lincolns and said, "In ten minutes, walk through the lobby pagin' a Mr. Isadore Brodsky. Then bring a fifth of Old Log Cabin and six Vernors up to room 521." They sank down into a couple of big black leather chairs and gleefully listened for the page. Izz got a huge thrill when he heard his name announced in the lobby of such a fine hotel. They then took the elevator up to the fifth floor and admired the furnishings of their room, so unlike what they had become accustomed to at the Embassy. Soon the bell captain arrived, put the suitcases on folding luggage stands, and opened the drapes. Before leaving he said, "Sir, I can put you in touch with two very nice young ladies for a lot less than the cost of your room." Izzy was in the john mixing drinks, so Monk thanked him and said "I'm Mr. Brodsky's private secretary. We'll only be in town a short while, but I'll certainly advise Mr. Brodsky of your kind suggestion." When the captain left Izz came out laughing. He put his arm around his nephew's shoulder and said, "Monk, sometimes you make me proud you is my sister's kid."

It wasn't long before they started getting a buzz on. Monk poured another double shot of Old Log Cabin in a clean hotel glass, added two fingers of Vernors and asked Izz if he'd ever seen Big Al face to face – like

81

sitting at a bar telling lies and ragging his friends?

Izz said, "Hell yes, lots of times in Colosimo's. After I done that job for him and Nitti in the spring of '21, Frankie give me an invite to the Midnight Frolics Club over on the South Side. Of course, Big Al is there with his pals, like his brother Ralph who's managin' the Four Deuces, the Genna brothers, Johnny Lombardo, Jake 'Greasy Thumb' Guzik, and three bums who ain't his pals at all – Dion O'Banion, Hymie Weiss, and a loud-mouth bastard they called Sean Kelly from north of Madison Street. This guy O'Banion and a partner named William Schofield own a flower shop on North State Street opposite Holy Name Cathedral."

Monk interrupted Izz. "Oh yeah, I remember going there for the funeral of Nino Pavelka – the guy who ratted on Bunko Glodsek. You knew Nino's older sister, Bethelda, who ran the bingo games at the Blessed Mary in Canaryville." Izz acted like he didn't hear Monk and continued his story.

"This here O'Banion sets up all the final arrangements for wiseguys who get whacked, stuff like big horseshoes of flowers which say, 'Old Pal of Mine,' and 'We'll Never Forget,' from guys which probably had somethin' to do with the bum's deceasement. Anyways, Big Al is feelin' no pain and when this kid, Joe E. Lewis, who's been workin' such joints as the Green Mill and the Lincoln Gardens over on Cottage Grove, starts singin' *Sam You Made the Pants Too Long*, Big Al rolls up his pant legs with his garters showin' and starts singin' and shufflin'. Pretty soon he's floppin' his cigar up and down just like Groucho Marx. Al's the kinda guy where you can't buy a drink or nuthin,' so we all had a great time until we was fallin' down drunk.

"Funny thing though, this Kelly guy gets a snoot full and starts mouthin' off how the Dago bastards is buying all the product from the alky cookers in Little Italy and usin' it to spark up the beer they sell to the joints on the North Side, and then jackin' up the price. He claims there's cockroaches and dead rats in every barrel. O'Banion tries to shut the bum up but he keeps rantin' and ravin.' Next morning I read in the *Trib* that a guy is found up on North Broadway in a trash bin with a mouthful of dead cockroaches, a dead rat in each hand, and a neat little hole right between the eyes.

"Another time, Frankie tells me to show up for a little party tossed for Big Al's wife, Mae, at the Hawthorne Inn – Al's joint in Cicero. I go expectin' a little shindig kinda thing, but Al's hired Austin Mack and his Century Serenaders and Mezz Mezzrow's jazz band. Again, there ain't nuthin' you can pay for. If you want a smoke, the cigarette girl with a tray full of Havanas and hardly no clothes on drops a couple El Mundos next to your plate. If you want a drink, you got one with just the snap of Al's fingers. Booze keeps flowin' like there ain't no tomorrow, and the food is laid out on four long tables. Frankie tells me Big Al's always like that. If he likes you, there ain't no limit, but if you double cross him you might as well talk to your priest and sell your Chevy.

"Anyways, the high spot of the night is when Jan Garber and his band come over from the Karzas brothers' Trianon Ballroom as a surprise for Mae and play *You Are the Only One*. Big, tough Al takes out his handkerchief and acts like he's got somethin' in his eye. Georgie Jessel and Sophie Tucker, a couple of headliners from New York who have been working Colosimo's and the Green Mill Gardens, show up about midnight. Tucker sings some crowd-pleasin' words to *Pretty Baby*, and Georgie tells a few jokes and sings *Mammy*, pretendin' to be Al Jolson. Later, Jessel comes over and introduces this young stacked blond dame to Al. I guess she was probably Georgie's niece. You never seen nobody as polite as Big Al. He sets them down, buys drinks and wants to know all about what's goin' on in New York. You can almost hear a catch in Al's voice when he talks about the Big Apple.

"After a while this guy, Joey Guardino, I'm sittin' next to starts tellin' me what a great man Big Al is, which I already know, and how worried he is because of all the problems Al's got. He says the new rag sheet, *The Cicero Beacon*, ran a series on Al's cat houses and reported his girls ain't clean. The police commissioner's raidin' Al's joints again, he says, and them old church dames are sayin' Al was hurtin' the morals of young kids. Hell, I ain't never seen a kid below fifteen in any of Al's joints, and they was all polite and said 'ma'am' and 'sir.'

"Joey is really gettin' worked up now and he says Police Chief Wagner is gonna start enforcin' the old Sullivan Law and nail any of Al's boys which is carryin' concealed rods. And if that ain't enough, ten of Al's beer trucks got hijacked last week. Everybody thinks the Genna brothers' goons done it. I told him it just seems like a guy can't make an honest buck these days. Joey looked at me kinda blank like, downed a double shot of Canadian Club, fumbled for a cigarette and said he never seen a guy what's down on his luck that Big Al wouldn't give a sawbuck to. 'And you just watch,' he mumbled, 'Al's boys will take all this leftover grub down to Mike Pidgeon's mission over by the El on Wabash. Fat chance them silk stockin' bastards on State Street would even drop a quarter in the Salvation Army pot at Christmas.'

"By this time Joey is slobberin' all over me and when he tries to get up to piss, he grabs the tablecloth and pulls two or three drinks and a bowl of shrimp sauce all over my pants. After Al's guys bum-rush Joey out of there things start to slow down and get mellow. Jan Garber takes his turn on the bandstand playin' Mae's favorite, *Dartanella*, and in walks Vito Castelone with that dumb, fat little blond whore who Johnny Hennessey says Al keeps stashed on the seventh floor at the Metropole. They walks right up to Al's table and Vito says, 'Snorky, I want you ta meet my good friend, Candy Serganti.' I figure if ever a guy's wantin' to take the deep six, Vito must be standin' first in line. There ain't nobody who calls Al 'Snorky' 'cept his brothers and maybe Frank Nitti when they all got a snoot full. Now Al's gotta introduce both of them dummies to Mae."

Monk said, "Hold it a minute Izz, I gotta squeeze the turnip, but don't forget where you stopped. I want to know what happened to Castelone." Izzy admired the view of the Detroit River while he waited for Monk to return. When Monk got settled back in his chair, Izz continued his story without missing a beat.

"Al don't even look mad. He buys a round of drinks and a flower for the whore and everybody breathes a little easier. Jimmy Ondrono tells me the next day three of Al's wiseguys pick up Vito and the broad, takes them to St. Michael's church and has Father Benedito marry the dummies. One of the wiseguys even stands up as Vito's best man and Carmine DeLuca gives the dame away. Not only that, the boys tell Vito if Al ever hears about him hurtin' the whore, or if he threatens to leave her, he'll have one of the grandest funerals Chi-Town ever seen. Carmine tells Vito he's got a paid-up account at O'Banion's flower shop. Then they take the two of them over to Mt. Carmel Cemetery and let Vito get a look at a freshly dug plot with his name on a big bronze marker showin' his birth date and a blank space. Anyways, it was one swell party, and that was the last time I seen Big Al face to face."

M onk and Izz started getting hungry about 5 o'clock. So being in the chips they went over to Nate's Chop House on Monroe Street and ordered big Delmonicos with all the trimmings. Halfway through the meal, Izz pushed his plate away and said, "Remember when you was just a kid? Me and four or five young guys come over to Detroit City to work for old Henry Ford in his T model plant on Woodward and Manchester? They started me out puttin' bands in the planetary gearboxes of T model trucks. It was back-breakin' work and we put in ten to twelve hour days, but five bucks a shift was twice what the Dodge brothers was payin'. Them was good days and a bunch of us guys and five or six nurses in trainin' at the Sisters of Grace Nursin' School on East Grand Boulevard went most every Sunday to Belle Isle and had ourselves a picnic and canoe ride. I was kinda keen on a pretty little black-haired girl named Esmeralda Sweeney, and one of my pals, Jock Adamson, who was installin' Otis Elevators in the Highland plant, had his eye on Esmeralda's girl friend, Marguerite Crawford. Jock played the harmonica and another guy, Johnny Slocum, played the banjo pretty good. We got our canoes side by side and laid the paddles flat across them both and tied them down. We kinda drifted along and when the moon come up it just seemed like singin' was the thing to do."

Izz was quiet for a short time, then wiped his eyes and began singing softly. Monk never knew Izz had a voice and was embarrassed at first. Monk kept his head down, but looked around the room to see if anybody was noticing. As Izz's voice grew stronger, you could hear the sadness in it and everyone in the restaurant stopped talking and eating. Monk knew he would never forget those words:

'*I had a dream, Dear, you had one too.*
Mine was the best dream because
it was of you.
Come Sweetheart, tell me,
now is the time,
You tell me your dream,
And I'll tell you mine.'

When Izz finished, all the folks clapped their hands quietly, but with respect, kind of like they had just heard that an older sister had finished her vows and was accepted as a nun. At that moment Monk swelled up with pride for his Uncle Isadore Brodsky.

They left the Chop House about 6:30 p.m. and started walking up Raynor Street with the collars of their Chesterfields turned up to their ears. After about a block Izz said, "I got a crazy idea, Monk. What would you think about us goin' out to Hamtramck and seein' if any of my old pals is still there?"

Monk was being honest when he said he'd be pleased to tag along and meet some of the old gang he'd heard so much about. Just before they got to Gratiot, Izz saw one of those Christian Science Reading Rooms and said, "Let's go inside where it's quiet for a few minutes. There's somethin' I'd like for you to read." Being dressed to the nines like they were, the lady at a table full of books and pamphlets smiled and said, "You are most welcome here, friends. Please feel free to relax and stay as long as you like. I would be pleased to answer any questions you might have."

They thanked her, took one of her pamphlets and found a couple comfortable chairs by the fireplace. Izz pulled out a dirty crumpled envelope, removed a letter and said, "Monk, I think this might clear up some things you and your ma has been wonderin' about."

Monk started reading the prettiest handwriting he had ever seen.

Ste. Menehould, France
October 4, 1918

My Darling Izzy,

I've been so worried about you lately. With all the shortages, I know you aren't eating properly. Please try to get enough rest and if your back continues to bother you seek the advice of a good doctor. It's just like you to be so sweet to Mrs. Hrbec's daughter. The war is horrible, but I've seen miracles performed here and I'm sure new procedures will help Addie regain full use of her leg when this is all over.

Dearest, don't be so hard on yourself. I know you have tried to enlist, but you are doing vital war work. The Eagle boats you are helping build will surely have a devastating effect on Germany's horrible submarine fleet.

Remember Betsie Crawford? You knew her as Marguerite Crawford. She grew up in northern Michigan along the banks of the Betsie River, so when the boys in the ward found that out, she became "Betsie" to everyone.

Betsie has been my closest friend since those wonderful days (especially those precious Sundays) when I was in training. We came over together on the George Washington *and now share quarters (such as they are) here in Ste. Menehould.*

You'd never guess in all this world what happened last week. I heard a soldier plunking away on a banjo in the ward, and when Captain Tydie made his rounds and removed the bandages from the soldier's eyes, who should it be but Johnny Slocum. Johnny could only see faint images at first, but each day his vision improves and Dr. Tydie says he will soon be whistling at the nurses! We have had a grand time remembering those delightful picnics (and I remember those heavenly nights) on Belle Isle and the Detroit River. Remember the day you proved it was impossible to stand up in a canoe and chug-a-lug a bottle of Vernors ginger ale at the same time?

Last Tuesday, Johnny organized a sing-along in the ward. Of course, Johnny is the lead with his banjo and Sgt. Joe Draper plays the harmonica. A couple of the British boys who are ambulatory requisitioned spoons from the mess hall, so they've got a regular little band going. Captain Tydie says the sing-along has done more for morale than Mata Hari. I must say, darling, it's helped me too, but for a different reason. Songs like Drifting and Dreaming, 'Till We Meet Again, My Buddy, and especially I Had a Dream, Dear, make cherished memories come alive again.

I'm enclosing five pictures. One is of the damaged building here in Ste. Menehould where Miss Marion Crandall lost her life. She was a lovely lady and the first A. E. F. welfare worker to die in a combat zone. Betsie and I enjoyed many delightful evenings with Marion in her two-room flat.

The picture of several men standing in front of the Hotel de Metz in Ste. Menehould has great historical significance. Victor Hugo and other leading French writers produced some of their best works here. Alexandre Dumas wrote of Louis XVI stopping in Ste. Menehould to eat "pigs'-trotters." You might share this picture with Mrs. Hrbec. I am sure she would be proud to present it to Mrs. Edsel Ford.

The picture of a man walking in front of demolished buildings was taken in Verdun – a city on the Meuse River which was fought over several times by the Allies and the Central Powers. Verdun was finally taken in 1916 by British and French troops, but with a horrible loss of life.

If you look closely at the fourth picture, you can just make out the Hindenburg Line a few miles southwest of the Argonne Forest. Our forward base hospital at Ste. Menehould is located at the far western edge of the Argonne.

The fifth picture is one of Betsie and me acting a little silly during a skit in which we pretended to be the Kaiser's military advisers. That's Betsie with the fake mustache and monocle.

We have three young German soldiers in the ward. They were left for dead when their comrades were pushed back by our 307th Infantry. Their injuries, while serious, are not life threatening. I believe they are as uncomfortable with us as we are with them. It's strange how one can despise a faceless enemy, but have compassion for an individual. I find that I can tend to their medical needs without malice. One of the boys showed me a picture of the girl he hopes to marry some day. I pray for the time when the hopes and dreams of all those engaged in this senseless struggle will be achieved.

We had some excitement in the ward yesterday. Captain Eddie Grant visited with the boys and told stories about his baseball days as a third baseman with the New York Giants. You know me, I don't know a bunt from a punt, but I was intrigued when he spoke about names I'd heard you mention. I've written some down – John McGraw, Walter Johnson, Ty Cobb, Christy Mathewson, and Wee Willie Keeler. Wee Willie sounds to me like he should have been in a fairy tale.

Captain Grant was just wonderful. He autographed casts, slips of paper, and even one boy's letter home to his dad. The Captain ate our rations with us – tinned beef and gravy, hard biscuits, boiled potatoes and tea. We discovered he was a strange combination of baseball player and lawyer, having graduated from Harvard College!

Captain Eddie did an unusual thing when he left. He saluted all the boys in the ward and thanked them for their patriotism and devotion to duty. Captain Tydie told me later that General Pershing had ordered Captain Grant's outfit, Company H of the 307th Infantry Regiment, to rescue the Lost Battalion "at all costs." As Captain Tydie explained it, the Lost Battalion, a unit with about 550 soldiers, had advanced too rapidly into enemy territory and was completely surrounded by German troops. The Captain said, in his estimation, any rescue attempt would end as a suicide mission.

I believe the hardest thing to bear is being with a person one day, or even just moments, before they are gone. It's increasingly more difficult for me to believe we are making the world safe for democracy as President Wilson insists.

Darling Izzy, I don't want you to misunderstand what I am about to say. I am not the same wide-eyed girl you held so tightly in your arms at the Michigan Central Depot in May of 1917. I don't regret my decision to volunteer for overseas duty, but it would be impossible not to become a realist after months of witnessing amputations, dressing hideous wounds, and seeing young kids not much older than your nephew, Monk, gasping *for breath and drowning from fluids in their lungs after being exposed to mustard gas. Your love for me is the greatest gift I could ever receive and that is why I want you to go forward with your own life. Please seek out a wonderful girl who adores you as I do, and create a future filled with happiness and promise.*

You, my darling Izzy, are the reason for my very existence. I will love you always,

Your Esmeralda

Monk's eyes were so full of tears he could hardly see the end of the letter. The lady at the desk came over to see if she could help, but he waved her away. Uncle Izzy said that was the last letter he ever got from Esmeralda Sweeney. Now Monk finally understood why Izzy had never married and had been such a rolling stone all these past years.

T he cold night air was welcomed by Monk as he and Izzy hopped the Gratiot/Joseph Campau trolley. They were both deep in their own thoughts during the twenty-minute ride to Hamtramck. Reaching their destination at Joseph Campau and Casmere Street, Izz said, "Now we is in my old stompin' grounds, Monk. Bennie Cermak's Tip Top Club is just three short blocks north."

When they reached the old familiar building, a small buzzing red neon sign weakly announced the renamed Par-a-dise Cafe – the middle "a" flickering on and off. Upon entering, Izzy was relieved to find the club pretty much as he remembered it. He walked up behind Bennie, put him in a bear hug, and in that loud, gruff voice of his said, "Izzy Brodsky is back and is buyin' drinks for the house. But what's with this Par-a-dise Cafe shit, Bennie?"

"Izzy, you old bastard," Bennie cried, "You're a sight for sore eyes. We ain't seen you since Ma Barker got her tit caught in the wringer. Look who's here everbody, Izzy Brodsky. We had to give up the name 'Tip Top Club', Izz, after prohibition started. We're a supper club now," Bennie said with a wink.

It was beautiful for Monk to see all the old friends crowding around his uncle, slapping him on the back, asking where he had been, what he was up to, and telling him how great he looked. Bennie and Rosie grabbed a tray full of coffee mugs and lit out for the back room. Bennie broke open a couple fifths of Old Log Cabin he just got from the Sugar House Gang over on Brush Street. After a few snorts with alky chasers, tongues were loosened and stories about working the assembly line at the Ford Highland plant came fast and furious.

Denny Zakowski told a good one about Charlie Sorenson who was always ragging the guys to work faster. Denny said, "Charlie was leanin' over inspectin' a differential when Tommy Hedrin slipped a hydraulic nozzle in the back of his pants an' pumped 'bout two quarts a 600-weight oil inta his unnawear. You never seen nobody madder 'n Charlie. He called Tommy names I never even heard in the army and told him he was fired, and to get his Irish ass outta the shop an' never come back. Tommy was laughin' so hard he peed his pants and told ol' Cast Iron Charlie he was way ahead a him 'cause he had quit before that six-hunderd-weight oil had a chanct ta start lubricatin' his private parts."

Billy Roden took a big gulp of Old Log Cabin and said, "I ain't knockin' Mr. Ford's $5 a day wage. Lord knows it was more'n twice as much as I was makin' at the Red Stone Nickel and Chrome Plating Company – an' only workin' nine hours a day instead a' twelve. But that $5 come with strings all over it. We was actually paid $2.34 for a day's work an' $2.66 for what was called a 'profit-sharin' bonus' which we got only if we lived in a way agreeable to Mr. Ford. Some a' you guys remember Wilfred Olander, you know, the guy from Belleville, that little village 'bout ten miles west of Henry's new Rouge plant? He used to say, 'I'm from BELLEville, an' I got the biggest dong in town to prove it.' Once Reverend Marquis – the head a' the Ford spy department – sent one a' his guys to check up on Wilfred, to see if he was spendin' his profit bonus money the way he should. Wilfred told the reverend he was investin' in houses an' lots. It turned out he was spending his bonus on whorehouses and lots of whiskey. Poor old Wilfred was gone before the next payday come."

Rosie butted in and said, "Billy, that may be a funny story, but Reverend Marquis wasn't no spy, he was an adviser. Mr. Ford just wanted to make sure his workers and their families was livin' good and decent lives. You know, keepin' their places clean, treatin' their kids good and not squanderin' money like your friend on booze, gamblin', and whorehouses."

Big Honnie Janousky laughed and said, "Speakin' of whorehouses, one day after pickin' up our two weeks' pay in brand new crisp bills – remember how Mr. Ford always paid in new bills?" Everybody nodded and Honnie went on. "Mickey Collinder and me had a few belts in the back room of Angelo's Sweet Shop over on DeQuindre Street an' decided to go high hat. We had plenty of foldin' money so we went over to Hattie Miller's Red Carpet on Mack Road. We didn't have no trouble gettin' in, but Mickey was wearin' his Ford badge – you know how proud he was of that damn thing. Well, as soon as Hattie's floor man seen the badge, he says, 'Whatta you god damn no good Ford bastards think you're doin' in a high class joint like this?' Before we knew it, four guys as big as them Jap Sumo wrasslers grabbed us by the ass an' back of the neck an' bum-rushed us out on the sidewalk. We brushed ourselves off an' went over to the Bucket of Blood on Melrose where for ten cents you could get a' alky-spiked beer an' a damn good lay for two or three hours' work on the line."

By that time, everybody was feeling no pain so Billy Roden piped up, "I think I was tellin' a pretty good story when I was butted into by Rosie an' Honnie." Everybody gave Billie a big formal-assed bow and Rosie said, "I'm soooo sorry, Billy, please don't mind me. Go on with your damn story." After knocking down a generous shot and wiping his mouth with the back of his hand, Billy continued. "One Saturday when line four was closed down I was over at Jorge Swenson's place on Courtland Street. We was havin' a taste of Jorge's bathtub gin – I told him he shoulda pulled the plug on this batch and used it to clear out his sewer pipes. Anyways, we looked out the window to see what all the commotion was about and there's a shiny new 1920 Ford sedan sittin' at the curb. In a few seconds out steps a woman, maybe twenty-five or so, carryin' a black leather briefcase. We know right away this is one of Mr. Ford's spies – okay, Rosie, one of Mr. Ford's social advisers. Annie, Jorge's wife, begins dustin' and straightenin' things up like there's no tomorrow. She just gets her apron off when there's a knock on the door. Jorge and me both put our gin glasses under the couch and Jorge skedaddles into the bedroom. Annie opens the door and in walks this woman who says her name is Miss Emerson and she's from the Ford Motor Company Sociological Department. Annie gives her a blank face so she says, 'Actually, I'm a social worker and I just want to ask a few questions and perhaps give you some suggestions on how you and your family can live happier and more productive lives.' Annie mumbled something like she's already as happy as a clam, but by now Miss Emerson has on her black-rimmed specs and has spread out a blue and white form that covers half the round oak dining room table.

"Miss Emerson begins askin' questions like 'What is your stated religion? Are you legally married? Are you and your husband compatible?'

(which Annie raises an eyebrow at) 'Are you and your husband American citizens? Do you both speak and understand English? How is your general health? Do you save money each payday?'

"Jorge has been listenin' to this malarkey in the bedroom and can't stand it no longer, so he opens the door and walks out bare-assed naked. 'cept for his white socks and work shoes."

Rosie said, "Billy, you is makin' this damn story up, and you should be ashamed of yourself."

Billy put his hand over his heart and said, "On my mother's grave, Rosie, I'm tellin' you the God's truth."

Just about everyone in the room except Rosie told Billy to go on with his story. "Jorge sits on the kitchen chair opposite Miss Emerson just as calm as you please, introduces hisself and looks Miss Emerson right in the eye. You got to know Jorge is hung like a Belgian draft horse and he ain't one little bit bashful." At this point Rosie hurried into the back room for some more refills and Izzy's pals leaned eagerly forward. "Jorge casually lights up a cigarette and asks the Ford lady to go on with her questions. Miss Emerson, who's acted like a cold miss-goody-two-shoes up to now, has turned as red as a beet and begins shufflin' papers and clearin' her throat. Jorge offers her a Camel and as she picks up the pack, half of the cigs spill out on the floor. Jorge gets up to help her and she says, 'Oh, no, no, no. I'm sorry to be so clumsy, I'll get them. Thank you anyway.'

"As Jorge leans forward to give her a light, you can tell she don't know where to look. Her eyes is dartin' up to the ceilin', back to Jorge's huge stoming, and back to the ceilin' again. After a few quick puffs on her Camel, Miss Emerson had regained a little control and says in a higher and faster voice, 'I only have a few more suggestions for a more healthy and happy life. Be sure to use plenty of soap and hot water not only on eating utensils, but on floors, around toilets, and especially on things you touch.'

"She now gets even more flustered and begins crammin' her papers into her leather case. She thanks the Swensons for their cooperation and hurries out the door. Annie runs after her and hands Miss Emerson her coat and perky little hat. As she climbs into the Ford she gives Annie a nervous little smile, a half-assed wave, and is on her way to the next household."

By now, everybody in Bennie's but Rosie was laughing and slapping their sides and pouring Billy another drink. When the crowd quieted down a little, Eugene Tomassi said, "I can't top a story like Billy's and

Denny's, or Honnie's, but I got one I think you'll all appreciate. You all know the name Harry Bennett." Everybody groaned and Pete Yanovitch said, "*Know* the little son-of-a-bitch, I'd like to cut his balls off with a dull knife."

With a few more nasty comments and nods of agreement, Gene continued. "Mr. Ford hired Bennett just after the war – maybe late 1919 or early '20. He had been a pretty good welterweight in the navy, but cocky as hell an' not the least bit unwillin' to take a crooked buck. In the short time he was in New York, he had made some pretty good contacts with hoods an' wiseguys. He threw around names like Lucky Luciano, and the Capone brothers, Al, Ralph, Frank and Jim. Mr. Ford was in New York on business at the time and one of his greatest worries was the possibility of some creeps kidnapping his grandson, Edsel's little boy, Henry Ford II. After some nosin' around, Mr. Ford was put in touch with Harry Bennett. For some reason, Mr. Ford liked the little bastard right off. Some say maybe he seen in Bennett strengths he wished his son Edsel had. Anyways, he offered Bennett a job headin' up security at the big new River Rouge plant. I got ta admit, there was never no kidnapping threats on little Henry, or later on Benson, Josephine or Billy Ford neither.

"Things really changed at the Rouge in a hurry when Bennett come in. If any guy even mentioned the word 'union' in the spray department, he was gone before the black paint dried on a T-Model body. And you remember, Eddie, that time them commies was talkin' up a meetin' on the midnight shift?" Eddie nodded in agreement and Gene went on. "They was plannin' to meet at the Athletic Club over on West Grand Boulevard. Three a' the guys was found beat an' bloody outside the East Gate the next mornin'." Gene kidded Rosie about being a little stingy with the drinks and then said, "There wasn't a line worker who didn't fear Harry Bennett or hate his guts. An' now I'm gettin' to the good part of the story. You know how Mr. Ford liked to give University of Michigan football players summer jobs. He an' coach Fielding Yost were friends an' kinda alike in some ways. They was both winners an' took no crap off nobody. Well, one day Bennett heard about a kid football player who was causin' unrest on the transmission line. He was tellin' the guys they should be gettin' more rest breaks and piss calls – stuff like that. An' he said when the time-study guys suggested a speed-up, they should slow down – things he probably learned over in Ann Arbor. Bennett called the 6'4" 240-pound guard into his office and read him the riot act. He ripped the kid up one side and down the other, an' said if he as much as opened his trap on the line again, his ass was gone. When Harry stopped for a breath, this big kid reached over the little prick's desk, picked him up by that blue shirt and white collar he always wore, hit him three times in the nose, and tossed him in a corner. The kid walked out of Bennett's office and the Rouge Plant with a smile on his face and hitched a ride back to Ann Arbor. Right after that was when Bennett started keepin' a loaded pistol in his desk drawer, a buzzer within reach, an' two goons standin' outside his door. Oh yeah, when Mr. Ford heard what happened, he said, 'Well Harry, you win some and you lose some.'"

The whole crowd gave Eugene a big hand and settled down to some serious drinking. A while later Izzy asked Bennie if he ever saw Johnny Slocum after the war. Everybody got real quiet and Bennie said, "Izz, Johnny got killed in the last big battle of the war in a place called the Argonne Forest a month before the Armistice. His mother was sent his silver star an' a citation from President Wilson. The citation said he gave up his own life trying to save two nurses, one of which was killed an' the other seriously injured."

Izz sat there for several minutes, just staring at his drink. He finally asked Bennie if he knew the name of the nurse who was injured. Bennie called Rosie over and she said, "Izz, I'm really sorry, but neither of the two nurses' names was ever give out. We checked over at the nursin' school, but they didn't have no information."

All the fun just seemed to drain out of the party. Izz asked Rosie if Mr. and Mrs. Hrbec still lived on Pulaski Ave. He said he once had a room there and Mrs. Hrbec even let him fry an egg if he wanted.

Rosie stopped washing the coffee mugs and said, "I believe Mr. Hrbec passed about two years back, but his missus was still livin' there the last I knowed."

Izzy asked Bennie if he could make a local call and Bennie said, "Izz, you go inta my office and make any call you want." Izz rang up central and got Mrs. Hrbec in no more than a couple of minutes. When she heard Izzy's voice she could hardly talk she was so excited. She said for Izz and his nephew to come on right over because she always stayed up until 11 or so listening to WWJ, and sometimes, if the weather was just right, and she could get the Atwater Kent tuned, she could even get WGN in Chicago.

Izz smiled and pointed the receiver up so Monk could hear. Mrs. Hrbec went on. "Last New Year's Eve me an' Mrs. Berg, my neighbor, even got King Oliver and Louie Armstrong playing at the Lincoln Gardens in

Chicago. Now Izzy, you and your nephew get on over here. I can't hardly wait to see you. Do you remember how to get here?"

"There ain't no way I could ever forget. We'll be there in fifteen or twenty minutes."

Before leaving, Izz turned to everybody in the room and said, "Bennie, Rosie, Billy, Danny, Honnie, Mickey, Eugene, an' all the rest of you good friends, I wouldn't trade this evening for anythin.' I want you all to know how much you mean to me, an' how much I appreciate what you all done for me a few years back."

CHAPTER SEVEN

It was only five or six blocks to Mrs. Hrbec's house – just long enough for Monk to get the cobwebs out. He asked Izz what everybody at Bennie's had done for him a few years back.

"Monk, I just might tell you about that sometime."

Monk was very impressed when he saw Mrs. Hrbec's house. It was a little white frame and the driveway had two cement lanes separated by grass leading back to the garage. It looked like she probably had flowers in window boxes in the summertime. There was even a couple of little trees on either side of the front sidewalk leading up to the house. When Mrs. Hrbec opened the door she wrapped her arms around Izz and hugged him like her long lost brother had just returned. Turning to Monk and taking both his hands in hers, she said, "Monk, I'm so pleased you have come with Izzy. Both of you boys sit down and make yourselves comfortable. I've got hot coffee ready and this morning I just happened to make a batch of Izzy's favorite cookies."

Mrs. Hrbec was just as Monk had pictured her – a plump little lady with a round face and gray hair pulled back in a bun. The twinkle in her eyes and her quick little steps as she hurried to the kitchen reminded him so much of his Aunt Marie. He knew he was not a good judge of age, but thought her to be a little south of fifty – only because Izzy had said she had a daughter ten years old when he first came to Detroit City in 1914.

While they were waiting for Mrs. Hrbec to return with the cookies, Monk's eyes wandered over the small, neat room. The oval throw rugs in front of each chair were probably made by Mrs. Hrbec. There was a large picture of Jesus over the fireplace blessing little kids, and family pictures crowded the end table across from her Lincoln platform rocker. The room smelled faintly of those little purple flowers that Monk couldn't name, but recognized as the kind he would always see at Easter time.

After filling their coffee cups a second time, Mrs. Hrbec and Izz could hardly draw a breath for talking. She asked Izz if he remembered when he had stomach pains and her mister took him to Our Lady of Grace Hospital and had his appendix taken out. Her mister, she said, thought of Izz just like blood kin. Izz looked over at Monk and said, "Mrs. Hrbec fixed up the cistern room in the back and took care of me for two weeks until I could go back to work."

When Izz asked about her Addie, Mrs. Hrbec's face lit up and she said, "Izz, you'd hardly even recognize her now. She's all grown up, married, an' living in Dayton, Ohio with George Wolinski, the swell kid she met while working at Woolworth's Five and Dime over on John R. and 29th Street. They got themselves a little apartment and she just wrote and said George was made assistant stock manager in a Sears mail order store. Her leg is still a little crooked, but she hardly limps any more and the pain is almost all gone, thanks to what you did for her. Like you asked, I never told her who paid for the operation and all the doctoring and therapy.

"Say, do you remember when she was about ten or eleven? Almost every Sunday after she came home from Bible school you would give her a shiny dime. She'd hobble all the way to Mr. Czonka's candy store on Ferry Street and buy a 5-cent dixie cup of strawberry ice cream and one of those chocolate covered caramel bars. You laughed when she scrunched up her face as she licked that little wooden ice cream spoon, but oh how she looked forward to that weekly treat. Sunday night after supper, she cut that caramel bar into five little pieces and put one each day in her lunch box. When Friday came she always gave the fifth piece to a little girl in her class whose parents had come over from Poland a few months back."

Mrs. Hrbec was just getting her second wind, and went on. "I wish you could have been here for Addie's wedding. My mister was feeling pretty poorly by then, but he was bound and determined to stand up with his little girl. On the big day I had to help him out of bed and give him a shave. He couldn't even raise his arm up. He looked so nice in his new blue serge suit, white shirt and a tie Addie had given him for his 58th birthday. He even wore that Ford tie pin you gave him. We laid him away in that same outfit some three weeks later."

By that time Monk was trying his hardest to hold back from blubbering. He noticed Izzy look away a couple of times, too. Mrs. Hrbec warmed up their coffee and said, "When it came time to bring his little girl up the aisle, my mister's back was ramrod straight and he had a sweet smile on his face. I knew he was in pain, but he didn't let anybody see it. Addie said later she was proud but a little embarrassed when Father Wojdyla asked, 'Who gives this bride away?' and my mister said in a voice you could have heard over on Sobieski Street, 'Alexander J. Hrbec and his missus do!'

"The reception was held over Greenbaum's delicatessen on Doremus Street. During her junior and senior years at St. Aubin High, Addie worked for Mr. Greenbaum and he promised she could someday use the empty room over the store for her wedding party. Vertusso's Mortuary loaned fifty folding chairs and four dozen of those little fold-out fans with their motto, 'Don't do anything until you call us,' stamped in gold on the back. Jan Masersky and his 5-piece Society Band played for six hours – the last hour for free providing he and his group had access to the cold cuts and beer. Mr. Greenbaum joked and said, 'This is where the kielbasa meets the gefilte fish.'

"You would have been proud of the way Addie's leg held up, Iz. Of course she saved the first dance for her daddy. We all held our breath, but my mister even managed a few waltz steps. I wish you could have seen Addie's dress when the party ended. She had dollar bills pinned all over and some even tucked in her hair. It was a beautiful wedding, and the children had a nice honeymoon cruise down the Detroit River to Bob-Lo Island, but they had to be back at work on Monday morning."

Mrs. Hrbec looked out the window, didn't see a car, so asked how Izzy and Monk were traveling. When Izz said by trolley she promptly walked them out to the back of the house. In the garage was a shiny black 1921 Hupmobile 6-cylinder, five-passenger club coupe, smelling inside like a new pair of shoes and looking as pretty as a picture.

Mrs. Hrbec said she'd been having a neighbor man drive it every month and he kept it tuned and greased. She ran her hand across the mohair upholstery, smoothed down the front cushion and said, "Izzy, I just know my mister would have wanted you to have this car, and it's yours if you'll have it."

In the garage was a shiny black 1921 Hupmobile 6-cylinder, five-passenger club coupe, smelling inside like a new pair of shoes and looking as pretty as a picture.

Izzy must have been getting a cold, because Monk saw him turn his back and blow his nose a couple of times. His voice was soft and Monk had to strain to hear him when he said he'd be proud to own her mister's car if she would accept a donation to All Saints' Church. Monk saw Izzy put a couple General Grants in her hand and Monk was glad he still had some folding money. When Izz asked what time it was, Monk pulled out grandfather Harpinski's gold retirement watch and said it was going on 12:30. Izz took both of Mrs. Hrbec's hands in his and said, "I didn't know it was so late. Monk and me has got some business in the morning early, so we better get goin.' The next time you write Addie, tell her I'm happy and proud of her and that I send my love."

Mrs. Hrbec, in a stern but friendly voice, said, "Isadore Brodsky, you and Monk march right back into the house. Your room is just like it was when you lived here and I fixed up Addie's old room for Monk. I'm not taking no for an answer, so you boys skedaddle in and get to bed. I'll call you in plenty of time in the morning." Izzy winked at Monk and they both skedaddled.

Addie's bed was all ruffles, and the feather mattress just about swallowed Monk up. Maybe he was trying too hard, but he just couldn't drop off. He tried standing on one leg for about five minutes and even pretended he was seeing big white clouds drifting by on a summer day, but nothing seemed to help. He kept remembering Izzy telling his friends he'd never forget what they had done for him a few years back. He finally got up and went out to the kitchen thinking maybe a glass of milk would help. Mrs. Hrbec came out of her room in pajamas, buttoning up her robe, and asked, "Is that you, Monk? I heard you thrashing about and figured you couldn't get to sleep. Let me warm that milk up for you and put a little chocolate in it. I'll have one, too."

Mrs. Hrbec said she was so excited to see Izzy that she was having trouble falling asleep herself. Monk knew she wasn't just being polite when she asked about his family and where he had grown up. Here he was in her house only a couple of hours and already he felt like kin. When Monk asked if she was born in Detroit, she said, "Oh, no, Monk. I was born in the little village of Gora, about forty miles south of Warsaw, Poland. I guess I'd be living there yet if my parents hadn't saved enough money to send me to the States to live with my aunt here in Hamtramck."

Mrs. Hrbec took a sip of her hot chocolate and continued. "I remember the day my father returned from Warsaw with my immigration papers. I was only sixteen and was needed on the farm, but both mother and father knew I had no future in Gora. Old Doctor Lukasik examined me for tuberculosis and eye disease, which he said was the first thing they checked for on Ellis Island in New York harbor.

"I was put on a train for Gdansk in early September with my steamer ticket, one suitcase, two rolled blankets, and $48 in American money. The *Casmere Pulaski* was an old ship, so the eighteen days on the ocean were very hard. Third-class passengers were put in the steerage hold with hardly any comforts. We slept on the steel deck not two feet apart, and the stink, after a few days, would make a pig gag. The biggest worry was somebody stealing your papers and money, so my mother had sewed them both inside my underwear. The toilets were at the far end of the big room, separated by a canvas curtain. Men and women had to take turns using the toilets, which were wood seats fastened over an open pipe with salt water rushing through. Salt-water showers were only turned on from 6 to 8 o'clock at night. With maybe 200 grown-ups and kids in the hold, only a few could bathe each night. Using salt-water soap and sea water left you feeling sticky after a shower, but at least we didn't smell quite so bad. Meals were another hardship. Just about everybody brought some hard salami and bread, but that only lasted a few days. Breakfast was a kind of corn gruel mush, maybe an apple, raw milk for the kids under twelve, and coffee or sometimes tea for the adults. The supper meal started at 4 o'clock and was always thin potato or turnip soup with a piece of hard bread, and some days a small piece of salted meat. It was the hot coffee I really looked forward to.

"Every woman and girl was fearful of going to sleep. About a week out, we heard the muffled cries of a young girl. By the time the older men got to her she was sobbing and holding her private parts. The last I saw of the filthy man who attacked her was when he was sitting in a corner bleeding from his ears. The men must have carried him up to the top deck during the night and thrown him overboard. We didn't have any more trouble after that.

"One of the happiest days of my young life was when we sailed into New York harbor. I'd learned about the Liberty Lady in lower school, but now on a bright September morning there she was lifting her torch over her head in all her glory. We had been allowed up on the main deck, so everybody ran to the right side of the ship shouting, '*Panna Wolność*,' '*Signorina Libertà*,' '*Fraulein Freiheit*,' and languages I'd never heard before. I knew a few English words and yelled louder than anyone around me, 'Miss Liberty, Miss Liberty.' The ship was leaning so bad I thought for sure it would turn over. The captain and members of the crew were shouting through horns for us to return to the middle of the ship.

"When the *Casmere Pulaski* docked in New York we were herded onto a ferry and taken to Ellis Island. The building was the biggest I'd ever seen, with the ceiling so high birds were flying back and forth. The first thing I remember was getting the wonderful hot meal of soup with real meat in it and fresh brown bread. The milk was cold and came in little glass bottles. When it was time for our medical exam we lined up four across. The men went left into a long room and the women and children went in a room to the right. We passed between women doctors on both sides and got a quick examination. After running in place they checked our heart and lungs, and looked in, up, and all over. If you passed they put a green tag on your coat. I saw some people with red tags crying and being put in another line. There was a big group of people from Northern Italy, with worried looks on their faces. Each of them had a tag on their coat with W.O.P. printed on it. I found out later the letters meant 'with out papers.' After the health exam we passed into a big room with signs like '*Polska*', '*Italia*', '*Deutschland*,' and other places the immigrants came from. Friendly people speaking in our native language asked our final destination. A lady with a nice smile hung a sign that said 'Detroit' around my neck and wrote 'Polack' on my tag.

"The next wonderful thing that happened to me that day was when a lady in a blue uniform and little white hat gave me a cloth bag and directed me to a dormitory with clean double-deck beds and wooden lockers. When I sat on my bed and opened the bag I found a piece of white soap, a piece of yellow laundry soap, toothbrush, toothpaste, a comb, a little book with Polish to English words, and four pieces of hard candy. I wasn't even embarrassed when I yelled out, 'I now American!' That night I took the first hot shower I'd had in twenty days, washed my under things and snuggled down in a clean bed on a real mattress.

"The morning I was to leave for Detroit, a lady in a blue uniform assigned a strong young man to accompany me and several other Detroit-bound immigrants on a ferry to New York City and the Pennsylvania train station. She warned us that over-friendly people could spot a new arrival and would offer to help carry suitcases. We were called 'geese' or 'lambs' which meant we could be plucked clean or easily fleeced. Of course we would never see the 'friend' or our suitcases again. I boarded the New York Central train and arrived in Detroit City a wide-eyed sixteen-year-old Polish girl who knew about six English words."

"Mrs. Hrbec, you were such a young kid when you landed in the States. What kind of life did you have with your aunt?" Mrs. Hrbec was silent for a little while and then went on with her story.

"Oh, I had a wonderful life, Monk. My Aunt Iris was a sweet lady. She came to the States like I did, but twenty years before. She married a good man and had a happy life until he passed on a few years back. The first thing Aunt Iris did was enroll me in a night-school English class which met at St. Stanislaus Church three days a week. When I learned enough English to get by, I was hired as a cleaning lady at the J. L. Hudson Company on Woodward Ave. The Hudson family was so good to me. Mr. Hudson always stopped and asked how my English classes were going, and was I happy with my job. He was a wonderful man and you knew he was really interested. After about ten months Mrs. Hudson asked me if I would like to work and live in the Hudson's beautiful home on Boston Boulevard. I did general house work at first, but when Mrs. Hudson found out I made all my own clothes she put me in charge of her personal wardrobe.

"After I married Mr. Hrbec in 1902 we moved in with mother Hrbec, but I continued to work days for the Hudsons and weekends when I was needed. The Hudsons had two adorable nieces who in 1905 were nine and fourteen years old. They both loved to visit the mansion and often stayed over the weekend when their parents were away. I saw to their needs and we became very close. When their father, William Clay, died in 1908, Mrs. Clay and the girls, Eleanor and Josephine, came to live with the Hudsons. Mrs. Clay enrolled Josephine in Miss Annie Ward-Foster's dancing and social graces class that met every Saturday afternoon from mid-January to the first week of May. At first, Eleanor, being so young, just enjoyed accompanying her sister and playing quietly by herself, but as so often happens, younger girls grow up more quickly when they have older sisters to look up to. By the time she was thirteen, Eleanor was fully enrolled in Miss Annie's class and was becoming quite accomplished. It was my job and pleasure to chaperone the girls in a beautiful chauffeur-driven Hudson motorcar to and from Miss Foster's every Saturday. The class ended at 3:30 and on our way home the girls enjoyed stopping at a little Greek ice cream parlor next to Grand Circus Park. Josephine always ordered a banana split and Eleanor always had a tin roof – vanilla ice cream topped with hot chocolate sauce and salted red-skin peanuts. It was more than just chance that a young man in suit, tie, and white gloves from the dancing class showed up each week for ice cream. He was always very polite and proper when he spoke to Josephine. Eleanor had great fun teasing her sister when we returned to the car singing 'Josie's got a boyfriend, Josie's got a boyfriend.' Josephine blushed and said, 'Oh Ellie, he's just one of the dumb boys who steps on my feet in dancing class. Besides, who would want a boyfriend named Edsel? That sounds more like the name of an automobile!'

"It wasn't long before we began seeing quite a bit of Master Edsel. Mrs. Clay said he was a very desirable young man and he appeared at most every party and informal gathering. When Miss Eleanor was fourteen, Josephine had moved on to other interests and Mr. Edsel was giving his entire attention to Eleanor. They played croquet, rode horseback, and even played billiards together. Mrs. Clay instructed me to always keep a strict eye on the children when we picnicked on the Fairlane property in Dearborn where Edsel's parents planned to build their future home. I was a little afraid of Mr. Ford at first, but he treated me so nice. One afternoon when Eleanor was chasing peacocks and Edsel was helping his mother set up the picnic lunch, Mr. Henry told me he grew up on a farm not five miles away. I had to pinch myself to believe I was talking to one of the richest men in Michigan, and maybe in the entire country.

"When Miss Eleanor was nineteen or twenty she graduated from Miss Liggett's finishing school and surprised everybody by marrying Mr. Edsel Ford that November of 1916. I had the honor of fitting Miss Eleanor's beautiful gown and attending the elegant ceremony as a guest."

Mrs. Hrbec pulled open the grate, put several pieces of coal in the large cook stove, and continued. "Your uncle Izzy started working on the line in the Ford Highland plant in 1914. By early 1917 he was getting bored with production work, and not only that, but the young nurse he was seeing…" Monk interrupted and asked if the young lady was Esmeralda Sweeney. "Why yes," Mrs. Hrbec answered. "Did you know her?"

"No, but I know all about her."

"Well," Mrs. Hrbec went on, "when the big war started and Esmeralda was sent overseas, Izzy felt like he wasn't doing enough. He was just about over the draft age and he had a disability deferment. He tried to enlist in the U. S. Army and even went over to Windsor, Canada, but neither country would have him. I got to wondering one day how I could help Izzy out of his misery. I read in the *Times* that Mr. Henry Ford had built a factory on the Rouge River to make Eagle boats for the U. S. Navy. Now, Izzy and me used to sit in the kitchen after his middle shift ended and over coffee he'd tell me interesting things he had done. I remembered one story about how he and a friend named Gar Wood had worked on a motor that could make a rowboat go over 25 miles an hour. On a hunch, I called Miss Eleanor at her home in Indian Village and told her about Izzy. We had a nice long chat and she promised she would talk with her mister. It wasn't but two or three weeks later Izzy came home all smiles and said, 'Mrs. Hrbec, you are now lookin' at a hydraulic engineer at the Ford Eagle Boat Company. Mr. William Knudsen hisself asked for my transfer.' Izz took my mister and me over to Bennie Cermak's Tip Top Club on Charest Street – where Izzy called from tonight. I never saw Izzy so happy. We had steaks and beer and Izzy kept buying drinks for everybody in the house."

"I can believe that, Mrs. Hrbec, Izz never left anybody thirsty." Mrs. Hrbec leaned forward and whispered, "Monk, your uncle Izzy is a proud man and I wouldn't ever want him to know he had help getting that Eagle Boat job." Monk promised never to say a word.

"Speaking of helping others, it was Mr. Hudson who was responsible for us getting this house. Mr. Hudson had a high-up position in the Bank of Detroit. In 1911, a short time before he died, Mr. Hudson made it possible for us to get a 25-year mortgage with no money down. Mr. Hrbec just couldn't believe it, but I told him it was because of his reputation for honesty and steady work that did it. Five years later we were called into the bank and Mr. Ambrose surprised us by handing over our paid-up mortgage. Mr. Ambrose said it was stipulated in Mr. Hudson's will that if we kept up with our payments for five years, the J. L. Hudson Company would pay off the remainder of the loan.

"I was seventeen and working in Housekeeping at Hudson's when I first met Mr. Hrbec. He had been with H. G. Lipscomb about four years and delivered cleaning supplies every Thursday. At first I wasn't attracted to him because he was quite a bit older. He had a great sense of humor, though, and kinda walked with a swagger. All the girls loved his pencil-thin mustache and the way he kidded them. After I took the job in the Hudson home Mr. Hrbec and I kept company for several years before we married. My mister didn't have much schooling, but after delivering cleaning supplies for several years he got promoted to clerk at the Lipscomb main store. His people marveled at the promotion and said he actually went well beyond his ability, and I guess they were right about that.

"Other than our house and Addie, who we just adored, I guess the biggest run of luck we had was when my mister got that 1921 Hupmobile. It was only two years old and when our neighbor, Tadzik Koste, passed on, his misses said we could have the car for $250 if Mr. Hrbec would paint her house. Well, we jumped at that. We put up $75 and the Guardian Bank gave us a 4% loan on the rest. Mr. Hrbec was feeling fit at the time, so him and two friends from his Eagle Lodge did the paint job on weekends.

"We had some good times in that car. On a Sunday morning we'd drive over to Belle Isle for a picnic – sometimes with Addie and her George. On the way home we often stopped at the Detroit Zoo in Royal Oak. On special occasions we might ride over to Pontiac and take in a flicker starring Rudolph Valentino or maybe Wallace Beery and Marie Dressler.

"The farthest we ever went was to Ann Arbor in 1923 to see a football game between the University of Michigan and Illinois. My mister used to read the sports pages in the *Detroit Times* before and after every Michigan game, especially the stories by O. B. Osbourne. It got so Mr. Hrbec just loved the boys at Michigan, and I believe he thought more of coach Fielding H. Yost than he did President Harding or President Coolidge. Hearing him talk to our neighbor Mr. Orinski so much about sports, I got to know the names of some of the football boys myself. There was a couple of freshmen kids who both men said would be future stars. One was named Oosterbaan, I think, and the other was a Jewish kid named Benny Friedman. The captain of the team was Harry Kipke. My mister said to especially watch him because he had an arm like a slingshot and could drop-kick the ball into a bushel basket from thirty yards out.

"Mr. Orinski once worked for a big New York newspaper. One day he said, 'How'd you and your misses like to see a college football game?' He had been working for the *Detroit News* and he said an old friend from his New York days by the name of Grantland Rice had offered him four tickets to the Michigan-Illinois game and we could pick them up at the gate. Well, my mister hardly got any sleep waiting for Saturday to come. He was almost too scared to go to a big college place. His father made him quit school at the end of the sixth grade and got him his first job as a wiper in the train yard in Schenectady, New York. He used to kid about not being able to spell the name of his hometown until he was twenty-five.

"I wish you could have seen Mr. Hrbec when Saturday morning came. He was decked out in blue pants, yellow shirt, blue jacket and yellow shoes. He had on a blue cap with a yellow button on top and even had two University of Michigan flags attached to the front fenders of the Hupmobile. We left for the game about ten Saturday morning, Mr. Hrbec, me, and Mr. Orinski and his misses, Bettina. I still remember going down Gratiot, around Grand Circus Park and over to Michigan Ave. singing the Michigan fight song. By the time we reached the outskirts of Ypsilanti, Mr. Orinski said, 'We can't go to no college football game without a little libation.' The men stopped at a roadhouse called the Orange Lantern and said they needed to get some cigars. Bettina and me sat in the car for about thirty minutes before the men came out with red faces and talking kinda loud and smoking cigars.

"We got to Ann Arbor about thirty minutes later and sure enough, four tickets were waiting for us at Ferry Field. I had never seen a football game before, and here we were sitting in bleachers with six-thousand or seven-thousand young folks yelling and screaming as the Michigan kids came on the field. The Illinois boys came out and you could almost hear a pin drop. Bettina and me tried to act interested, but to tell you the truth we didn't have the slightest idea what was happening. Our misters were having the time of their lives, though. When the game was half over, they both went down on the field and led a Michigan cheer which the crowd seemed to enjoy. The Michigan boys played as hard as they could and young Harry Kipke even scored a touchdown, but the Illinois player they called 'Red' Grange just couldn't be stopped. Our boys got beat pretty bad, but it was all great fun and I'll never forget that fall day in Ann Arbor."

Mrs. Hrbec checked the clock in the living room and said, "My, Monk, I had no idea I'd been bending your ear so long. If you can put up with an old lady's babbling for a little longer there's something I think you need to know about your uncle Izzy's life here in Detroit. It's not about the wonderful things he's done for my family, but some things the police are still interested in. What I'm about to tell you has got to stay within these walls."

Monk said, "Mrs. Hrbec, you don't need to worry about me. Izzy has been the best uncle a kid could have. He came up the hard way and got mixed up in some things my ma called 'shady deals,' but he never hurt anybody, and underneath it all he sure is a good guy. I can promise you that whatever you tell me won't go out of this house."

"I believe you, Monk," Mrs. Hrbec said as she shook the grate and added more coal. "I can see that Izzy means as much to you as he does to Addie and me."

Mrs. Hrbec cut slivers of chocolate from a large bar and expertly directed them into a pot of simmering milk. She disappeared for a few minutes and returned with two blankets, tucking one around Monk's legs. Then she went on with her story.

"Izzy took a room with us in 1914 when he started working for Mr. Ford, and right away he and Addie became pals. At first, I think Izzy felt sorry because of Addie's deformed leg, but his feelings got a lot stronger as time went on. I hate to say it, but Addie seemed closer to Izzy than her own dad. Mr. Hrbec always blamed hisself for Addie's accident that happened when she was only six years old. My mister was supposed to be watching her when a puppy our neighbor gave her ran out into the street. Like any kid she went after it and was hit by a horse-drawn wagon. Her right leg was crushed and broken in three places. The doctor said she might never walk normal again. As she got older, we were told special surgery might help but there was no way we could afford it. My mister was never what you'd call a good provider and with the little bit I brought in we just managed to scrape along. Instead of showing Addie more love, Mr. Hrbec pulled away from her. I'm sure it was because he felt so guilty.

"Addie was ten when Izzy came to us. Over the next four or five years he did everything possible to help her. He even took a part-time job after working ten hours a day for Mr. Ford just to pay for doctor visits. Of course, we always let Addie think her dad was paying the bills.

"Mr. Ford closed down his production lines during harvest time in late summer so laid-off workers could help on the farms. Toward the end of August in 1918 Izzy had some free time. He heard about a hands-on doctor in Kalamazoo who had performed all kinds of miracle healings. I was able to contact this Dr. Vandermeer and tell him of Addie's condition. He kindly agreed to see Addie Wednesday afternoons at 1 o'clock. He said we would have to commit to a 5-week program and each session would cost $5. I assured the doctor that I would send a letter with Addie's uncle, Mr. Isadore Brodsky, authorizing him to be Addie's guardian in my absence.

"You can imagine how scared Addie was on that first Wednesday, Monk. She had never been away from Hamtramck, let alone on a train. Of course, she was comfortable with Uncle Izzy – the loving name she had called him for several years.

"That first Wednesday morning my mister and me walked the brave travelers over to the Joseph Campau trolley, and I can tell you I had an ache in my heart as I hugged and kissed my little girl good-bye.

"Izz later told me about their day. They caught the 9 a.m. at the Michigan Central Depot and Addie sat entranced for most of the three-and-a-half hour trip to Kalamazoo watching for farm animals – especially white cows when Izzy promised her a nickel for each one she spotted. Addie was impressed with the Negro porter in white coat and black pants as he walked down the aisle offering cold bottles of Moxie and Nehi grape soda for ten cents. Addie laughingly said she would treat since she had already spotted five white cows. They easily made their 1 p.m. appointment. Uncle Izzy insisted they take a Checker cab – another first for Addie – from the depot to Dr. Vandermeer's downtown office on Park Street.

"Nurse Barneveld greeted them warmly, set up Addie's file and said she had a granddaughter about Addie's age. She ushered them into a clinic room and took Addie's blood pressure, pulse rate, and temperature. She then pulled a privacy curtain around a cot and instructed the nervous Addie to put on a hospital gown over her underthings. She patted Addie's arm and said her uncle would remain with her during the entire procedure. Within a few minutes a tall, slightly bent sixtyish man entered the room and introduced himself. Addie would always remember his white hair, white mustache, fatherly manner – and most importantly the worst ten minutes of her young life.

"Dr. Vandermeer examined Addie's right leg while asking Izzy questions about his years working for Mr. Ford. He said he had been one of the first in Kalamazoo to own Mr. Ford's new Model T in 1908. Dr. Vandermeer completed his examination, pondered a moment and said he was confident that he could restore the muscles and nerves of Addie's leg to near normal condition. He warned, however, that they shouldn't expect dramatic results within the first few weeks. He carefully explained the three procedures he would use. The first and second would take place simultaneously. After nurse Barneveld applied warm compresses and a soothing oil, he would begin treatment with gentle massage and uninterrupted deep prayer. Dr. Vandermeer cautioned that during this approximately twenty-minute procedure absolute silence was imperative, but both Addie and Uncle Izzy were encouraged to close their eyes and engage in their own silent conversation with God asking for the miracle of healing. Addie would begin to feel a slight pulsation of the spiritual flow being transmitted through his sensitive hands and fingers. Addie was comfortable talking with God nightly and always included her mother, father and Uncle Izzy in her prayers, but Izzy said later he not only began to have serious doubts about Dr. Vandermeer but had never talked with God and didn't even know how to begin.

"Dr. Vandermeer said that during the final ten-minute procedure the mysterious power of electricity would be directed to Addie's entire leg. He said he knew Addie was a strong young lady and he was confident she could endure the temporary tingling and warmth generated by the healing vibrations of the electric current; and of course Uncle Isadore would be sitting beside her throughout the entire time.

"Dr. Vandermeer left the room for a few minutes, giving Izzy and Addie a chance to talk about the electric shock treatment. They agreed they had nothing to lose and should go ahead and trust the doctor."

Monk said, "Mrs. Hrbec, your Addie is one brave young lady. I don't know if I could have taken that electric current – especially at her young age. One time I was trying to fix my ma's new electric toaster, and got a jolt that just about popped out my eyeballs! Also, I have to smile when I think of Uncle Izzy asking God for a favor. I can see him making a few demands and maybe making a promise or two – like giving up drinking or smoking or some other bad habit for a few days, but asking for a favor sure ain't like Izz."

"Well, Monk, we were all desperate to help Addie and I admired Izzy for the way he acted. When Dr. Vandermeer reentered the room, he removed a hinged polished oak box about the size of a woman's vanity case from a white cabinet. When opened, the top section revealed a compartment from which Dr. Vandermeer removed two small silver cylinders with wood handles, a tangle of wires, and two round, flat sponges attached to metal discs with wood handles. The doctor relieved Addie's wide-eyed look of apprehension somewhat when he said Uncle Isadore would experience the same tingling sensation and warmth she would feel as she held the cylinders and Uncle Izzy held her wrists. Dr. Vandermeer said Isadore's many years of work experience for Mr. Ford would help him understand the technical aspects of the Faradic battery machine. He went on to explain that the electrical response was generated by a simple 1 ½ volt telephone battery encased under the bedplate and connected to several switches and binding posts. The intensity of the current was adjusted by the vibrations of the contact spring and a four-inch coil. Moving the pointer parallel to the core of the coil to the right from zero to four-hundred units would be carefully monitored by nurse Barneveld while he administered the current flow to Addie's leg. At no time would the current exceed 125 units.

"Addie rather enjoyed the warm compresses, massage and intensive prayer. Izzy had great difficulty communicating with a Greater Power but later admitted he went along because he felt it couldn't hurt. The electrical machine was a different matter altogether.

"Dr. Vandermeer attached wires to the two primary posts and the two silver cylinders and told Addie to grip the cylinders firmly in each hand. The machine was turned on and as Izzy gripped both of Addie's wrists, Dr. Vandemeer slightly increased the electric current to about fifty units. They both could feel a tingling sensation and see a twitching of their hand and arm muscles. The machine made a buzzing noise and Dr. Vandermeer said, 'Now that you have experienced the electrical sensation and realize it is harmless, I will proceed with the treatment to Addie's leg.'

"He attached electrodes to the sponge-covered discs, dipped them in a salt-water solution and held both insulated handles in his hands. The ends of the two electrode wires were plugged into the posts on the bedplate and the core set at fifty units. Dr Vandermeer placed one sponge on top and one on the underside of Addie's leg. As the current was increased to125 units, the buzzing became louder and Addie's leg turned from pink to bright red. Izz put his hand on Addie's moist forehead and tried to calm her, but her entire body began to shake and the buzzing sounded like a hive of angry bees. Izz wanted to pull the electrodes out of the machine and grab Dr. Vandermeer by the throat, but at that moment

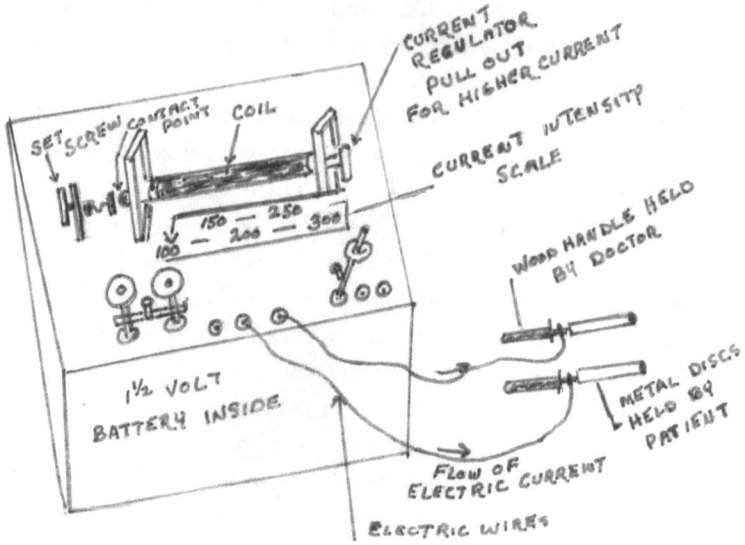

The electrical machine was a different matter altogether.

the doctor slowly lowered the current to zero. Nurse Barneveld put a cool towel on Addie's forehead and told her to rest for fifteen minutes.

"Dr. Vandermeer charged $5 for each treatment, but after six weeks we couldn't see that the doctor had done any good at all. Izzy never gave up hope though, and even promised Addie that when she grew up and got married she would walk down the aisle on her dad's arm without a limp or pain.

"In the fall of 1919, the Henry Ford Hospital opened on West Grand Boulevard. Izzy took an afternoon off and went over to talk with one of the doctors who was just out of the army. Izzy later told me that when he was introduced to Dr. Tydie, he could hardly speak. It was the same Dr. Tydie who Esmeralda Sweeney had written about in her letters. Dr. Tydie remembered Esmeralda mentioning Izzy and Addie, and even knew about Addie's deformed leg. When Izzy recovered, he told the doctor he hadn't heard from Esmeralda for over a year and did he have any information about what might have happened to her? The doctor said he had been reassigned to a forward hospital unit in October of 1918 to receive the wounded men from the Statue of Liberty Division known as the 'Lost Battalion.' He'd heard that the field hospital had been over-run by Germans and that every soldier who might return to duty was either bayoneted or shot. Amputees and men too ill for duty were allowed to live because each disabled man would require three or four attendants to care for him. He said he'd heard several nurses had been killed during the initial stage of the engagement, but he had no information about Esmeralda. The Armistice was declared the following month and he was returned to the States in December. Dr. Tydie said surgeons at the front had performed more emergency operations in a few weeks than most doctors would be called upon to deal with in a lifetime of practice. New techniques were perfected, especially on arms and legs. He said he definitely wanted to examine Addie and made an appointment to see her the following week.

"After a thorough exam, Dr. Tydie said the X-rays confirmed his belief that a series of operations would restore the function and appearance of Addie's leg. He cautioned, however, that she might continue to have a slight limp until the muscles readjusted to the new configuration of the leg. Dr. Tydie described how research doctors at Johns Hopkins Hospital in Baltimore, Maryland, had fashioned screws, plates, and all necessary hardware out of vanadium steel for use in bone reconfiguration surgery. Izzy said that was the same kind of steel Mr. Ford used to make his T model parts so tough. The doctor went on to say Addie would need at least three operations, maybe two weeks in the hospital, and several weeks of therapy.

"You can imagine how thrilled and happy we all were, but as so often happens, there was some discouraging news. Dr. Tydie said all doctors at Ford Hospital were paid a set salary so that was no problem, but he estimated that the entire procedure, including hospital time and continued therapy, would run about $1,500. He further told Izzy that Addie's legal guardians would have to sign a waiver guaranteeing full payment to the hospital. The doctor might just as well have said $15,000. My mister and me had a grand total of $65 in the Guardian National Bank. We figured we were done for, but then Izzy said, 'I promise you that Addie's gonna have those operations and she'll walk normal again. I guarantee it. I swear on my dear mother's grave, but you'll have to go along with my plan.'

"We promised we would go along with everything Izzy had in mind and wouldn't ask any questions. The first thing Izzy did, and this will shock you, Monk, was to become Addie's legal daddy."

Monk caught his breath and said, "How in hell – pardon my English, but how did that happen?" Mrs. Hrbec was unperturbed by his strong language and went on.

"Izzy found a lawyer who drew up adoption papers which gave him guardian rights to Addie, so my mister and me signed off as Addie's parents. Izzy promised to give Addie back to us when the operations and therapy were completed. Now, you've got to know that Addie never knew anything about the plan. When Izzy went back to the hospital with the legal papers they accepted him as Addie's guardian and his sworn statement to pay all expenses. The next time Dr. Tydie saw Izzy he laughed and said, 'Izzy, I don't even want to know how you pulled this off.'

"The rest of the story is what has to be kept between us, Monk. There're things that happened that cause me to wonder, but I'm not ashamed of not offering any help to the police."

Monk assured Mrs. Hrbec that whatever she told him would go in one ear and right out the other.

"Did you ever know a person named Morris Rudensky?"

Monk thought about it and said he didn't think so, but then he remembered Izzy had a friend "Red" Rudensky. He recalled that he and Izz were killing time over a couple of drinks in the Four Deuces one evening maybe a year or so ago. Delphine brought them over two free ones and said the gent at the end of the bar gave her two bits to make the delivery. This red-headed guy was walking toward them with his drink when Izzy jumped up and yelled, "Red, you ol' son-of-a-bitch," and gave him a big bear hug. Izz introduced Red to Monk and said they'd been buds in Chi-Town before he came to Detroit in '14. Before long they were having fun talking about the old days and the guys they both knew. The drinks were coming pretty good when Izz said, "You remember that special job you done for Capone in '21, Red?"

Red laughed and said, "You mean the night I blew the safe in Al Capone's apartment at the Metropole Hotel and retrieved the sapphire necklace?" Red couldn't resist telling such a good story, so after he took a pull on his alky beer, continued.

"Al got started drinking pretty early that day – which he didn't usually do. It was his and Mae's anniversary and Al got pretty well potted by 7 o'clock. He had promised to take Mae to Danny Cohen's Green Mill over on the Northside that night and was planning to surprise her with the sapphire necklace he had put in his safe the day before. He got so stewed, though, that he couldn't remember the combination. Frank Nitti gave me a hurry-up call and told me to meet him at the Metropole, so I grabbed my tools and was at Al's on the fourth floor by 7:30. That damn National Bond safe of his must have weighed 2,000 pounds and had a door eight inches thick. I told Nitti the precinct captain over on Wabash Avenue was going to get a wake-up call when the damn door came off, but he said there wasn't any other way, so I let her rip. Well, the story had a happy ending. Mae got her necklace, Al gave me a diamond-studded belt buckle, and the cops were laughing for a month about Al's safe getting blown open."

Izz turned towards Monk and said, "Monk, Red is the best box and soup mechanic in the business, bar none." Monk told Mrs. Hrbec that he didn't find out until later that a "box and soup mechanic" was a safe cracker who used nitroglycerine. Izz asked Red what he had been doing lately and Red said, "A little of this and a little of that. Screwy Moore and his Circus Gang put me on retainer, and we have a job coming up that will keep me in groceries in Miami Beach for a couple of months this winter." Izz laughed and said, "Sure, Red, and then some, providin' you stay away from the dog track and Melba McNamara's cat house." Red said he had a meeting coming up at midnight with Angelo Genna, and left. Monk told Mrs. Hrbec that was the first and only time he had seen Red Rudensky.

"That's got to be Morris Rudensky, Monk, or 'Red' as you know him, and I think he figures in what happened – at least the police seem to think so. I can tell you that Mr. Rudensky was sitting in the very same chair you're in now having a cup of coffee two or three nights before the break in."

"I've got no idea what you're saying, Mrs. Hrbec. Do you think Izzy was mixed up in something crooked?"

"I'm sorry, Monk, I'm way ahead of my story. Let me back up some. During the early winter of 1919, Dr. Tydie performed the operations on Addie's leg and she came through with flying colors. As promised, Izzy paid the $1,500 to the Henry Ford Hospital. Now, here's where things get kind of mixed up. Two nights before Izzy paid the hospital bill, the Guardian National Bank vault was blown open. When the bank manager and the police showed up, the door was hanging by its hinges and money was scattered all over the floor. After an accounting was made, it was reported that only $1,500 was missing."

"Oh my god, did the cops think Izzy was behind the job?"

"Well, sure, but they didn't have solid proof. When the police asked Izzy where he was between 11 p.m. and 12:15 a.m. the night of the heist, he said he'd been at Bennie Cermak's Tip Top Club from about 8 p.m. to 1 a.m. when Bennie closed up. The cops questioned everybody who was there and all the stories were the same. Each person said they could swear Izzy was in the club because they were having a cribbage tournament. Izzy had played eight different people and won the top prize of $10. Johnny Bredernitz said Izzy beat him the last game just before closing time. The police were very interested in how Izzy could pay a $1,500 hospital bill on the wages he was earning at Ford's. He told them he played the horses every Saturday during racing season, and bingo at the St. Stanislaus Church on Thursday nights. Millie Buckrus said she'd never seen a luckier bingo player, and Joseph Lansky signed a statement saying he always went to the races with Izzy and only saw him lose once or twice."

"It seems to me," Monk said, "the cops have only what they call circumcising evidence – nothing that would hold up in court." Mrs. Hrbec smiled and said, "You're right about that, Monk, and Sergeant Malone was hopping mad. He came over and talked with me and I answered all his questions about Izzy – like how long I'd known him, was he honest, and did he ever have large sums of money, things like that. I was truthful, but I didn't offer any helpful information. The sergeant was interviewed later by a *Free Press* reporter and said everyone at the Tip Top Club had an identical story – almost like it was rehearsed. If just one person had told the truth, he said, he'd have enough evidence to arrest Izzy. Then he was quoted as saying something that really made Izzy mad. 'If Isadore Brodskty isn't brought to trial, I'll hound him for as long as it takes, and make his life miserable until he is behind bars.'

"The next day there was another story in the *Free Press* – here it is – I cut it out and underlined what Sergeant Malone said."

I'd like to set the record straight concerning the story in the Free Press *on December 18. I was misquoted from start to finish. I don't doubt in the least the honesty and integrity of the fine people interviewed at the Tip Top Club. I believe in the rule of law and Mr. Brodsky is entitled to due process. As for the matter of the Detroit Police Department "hounding" Mr. Brodsky, that is absurd. We are professionals and seek out evidence in a professional manner. Mr. Brodsky is free to come and go without any so-called police harassment. When a suspect is tried in a court of law and found guilty by a jury of his peers and incarcerated for his crime, we feel we have served the public interest. If a suspect is found not guilty, we are delighted and encourage him to resume a normal life without malice.*

Monk could hardly believe what he read. The story made the Detroit Police Department sound like a Salvation Army rescue mission. He told Mrs. Hrbec that he remembered Izzy coming back to Chicago about that same time saying he was fed up working for Mr. Ford.

"That's right, Monk. Izzy didn't believe a word Sergeant Malone said. He left early the next morning and didn't even take time to pack all his things or say good-bye. Sergeant Malone came around a couple more times, but I never said a word about Morris Rudensky being right here in this room. Another thing I kept mum about was Izzy's feelings toward banks. He always hated the high interest rates they charged. He once saw a story in the *Detroit Free Press* that compared all the business dealings of the banks and loan companies in and around Detroit. When it came to foreclosures on home mortgages, the Guardian National was the worst of the lot.

"In another newspaper story, Sergeant Malone was quoted as saying he had contacted police departments in big cities concerning bank robbers and safe crackers. The Chicago police sent back a profile of Morris Rudensky which fit the kind of job done on Guardian National to a T. The sergeant said Rudensky's M.O. was just like a fingerprint. It seems every safe cracker has his own way of doing things.

"The Detroit police sent out a 'want' on Mr. Rudensky and found him in Miami Beach but couldn't hold him. A woman named Melba McNamara swore he had been living at her place at the time of the robbery, and six of her lady boarders said they had reason to know that was the truth. That's the whole story of what happened. Do you think Izzy could be involved?"

Monk began putting the pieces together in his head: Izzy's love for Addie, his friendship with Red Rudensky, the way he felt about banks gouging poor people, and the bank robbery of $1,500 – could it all be a coincidence that Addie's hospital bill came to that exact amount? And what about Izzy thanking his friends at the Paradise Club for what they had done for him? Mrs. Hrbec was searching his face for an answer so he finally said he'd never tell another living soul this, but he knew for a fact that Uncle Izzy hates cribbage with a passion and he'd rather have a dirty thumb poked in his eye than play one game, let alone sit still for a five-hour tournament!

CHAPTER EIGHT

After tossing and turning and thinking about what Mrs. Hrbec had told him, Monk managed about four hours of sleep. At 6:45 he was awakened by the aroma of a bubbling coffee pot and the sound of a bushy-tailed uncle splashing in the shower. Mrs. Hrbec sounded wide awake when she yelled in and told them they had less than ten minutes before the bacon and eggs were ready.

By 7:30, with the hugs and good-byes done, they were rolling down Conant St. in Izzy's beautiful 1921 Hupmobile. They picked up Mt. Elliott at Dunn St. and Izzy was annoyed when Monk suggested he was driving a little too fast. Monk could still hear Mrs. Hrbec asking if they had done anything that could get them in trouble with the police. She said she would miss them, but it would probably be best if they both got back to Chicago as soon as possible. After crossing East Grand Boulevard Monk spotted the Lutheran Cemetery and asked Izzy to pull the Hupp in for a few minutes because something was really bothering him. Izzy parked in back of the caretaker's shed, grabbed the buffalo robe from the back seat and said, "Monk, I figgered you had sumpthin' on your mind. What's troublin' you?"

Monk pulled the robe over their legs and fumbled for a cigarette. "This whole caper has been a real adventure," he said, "and lots of laughs, but I've been wondering if we're getting in over our heads. What we've done is against the law and I know we haven't hurt anybody, but what if we get caught and end up doing a stretch in Joliet?" Izzy thought on it for a time and said, "Monk, I sure don't want you worryin' none, and if you want out, I'll put you on the *Wolverine* for Chi-Town tonight. I'm goin' ahead with the job and I'll cut you in on half the take whether you stay or go. No hard feelings neither. This was your idea from the start – I just helped move things along a little. I can't say there ain't some danger involved. Just about everythin' you do in life has a down side and if you lose any sleep over it, you sure should pull out. About what we're doin' being legal or right or wrong, I've done a lot of thinkin' on that, and readin' too about the Volstead Act – Prohibition to you an' me.

"Before they put a lid on booze, anybody who wanted a drink could get one. The government was happy because they got a piece of the action on every bottle sold. The tax money went for schools, roads, hospitals, or anythin' else the government spends money on. I ain't sayin' booze is good for you, and there's a lot of rum-dums who drink up their family's food and rent money, but I guess they woulda spent the money on gamblin' or whorein' or somethin' else if not on booze. But what about the millions of people who just want a drink at dinner time – or guys like us who maybe sometimes get tanked – but look at the fun we have raggin' each other, not to mention how brave we get with the broads.

"At the end of '19, here comes a guy from Minnesota named Andrew Volstead who decides the government should be able to tell you what you could or couldn't do. It wasn't like not killin' or stealin', stuff that everybody knows about. It was about not drinkin'. That's like tellin' a guy he can't eat different kinds of food 'cause they might hurt him, or that he can't ride in a car or train because he might get killed. Now, about the legal part of it. After January, 1920, did people stop drinkin'? Hell no, they just kept drinkin' in back rooms of candy stores and joints that paid protection money to the police. There's another funny thing. The judges, mayors, and police commissioners, and even President Harding hisself, kept right on drinkin.' I even read where a senator from Texas who voted for prohibition was caught with a white lightnin' still on his property."

Monk blew on his hands and said, "Izz, you sure make a lot of sense. I never thought about it that way."

"There's somethin' else to think about, Monk. You know that a lot of judges get appointed. Suppose you're walkin' down a fancy street in North Chicago in your work clothes lookin' for work, maybe shovelin' snow in January or rakin' leaves in October, it don't matter. A cop car comes along and picks you up for what they call vagrancy. The cop is just doin' the job he's paid to do. The judge, though, is beholdin' to the neighborhood rich people. He asks a couple of questions like how much money you got in your pocket or what's your home address. If he don't like your answers he might give you thirty days on a work gang. The judge is the law, but is he right? You probably learnt about the Supreme Court and all that in Roosevelt High?"

Monk nodded and said with a laugh that he sure hoped Izz wouldn't ask him any questions about it because he was pretty sure he got a D in Social Studies. Izzy went on.

"The Court's got nine judges, so when they vote there won't be no tie. Now suppose the vote on a case comes out five to four, one way or the other. Does that mean the four guys is wrong and the five guys is right? What about the fifth judge? It seems like the whole case is finally decided by one guy who might change his mind in the future. How about a no-good bastard who kills a innocent woman or kid? Five people seen him do it, but his high-priced lawyer gets him off on what they call a technicality. It's legal, but is it fair? I went to the library and read the Volstead Act. I can't understand all of it, but if you know the right doctor, he can legally write a prescription for a pint of whiskey every two weeks. Also, churches can keep a supply of wine for their religious doin's. If you want to have a party in your own home for business or pleasure, it's legal to keep several bottles of whiskey on hand. It's against the law to make or transport booze, so how the hell did the guy get the whiskey in the first place?

"The law says it's legal to drink booze, but guys like Al Capone are locked up if they transport or sell it. Al says he's just a businessman sellin' a product people want. Anyway, Monk, that's what I think about what's legal and what ain't – what's right and what's wrong. Your teeth are startin' to chatter, so let's head back to the hotel and I'll mix you a stiff illegal drink."

Monk, with a nod of agreement, said, "I wish this damn manifold heater would work when the car is sitting still, Izz. I am getting cold, but from the way you explained things, I sure as hell won't be going back to Chi-Town alone. We might be doing something against the law, but it doesn't seem to be much of a crime – I'm with you all the way."

"I was hoping you'd feel that way, Monk, but what I said still goes. I ain't never gonna put pressure on you if you want out. However, there's one embarrassin' problem we got to discuss. When I checked my cash this mornin' at Mrs. Hrbec's I had $15.74. If this next job goes like I got it planned we'll be rollin' in dough, but it'll be a week or more before we get our cut from Al. I was wonderin' how much you got left."

"I've got about forty-two bucks after leaving Bennie and Rosie thirty dollars to cover the several rounds you bought for the house and covering the bets you lost to Tommy Hedrin and Honnie Janousky. I'm not complaining, but I did wonder about our stake when you gave Mrs. Hrbec those big bills for the Hupmobile – but I would have done the same thing in your shoes. If you want, we could move back to the flophouse until we get flush again. I gotta say, I've missed the view of that brick wall and the dirty back alley."

"O.K., Monk, that's a good idea. Let's pick up our stuff at the Book Cadillac and I'll talk to Fred at the Embassy. I think he'll carry us for a week or ten days. And thanks for giving the money to Bennie and Rosie. I know I get a little goofy when I'm drinkin' and sometimes spend more money than I got. I'll make it up to you after our next job."

When Izzy drove the Hupmobile by the Early Bird Cafe on the way to the Book Cadillac, Monk saw Betty Lou through the front window. He asked Izz to pull over for a few minutes and said he'd been thinking about asking Betty Lou out and maybe buying her some new clothes and taking her some place nice. He said it shouldn't cost more than fifteen or twenty bucks.

Izz thought that was a great idea and said, "Betty Lou's a sweet kid and you both deserve some fun. An idea just struck me. I'm gonna go down to Sam's Emporium – the hock shop next to Conn's Clothes, and see what we can get for our new duds and jewelry. We ain't gonna need none of this stuff while we're workin', and by next week we could buy out Sam's entire stock and then some. Since you're stepping out with Betty Lou, you better keep your threads another day or two. If you don't need any wheels today, I could use the Hupp to take care of some last-minute details. Do you think you could meet me and Gussie tonight at the Embassy about 11 o'clock?"

"No problem, Izz, I'll be there by ten, easy, and fill you in on my day."

Betty Lou was all smiles when she saw Monk come into the Early Bird. He had had such a big breakfast, compliments of Mrs. Hrbec, so he wasn't hungry and ordered just a sinker and coffee. While licking the chocolate frosting off the donut Monk said, "Betty Lou, I don't know how you can look so pretty and fresh this early in the day." Betty Lou sashayed away, gave him a sweet smile over her shoulder and returned with two cups of coffee and a big slice of apple pie. She sat down, straightened her dress, fluffed up her hair a little and said, "Monk, you look like a big Ford exec in those fancy duds. Is there something you ain't telling me?"

He said it was a long story, but if she was really interested maybe Pete would let her off for the rest of the day and they could go somewhere. Betty Lou didn't take any time at all to get to the back room and talk to her boss. She returned all smiles and said, "Pete told me I could knock off at 12:30 after the lunch crowd thins out, and I don't have to be back until 8 o'clock tonight when Mildred finishes her shift." Monk squeezed her hand, turned a little red and said, "Here's $1.30 for the sinker, pie and the blue plate specials you gave me and Uncle Izzy Monday night." He left a ten-cent tip and said he'd pick her up at 12:30 sharp. Betty Lou punched the keys on the National cash register and hurriedly said, "Wait a minute Monk," and caught him at the front door. She pressed fifteen cents into his hand, flashed a pretty smile, and said, "The apple pie was on me."

Monk spent the next couple of hours in Sharkey's pool hall playing eight-ball, but couldn't concentrate and lost four out of five games plus three alky beers.

B etty Lou was wearing her old gray coat and standing just inside the storm door of the Early Bird when she saw Monk making his way across Howard Street. He entered the vestibule, said hi, squeezed her hand, and pinned a crimson American Beauty rose on her worn lapel. Betty Lou turned the color of the rose and Monk said, "Betty Lou, if I didn't know better, I'd have thought you were one of the headliners over at the Avenue." Betty Lou gave him a sweet smile and said, "Monk, you sure are full of it, but don't stop feeding me that blarney. What'll we do first?"

"I was thinking of going over to Hudson's department store for some things I need."

Hudson's was a six-story building covering an entire city block. There was probably nothing you wanted that Hudson's didn't have. Monk asked the elevator captain for ladies' outerwear and was directed to the third floor, east. Betty Lou had a puzzled look and when she started to speak Monk touched her lips with his forefinger. The lady floor manager gave Betty Lou a disdainful once-over, but noticed Monk's fancy clothes so realized she could probably make a sale. Monk said, "I'd like to see some warm winter coats that would fit this young lady."

Betty Lou looked up at Monk and whispered, "Monk, I can't afford a new coat, especially here at Hudson's."

"Hush up, Betty Lou, and pick out the coat you like best. I've got some extra cash burning a hole in my pocket. And miss, fix the lady up with a warm hat, a scarf, and a pair of those blue wool gloves."

When they got outside on Woodward Avenue Monk took Betty Lou's hand, held it above her head, twirled her around a couple of times and said, "Betty Lou, let's get outta here before Mr. Hudson puts you under contract to model his winter clothes."

With a fresh sparkle in her eyes and a little girl's playfulness, Betty Lou scooped up a handful of snow and awkwardly threw a snowball at Monk. The fight was on. People walking by smiled and raised their arms pretending to shield themselves from danger. Betty Lou half ran, and as she turned to see if Monk was following, lost her balance and started to fall. In a split second she was in Monk's strong arms and he could feel the wonderful soft curves of her body. As their eyes met, Betty Lou teasingly said, "Monk, if you keep holding me like this, people will think we're doing a love scene for a Hollywood flicker." As they walked arm in arm down Woodward in exaggerated unison steps, Betty Lou happily said, "I got a great idea. There's an open-air rink out at Gratiot and Pennsylvania. How would you like to go ice skating?"

"I haven't been on skates for a couple of years, but I'm game for anything you want to do, Betty Lou. Let me grab us a Checker."

"No way, Monk Harpinski. Why spend good money on a cab when we can ride the Gratiot trolley for a nickel?"

The streetcar was crowded and at every stop the folding doors let in a blast of cold air. The two rows of wooden seats were separated by a worn linoleum aisle. Above the aisle were looped leather straps for stand-up passengers to grab when the trolley lurched to a start or stop. Monk smiled to himself when he read the curved cardboard ads that lined a horizontal space above the windows just below the roof line. There was one for Conn's Clothes and another for the Embassy Hotel! Since it was about a thirty-minute ride, he and Betty Lou moved to the more comfortable seats that extended across the back of the trolley. A small coal stove helped warm that part of the car. After passing Mt. Elliott, the passengers thinned out and the only noise was the steel wheels scraping the tracks and the snapping and crackling of the electricity as the overhead arm crossed intersecting power lines – that and, of course, the droning voice of the motorman announcing street names.

"Why spend good money on a cab when we can ride the Gratiot trolley for a nickel?"

Monk removed the blue woolen glove from Betty Lou's left hand and held it close to his side. This was a new experience for Monk, the brash ladies' man who up until now thought of only one thing when he met a new girl. Betty Lou's hand was warm and moist, and when she gently squeezed his fingers a sensation only experienced during very private moments pulsated through his body. When Monk recovered enough to speak he said, "The only real time I ever skated was when the sewage ditch froze over in Canaryville down by the packing plant on Pulaski and 47th Street, and it had to get below twenty degrees for any ice to form. There was only one kid who had real store-bought skates, Iver Jensen, whose uncle had given him a pair of Canadian CCMs for Christmas. The rest of us made our own skates. We'd get a block of hard maple about ten inches long, four or five inches wide, and two-and-a-half inches thick. Danny Cigenski's old man over at the furniture factory would run a saw through the middle of one side about an inch-and-a-half deep. We'd get a scrap piece of flat steel and have Mr. Craven at the blacksmith shop curve it up on one end and sharpen one side. We'd then force the dull side into the block and have Mr. Craven drill through the block and steel runner in a couple of places and pound rivets through the holes. The skates stayed on pretty good by nailing a belt and buckle on the wood block and cinching it over our shoes."

"Well, you're in for a big surprise, Monk. The rink rents real store-bought skates at fifteen cents for two hours, and you can lace them up as tight as you want."

The rink was about thirty yards wide and forty or fifty yards long. Every night the ice was scraped clean of snow and flooded. Admission was thirty-five cents for all day, and they had a little covered warming shed where you could sit and drink hot chocolate and eat five-cent hamburgers. A Thomas Edison phonograph with a large morning-glory-shaped horn played four-minute blue cylinder records – songs like *Over the Waves*, the *King Cotton March*, and the *Blue Danube Waltz*.

Betty Lou had to help Monk stand up for the first few minutes, but he got the hang of it and only fell when he leaned back too far or lifted his feet too high. Betty Lou zipped around the ice frontward and backward and even made a couple of neat pirouettes. Monk felt a surge of anger when a boy with slicked-down black hair slid to a stop in a spray of ice and asked Betty Lou to skate. She looked shyly at Monk and he said, "Betty Lou, skating with me is like helping out at a convalescent home. Go ahead and have some fun. I'll just watch."

It didn't help matters when the dandy held Betty Lou's hand and put his arm around her waist. Everybody on the ice stopped and watched as the pair glided effortlessly, with him skating backwards and lifting her part way up his body. After a couple of turns, Betty Lou sensed Monk's feelings and returned to help his unsteady progress around the edge of the rink. The highlight of the afternoon was when they sat drinking steaming hot chocolate from white porcelain mugs while searching each other's eyes. The precious moments were rudely interrupted by the fading light of the mid-winter sun. Monk reached for his grandfather's gold watch and said, "I hate to say it, but it's going on 4:30, Betty Lou. Don't you think we should hop a trolley back downtown before the rush hour?"

"You're right, Monk. It's just that I've had so much fun I don't want this day to ever end." Monk touched her on the tip of her nose and whispered, "Maybe it won't have to."

As Betty Lou was leaning forward unlacing her skates she said, "Monk, there's something I'd like to ask, but I don't want you to get mad or upset or anything like that."

"Betty Lou, you can ask me anything you want, there's no way I could ever get mad at you."

"Well, 'Monk' is a strange kind of name for a guy. You weren't born with it, were you?"

Monk laughed. "No, Betty Lou, my ma did some crazy things, but naming me Monk wasn't one of them. When I was in the fifth grade one of those Hollywood flickers was showing at the Orpheum Nickelodeon on North Halstead. It was all about a little kid who was brought up by a bunch of apes in the jungle after his mom and dad were killed. The kid was named Tarzan, and he grew up learning the ways of animals. He wasn't dumb, but he could only speak a few English words. One of his best pals was a little happy ape who followed him everywhere and jumped up and down screeching and jabbering when he saw a lion or tiger, or some other kind of danger. Anyway, Monday morning in school before the teacher came in, I hopped up on a desk, started jumping and screeching, and scratching under my arms. From that day on I've been called Monk – even by my mother."

"I think Monk is a perfectly fine name and I don't think of a monkey at all when I say it. I just think… well, of a really nice guy."

As Monk was lacing up his shoes he was jolted back to reality by a rough poke on the shoulder. He looked up to see gap-toothed Victor Ciambi grinning down at him. Monk stammered, "Hi Vic, I didn't know you were a skater."

"Hi yerself, Monk. You'd be surprised at the stuff I kin do. Who's yer girlfriend?"

Monk stammered, "This is Betty Lou Olsen. She works for Pete Consani over at the…"

"Oh yeah, at the Early Bird – I know," said Victor with a leer. "I've been givin' her the eye fer the last couple of days. What ya doin' out with this dumb Polock, Betty Lou?"

Betty Lou began to bristle, but Victor cut her off and said, "I was jus' raggin' ya, Betty Lou. Monk and me is good pals. As a matter of fact, you could say we is kinda business partners. I'll see ya in a couple of days, Monk. If you want ta have a good time with a real man, Betty Lou, give me a nod."

Betty Lou was furious as they left the rink and boarded the Gratiot-Woodward trolley for Times Square.

"What did he mean you were business partners, Monk? How could you even stand being around a smelly little bastard like that?"

"Now mind your tongue, Betty Lou. I don't like to hear you talk like that. Victor's a dumb blowhard and we aren't partners or even friends. We're working on a little job with a bunch of other guys. I'll tell you about it another time."

Betty Lou had calmed down by the time they crossed East Grand Boulevard. She squeezed Monk's hand and said, "We've got a few hours,

Monk. If you want, we could go up to my room and talk. Mrs. Hathaway, my landlady, is very strict, but I really like her and she has been real good to me."

M rs. Hathaway's aged three-story brownstone house had seen better days. When Judge Hathaway commissioned its construction in 1890, people thought it to be a Detroit showplace. Curved white steps fronting on fashionable Bagley Street led to a veranda enclosed by a three-foot balustrade. The solid oak front door with a large cut-glass oval and brass hardware opened on a marble vestibule. An ornate armoire serving as a repository for outer garments, boots, and umbrellas reflected in a full-length mirror. Dark oak doors and wainscoting gave a formal atmosphere to the living and dining areas. The huge carved sideboard and inlaid mahogany table had come from the judge's parents' home. A leisure room with beamed ceiling, to the right of the long hall, displayed wall sketches by Frederic Remington and bronze statuettes of cowboys and long-horned cattle. Comfortably worn leather easy chairs rested on a patterned teakwood floor. Built-in bookcases on either side of a massive fireplace and a green felt Brunswick billiard table completed the room's masculine decor.

Being only five blocks from the heart of the city, the home became a favorite gathering place for politicians, industrialists, financial gurus from the newly established Detroit Stock Exchange, and nouveau-riche merchants. Only in Mrs. Hathaway's fading memory could be heard the laughter and stimulating conversation of the city's elite. It was here that Henry Joy, his brother-in-law Truman Newberry, Dexter Ferry, and a few close friends hatched the plot to gain control of the Packard Motor Car Company. J. L. Hudson first talked of a closed-body automobile over brandy snifters with Roy Chapin and Roscoe Jackson.

The only man to hold the position of mayor of Detroit and governor of Michigan simultaneously, Hazen Pingree, was advised in this very room by the judge to opt for the higher office. Usually after cigars and libations, wives were invited in to enjoy the warmth of the fire. In 1903 or 1904, Charlotte Hathaway, Eliza Clay, and Ann Dodge formed a triumvirate to encourage the development of Belle Isle for family use. The first public-funded aquarium would remain a cherished accomplishment in Mrs. Hathaway's dimming memory.

Monk was surprised that such a large house occupied so narrow a lot. Betty Lou said, "Come around back, Monk. I guess folks in the early days did most of their good-weather-living in the back yard." A crushed limestone driveway hugged the side of the house and curved through what was once a formal English garden. The horse and carriage barns beyond the garden were fully one-hundred and fifty feet from the back patio. These long rectangular city lots were a holdover from French King Louis XIV's reign, when narrow grants of land permitted more French settlers access to streams and rivers for irrigation and dockage.

The door to the carriage barn hung precariously on one hinge. Monk could see in the fading glow of the January day the outline of a once-grand two-seated surrey. Journals, papers, and leather-bound books, now molded by time and weather, lay on the surrey floor and seats. Bridles, nickel-plated harnesses, traces, breeching straps, bellybands and blinders hung neatly from cast-iron wall hooks. Long-discarded furniture – a Lincoln platform rocker, tables and summer wicker – lay in disarray, silently gathering dust. Monk and Betty Lou had neither the capacity nor clairvoyance to comprehend the human history that lay in silent ruin. Who but the muses, and possibly Mrs. Hathaway, could know of the countless hours spent planning and planting the hundreds of flowers, shrubs and trees that now formed a mass of untended vegetation? Who would even care that the once lovely garden was illuminated with Chinese lanterns on party nights, while the movers and shakers of a newly vibrant Detroit talked of politics, business and social issues? And who now remembered the great pleasure the judge took in the methodical grooming and the harnessing of the tempestuous chestnut mare, Zingara, in the carriage barn, and the thrill of the ride along East Jefferson as the proud horse's head and mane swung from side to side in perfect unison with her high-stepping gait? Sadly, the small pleasures of the good life that had seemed so endless had come to an abrupt halt on a cool September evening in 1915 when the judge suffered a massive heart attack while climbing the front steps of his beloved home.

As darkness began to settle, Betty Lou suggested they go inside. She pulled down the spring-loaded doorbell lever to alert her landlady, used her key, and stepped into the vestibule. Wrapped in a gray shawl and walking slowly with a cane, Mrs. Hathaway greeted the young people.

"Monk, I'd like you to meet my landlady, Mrs. Hathaway. Monk Harpinski and I would like to visit in my room if we may." Mrs. Hathaway looked Monk over carefully, gave a nod of approval, but said, "Monk... Monk? What kind of a name is that for a grown young man? What is your birth name?" Monk shifted uneasily and said, "My given name is Kelsen,

Mrs. Hathaway, but I've been called Monk since the early grades."

"Well, young man, I shall call you Kelsen, a perfectly fine Christian name, if you don't mind. And Betty Lou, of course you may have a guest – as long as you abide by my rules of decorum: no smoking or drinking, the door is to be left open and one foot must remain on the floor at all times."

Betty Lou blushed and said, "Of course, Mrs. Hathaway, I know the rules. When Monk – er, Kelsen leaves, I'll come down for a cup of tea with you before I go to work about 7:30."

Betty Lou's second-floor room was to the right at the end of the long hall with a view of the once-beautiful English garden. The back stairs led down to the carriage driveway and were used by night-shift workers so as not to disturb Mrs. Hathaway's sleep. Directly across from Betty Lou's room was the bathroom. Gloria Smedley and Rosa Schmerburg occupied the two rooms toward the front of the house. Betty Lou's room was comfortably but simply furnished with a mahogany writing desk under the back window, a four-drawer dresser with mirror opposite her brass bedstead and a chintz-covered chair and lamp to the left of the door. The large armoire on the side wall seemed out of place, considering the contents of Betty Lou's meager wardrobe. A medium-sized Navajo rug purchased in Winslow, Arizona by the judge and Mrs. Hathaway in 1902 helped warm the oak plank flooring. The multi-finned steam radiator kept the small room unbearably hot.

Monk wasn't inclined to sit in a chintz chair and was somewhat embarrassed when Betty Lou patted a spot next to her on the bed. With both feet on the floor and the door open, Monk fumbled for Betty Lou's hand – more in a gesture of friendship than of romance. After a long silence, Betty Lou looked into Monk's eyes and said, "Monk, there's something I want – no, I've got to tell you."

CHAPTER NINE

M onk said, "Betty Lou, you don't have to tell me anything. I like you a lot and we probably both have some things we've done, at least I have, that I'm not so proud of, but, we don't have to spoil a day that's been so much fun."

"That's why I need to tell you about something that's been eating a hole in me. It's because I have deep feelings for you. I told you once that I came down to Detroit to try and make something of myself, but that's not entirely true. I came down here before I started showing – to have a baby out of wedlock."

Monk had a stunned look on his face and said, "Betty Lou, don't; you don't have to ..."

Betty Lou put her finger on Monk's lips and continued. "First, you need to know more about me. I was born in the little iron-mining town of Negaunee in the Upper Peninsula. My father's people were miners in the iron ore region of Kiruna, Sweden, for as long as anyone can remember. When my grandparents came to America and settled in upper Michigan, it was just expected that their son, my father, would become a miner. As a little girl I remember how proud I was to take my father his tin dinner pail on my way back to school at 12:30 each day. The owners of the Cleveland-Cliffs Iron Mine let the men come out of the pits for a thirty-minute dinner break. Every morning mother baked a large pastie. That's a kind of pie dough filled with beef, pork, or chicken, mashed turnips, potatoes, gravy, and sometimes onions and carrots."

"Betty Lou, you're making me hungry."

She squeezed Monk's hand and went on. "Mother folded the dough, crimped the edges and baked the pastie for two hours in our big wood-burning kitchen stove. The miners' tin dinner pails were a little larger than square and were easily carried by a wooden handle mounted on stout moveable wires attached to the sides. The bottom section was filled with scalding hot soup – usually potato or turnip. The top section fit snugly into the bottom and contained the pastie, kept warm by the hot soup below. An air-tight lid on top had a tin cup firmly mounted in an upside-down position for cleanliness. The pails were large enough so the men could have a second dinner halfway through the afternoon. Each group of six or so miners kept a pot of tea brewing on a coal fire. When I handed my dad his dinner pail he always gave me a hug and kiss and pressed a nickel into my hand. Every day I did the same thing. I stopped at the company store and bought two licorice whips for my little brother Tommy, and a bag of horehound candies for me and my younger sister Edie. Every once in a while Mr. Fribourg would slip in a piece of caramel.

"One day there was a loud explosion in pit number three. Daddy didn't come home that night. After we buried Daddy, Mother had a nervous breakdown and couldn't take care of us kids. We were placed in the Evangelical Home for Orphans on the edge of town. It was eight months before mother collected her wits and began her seamstress business. We weren't exactly orphans, but we sure felt like we were. The Home was a big faded red brick building with two huge spruce trees on either side of the front door that grew all the way up past the second floor. I remember wondering if the gospel ladies decorated the trees during the Christmas season and, if they did, how they would manage to reach the top branches.

"One of the first things I noticed when we entered the front door was the long shiny brown hallway that made your shoes squeak when you walked on it. Mrs. Johnson, supervisor of the home, had a large office on the left. Then came the nurse's examining room. A small library, two study rooms, and a playroom for the little kids occupied the right side of the hall. Between the library and study rooms, a short hall led to the chapel. At the end of the long hall, double doors opened on the dining room with rows of wooden tables and benches for the kids. Hinged, double serving windows and a counter separated the kitchen and dining room.

The Ladies of the Gospel ate at small tables near the outside windows. Mrs. Johnson usually ate in her office, or in her cottage out back. All the girls slept in a large dormitory room on the second floor. The gospel ladies, nurse, and cooks had small rooms just off the dormitory. The boys' dormitory room was on the third floor reached by the back stairs.

"Living at the home was hard on all the kids, but particularly on the ones who had lost both parents. Tommy, Edie and I felt lucky to be together, and I could keep an eye on them. The gospel ladies were nice to us but they were very strict and we were all a little afraid of them. Four girls about my age, Sallie Wilson, Roxanna Peters, Mandy Holland, Lucia Ferrano, and I formed a bond of friendship. We didn't do bad things, but we pushed our luck as far as we could. Six days a week we had either fried cornmeal mush or thick gooey porridge. We all looked forward to Sunday when we had an egg, bacon, toast and fresh-squeezed orange juice. I hate oranges to this day because we all had to swallow a spoonful of castor oil with the juice.

"All five of us girls had a sweet tooth and loved the dark brown sugar on porridge day. The trouble was, we could only take one spoonful out of the bowl and had to use our knife to level it off. The gospel ladies followed the bowl with a sharp eye, so each of us figured a way to cause a distraction. Sallie could force milk out through her nose and go into a coughing fit. We sat apart, so when Sallie went into her act and the ladies rushed to her aid, the girl with the bowl in front of her would take two heaping spoonfuls and press the sweet sugar against the roof of her mouth and pass the bowl on. Even the little kids kept a straight face and never squealed on us. Other times one of us, or even one of the other kids, would spill a glass of milk or drop a plate on the floor – anything to give us that split second we needed.

"All the children were assigned special jobs that were rotated each week. The little ones dusted and carried out trash while the older kids changed bed clothing, worked in the kitchen or basement laundry. The assignment I liked best was reading and entertaining the little ones and giving them hugs and kisses when needed. One day, while cleaning and straightening up the nurse's room, Roxanna found a green rubber glove in the trash. She tucked it in the waistband of her underwear, and when she returned to the dormitory, hid it under her mattress."

Betty Lou glanced at the brass alarm clock on her dresser and said, "My gosh, it's after 6 o'clock. I've been chattering on like a magpie and haven't let you get a word in edgewise. If you'd like, I could make us some tea and give your ears a rest."

"Oh, no thanks," Monk said. "I'm not much of a tea drinker but I'm really interested in what you've been telling me – especially why Roxanna hid that rubber glove under her mattress. What did she have in mind for it?"

"You're sweet for asking, Monk. Roxanna was a wonderful friend, but always full of mischief. I think you'll get a kick out of what she had planned. I suppose the food at the home was nourishing, but it was awful monotonous and you knew every day what it was going to be. Supper, without fail, on Friday was one medium boiled potato, boiled cabbage, succotash and four horrible, slimy little fish called sardines. Dessert was always lemon jello. The only difference was the little kids had smaller portions and two sardines. All the kids were expected to finish every bit of food on their plate or risk being assigned some extra work.

"Each table had a metal pitcher of milk and a basket of bread, but the plates were filled in the kitchen and put on the long shelf in front of the two swing-out windows. Four or five children on serving duty would pick up the plates and bring them to the kids and to the gospel ladies by the windows. Before going to supper the next Friday, Roxanna pinned the green rubber glove inside her blouse near her neckline. Giving the blessing was on a rotation basis. The little kids and boys could finish in less than ten seconds, but on Friday the ladies always asked Lucia Ferrano to do the honor. She blessed the food, Mrs. Johnson, each of the gospel ladies, the cook, the grocery delivery boy, the iceman, and sometimes the poor little kids in China. The ladies said the Lord would be pleased and that they were proud to have such a fine Christian girl lead them in prayer. Everyone except Roxanna and Lucia closed their eyes and bowed their heads. While the blessing was in progress Roxanna stuffed the slimy sardines into the four fingers of her rubber glove. On the way back to the dorm, after supper, she liberated the vile fish in the toilet. Each week one of us took our turn using the glove.

"One Friday night when it was Roxanna's turn again, Mary O'Donnell, one of the gospel ladies, asked Roxanna to help her fold laundry in the basement, because Sallie Wilson said she felt sick. There was nothing Roxanna could do but follow Mary O'Donnell down to the hot laundry room next to the furnace and start folding sheets and such. By the time they finished, the fish in Roxanna's green rubber glove began getting kinda ripe. Mary O'Donnell thanked Roxanna for helping, put her hand on Roxanna's shoulder and said, 'My dear, I do hope you will begin thinking more about your own personal hygiene.' Roxanna blushed so hard her face looked like it was about to explode!

"I guess the worst thing about the home was the clothes we had to wear. All the girls wore white blouses and blue jumpers. You could hear the boys walking thirty feet away as their thick corduroy pant legs rubbed together. When the weather turned cold all of us were forced to wear gray long underwear. On our way to school, when we passed out of eyesight of the home, all the older girls rolled up the underwear legs and pinned them to their slips. The names we were called in school were hardest on the little kids. We were all referred to as 'Evangies' or 'Orphies' – and those were the kindest names.

"By the time I started ninth grade, and was living back home with Mama, some of the older boys began to take notice of me, but I didn't know why. I studied hard and got good grades, and Miss Jackson even let me work on the school serving line in exchange for lunch. Before the semester ended she said if I worked in the kitchen one and a half hours each day after school, Tommy and Edie could also get a free lunch. I began to hope that someday I could work in a cafe like Dolmers on Main Street, or even maybe in the Cleveland-Cliffs office as a secretary.

"In the spring of my junior year a boy named Bradford Ferguson drove by every day after baseball practice as I walked home from working in the school kitchen. Bradford's father owned a men's clothing and shoe store in Negaunee and also was a city council member and deacon in the church. One rainy day Bradford stopped and said, 'You look like a drowned rat, Betty Lou. Jump in and I'll run you home.' Well, I didn't even think he knew my name. He was the Bears' quarterback and star baseball pitcher and always hung out in the lunchroom with the guys on the football and baseball teams. Of course I'd noticed that the cheerleaders and the girls in the Masquers Club always seemed to press up too close to him. I had a load of books and my hair was hanging in my eyes, so I hopped in his little Model T Ford coupe, grateful to get out of the rain. Bradford was a perfect gentleman and even carried my books to the door.

"Nothing much happened after that. He gave me a few more rides home and I put a little bigger piece of meat loaf on his plate during lunch. One day in early May when he took me home, we parked out in front for a little while and talked. I could see Tommy and Edie peeking out the front window. Bradford took my breath away when he said, 'Betty Lou, I'd like you to be my date for the senior prom.' I just sat there kinda tingling and he said, 'I've already asked our principal, Mr. Tomaselli, and he said it would be all right to bring a younger guest if she had permission from her parents.'

"When I told mother, she had a worried look on her face and said, 'Honey, the girls who go to proms wear expensive gowns, new shoes, and even have their hair done at Vera's Beauty Shop.' Mom could see the disappointment in my eyes and she said, 'Let me sleep on it, and we'll see what we can do.' I at least had some hope. I was on pins and needles for the next few days. Then on Saturday, Mom met me at the door when I returned after delivering some altered dresses to Reverend Beason's wife. She was just beaming when she took my hands in hers and said, 'Baby, I think I've solved our problem. I traded Miss Alfredson, you know, Mr. Tettleman's secretary at the Mine office, some alteration work for a pair of her blue pumps.'

"'But what about the prom dress, mother? There's no way we can afford one.'

"'I've got that problem solved too. I can make you a beautiful dress out of the lace curtains on the front and side windows. They can be bleached and then dyed a pretty baby blue. I have in mind a square neckline, a fitted bodice with puffed sleeves and tiny blue buttons down the front. The hem might be trimmed with white or blue ribbon and maybe a ribbon comb would look nice in your hair. A soft white undersheath will give a lovely contrast to the blue lace. What do you think?' 'Oh, Mama, I can't wait to see it finished,' I squealed.

"The seniors were let out at noon the day of the prom and Miss Jackson said I could skip my after-school job in the kitchen this one time, so I raced home at 3:20. Mother was just tacking the last of the ribbon on the hem of my beautiful dress and said, 'Betty Lou, take your bath so we can make some final adjustments. After that, light the kerosene lamp and put the nose of the hair curler down in the glass chimney to heat.'

"After toweling off, I looked in the mirror and for the first time I actually felt like a woman." Monk had enough sense to keep his mouth shut, so Betty Lou went on. "I could feel and smell my hair curling as mother clamped a few locks around the hot barrel of the curling iron, wound it up in the scissors grip and held it for ten or fifteen seconds. By 6:30 mother was satisfied. My gown was finished. I slipped on my beautiful new dress and blue pumps and stood before the full-length mirror that was on the back of the closet door. I couldn't believe I was the same stringy-hair girl who dished out salisbury steak, potatoes and peas that same noon in the school cafeteria lunch line.

"I was too excited to eat more than a few nibbles of cinnamon toast and drink some tea. At 8:30 I heard Bradford's car out front and then a knock on the door. There was Bradford in a tuxedo handing me an orchid corsage. He gave mother a small book of poetry and Edie and Tommy each a shoehorn from his father's store. Then he broke the exciting news – we were to lead the senior grand march! When we arrived at school most of the boys and their dates were in the gymnasium drinking punch and eating strawberry ice cream out of dixie cups with those horrible little wooden spoons. Several boys and girls came up to us – the boys were hitting each other on their upper arms and acting a little crazy. The girls commented on my dress and Jenny Lindstrom said it looked almost like it was store bought.

"A little after nine the Northern Lites – a group of five boys in the regular school orchestra – began playing *A Pretty Girl is Like a Melody* and Mr. Orbach, the 12th grade counselor, yelled through a bull horn for everybody to line up for the grand march. I can't tell you how wonderful I felt to be on the arm of the Bears' quarterback and the twelfth-grade president. The Northern Lites switched over to *For Me and My Gal* as we marched through a big horseshoe of flowers and then finished with *Ain't She Sweet*.

"As the evening wore on, some of the boys added something they called sloe gin to the cups of pink punch. It tasted a little like the nickel bottles of Nehi orange from Mr. Fribourg's front porch ice chest. By 11:30 it was getting awful hot in the gym and I began feeling a little bit dizzy. When Bradford said, 'Betty Lou, let's take a little ride and get some air,' I was more than ready even though I knew we couldn't get back into the dance once we had left.

"Everything smelled so clean and sweet after the early evening rain. Bradford opened the split windshield and the night air felt cool and refreshing. Before I realized it, Bradford had driven down to the shore of South Lake. He spread a blanket near the water and we watched as the moon came up. I was feeling groggy and almost sick. Before I knew it, Bradford was kissing me all over and fumbling with my dress and panties. I told him no, but my voice sounded like it was coming from somebody else. What Bradford did to me hurt something awful and when he was finished I rolled over on my stomach and cried. I had never felt so dirty. Bradford tried to kiss me again, but I ran into the lake and washed myself off. Bradford kept saying he was sorry and that he thought I wanted him to do it. When he offered his handkerchief and tried to wipe away my tears I screamed and scratched him on his left cheek."

Monk didn't know what to say, but when he put his arm around Betty Lou's shoulder, she began sobbing and pressed herself into his chest. Monk finally said, "Betty Lou, if I could find that Bradford fella, I'd beat the living piss out of him." When Betty Lou's body began to relax she went on. "I didn't know what to do. I had broken the heel off one shoe and my dress was a mess. When we drove up to the front of my house, Bradford said he was sorry, but that I shouldn't tell anybody, especially my mother, what had happened. He also said I was partly to blame.

"I was relieved that mother, Edie, and Tommy were asleep. As I lay in bed I concocted a story they might believe. The next morning at breakfast I said as we were leaving the dance, some devilish boys had stretched a rope across the pathway to the parking lot and we fell in the wet grass and mud. I said I had broken the heel off my shoe and couldn't find it in the dark. Of course, Tommy said he'd go after breakfast and look for it. I didn't know if mother believed me. All she wanted to know was if I had had a good time.

"There was still a week to go in the school year after the prom. On Monday, Bradford had a bandage on his cheek and didn't even talk to me when he went through the lunch line. About the only pleasure I had was giving him a gristly piece of meat with his potatoes and peas.

"After graduation, the seniors went every which way. I heard that Bradford's father got him a summer job at the Cleveland-Cliffs Mine in Iron Mountain, about sixty miles from Negaunee. He had been given a scholarship to the Colorado School of Mines and had to be in Golden, Colorado by mid-September. I was lucky to get a waitress job at Dolmer's Cafe. I was barely seventeen and only had school lunchroom experience.

"The summer months passed pretty fast and in early September, just before school started, I woke up one morning and was sick to my stomach. After three or four days I wasn't any better so mother took me to old Dr. Lahti on Calumet Street. It didn't take him long to discover that I was pregnant. He said I wouldn't start showing for another few weeks, but maybe I shouldn't enroll in school for the fall term. Dr. Lahti told me since I was under age he was obligated to report his medical findings to my mother. I guess mother must have been in shock. When Dr. Lahti told her she just sat in a kind of daze. He was so kind and considerate and suggested we come back and see him in a few days when we could think more clearly. As we were leaving he said not to despair because there were ways he could help us."

Betty Lou's voice was stronger now and Monk realized she wanted him to hear the entire story. He held both of her hands in his and let her go on.

"I was embarrassed, ashamed, hurt, and angry as hell. We took Dr. Lahti up on his suggestion and mother and I came back to see him on Friday. He took us in a little room after his nurse had gone home and said, 'Mrs. Olsen, I think I can help Betty Lou, but I'm going to have to ask some very personal questions and I'm going to tell you things that must be kept confidential. When you lost your husband in that terrible mine disaster a few years back and had to put the children in the Evangelical Home, all expenses were taken care of by a secret group of men who call themselves The Golden Rule Outreach Circle, of which I am a member.'

"Mother was startled and tried to speak, but Dr. Lahti went on. 'Other members of the group include lawyer Will Bradley, Reverend Timothy Beason, the pastor of the Episcopal church, Father Alistaire Trent of St. Anthony Catholic Church, and Grady Crocker, the President and Director of the Great Northern Bank and Trust. I think you would agree that these men have considerable influence within our community. We are not a secret group because of any mystical persuasion, but only because we find we can do the most good for others without the glare of publicity. We only ask that those we assist try to pass along their blessing and assistance, however small, to others in their time of need. We do not ask for any financial remuneration. It's a system that we call 'helping others to help themselves.' Now Betty Lou, the first step is for you to tell me who is responsible for your being with child. We will go on from there and take the necessary steps to relieve you of your psychological burden and help you on your way to a happy life.'

"I looked at mother and she nodded her approval. When I said it was Bradford Ferguson, and how he had forced himself on me, Dr. Lahti had a look of concern on his face and said, 'Having lawyer Will Bradley, Grady Crocker, Father Trent and Reverend Beason, Pastor of the Ferguson family's church, on our side will help immensely.' Dr. Lahti's advice was for me to first confront Bradford, find out his intentions, and then come back and we would decide on a plan of action.

"Bradford came home every weekend from his job in the open pits in Iron Mountain. I knew he hung out in Grayson's drug store on Saturdays so I called Mr. Grayson and asked to speak to Bradford. When he came on the line he recognized my voice right away, so before he could hang up on me I told him to meet me in the school bleachers at 4 o'clock – or he might not be going to Colorado in the fall.

"I knew I had gotten his attention when I heard his car pull up and park on Talbot Street. When Bradford approached me he said angrily, 'Betty Lou, what in the damn hell do you mean I might not be going to Colorado?' I said, 'Thanks a lot for saying hello, Bradford,' and proceeded to tell him I was pregnant and his little fun at the lake on prom night was going to make him a father. Bradford sat down, looked at the ground for a minute and then blurted, 'Betty Lou, how could that be – I mean, you didn't even enjoy it. Besides, what makes you think it was me?'

"I was so mad I said, 'You spoiled bastard, of course it was you. Do you think it was some kind of Immaculate Conception? I haven't even held hands with a boy since way before that night.'

"He said, 'O.K. Betty Lou, O.K., just calm down. Let me think about it. I promise I'll talk to you in a couple of days. Do want a ride home?'

"I just glared at him and he hurried back to his car.

"On Monday at the cafe, Mr. Dolmer said someone had left an envelope for me. When I opened it, a typed note said, 'Please drop by Ferguson's Clothing Store after work today.' When I entered the store, Mr. Ferguson was busy with a customer so I pretended I was interested in a tie on a rack by the sportcoats. As the customer approached the door, Mr. Ferguson came up to me all smiles and said, 'Betty Lou, it's so nice to see you. Thank you for dropping by. Please come into my office.'

"I was uncomfortable – Mr. Ferguson had never said two words to me in my entire life. When I sat down Mr. Ferguson came right to the point. He said, 'Betty Lou, what's this I hear about you implicating Bradford in the condition you find yourself in? That is the most outrageous accusation I have ever heard. I have talked with Bradford and he says he felt sorry for you so asked you to go to the senior prom. That is the extent of his involvement with you. I can also tell you that three of Bradford's rather unsavory friends have said you left the party in a drunken condition. When they followed you outside, you invited all three of them to partake in an orgy of uninhibited pleasure. I can tell you, young lady, and I use that term loosely, if you persist in this false accusation against my son, I'll expose you for what you are.'

"I could hardly hold back the tears. As I ran to the door, I yelled, 'Mr. Ferguson, ask your precious boy how he got those scratches on his left cheek on prom night!'

"When I told Dr. Lahti what had happened, he said, 'All right, Betty Lou, you've done all you can. Don't you or your mother talk to anyone about what has happened. I'll take over and let you know from time to time what progress I am making. In the meantime, go on with your life and trust me.'"

Monk got up, walked over to the window and looked out at the backyard. "Betty Lou, you didn't have to tell me about anything that happened to you before we met, and now I can hardly wait to hear the rest of your story. What did Dr. Lahti and his friends do next?"

"Well, Dr. Lahti was a little like the director of a school play. Each of the men was given a part and they all reported back to him. I'm sorry I can't give you the details, Monk. I don't know them myself, but the men must have put the fear of God into Mr. Ferguson. A few days later, Mother and I stopped in Dr. Lahti's office, as he had requested. In that calm, sweet voice of his he said, 'Mrs. Olsen and Betty Lou, thank you for coming by. I just wanted to bring you up to date and perhaps relieve your minds. My associates have had some very meaningful conversations with Mr. Ferguson and without going into detail I can assure you he has shown a very cooperative spirit. There are, however, certain facts we must acknowledge and come to grips with before we proceed. Mrs. Olsen, I know you have lived in this town for many years. I'm proud to say that I helped bring your three fine children into this world.'

"Mother smiled and said, 'And you continued to be there for us through diaper rash, measles, whooping cough, and I don't know what all, doctor.' Dr. Lahti squeezed mother's arm and went on. 'This is a small town, Mrs. Olsen, and there is a stigma against unwed mothers, more so than against excessive drinking, gambling – even stealing and lying. You must be aware of the viciousness of this intolerance and what it could mean to the future of you and your family. Mr. Ferguson remains adamant against a marriage and insists he will go to the wall to protect Bradford. That does not mean, however, that he is unwilling to compromise, but unfortunately at this time his compromise only involves a rather large contribution to the church fund. I've already discussed the medical procedures that would remove the fetus by the end of the fourth month, Mrs. Olsen, but Betty Lou is determined to carry her baby full term. I admire her courage and agree with her decision completely.

'There is another avenue which I wish to present to you both. Father Trent and Reverend Beason have discretionary money that they send to a Catholic mission in Detroit staffed by the competent Sisters of Mercy.

Their facility is beautifully run with love and medical expertise. They accept unwed mothers-to-be with one important caveat – mothers must relinquish all legal ties and give their newborn up for adoption at birth.'

"I gasped and threw myself into mother's arms and cried, 'Oh Momma, no, I couldn't, please Momma!' Mother stroked my hair while holding me close to her bosom. When my sobbing subsided, Dr. Lahti suggested we consider all options and perhaps seek guidance from Reverend Beason and Father Trent."

What Betty Lou and Monk would never know was that the men seeking justice had confronted Mr. Ferguson, and with an iron hand in a velvet glove helped him reach an equitable decision. Will Bradley called Mr. Ferguson into his office and informed him that he was being retained to represent an underage high school girl in an alleged sexual misconduct case that also involved illegally providing a minor with alcohol. Mr. Bradley made it clear to a highly agitated Mr. Ferguson that his son, Bradford, would be charged in the case – if, of course, it came to trial. Will Bradley counseled Mr. Ferguson to hear him out. He mentioned the scratches on Bradford's cheek observed the day following the prom, which were verified by Bradford's friend, Sam Offerman. Several boys and girls he had questioned stated that alcohol was indeed made available to them by Bradford. Two girls said they saw Bradford pour "something" in their punch from a silver flask. The boys laughed and joked about how quick the sloe gin would act. All had agreed that they saw Bradford and Betty Lou leave the prom early, and Jenny Lindstrom said she had seen Betty Lou throw up in the girls' bathroom.

Mr. Bradley told the subdued father that he would be compelled to question, under oath, the three friends whom Bradford claimed would swear they had had illicit relations with his client. Finally, whether found guilty or innocent, Mr. Bradley said it would be impossible to keep the accusations made during the trial from the eyes of authorities at the Colorado School of Mines and Bradford probably should not count on a scholarship or admittance that fall. Mr. Ferguson slumped in his chair and showed no sign of the belligerent attitude displayed at the outset of the conversation. Arnold Ferguson's voice was barely audible when he said he would contact Mr. Bradley in a day or two. He bid Mr. Bradley good-bye and retreated into the overcast of a bleak September day.

Later Grady Crocker summoned Mr. Ferguson to his well-appointed office in the Great Northern Bank and Trust Company. As Mr. Ferguson entered, Mr. Crocker, a graying man with an authoritative presence, offered his hand across his desk without rising and said, "Arnold, it was good of you to come by. I know how busy you are. Have a seat, have a seat. How are Alice and the children?" After a few more informal inquiries about nothing in particular, Mr. Crocker tilted back in his leather swivel chair, and holding the end of a pencil in both hands near his chest said, "Arnold, a down-state conglomerate has shown an interest in purchasing the Mack building. Motion pictures have become the rage largely due to a couple of gents by the names of Buster Keaton and Charlie Chaplin. A representative of the conglomerate tells me that within a few years, flickers, or motion pictures as he calls them, will be in every town and village in the United States. His group is looking for suitable locations in downtown areas, or at least within comfortable walking distance from town centers. I feel obligated to tell you that our board is seriously considering a package deal which would include the Mack building and the two structures to the east of it. The smaller buildings would be torn down to make way for a parking lot.

"I know you have six more months on our rental agreement for the first and second floors of the Mack, but in all fairness I thought you should be included in the loop. This is not a done deal by any means, but as they say, 'Forewarned is forearmed.' Oh, while you're here, Arnold, Father Trent spoke to our Downtown Club luncheon yesterday and discussed the need to replenish the Special Project Fund that St. Anthony's and the Episcopal Church are involved in. Since you missed the luncheon, I said I'd ask if you would again take a leadership role in the drive this year. I hope I wasn't acting presumptuously."

Mr. Ferguson shifted uneasily in his chair. "Oh, no, Grady. I'm sorry I missed the luncheon. Father Trent is a forceful and compelling speaker. I'd be more than happy to do my part. I'll contact the church leader promptly." Changing the subject, he said, "Of course, I'm greatly concerned about the possibility of losing my business location. Let me ask, if another venue was to be found – one more attractive financially to the conglomerate, close to downtown, with adequate parking and more in line with the thinking of the Architectural Board, would the bank support such a proposal?"

Mr. Crocker sat upright in his chair, put his hands palms down on the desk, and said, "Arnold, what an innovative idea. I like it, I like it. I'm sure my people would consider backing such a plan. We do have misgivings about altering the historic significance and ambience of the

Superior Street district. Please get back to me with a plan of action as soon as it is convenient for you. This certainly opens up an entirely new perspective." Walking back to his clothing store, Arnold Ferguson had the feeling he was facing pressures over which he had lost all control.

During a late night meeting of the Golden Rule, Dr. Lahti prefaced his remarks to the members of the club by saying, "Gentlemen, a great injustice has been done, and a naive young girl, her unborn child, family, and perhaps our town have been placed in jeopardy. We have agreed that hard-nosed pressure, coupled with persuasion, implied financial ramifications, and the unqualified belief in the innate goodness of man, might help us reach an equitable solution. Will Bradley will now present his report, followed in order by Grady Crocker, Reverend Jonathan Beason, and Father Alistaire Trent."

Will Bradley began by saying, "Arnold Ferguson came into my office yesterday morning and said the unsavory matter in which his son was allegedly involved, if carried to a conclusion in a court of law, would only cause pain to everyone. He said his son had decided to forego his Colorado scholarship and remain employed by the Cleveland-Cliffs Iron Company for a two-year period before continuing his education – probably at Northern Michigan College in Marquette. He will contribute half his wages for a two-year period to any charity designated by Reverend Beason and Father Trent. Mr. Ferguson said he would not pursue any action against my client nor would he use any language to denigrate her character. Not a full-blown confession of guilt, but close enough, so I accepted his attempt at redemption."

Grady Crocker reported, "Mr. Ferguson came up with an excellent site plan for a new complex and parking lot on J Street after I mentioned the possible sale of the Mack building. He said his silent partner, Dwight Dawson of Value North Realtors, would handle the land acquisition. Mr. Ferguson further stated he would forego his normal commission and happily donate to the city a large adjacent lot he and his wife had owned for years. He hoped that the Park Commission might develop the property into a small city park. I complimented Arnold on his integrity and civic pride and told him that I would contact the conglomerate. I then mentioned that I believed they would likely send a feasibility expert to consult with him."

Reverend Beason and Father Trent reported that Arnold Ferguson had requested a meeting with them in St. Anthony's rectory on Tuesday morning. After a short discussion on religious ethics, personal obligations, and the always-present fear of damnation without redemption, heads were bowed in silent prayer. Reverend Beason then reported that Mr. Ferguson had apologized for missing Father Trent's presentation at the weekly Downtown Club meeting. He said Grady Crocker had informed him that the drive to replenish the Special Project Fund was slated to begin the first of the month, and that he would be honored to once again assume a leadership role. After writing a personal check for $1,000, he asked what the primary emphasis of the fund would be this year.

Father Trent said Mr. Ferguson seemed startled, but kept his composure when told the fund would be used to further the work of a Catholic agency in Detroit whose mission was the pre- and post-natal care of unwed mothers, and the placement of newborns in adoptive Christian homes. Before leaving, Arnold Ferguson mentioned that perhaps Grady Crocker and Will Bradley might be informed – in a very discreet way, of course, about his rather generous pledge. Father Trent closed by saying money had been set aside to cover all expenses in Detroit as well as expenditures for wardrobe, transportation, and incidentals, should Mrs. Olsen and Betty Lou accept the heartfelt benevolence offered by both churches.

Dr. Lahti complimented the men for their efforts. He said, "Your selflessness has justified our faith in the Golden Rule. I will present the opportunity to Mrs. Olsen and Betty Lou for their consideration. Betty Lou's life will not be made whole again, but it is both an ending and a new beginning for her. Thank you all, and good night."

B etty Lou continued her story. "Late in the afternoon on Wednesday, I think it was, Mother and I visited Dr. Lahti in his office. His voice was so reassuring as he greeted us, asked us to sit down and said, 'I'm not going to take your time with all the details, but I think the men of the Golden Rule have come up with a moral and financially acceptable plan that I hope you will consider.' He told us that Bradford had given up his scholarship and had decided to work in the Cleveland-Cliffs mine at Iron Mountain, giving half his earnings for a two-year period to the churches' special project fund. Bradford's father had also contributed a rather large sum to the fund. Dr. Lahti took my hand in his and said, 'I'm well aware, Betty Lou, that the efforts of the Golden Rule members will not relieve all of your fears and apprehensions, but you now have an opportunity to get on with your life.' I just had to hug Dr. Lahti. Mother and I both agreed I should go down to Detroit."

Monk squeezed her hand again. "I think you made the right decision, Betty Lou. You sure were lucky to have Dr. Lahti and his friends on your side. I can just about hear old man Ferguson reading the riot act to Bradford. What he did and the way he acted was dead wrong and he's gonna get reminded of it every day when he's working in those dirty pits for half pay. It serves the bastard right, and it cost his dad a bundle, too, which he won't forget for a long time. When did you leave for Detroit City?"

"Well, I thought I was beginning to show a little, so Mother made up a story about me going to Detroit to help out my Aunt Gert who was ailing. I really did have an Aunt Gert, but she lived in the little town of Chelsea, about sixty miles from Detroit, and was as strong as a horse. As a matter of fact, she worked for a landscaping outfit and Momma said she could do the work of two small men and a medium-sized mule! Mother and I met with Reverend Beason and Father Trent the next day and by the weekend I had new clothes, some expense money and a train ticket.

"I can't tell you the next few months were easy, Monk, but the sisters at the Holy Redemption Mission over on Brainard Street treated me just great. The hardest thing for me was giving up my baby without ever being able to hold and love it. One of the sisters came into my room the night before I left and secretly told me I had given birth to a golden-haired, blue-eyed little girl. I felt so relieved when she said a young couple from Melvindale would be adopting my baby. The husband had a good job with the Ford Motor Company and they were both fine Christian people.

"Before I left the Mission, Mother Superior Angelica got me a room here at Mrs. Hathaway's, and even recommended me to Pete Consani for a job at the Early Bird.

"Monk, I've never had a better day than this one, and I really mean it. But in case you try to look me up before you and Izzy go back to Chicago and I'm not here, there's one more thing you should know. My little sister, Edie, is growing up too fast. Momma tells me she's threatening to run off with a seventeen-year-old dropout kid who's driving a grader for Cleveland-Cliffs. She just turned fifteen and thinks she knows all about life. I feel like I set a bad example for her. Anyway, I told Momma that just as soon as I saved up enough for a ticket, I'd come home and try to talk some sense into her. I don't want Edie to end up in a dead end like me. Pete told me he'd give me a couple of weeks and hold my job for me if I wanted. I thought you should know just in case ..."

Betty Lou's cheeks were glistening with tears as she turned her upper body toward Monk. Still keeping one foot on the floor, Monk tenderly pulled her to him and could feel the delicate softness of her breasts rising and falling in unison with his own accelerated breathing. She had the expression of an innocent little girl as he lightly brushed her closed eyes with delicate butterfly kisses. Her slightly parted, moist lips encouraged further exploratory kisses and then, in a flood of uncontrolled passion, their bodies embraced in an ecstasy that neither had before experienced. As a finality, the pyrotechnician of human intimacy unleashed a missile that shot upward into a darkened sky, reaching its apogee, then bending in a graceful downward arc showering the heavens with multi-colored lights that slowly lost their brilliance as they tumbled into a sea of not unpleasant darkness.

As their bodies regained vitality, they walked hand in hand through an emerald green valley of buttercups and pink roses. When passions receded into reality, Monk gently stroked Betty Lou's hair and said, "Betty Lou, you are one wonderful girl," – and then with a little teasing smile added, "and an A-1 contortionist too. One more thing. Before I stole that first kiss I want you to know I put Grandfather's gold watch on your night table under your hankie. That just might help get that train ticket home a little sooner."

While straightening her frock and fluffing up her hair Betty Lou said, "This has been the most special day of my life, Monk. I'll treasure it always." Monk pulled Betty Lou close. "This has been an extra special day for me too, and I can guarantee that you haven't seen the last of Monk Harpinski." He kissed her on the tip of her upturned nose and disappeared by way of the back staircase.

CHAPTER TEN

Monk grabbed a coney dog and a mug of java at Dago Tony's on Second Avenue and ran up the stairs at the Embassy. Izzy said, "Damn, Monk, I'm glad to see you. Frank Nitti called and said for us to meet Abe Bernstein in the Pump Room of the Leland Hotel at nine. Big Al give Abe the go-ahead to advance us the $4,600 for fifty cases of Johnnie Walker Black and expenses. Since you still got your fancy duds, you do all the talkin.' Abe will think I'm some kind of rum-dum in these rags. What time is it now?"

"Izz, I almost hate to tell you, but I gave Grandfather's watch to Betty Lou. It's a long story and I'd rather talk about it some other time."

"You don't have to explain nuthin' to me, Monk. Whatever you done, you had a good reason. Let's get over to the Leland. I told Gussie we'd meet him back here at 11 o'clock and give him the cash for the booze and the part-pay for our crew and the Cannucks."

When the boys walked into the Pump Room, the floor manager gave them a fish eye until Izz told him they had a meeting with Abe Bernstein. The guy fell all over himself and directed them to a dark corner booth. Abe, dressed in black pinstripes with white tie, offered his hand and motioned for them to sit down. He said Mr. Capone had contacted him and he was more than happy to do a favor for an old friend. After buying a couple drinks, Abe said his Purple Gang was available to assist them in any way. Izz was amazed when Abe said he remembered Izzy had a problem with Detroit's finest a few years back and wondered if the matter had been settled. If not, Abe said, he was having a late supper meeting with the police commissioner and would suggest that he close the books if the case was still pending. Izz said he would appreciate a good word on his behalf, and with that, Abe placed a dark brown satchel between them, ordered two drinks, said to give his regards to Mr. Capone, and disappeared. Monk and Izzy returned to the Embassy, locked the door, and dumped $4,600 dollars onto the bed.

Gussie arrived at 11 o'clock sharp and after two or three Old Log Cabins, straight up, said he had fifty cases of Johnnie Walker Black lined up in Windsor. The Cannucks would have the merchandise in the garage at midnight Saturday, providing Reggie got the cash by 10 p.m. Thursday.

Izz said that wouldn't be a problem, but cautioned Gussie to give Reggie $1,800 on Thursday and the rest when the pouches started moving. He also said it wouldn't hurt to mention that Al Capone and the Purple Gang had some heavy contacts in Windsor.

Gussie agreed, lit a Camel, leaned back against the wall, exhaled a white cloud through his nose and said, "I've been havin' a little trouble findin' a full crew. I got four a' the wiseguys back, includin' that smart-ass Victor Ciambi, an' his friend Geno Evola, but I can't locate Angie or the big Kraut they call the Iceman."

Monk swished the amber liquid in his glass and said, "I guess we can't be too particular, but I've got a bad feeling about that damn Ciambi. I think we would be a lot better off if his old man had shot the stork."

Izzy laughed, "Oh, Victor ain't that bad, but I agree we maybe should all keep an eye on him."

Gussie said, "Abe Bernstein's brother Roy give me the name of a Detroit cop on the take, a Joe Yaro, Izz. I called him and he said he could meet with us here tomorrow night if it's O.K. with you."

"Fine, there ain't nuthin' better than a dirty cop with inside information. Tell him to be here about 10 o'clock. And Gussie, when you contact Reggie in Windsor, check to be sure Scalese's brother-in-law, Mario Sillari, and his people have made up three-hunnert more pouches. Scalese says there's plenty of room on the ropes for the extra pouches. Remind Mario that Scalese and me have a firm agreement."

"O.K., Izz, everythin' looks good. I'll try to locate two or three more wiseguys and see you and Monk back here Friday night."

O n Thursday about midmorning Monk hocked his fancy clothes and jewelry at Sam's Emporium on West Jefferson. Sam was in a friendly mood so he gave Monk $25 in cash, a set of used work clothes and a heavy army surplus overcoat. Monk met Izz in Lefty O'Doul's at noon for a couple corned-beef sandwiches, washed down with several alky beers. Izz settled their chit with Lefty and picked up another fifth of Old Log Cabin.

On the way back to the hotel, at Izzy's urging, they stopped in the back room of the United Cigar Store just off Times Square for a game of 50-point, call-shot, straight pool. Izz made the competition close, but Monk once again was stuck with table time and a double order of drinks. The teletype machine chattered the results of the third race at the Flamingo Dog Track in Miami, while Izz gleefully sipped his reward for a misspent youth. After the gent in the green eyeshades put up the line for the fifth race, Izz laid a two-dollar bet to win on a long-shot greyhound with the enticing name, King Rufus lll. By 4 p.m., Izz had collected $14.50. A duly impressed nephew and his swaggering uncle returned to the Embassy.

Monk, still slightly perturbed with himself for losing a close pool game, and eager for revenge said, "What would you think of a few hands of stud poker – just to pass the time?"

Izz jumped at the chance and said, "Great idea, Monk. Go downstairs and give old Fred two bits to knock on our door at exactly 6 o'clock. Whoever's behind when he knocks has to spring for a blue plate special at the Palms and a bunch of flowers for Ann Howe at the Avenue."

"I've got your ass, this time, unk. Have a drink ready and those bicycles in a neat pile when I get back."

A t 10 o'clock Thursday night, Joe Yaro showed up at the Embassy. Izz greeted him warmly, and pointing to Monk, said, "Joe, this is my sister's kid, Monk Harpinski. He's a little outta sorts because he had to bounce for a couple of blue plates, the price of admission, and a bunch of flowers for a big-tittied broad over at the Avenue."

"Don't pay any attention to Izz, Joe. He beat me at five-card stud and he's got his tail up. We're having a drink – can I pour you one?"

"Sounds good, Monk. From what Gussie tells me you got a' operation goin' that sounds mighty interestin.' I'd like to hear more about it, an' if you can use me, I got some free time, an' I can always use a few extra bucks. You know, this here damn city don't hardly pay a cop enough to live on."

Izzy gave Joe the lowdown on the job coming up and, after a couple more drinks, Yaro said, "There's talk down at the precinct about a New York kinda job that went down last week that you boys might be interested in. The Adonis brothers' barber shop an' athletic club in Corktown out by Navin Field has a history a' fast an' loose deals. The brothers, Pete an' Julius, are legit out front, but run the numbers an' the horses in the back room. You can also get drinks an' a lay upstairs for two bucks, if you want the regular.

"Anyways, last Tuesday about nine in the mornin' a guy comes in for a shave. Julius sits him in chair number two by the window, tilts him back an' puts steamin' towels on his face. It ain't but a few minutes later a big ugly guy comes in an' don't say nuthin' but, 'Shave, shave.' Julius puts him in chair number one, an' sez he has to go out back for more hot towels. He ain't gone three to four minutes an' when he comes back, the big guy's nowhere to be seen. Julius gets a lotta kooks so he don't think much of it. He asks the guy in chair number two how he's doin,' but he don't get no answer. He pulls the towels offin the guy an' he's staring up at the ceilin' with eyes as big as them glass aggies we usta shoot as kids in grade school. Patrolman O'Grady happens to be out back laying a bet or somethin', so he checks the guy over an' there's blood seeping down his front. O'Grady rips open the dead guy's shirt and there's a little round hole about as big as a ice pick would make that looks like it goes right inta the stiff's ticker."

"Damn," Izz said, "I think I know who done that job. It's gotta be the Iceman!" Yaro continued without even blinking. "Anyways, detectives Dursten and Miller get there in a half hour or so, an' by 'bout 10:30 they collar a rum-dum who says he seen a big ugly guy run outta the shop and go into the Rex flophouse down on the corner. The boys question the old man on the desk and he sez a big guy, who could hardly speak English, give him a week's deposit on room 319 two days ago. Funny thing, the old man sez that same guy threw his passkey at him an' run out the door about 45 minutes earlier – an' he still had five days left on his rent! Dursten and Miller run up to the third floor, bein' careful to step over bombed-out drunks, empty Thunderbird jugs an' stuff you don't even need to hear about. The door to 319 is open so they go in, but there ain't nobody inside. A half-quart of milk an' some crackers is on the table and the bed is a mess, but that's about it. As the boys are leavin,' Dursten sees a cage like they keep parrots in, with a fiver stuck in between the wires.

Inside there's a big white bird like you see hangin' 'round garbage dumps hoppin' up and down tryin' to get out. There's a dirty crumpled up piece a paper on the table by the milk bottle and it reads, 'Set bird free – keep fiver.' Well, the boys pocket the fin an' go back to headquarters by way of West Jefferson. They carry the cage down to the river an' when they open the door, the bird flies in a big circle around their heads an' then straight up inta the sun. Miller sez, 'Ain't it strange that a guy which pokes a hole in another guy would wanta keep a wild bird cooped up in a cage as a pet?' That night they get a make on the stiff whose name is Angie Zambelli outta Toledo. He's got a rap sheet as long as your arm."

Monk let out a low whistle. "Damn, I knew Angie was ragging the Iceman every chance he got, but I sure didn't think the Kraut would poke him."

"It don't really surprise me none," Izz said. "I seen the Kraut lose his temper over a lot of little things. Last week, just before he and Angie lit out for Windsor with the wire and telephone, Gino Evola accidently bumped into the Iceman. He got red in the face and cussed Geno up one side and down the other in German. Poor Gino just stood there shakin' his head."

Joe Yaro downed a couple more drinks and before leaving said, "Thanks for includin' me in, boys – an' you don't need to have no worry about the cop workin' the nightshift by the river queerin' the deal. Corporal Carmichael's got a tight lip. He an' me has worked together on lots a' outside jobs. I'll see you gents Saturday night at the warehouse."

I zzy pulled the dirty cord on the dim ceiling light, climbed in bed and said, "Monk, we got more time than we're gonna need. I seen in the *Times* while we was in Lefty O'Doul's that a blizzard is expected by Saturday night. It's startin' to snow pretty good right now. I was thinkin' about walkin' over to Windsor early tomorrow to make sure there ain't no slip-ups. What would you think about movin' everythin' up by one day to Friday, if Gussie an' the Cannucks is agreeable?"

Monk, laying on his back on his narrow cot, took a deep drag on his Camel and said, "I don't see any reason to put it off, Izz. We start one day earlier and we get our payoff one day sooner. Everything is just about ready here, and while you're in Windsor I'll round up three more wiseguys, call Joe Yaro, and tie up any loose ends. You don't need to come back until dark on Friday, and we'll still have plenty of time to start pulling the booze around midnight. If we wait until late Saturday night, there could be a pile-up of snow."

"O.K., Monk. It's a done deal if Gussie gives a thumbs-up. I'll be back in Detroit after dark Friday night."

The first thing Monk did Friday morning was contact Joe Yaro. Joe said Friday was just as good as Saturday and he'd be at the warehouse by eleven o'clock. Two of the original wiseguys, Geno Evola and Victor Ciambi, were hustling drinks as usual at Sharky's Pool Hall on Shelby Street. Victor was concentrating on a tough side-pocket 8-ball shot and barely looked up when Monk said the job was rescheduled for that night. Victor caught the side pocket tit and left an easy corner shot for his opponent. Enraged, Victor said, "God damn it, Monk, don't talk when I'm shootin.' You just cost me two bits an' a' alky beer. I don't give a shit when we do the job, but I did have a mind to try some a' that sweet meat, Betty Lou, tonight."

Monk grabbed a cue from the rack and slammed Victor up against the wall with the cue stick, making Victor's eyes bulge out and his Adam's apple quiver. In a low controlled voice Monk said, "You dirty little son-of-a-bitch, if you ever talk like that about Betty Lou again I'll run twelve inches of pool cue up your stinking ass."

Geno pulled Monk away and said, "Monk, Victor don't mean nuthin.' He's jus' got a big mouth an' don't know when ta shut up." Still glaring at Ciambi, Monk slammed the cue on the table and growled, "Just be at the damn warehouse by eleven tonight and ready to go to work."

Monk still needed two or three more wiseguys so he hopped the Woodward trolley to Highland Park and paid a visit to the Oakland Sugar House. The Purple Gang's headquarters was a one-story brick building three blocks from the Ford Model T factory. A swarthy man in his middle forties with the familiar bulge of a shoulder holster asked Monk his business and patted him down. Isadore and Ray Bernstein were pounding bungs in whiskey barrels stenciled "Old Log Cabin" as Monk entered the back room and introduced himself. The brothers couldn't have been more friendly and offered Monk a dipper full of whiskey from an open barrel. Ray said with a wink, "I think you'll like this batch, Monk. It's been aged five days."

Abe Bernstein had told his brothers about Monk and Izzy's caper and that they were supplying Capone with Johnnie Walker Black from Canada. Isadore said, "Monk, we got nuthin' but respect for Mr. Capone and we know how Izz Brodsky rigged up Al's beer trucks so that prick,

Dion O'Banion, couldn't jack 'em. What can we do for you?"

When Monk said he needed three more guys for that night's run, Ray said, "Go out back with Isadore an' tell Johnny Milberg, Anson Neuman an' Bennie Fleisher where and when you want 'em, an' they'll be there with bells on. Isadore, wrap up a couple fifths for Monk and Izzy." On the way back to the Embassy Monk thought to himself, "It sure pays to have friends in this line of work."

M eanwhile, before daybreak Friday morning, Izzy walked across the ice to Windsor in what was called a "whiteout" – blowing snow that made visibility more than ten feet impossible. After warming up in an all-night joint with coffee and a ringer, he went to Scalese's leather shop on Tecumseh Road and was satisfied that Mario Sillari would have the extra three-hundred pouches sewn on the pull ropes by 3:00 that afternoon. Gussie had already seen Reggie and he thought moving everything up by a day was a good idea. Reggie said his boys could start carting the Johnnie Walker to the river garage by noon. When Izz looked surprised, Reggie said, "Izz, this ain't no U. S. of A. We ain't got no goofy export prohibition law here. Our Coast Guard an' Customs guys don't give a damn if we send booze to you Yanks."

Izz said he'd see Reggie and his guys after lunch and he and Gussie would help move the fifty cases to the river. After grabbing fish and chips in the Picadilly Room of the King Edward Hotel, the boys loaded the Ford truck with Johnnie Walker and after three runs had everything secured in the river garage. About 3:00 p.m. Izz said, "Gussie, I got a few hours to kill before startin' back across the river. Since the snow is stopped I'd better wait until dark so I don't raise no suspicions. You got any great ideas?"

Gussie's eyes lit up. "It jus' so happens, Izz, that the Buckingham Palace strip joint on Wyandotte Street has a continuous show from 4:00 ta midnight, an' I hear them Canadian broads ain't a bit bashful."

"You hear, Gussie, you hear. Hell, I bet you got a seat down front with your name on it. As Monk would say, let's get our asses in gear."

The show started with all the strippers dressed in Scottish kilts and carrying bagpipes. As the four-piece band played *God Save the King*, Gussie leaned over and whispered, "If ya want to start a riot, Izz, stand up and say, 'If God can't save the King, the Yanks sure as hell can.'"

Izz hushed up Gussie and said, "I ain't here to start no trouble. I just wanna see a little tit." During intermission Izz bought a box of stale chocolate-covered caramels and a pack of Frenchie cards for Monk that had some interesting action when you flipped them fast with your thumb. Part way through the second half of the show, Izzy grumbled, "These Canadian dames ain't got nuthin' different than the broads in Chicago or Detroit, as far as I can see."

Gussie said, "That's the problem, Izz, they's some things you can't see. Take that Chinese stripper, for instance. I heard that while all white girls is up and down, them Chinese dames is crosswise." That got Izzy's attention until the final curtain. Gussie talked Izz into a hot bowl of chop suey at Wang Ho's across from the Palace and Izz was mildly upset when told the delicacy actually originated in San Francisco. "That sounds like another one of your damn Chinese stories, Gussie. I suppose next you'll tell me hamburgers come from Hamburg, Germany. Finish your coffee. I'd like to run down and check the garage one last time."

Finding everything in order, Izzy pulled a woolen scarf over his cap and ears and crossed the ends over his chest. As Gussie helped him into his greatcoat, Izzy said he'd call as soon as he reached Detroit. Leaning into the Arctic blast of swirling snow that had started up again during dinner, and with hands jammed deep in his side pockets, Izz made his way across the frozen river in the bitter cold of the January night.

I zz arrived at the Embassy by 9 o'clock, stomping and rubbing frost out of his eyebrows. Monk poured and handed him a half tumbler of Old Log Cabin. "Compliments of Ray and Isadore Bernstein, Izz. Oh, and the guys they promised for tonight are over in the warehouse getting briefed by Joe Yaro." Izzy took a large gulp, squeezed his eyes closed, looked up at the ceiling and croaked, "Them boys make a damn good grade of booze. I ain't surprised they sent some of their guys to help. Abe Bernstein said all we had to do was ask. We got ourselfs a lucky break tonight, Monk. The temperature is hoverin' around 10 degrees and there's just enough snow so them pouches will slide along like a piece a' butter on a hot griddle. Just as soon as I warm up a little we'll take a hike over to the warehouse."

Monk introduced the three Purple Gang members to Izz, and after they had proven they could tie ten perfect square knots in succession, he said, "All right boys, let's get the show on the road. Joe, you and Anson load fifty empty cases on the truck and drop one off every few feet from the warehouse to the river. Johnny, you and Bennie operate the wind-up machine. Keep a three-hundred-foot rope reel on the left axle and when the reel empties, throw on the next one and square-knot the ropes together. Joe, when you and Anson finish your job, you, Victor, and Geno start pulling the rope to midpoint in the river. When the rope tightens you'll know when to stop. Anson, we'll need you here when the pouches start arriving. Izzy's calling Gussie in Windsor so Reggie and the rest of the Cannucks will start pulling their rope and meet you at midpoint."

When the two gangs met, the ropes were tied together and a stout line then connected the Detroit warehouse with the Windsor garage.

Victor Ciambi and Geno Evola were told to continue walking to Windsor and help pack the Johnnie Walker in the leather pouches. By the time Anson Neuman and Joe Yaro returned to the Detroit shore it was snowing harder and the temperature had shot up to about twenty-five degrees. Monk lit one Camel after another and wore a path in the snow, but Izz remained calm and assured Monk the warm-up would just help the pouches slide across the ice that much more easily. In Canada, Gussie and Reggie lined up the six hundred-foot ropes with the pouches attached to the steel rope rings. Victor, Geno and the Cannucks carefully inserted a fifth of scotch into each pouch and securely tied the drawstring. When the first hundred-foot pouch rope was filled it was dragged to the ice and tied to the pull rope. Gussie then called Izzy and said, "Start pullin', Izz, but real slow while we feed the pouch ropes onto the ice."

Izzy gave Monk a hand signal to start slowly winding in the tow rope. Now a bundle of nerves, Monk grabbed the steering wheel in a white-knuckle grip, mashed in the clutch pedal and began rewinding the first reel. Joe Yaro and Bennie Fleisher had the empty wooden crates lined up and ready for the arrival of the first pouches. Izzy estimated that Gussie, Geno, and Victor could walk twice as fast as the pouches were moving. By the time the final bottles left Windsor the boys could follow, making sure there were no snags, and still reach Detroit in time to help unload. After winding in about six-hundred feet of rope, the old truck started shaking violently and finally stalled. The motor needed to be hand-cranked, but Izzy wouldn't let Monk near it because he said he'd seen fellas grab the crank like a baseball bat, give it a twirl and end up breaking a thumb or even an arm. He said the reason was because the T's magneto electrical system, peculiar to the T Model Ford, sometimes fired a spark a split second too soon and sent the flywheel spinning backward.

Izzy gripped the crank, tucked his thumb in back of his forefinger and brought the motor back to life. Monk wound in another couple hundred feet of rope and the truck started vibrating and bucking again.

Within seconds, the smell of hot oil permeated the air and black smoke poured out of the gear box. Izzy cussed and mumbled, "the damn bands on the planetary clutch discs must have burned out." He cut the tow rope and yelled at two wiseguys to push the truck to one side.

"Monk," Izz hollered, "get the Hupp and back down to the river!" Monk rushed to do as he was told. In desperation, Izz tied the tow rope on the Hupp's rear axle and motioned Monk forward. With its powerful 6-cylinder engine the black coupe easily resumed pulling the tow rope. When the Hupp reached the warehouse, Johnny Milberg untied the rope and Monk backed down to the river. Izzy attached the waiting rope to the axle and yelled for Monk to continue the routine until the pouches began to show up. After several runs, ice began to form under the Hupp's spinning wheels. Izzy screamed at Yaro, Milberg and Fleisher to grab shovels and start spreading sand on the pathway. Monk gently depressed the accelerator and was able to nurse the Hupp up the sanded slope and pull in a few hundred more feet of rope. Izzy estimated the pouches had reached the halfway point on the ice when the temperature suddenly shot up to over 40 degrees and a heavy rain began to fall. Izzy jumped into the coupe with Monk and the wiseguys ran for the warehouse.

"What in the damn hell is going on?" Monk panted, the tension making his breathing short. "It's supposed to get colder in mid-January, not warmer. I've never seen anything the likes of this. What do you make of it, Izz?"

Izzy's face was grim. "I heard about this kind of goofy weather, but I thought it only happened further up in Canada. I think the Cannucks call it a Chinook. It only lasts a little while and then it gets cold as hell again. I don't want you to get scared, Monk, but if we don't pull the pouches in real quick we is in big trouble. I'll get the boys outta the warehouse, and you start pourin' the juice to the Hupp."

With Milberg, Fleisher and Yaro frantically shoveling sand in the tire tracks, Monk was able to pull a couple more ropes through the slush. Just as suddenly as the temperature had shot up, a frigid blast of Arctic air dropped the mercury to ten or fifteen degrees, freezing the slush. The added strain threatened to snap the tow rope. In desperation, Monk watched the temperature gauge of the Hupp creep into the red zone. He could feel the tires losing traction – the spinning wheels were no longer able to exert the power needed to keep the pouches moving. Monk nursed the accelerator, but in his heart and mind feared for the worst. Izz, the two wiseguys and Joe Yaro feverishly continued shoveling, and for a brief moment the tires seized the sanded ice. Then, in a sudden lurch forward, all was lost – the overburdened rope snapped!

Izz, his fingers numb and stiff, sat pathetically on the ice trying to tie the frayed rope ends together. Joe Yaro, Milberg and Fleisher continued dumbly shoveling sand while Monk jumped out of the Hupp and stood by in the ever-increasing snowfall, praying for a miracle.

Within minutes, Gussie, Victor and Geno ran up the riverbank in their wet, freezing clothes. Amid stomping feet and flailing arms, Gussie bellowed to Izz, "Every god-damn leather pouch is froze solid in the slush an' there ain't no way to drag 'em out. We better get our asses outta here before the sun comes up and the revenuers see what we done." Izz nodded and headed for the warehouse, but Monk grabbed his arm.

"Izz, there's seven grand worth of scotch – six-hundred bottles – sitting there like a bunch of damn ducks just waiting for the revenue agents. We can't just leave it!" he shouted.

"We've got no choice," Izz yelled back through the snow. For a minute, they just stood there screaming at each other.

Finally, Izzy got a hold of himself and, his voice eerily calm, said, "There ain't nuthin' we can do but leave everythin' as is, and high-tail it outta here. Tell the wiseguys and Joe Yaro to run to some place warm and we'll take care of them later." Of course they both knew that was as unlikely as Izzy winning the Irish Sweepstakes.

Izz, Gussie and Monk jumped in the Hupmobile and raced to the Embassy Hotel, leaving the ropes, crates, telephone and Ford truck abandoned in the snow. At the hotel Izz poured three stiff drinks and old Fred on the desk let them use the tub down one flight at the end of the hall for twenty-five cents each. They wrapped themselves in blankets and commiserated while their wet clothes steamed dry on the hot radiator. After the third drink Izz said, "Gussie, you done a hell of a job, but you can see the mess we is in. Suppose you take the Hupp for your share of the job. The wiseguys ain't gonna believe we is busted, so Monk and me better hightail it to Chi-Town before they nail our asses. We'll contact you when things quiet down." Gussie at first refused because he knew how much the car meant to Izz, but accepted the offer when Izz convinced him that he was also in danger and needed wheels to quickly put some miles between himself and the wiseguys.

For the first time in Monk's life, Uncle Izzy didn't have a clue as to what to do next. He just sat on the edge of the bed rocking back and forth. It wasn't like Izz at all, so Monk finally said he had an idea he wanted to float past him. Izz perked up a little, so Monk went on. He said, "This might be dumb-assed, but we are just about out of choices. It's 4 o'clock in the morning, so I think we could make a run over to Betty Lou's place without being noticed. Maybe we could stay out of sight for a few hours and then hop the *Wolverine* for Chi-Town." Izzy mumbled his approval so they gathered up their meager belongings. On the way out Fred said, "I ain't seen you guys tonight, so I got no idea where the hell you went." Good old Fred. They left the half-bottle of Old Log Cabin on the register desk.

They ran up the driveway to the back of Mrs. Hathaway's house and Monk threw snowballs at Betty Lou's window until she woke up. When she saw it was Monk, she ran down the back stairs and opened the door. Monk started to tell her what had happened but she said there'd be time for story-telling later. She warmed up some coffee on her little kerosene stove, grabbed some blankets from the hall closet and spread them on the floor. Monk and Izzy drank the java with trembling hands while Betty Lou slipped downstairs and called the Michigan Central Depot. After learning the *Wolverine* would leave Detroit at 7:30, she called for a Checker cab to be in front of the house at 7:00 a.m. sharp.

While they were lying on the floor, Izz said, "Betty Lou, you is one girl in a million. I can see why Monk is nuts about you. I'm thankin' you for both of us because Monk is too dumb to do it hisself." Betty Lou blushed and said, "Try to get some sleep, boys. I'll call you in time to catch the cab. I think you both are pretty nice guys too."

They got to the depot with ten minutes to spare, and after buying two tickets, some coffee and four powdered ringers, they had exactly $5.78 left, both thinking that here they were, only a few days before, a couple of dandies without cares and rolling in dough. By the time they got to the outskirts of Battle Creek, Monk started blubbering about their stinking clothes and how everything was turning out like crap, and how they would have made a couple grand apiece if the damn Chinook had held off.

Izzy, however, was just about back to his old self by then and said, "Listen here, Monk, we come to Detroit City a coupla weeks ago with forty bucks of our own money and we're leavin' with a fiver and some change. We had great fun with your idea and we seen a bunch of my old pals and had a barrel of laughs. You was lucky to meet a swell girl. Not only that, but Mrs. Hrbec done a fine thing tellin' me her mister really thought so high of me. The only thing I feel real bad about was havin' to give up Mr. Hrbec's Hupmobile to Gussie. So, don't be bawlin' about how bad off things is. I think we're the luckiest guys on this train."

What Monk and Izzy wouldn't know until later was that Victor Ciambi had traced them to Betty Lou's room. He got there about an hour after they had gone. Victor broke open Betty Lou's door and said, "You god-damn little whore, where are them two pricks, Monk and Izzy? You tell me quick or you'll wish ya'd never seen that ugly Monk." By the time he was done beating Betty Lou she had a broken nose, a fractured arm, and blood oozing out of her ears, but she never talked. Mrs. Hathaway heard the commotion in Betty Lou's room and called Pete Consani at the Early Bird Cafe. Pete ordered an ambulance and Betty Lou was rushed to the Ford Hospital on Grand Boulevard. It was two weeks before she could return to Mrs. Hathaway's house, and another week before she felt up to leaving for home in upper Michigan.

Monk and Izz pulled into the La Salle Street Station just after noon, hopped a Halsted trolley to 22nd Street and got home before Monk's mother returned from her job at the Hormel packing plant. After three or four hours of badly needed shut-eye and a change of clothes, Izzy tried to convince his sister that everything was great, but she knew better and gave him the silent treatment.

Izz would have rather have a cold carrot run up his ass than give a call to the Hotel Metropole and tell Frank Nitti what had happened, but he knew if he didn't, they would be marked men. As soon as Frankie heard Izzy's voice he started ranting and raving. "Did you dummies see the afternoon *Trib*? There's a picture on the front page taken by John Brisbaine in one a' them new autogiros showin' six-hundred pouches a' Johnnie Walker stuck in the ice on the Detroit River. Reporters talked with the revenue guys an' they said Capone was more'n likely behind the caper 'cause he gets a lot a booze outta Canada through Detroit. One guy sez it's the biggest screw-up since them Black Sox jokers tried to blow the '19 World Series." Frankie calmed down a little and went on. "Big Al is hoppin' mad an' I'll do what I can for you two geniuses, but Al sez he's not only lost a bundle on the booze, but you made him look like a complete asshole. He's already got calls from Tony Sollima, Dingbat O'Berta an' that no good bastard, Felippe 'the mole' Grogonio. Grogonio was laughin' so hard he probably pissed his pants an' said he always knew Al liked his scotch on the rocks."

Frankie told Izz and Monk to show up at Poppa Caletti's Bella Napoli on Ashland and 35th Street at 10:00 that night. They knew there was no hiding from Big Al, so after hitting Ma up for a fiver, they trolleyed down to Mulrooney's Pool Hall on Western and tried not to think about what might happen. They played a few games of 8-ball and drank a couple quarts of spiked beer. Monk missed hitting the cue ball about six times and Mulrooney bum-rushed them out when he ripped a four-inch gash in the felt.

By dark, they'd had a few more pulls of beer and showed up at Caletti's fifteen minutes early. When Poppa saw them he got rid of his supper crowd and put a "Closed" sign in the window. They were sitting in a back booth nursing a gin when Big Al came blustering in with two goons beside him, and a third standing by the front door. Monk noticed uneasily that the two with Al had their hands jammed in their coat pockets and the guy at the door must have been hanging on to a sawed-off shotgun or one of those "Chicago typewriters" under his coat.

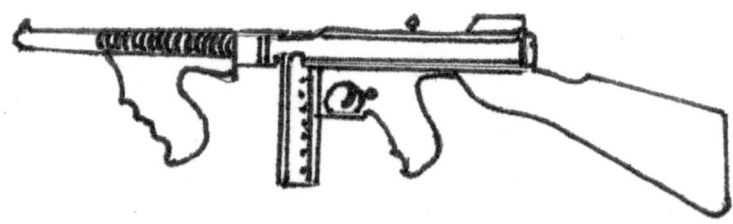

The guy at the door must have been hanging on to... one of those "Chicago typewriters" under his coat.

Al looked seven feet tall when he sat across from them. After a minute or two he slammed the *Trib* on the table showing the autogiro picture. He lit a big cigar and they could see his black eyes glaring at them through the smoke. He didn't say a word, just sat there glaring. Monk could see the big scar on the left side of Al's face getting almost purple and all he could think of was how bad he had to piss. He knew Izz must have been feeling the same because he kept fumbling with a match folder – turning it over and over in his right hand. After a few minutes Al began a little laugh. Then the goons laughed a little. By the time Al and his goons were laughing pretty hard, Izzy and Monk cracked little nervous smiles. Al reached over and gave them each a poke on the shoulder and said, "Boys, I like a guy what's got a little Moxie – guys who'll take a chance no matter what. I figure you amateur mechanics cost me over twenty-five grand, includin' the cost a' the booze, a grand to Abe Bernstein, another grand to the Commissioner an' lost profits."

Capone downed a double shot of vodka without blinking an eye and said, "I pay my soldiers a hundred and a half a week, so I'm gonna give you geniuses a break. You get to live – on thirty bucks a week fer two years. I figger what I'll save on yer pay'll just about make us even."

Monk could feel a warm glow come over him, mostly in the region of his crotch. As Al and his goons were leaving, Big Al turned and growled to Poppa Coletti, "Set the boys up with spaghettis and a bottle a' dago red. That'll come outta your first week's pay, ya damn dummies."

PADDY
1926

CHAPTER ELEVEN

I had been in sales with the Gold Bond Company about a year by 1926, and spent most of January out on the road. Now I was finally heading home to Chicago. As I approached Lake Michigan country a bone-chilling wind gusting off the gray water formed white ripples of snow on stubbles in sleeping cornfields. The manifold heater in my company Ford wasn't quite breaking even with the 18-degree temperature. Evening rush hour traffic in East Chicago had diminished to a few recently started engines puffing white exhaust while waiting at stoplights. At the intersection of Industrial Highway and Columbus Ave. a bent figure in a shabby army overcoat leaned into the blasts of winter and hurried across on the amber.

Entering the Gold Bond parking lot from Dickey Street I had to smile as I nosed into Norman Stoddard's private space next to the office side door. Good old Norm would have raised holy hell if I had taken his reserved spot at 8:30 in the morning. Norm really wasn't a bad sort, but he was the kind of guy you just knew had been chased home from school in the fifth grade. It wasn't Norm's fault that his father had spoiled him rotten and then handed him the keys to the business on his twenty-second birthday, or that his young stepmother had persuaded his father to leave him behind and purchase a palatial home on the southeast coast of Florida.

I didn't begrudge or envy Norm's perks – his new yellow 1925

Packard convertible, the large carpeted second floor office facing Lake Michigan, the huge walnut desk with inlaid Moroccan leather top, the private washroom (with fold-out sofa), or even his efficient blonde nubile secretary – well, maybe a little envy for the convertible and Bobbi Jean with those beautiful high firm breasts and a walk you would follow into the jaws of death.

The Ford engine sputtered to a stop and as I stepped down into the dirty ruts of snow the headlights of a familiar bright red Jordan Playboy sports coupe flashed in my eyes. Bobbi Jean rolled down a frost-covered window and sweetly chirped, "Paddy, can't talk; I'm late for a dinner date. I put a message from your friend Monk on your desk spindle. Did you have a successful trip?"

"Very successful," I replied, "but I missed you terribly, Bobbi Jean." "Oh sure," she said, "you and my lecherous Uncle Peter! Be sure to lock up – and smooth out the wrinkles on the sofa before you leave."

With a twinkle in her eye and a naughty smile, Bobbi Jean churned up the snow, ice, and gravel, pointed the sporty coupe toward the Loop and disappeared into the night.

Monk's note was an invite to join him and his Uncle Izzy at Mooney's speakeasy that night. I grabbed a quick shave and a clean shirt and stopped at Sam Ryan's One-Arm Joint for a corned beef and bowl of onion soup. Sam had this great idea and his little eatery was the talk of East Chicago. His 6 p.m.-2 a.m. hours brought in not only secretaries and office workers on their way home, but also single guys like me. The late crowd of society showoffs, hoods and crooked politicians stopped by because of the good food and the novelty of the place.

Sam had picked up forty surplus school desks – the kind that combined a chair with a flat oval writing surface attached to the right side only. He lined them up four deep like a classroom along the left wall on a white tile floor. He and his pretty wife, Gail, worked behind a full-view counter and kept the food options simple: four kinds of sandwiches – the most popular being the Earl of Sandwich – three hearty soups, and steaming black coffee. Sam boasted with pride that he served only "fast food" and the coffee was free if your order wasn't ready within five minutes. I tried to convince Sam to franchise his idea, but he would have none of it.

I hadn't seen either of the boys for a while. I knew they had been up in Detroit on business, but I never suspected the kind of crazy story they'd have to tell me – I just looked forward to a few drinks and laughs.

When I was a kid, Izzy never missed my Roosevelt High football games if he was in town, and after losing my father he was the one person I could always confide in.

I came stomping into Mooney's out of an unseasonal snow about 10 p.m. just as Clem McCarthy's staccato voice was announcing the Jack Dempsey knockout of some punk-of-the-month club in the third round at Madison Square Garden. Monk caught my eye, so I joined him while Izzy was at the bar joyously collecting his bets. As usual, Izzy bought a round for the house and helped Janice Cashin carry six alky beers over to our table. Jan, Mooney's eighteen-year-old niece, was saving her wages and tips for college at the University of Michigan. All the regulars appreciated her – especially the way she walked. She also had a smooth way of encouraging the guys and cooling them down at the same time.

She might say, "Bobby, I can sure see why your wife fell for you. You must be a wonderful husband and daddy. What did you buy your little girls for Christmas?" Mooney kept a short leash on all the customers and had enough sense to know the receipts were always higher on Jan's shift.

By 11 o'clock the crowd had thinned some so Mooney asked Archie Donahue to take over the bar. Mooney pulled four alky drafts and joined us at our table. He was a hockey nut so the small talk naturally turned to the poor showing of the Black Hawks this year. Mooney said the biggest problem was goalie Dirk Valentine. He couldn't stop a damn slap shot with a bushel basket. It didn't help matters that the New York Rangers had just whipped Chicago 7-2 and were leading the league by 5 games. When Mooney calmed down, Izz changed the subject, held his glass up to the light and said, "Mooney, it seems to me a few months back the alky beer was darker, with a little more bite to it."

"Don't get me started on alky beer, Izz," Mooney said, but then continued. "About a year ago Frank Nitti and his goons paid all us speak owners in South Chicago a visit. We were told that for every two barrels a beer we bought, we had to buy one barrel of the new alky they was promotin'. We knew the Genna brothers, Pete and Jim, had set up copper stills in a couple hundred tenement shacks in Little Italy. They provided the yeast and corn sugar and paid the alky cookers $15 a day to keep a fire burning under the still and skim off the scum. Each joint could produce about 350 gallons of raw alcohol a week. The trouble was, the smell of the fermenting mash attracted rats, cockroaches and the like. The Gennas used coal tar for coloring, then sold the 190-proof alcohol for $6 a gallon to Capone, Bugs Moran, Hymie Weiss or anybody who wanted to spike up their beer. Capone's boys added three quarters of a pail of raw alcohol to a barrel, dumped in some ginger ale, pumped in thirty pounds of compressed air, then jacked up the price to $70 a barrel to us speak owners. We had to get 25 cents a glass just to break even – and that caused a lot of pissed-off customers.

"Ariel Barton over on Central and 23rd Street refused to go along. One early morning a black Buick sedan – the kind Al Capone always used – pulled up in front of his club. Two goons shattered the front window with Thompson slugs, tossed in a couple army grenades, and Ariel's business was gone in less than a minute. After that, the rest of us speak owners fell in line."

"I remember when that job was done," Izz said. "Ariel had closed up and went home about a' hour earlier. The last I heard, the poor guy was workin' in some sleazy joint over in the Levee district."

"I wondered what happened to Ariel," Mooney said. "He was a damn good guy; the last I knew, he was struggling to put his kid through medical school. To finish the story, all us speak owners complained to Nitti about the junk in the barrels. Frankie ain't no dummy; he always said, 'To get along, you gotta go along.' So he had his boys strain every barrel of alky beer before delivery. Of course the raw alcohol preserved whatever was left in the barrels, so it really wasn't no different than the pickled eggs and pigs' feet you guys enjoy with your beer every night. Anyway boys, drink up; and Izz, now you know why last year's alky was darker. I ain't sure, though, where the 'bite' you was so fond of came from and I don't even want to know."

A crowd of late bowlers came in so Mooney returned to the bar to help Archie. Jan sashayed over and sweetly asked if we wanted three more alkys. I quickly said "I think we'd rather have three tightly capped Tivolis, Janice, and we'll skip the pigs' feet and pickled eggs."

By one a.m. we were feeling no pain and all the fun stories had been told and retold a couple of times. Izzy had returned to the bar and was shaking the leather dice cup for drinks. Monk took a swallow of his Tivoli and said, "Paddy, Izz an' me had a sure thing blow up in our faces a couple weeks ago and we damn near bought the farm."

He told of the thrill and danger of the first run of booze across the Detroit River, and then what happened on the second run. He put his thumb and forefinger about an inch apart, and said, "Monk, we were this damn close to picking up thirty-five-hundred bucks when the roof fell in."

He described Izzy's master plan and told about the wiseguys, Reggie and his Canadian crew, the Chinook, scrambling back to Chicago, and the final encounter with Capone.

I was stunned and said, "Good god, Monk, how could you get mixed up in a dumb-assed scheme like that? You and Izz came within a whisker of getting yourselves blown away and Al still might change his mind and not be so forgiving! What are you going to do now?"

Monk yawned and said, "Thanks for your concern, ol' buddy. I think what I'm gonna do now is just go home, hit the sack, and try to forget our rotten luck."

I didn't see Monk for three or four weeks after that, but I always looked forward to an evening at Mooney's and a few laughs, so I called him at his mother's house and we agreed to get together the following Saturday night about nine. He sounded a little depressed so I hoped that a night out would pick him up.

On Saturday night I arrived a little early so ordered my usual. When Monk walked in shortly after nine and Jan dutifully brought over a couple of bombs, I said, "Monk, you look terrible. What's eating you, is Big Al riding your ass?" He lit up a Camel, took a gulp of his drink and said, "No, Paddy, I've got no complaint with Al. After what we pulled, we're lucky we aren't on the bottom of the barge canal with cement feet. We cost him over twenty-five grand and he coulda just as easily put our lights out. Instead, we're on his payroll for two years makin' thirty bucks a week. It ain't much, but it's better than pushing up daisies, and I can live with it.

"My big worry is Betty Lou. I finally got Pete Consani, Betty Lou's boss at the Early Bird Cafe, to take my call. He said she left for home in upper Michigan a few weeks back and he didn't have her address. Pete sounded like he didn't want to talk to me, and when I asked if Betty Lou was feeling well he flew into a rage and yelled, 'Is she feeling well, for crissakes, how could she be feeling well after getting the bejesus beaten out of her!'

"I could hardly believe what he said, and asked who had beaten her. It sounded like Pete was about to hang up, so I quickly explained why we had to leave Detroit City so fast. I said Betty Lou had given us cover until we caught the *Wolverine* for Chi-Town early Monday morning. Pete softened up and apologized for flying off the handle. He said he hadn't known our side of the story.

"A few hours after we left, he said, a guy named Victor Ciambi trapped Betty Lou in her room and beat the hell out of her. She refused to tell him where we were, and ended up spending over two weeks in the Henry Ford Hospital. Mrs. Hathaway cared for her until she partly regained her strength, then she left for her mother's place.

"Pete said, 'she made me promise not to tell you or anyone else where she went. She was afraid Ciambi or his friends might find her and her family, and was also concerned that if you found out what Victor had done, you'd come back to Detroit and kill the bastard.'

"I told Pete she sure had that right, and when things cooled down a little, that's exactly what I intended to do."

Monk drained his glass. Jan, serving customers across the room, nodded when he held up two fingers.

"Pete said Betty Lou had given him the telephone number of her doctor, a friendly old guy named Swerden Lahti. Pete had kept up to date on her recovery each week and Dr. Lahti said her arm cast would probably come off by the first of the month. The rest of the injuries were healing, but she was still pretty stiff and sore.

"I said Betty Lou had told me about Dr. Lahti, and how he and his friends had helped her in the past. Pete seemed to know what I was referring to.

"There was a long silence, then Pete said, 'Monk, there's something I think you should know. I got a hard-nosed cousin named Angelo Bianca who thinks God put him on this earth to protect women. He got to know Betty Lou at the Early Bird and kinda took her under his wing like she was a niece or kid sister. When I told him what had happened to Betty Lou, he damn near went nuts. He visited her every day in the hospital, bringing candy and flowers and keepin' her spirits up with his funny stories.

"'One day he traced Victor Ciambi to Sharky's Pool Hall down on Shelby Street. Angelo played 8-ball with him, bought a few rounds of drinks and the two of them took in a couple of burlesque shows at the Gayety. After about a week of pallin' around, Angelo set Victor up. He told him he had a shipment of hot merchandise coming across from Canada to a spot just east of the Bob Lo dock and needed a partner to help fence the stuff. Angelo said if he was interested, he would split the take down the middle with him.'

"I said, knowing Victor, I can just see him drooling over a deal like that.

"'Angelo went down to the dock about 10 o'clock one night and pulled tarps over a bunch of empty crates. Victor met him about 2 a.m. and when Victor started pullin' the tarps off, Angelo grabbed the bastard and cold-cocked him. Victor looked up with a hurt look on his face and said, "What in the damn hell did ya do that for?"

"'Angelo picked him up by the scruff of the neck and said, "let's see, you little prick, you broke her nose. The blood gushed out like a smashed tomato." Victor's now screamin' and sayin', "I don't know what the hell yer talkin' about." "Oh yeah, sez Angelo, you blackened her eyes." Two fists flattened Victor's cheek and eye bones. Now Victor's on his knees with a mouth full of blood and spitting out teeth, begging for mercy. "What did you do to her ears, you little shit?" Angelo slapped Ciambi's ears with the flat of his hands and broke both eardrums. "Now her arm; which arm did you break?" Victor was pleadin' for his life when Angelo jumped on his left arm and broke it in two places. "Here's a little something you couldn't do to Betty Lou, Victor." Angelo smashed both of Victor's balls with a lead-tipped black jack. The creep's alive but will be in the county hospital for a couple of months, so you won't have to take care of Victor Ciambi, Monk – the job's done.

"'I'm sorry I can't give you Betty Lou's address, but I have to honor my promise to her. Just a minute, the new girl on the cash register is having a little problem, Monk. Call me back at nine sharp. There's more I want to tell you.'

"I was beside myself with worry until my call went through at 9:00 o'clock. A strange female voice answered and when I identified myself the voice said, 'Oh yes, Mr. Harpinski, Mr. Consani is expecting your call. One moment please.' When Pete came on he sounded almost friendly and said he was sorry to have cut me off, but the new girl has trouble making change for anything over $5.

"'Just before Betty Lou left for home she gave me the pawn ticket on the gold watch you gave her. That was a hell of a nice thing you did, Monk. I know how much your grandfather's watch must have meant to you. Betty Lou used the money for some clothes and her train ticket. I just wanted you to know I paid the pawn ticket and sent your watch to Betty Lou last week.'

"I didn't say anything for a few seconds. The operator broke in and said, 'Your three minutes are up, please deposit $1.25 for three more minutes.' I listened to the varied musical tones as I dropped 4 quarters, 2 dimes, and 1 nickel into the coin slots. 'Pete, I give you my word I won't try to contact Betty Lou. I don't want to bring any more hurt to her and her family, but if you'd do two last things for me, I'd sure appreciate it.' Pete could hear the pain in my voice so said, 'Sure, Monk, I'll do whatever I can.'

"'Pete – Pete, if you would just tell Betty Lou there'll always be a place in my heart for her and that she's the finest girl I ever knew. And if you would send Dr. Lahti a check for a dozen American Beauty roses he could arrange for them to be delivered to her home. A card won't be necessary. Betty Lou will know who they're from. I'll wire the money to you by Western Union tomorrow.'

"'Consider it done, Monk, and I wish you every success in the future.'

"When I returned the receiver to the hook, three quarters and a nickel of unused time cascaded into the return port, where they remained as I slowly walked away.

"Well, that's the story, Paddy. I'm stuck with Capone for at least two years. I want to help Betty Lou, and pay Pete back for the pawn ticket, but what the hell can I do on thirty bucks a week?"

Monk put his face in his hands and I said, "You've been dealt a bum hand, Monk, but maybe I can help. We've been closer than brothers since we were kids so I think I can talk from the heart."

Monk wiped the corner of his eye with his left thumb and I continued. "Uncle Izzy has meant almost as much to me as he has to you. We both know he's had a hard life and has a tendency to look for an easy score..." Monk started to talk, but I held up my hand and said, "Let me finish, Monk.

"After your first brush with danger, I was hoping you'd realize you were getting in over your head. Selling your soul to guys like Capone, Nitti and the Bernsteins is pretty serious business. They are friends only as long as you can do them some good. They will waste you or anyone who gets in their way – or even displeases them. Here's what I would like to offer. I know I can get you into Gold Bond. Norm Stoddard is always looking for good men. The pay isn't great at first, but you could learn a trade or even go on the road with your own territory in the future – and that's maybe the most important thing: you'd have a future.

"Finally, I'll get you the twenty-five grand and you and Uncle Izzy can pay off Capone."

Monk looked at me with astonishment and said, "Paddy, how in the name of god can you lay your hands on twenty-five G's? And even if you could, it'd take me the rest of my life to pay you back."

I said, "I don't want you to be concerned about how I'll get the money, Monk. I know I can get it. The important thing is you and Izzy will be off the hook to Capone. And don't worry about repaying the twenty-five G's. It's not a loan. I won't go into any of the details, but let's just say it's an involuntary contribution from a bunch of worthless bastards."

I was disappointed when Monk didn't accept my offer. He said he thought he should stick by Izz and work off their debt to Capone together. The only thing I could think to do was discreetly wire Pete some money to cover the pawn ticket.

A few months later Izzy came up with another get-rich-quick scheme and the temptation was too much for Monk. He was off again to seek the end of the rainbow with his Uncle Izzy.

PADDY
1935

CHAPTER TWELVE

For six weeks after meeting Opie Cantrill at his gas station, I worked my new territory of southern Wisconsin and northern Illinois. The success of opening sixteen new company accounts was more than I had expected, but I still looked forward to the comfortable old stomping grounds of southern Michigan. Three days in East Chicago permitted me to catch up on book work and convince Norm Stoddard to consider financial support for Opie's incredibly simple but effective oil filter.

It was good to be back on the road again on Monday morning. I approached Opie's Double D station with the anticipated joy of telling him his invention had found corporate interest. Eagerness quickly turned to foreboding. Debris lay scattered on the asphalt driveway, and the previously polished gas pumps were dingy with grime. I looked through the front door of Opie's office. Everything seemed the same, but frozen in time. The overhead fan no longer turned lazy circles, and while merchandise still filled the glass case next to the cash register, the tabby cat no longer lounged on the back shelf. I walked along the cracked asphalt to Opie's workroom and looked through the dirty glass into the darkened area. When my eyes became accustomed to the gloom, I could see Opie's 6-cylinder Dodge motor and beautiful stainless steel oil filter smashed almost beyond recognition.

At that moment I heard the shuffle of feet on the asphalt behind me and an agitated voice growled, "Hey, mister, what's your business here?

179

Didn't you see the no trespassing sign out front?" I turned and saw a huge man dressed in black with a bulge in his coat at the hip line. It was not his large crimson-veined nose or the wispy mustache that stood out as much as the sinister droop of his left eye.

I said, "My name is Paddy O'Brian. I represent the Gold Bond Tool and Hydraulic Lift Company in East Chicago. I stop here often and visit my old friend Opie Cantrill. Do you know what happened to him and his wife?"

"I didn't know the gent, but I heard he missed his gasoline quota several months in a row. The company has a strict rule and calls in delinquent franchises."

"Do you have any idea where Mr. Cantrill might be or how I could contact him?" I asked.

"Like I said, I didn't know the gent and have no idea where he went. I'm just a company agent keeping an eye on the property until the company finds another distributor. You might have some luck at the Daniels-Douglas corporate headquarters in South Elgin, Illinois, but I doubt it. Unless you have further business, I'd say you'd best move on."

It was with heavy heart I pulled onto the highway. I looked in the rearview mirror hoping, but not believing, I would see a bent old man in dirty overalls waving an orange grease rag as I pulled out of view. After driving a few miles I regained my composure and vowed I would find and punish those responsible for Opie's unwilling and sudden departure.

Luckily, I knew what to do. It all began back in high school, when I was working in old Abe Schulenberg's lock and vault shop. It was apparent that Abe's health had been failing, so it came as no surprise when, shortly after my dad died, he told me that he would be taking some time off. His tuberculosis exam had come back positive, so when doctors said he needed bed rest for five or six months, he arranged to stay with his sister in Denver. Abe informed me a week before leaving that his old friend, Red Rudensky, would be running the shop while he was away. Abe smiled and said, "Paddy, you will probably hear some stories about Red, and they will be true. He's connected with the mob and is widely known as a 'technician' and the best 'box man' in the business. The long and short of what I'm saying is that Red is a safecracker and there isn't a lock or safe made he can't open in a matter of minutes. But there is something you should know. Red is a true friend and knows I need help. He'll run the business on the up and up until I return and you can learn a lot working with him. I'd trust Red with my life."

Abe was right. Red was a no-nonsense kind of guy with a ready smile and a firm handshake. It didn't take long to get to know and trust him. Early one morning, we received an urgent call from the First National Bank and Mortgage Company on Monroe Street. A nervous voice identified himself as Chief Financial Officer Kevin Lattaway and said the company vault wouldn't open. His concern was that customers would begin arriving at 10 a.m. and would panic if they didn't have access to their accounts. We put an "Open at Noon" sign on the front door and made tracks downtown. Watching Red work was an education in finesse. After quietly surveying the situation he placed the rubber tips of his highly sensitive stethoscope in his ears, cocked his head sideways and leaned close to the vault door. I moved the diaphragm of the instrument as directed while Red gently agitated the dial forward and backward. It was the first time I had been aware of his long, almost feminine fingers. Moments later Red had the answer. He said the worn gears had locked on the primary dial at about 89 degrees. This he ascertained by his keen hearing and the minute vibrations felt in his fingertips. Using a lead hammer as if it were a surgeon's implement and relying on his acute hearing and touch, he swung the vault door open at 9:45. A relieved Mr. Lattaway was advised to transfer the vault's contents to a safe haven. Then Red removed the gearbox from inside the vault door and said he could rebuild and reinstall the mechanism within the week.

As I worked with Red I came to realize he had a clear visual image of the working components of all locking devices. It was almost a sixth sense. It wasn't a schematic outline in his mind, but an almost visceral knowledge that seemed to make the internal workings a part of his psyche. When shop work was slow, I'd line up twelve totally different locks – keyed and combinations. With his picks and super-sensitive instincts, Red would open all twelve in less than ten minutes.

As our friendship and mutual trust grew, Red began to reveal his past. He had started innocently enough working as a legitimate locksmith, installing and repairing bank lock boxes. When Johnny Torrio brought Al Capone to Chicago in about 1920, Red and Al became close friends. As Capone rose in the ranks of the underworld, Rusty, as Al called Red, became a valuable asset. Prohibition had completely changed the way liquor was transported and stored in 1920. All traffic and warehousing were controlled by the federal government. Red said he proved his worth many times over by breaking into government-bonded liquor repositories without firing a shot or using any type of explosives. He estimated that he probably "liberated" several million dollars worth of government liquor for Al. Red went on to master the handling and use of nitro in bank jobs, but said the work was dangerous and he had no doubt he would someday end up in a federal prison or an early grave.

Red Rudensky's outward appearance was deceiving. Flaming red hair, ample nose, thick Jewish accent, and quick one-liners would have made him a headliner on the Keith burlesque circuit. Although he became a hardened criminal he remained a caring, loyal friend with a deep passion for helping others. Having left school at an early age, he nonetheless read widely and developed his intellect. While serving his sentence in the federal penitentiary in Atlanta, he founded and became the editor of the acclaimed prison paper, *The Atlantian*.

During the last few days we spent together before Abe Schulenberg returned to the shop from his medical respite in Colorado, I found Red's low-key counsel influencing the direction of my life. In essence he said, "Paddy, you have progressed in the past few months to the top of this profession. Your natural skills and innate ability separate you from being a competent locksmith to a near genius. As I see it, you have two paths before you. One will lead to a comfortable, middle-class existence, perhaps owning your own business one day; the other to an exciting, risk-taking adventure that, like Icarus, may entice your flight ever closer to the flame of destruction. The second choice will be not only exhilarating, but will provide you an opportunity to satisfy an inner need and help your fellow man."

I found myself, as a young romantic, intrigued with Red's words and said, "Whatever choice I make, I have to know the end of this story. What specifically do you have in mind for me?"

Red took a long drag on his ever-present cigarette, put aside his work project and said, "First, Paddy, you must find a position in a field unrelated to locksmithing. The work must be completely legitimate and give you an opportunity to travel and make astute observations. You would be motive free in the eyes of legal authorities for what is to follow. I know from our casual conversations that you harbor disdain, as I do, for shady moneylenders who bleed the poor with unreasonably high interest rates. These people will become your target of choice. With your uncanny ability to quickly enter a locked door and decipher the mechanisms of a small vault or other hiding place of ill-gotten money, you would be in and out of the establishment in a matter of minutes. Now here is the most important part of the escapade. Never take more than ten per cent of the total bounty and take cash only. The reason? The scumbags will never call in the law or even report a robbery for their relatively small loss. They will assume it was an inside job or an accounting error and take appropriate action. Either way, they will absorb the loss as a business expense.

"If it is convenient, take a list of the borrowers. More about that later. As soon as possible, place the cash in bank lock boxes preferably in several towns far from your home base. Never use any of the cash to enhance your own lifestyle and always work alone. A partner is potential trouble. Now you have reduced your perceived culpability to near zero. You are a pro at covert entry, you are without any apparent motive, the theft will not be reported, and you will not be raising any suspicion by changing your personal spending habits.

"Why take the names and addresses of the unfortunate borrowers? This is what makes the danger acceptable and your involvement rewarding. Buy money orders with return receipt sent to the borrower. Pay off as many loans as possible – with the moneylender's own ill-gotten profits. Could there be any better gratification? Now don't get greedy. Maybe one job every few weeks, in different cities, so a pattern isn't established. Any excess money could be used to anonymously pay hospital, rent or other bills of those needing help. I call this 'giving one's self away.' There it is, Paddy. Of course there is personal risk and at times you will be pushing the envelope, but the satisfaction of helping others is reward enough."

Red Rudensky left a few days later and returned to his life of crime. By '31 he was serving a 25-year sentence in the Atlanta Penitentiary and Alcatraz, sharing a cell with none other than his old friend Al Capone!

His last bequest to me was a small black case containing an array of tools, picks, skeleton keys, rubber gloves, stethoscope, and a note: "Future success – whichever road you choose, Red."

I never saw him again but I believe Red has an angel on his shoulder and eventually will be judged, not by his transgressions, but by his positive contributions to his fellow man.

And as for me, I gave up legitimate locksmithing for the dangerous but exhilarating future Red Rudensky had laid out for me. I enjoyed my work as a Gold Bond company rep, but the true benefit of the job was that the large territory of Southeastern Michigan gave me the freedom and anonymity to help families being financially exploited by unscrupulous moneylenders. On my last trip, I had deposited a total of $12,850 in lock boxes in the Wisconsin villages of Dalton and Johnson Creek, as

well as Mount Morris and Hinkley in Illinois. Helping Opie would not
be a problem.

When Gold Bond closed down for product inventory a few
weeks later, Norm Stoddard suggested I take a few days off.
The following morning I drove over to South Elgin and located the
Double D corporate headquarters on Gilbert Road. The building was
an unimposing two-story gray structure on a corner lot in a commercial
district. I casually drove along the adjacent street on the north side about
4:30 p.m. and observed two caged Doberman pinschers near the rear
entrance. Later that night a darkened building convinced me that the
only security was the free-ranging dogs inside the building.

The following day just before 6:00 p.m. I purchased two pounds
of cheap hamburger, returned to my hotel and mixed in several ounces
of laudanum. The opiate was as easy to obtain as illegal booze from a
pharmacist down by the Loop on State Street. I left a call for 1:30 a.m.
and parked the Ford two blocks from the Double D offices. The lock
on the back door was breached in a matter of seconds and I tossed two
laced hamburger balls through a partly opened door to the snarling dogs.
Within minutes I stepped over the languid bodies and proceeded to the
second floor and found the president's office. Again, entry was simple
and I had to smile as I removed the founder's portrait from the front
of the wall safe. Solving the tumbler action was elementary and as the
thick steel door swung open my appreciative thoughts turned to Red
Rudensky. Ignoring Red's counsel of taking only 10% of the proceeds I
later counted a total of $18,000. The total lapsed time, from entering the
building until drawing two bowls of cool water and patting the relaxed
canines on the way out, was about fourteen minutes.

The following morning a long-distance operator confirmed that one
Opie J. Cantrill resided at 1008 North Freedom Road, Milton, Kentucky.
I received a receipt for $10,000 from Western Union and the money was
on its way to Opie anonymously by noon. I deposited $2,000 in the poor
boxes of four churches in Elgin, and was back in Chicago with time to
spare for the Cubs' afternoon game with the Pittsburgh Pirates.

Driving south from Wrigley Field on Clark Street after the game,
I crossed Belmont Avenue and realized I was in the old North Chicago
territory once controlled by Dion O'Banion and later by Hymie Weiss
and Bugs Moran. Monk had told me he and Uncle Izzy had met Frank
Nitti in a bar on Belmont in the spring of '26 and began planning the

heist of Weiss and Moran's fleet of beer trucks. I decided to do some sleuthing, so I parked in front of a joint near the intersection of Clark and Belmont called the Flame Bar.

After my third beer I asked the bartender if he had ever heard of Jake Clepka. He said, "Hell, yes. This was Jake's joint when he took one in the back of the head about eight or ten years ago. There was talk Bugs Moran done the job. My boss bought the place from Clepka's widow."

I took a couple more beers to a back booth and looked around. This was where it all began, I reminded myself. As I slowly finished the beers, my thoughts turned to the events that followed, right down to their fateful conclusion.

1926

CHAPTER THIRTEEN

During March and April of 1926, Monk and Izzy worked South Chicago for $30 a week, picking up protection money, helping in Capone's Hawthorne Inn and occasionally taking part in hijacking Hymie Weiss' beer trucks when they strayed south of Madison Street. In early May, Monk and Izz took in a flicker at the Bijou on Clark Street. Frank Nitti had left word in Colosimo's to meet him in Jake Clepka's joint on Belmont around the corner from the movie house at 11:00 p.m. They knew a request from Nitti was an order from Al Capone.

Monk and Izzy were sitting in a back booth when Frankie came in with his goons, Johnny Esposito and Pauli Del Bono. Esposito sat staring at the front door. Del Bono sat sideways against the wall with a view of the entire room and back exit.

Nitti greeted the boys like they were his first cousins and ordered a round of drinks. Cherri, the stacked bar maid, leaned way across the booth to retrieve an empty – to a very attentive Monk and Izzy. Nitti said, "If that broad had legs to go with them knockers, she'd be a headliner at Minsky's."

"Speaking of headliners," Monk said, continuing the small talk, "can you imagine the Cubs trading a guy like Grover Cleveland Alexander to the damn Cards? The only pitcher in the last fifteen years anywhere near as good was Walter Johnson."

Izzy joined in. "For my money, great hittin' will beat great pitchin'

189

any day. All the Cubbies need is a couple of guys like Al Simmons, Heinie Manush and maybe Rogers Hornsby to win the damn pennant."

Frankie said he'd lost all interest in baseball after the Black Sox scandal, and leaned forward with a smile and said, "Izzy, I think I got a little deal that'll get you guys off the hook and back on Al's regular payroll. Since O'Banion got whacked last year, an' Hymie Weiss an' Bugs Moran took over the Northside, Al's been thinkin' a' ways to turn the table on them bastards. Now, here's where you guys come in, if you want. I ain't sayin' there's no danger involved, an' you could get your asses in a sling real easy."

Izzy looked at Monk and Monk shrugged his shoulders. Izz said, "Go ahead, Frankie, we ain't got much to lose."

Frankie went on, "Weiss and Moran control the two biggest breweries on the Northside, Sieben an' Manhattan. Every week they roll out twelve beer trucks from each brewery to a refrigerated warehouse on Belmont Ave. We figger each truck carries thirty barrels, so twenty-four trucks is deliverin' seven-hundred an' twenty barrels a' fresh beer every seven days. Al's found a way to juice up his product by addin' some raw alcohol, ginger ale, an' compressed air. He gets $70 a keg wholesale, which is $50,400 fer seven-hundred an' twenty barrels. Now, add maybe $1,500 fer each hijacked truck an' we got a one-night heist worth about $87 grand."

Izz said, "Frankie, you is talkin' big money here. How does Monk and me fit into a picture like that?"

"First Izz, we gotta have trusted eyes an' ears inside both breweries. This ain't no 'zim, zam, thank you ma'am' operation. It's gotta be precision all the way. We need ta know the exact day an' time the trucks is scheduled to move out. It won't be no problem gettin' you boys on the loadin' docks an' you can figger on workin' about a month before the heist. Al said he'll bump ya up to $150 a week and ya can keep yer dock wages."

Frankie dropped his voice and continued, "But here's the most important part of the operation. We know the overhead doors outta the breweries are one-inch steel clad, an' locked from the inside. A big Mack or International could smash through, but that would leave a mess an' make it tough to get the beer trucks out quick. Besides, we want ta surprise the bastards, an' hit both breweries at exactly the same time. Izz, since you done that hydraulic job on Al's trucks a few years back, he was wonderin' if you might have a brainstorm on how to get through the doors the fastest without usin' any blastin' powder an' causin' any commotion. The cost a' whatever ya need ain't of no concern."

Izzy drained his glass, rubbed his chin and said, "Frankie, lemme think on this and I'll get back to you. In the meantime, get us loadin' jobs at the breweries. I'll need to see them door locks from the inside and maybe take some measurements."

After about a week on the job, an idea was already bouncing around inside Izzy's head. The lock mechanisms were four feet, six inches up from the bottom of each door, and three inches in from either side. Four one-and-a-half-ton trucks – preferably closed delivery wagons that would look natural in the neighborhood – would be needed. Frankie lifted two suitable grocery trucks, one laundry truck and one plumber's truck.

Izzy remembered back to the days in 1916 when Mr. Ford had elevators installed in the Highland Park plant to connect the second floor machine shop with the main floor assembly line. Heavy milled parts like cam shafts and pistons could then be sent down to the line as needed. As a safety precaution, dozens of large 6-inch-diameter coiled springs, thirty inches long, were mounted together on the floor of the elevator pit to cushion the fall of an overloaded elevator car if the brakes didn't hold.

Jock Adamson, the Otis Elevator Company foreman, and Izz bonded as good friends during the installation. Jock even became one of the regulars on the Sunday canoe and picnic outings to Belle Isle back in '16 and '17. The gang knew Jock had eyes for Marguerite Crawford, Esmeralda Sweeney's best friend. Jock was now the superintendent of the Otis Company branch in Chicago, so when Izz contacted him and walked into his office, the two old friends had a lot of catching up to do.

Jock pulled a fifth of Canadian Club and two glasses out of his desk drawer and said, "Izz, hearing your voice on the phone sure brought back some good old memories. What have you been doing with yourself? It's got to be, what, seven or eight years since we had a drink together?" Izz filled Jock in on his life since leaving Detroit City in '19. He lied a little and left a few things out, but what the hell, a guy's got to have a few secrets.

After a couple of drinks, Jock said, "Izz, do you remember after the elevators were installed in the Highland plant, Charlie Sorenson, Mr. Ford's top gun, volunteered to test the safety springs in the number one elevator pit? He was a tough guy and wouldn't let any of his workers do anything he wouldn't do first. So we overloaded the elevator and showed Charlie how to operate the controls. He was to cut the power half way down from the second floor and let the car drop to the spring pit. We were standing by the open door on the first floor and you could hear Charlie suckin' air as he went by. When we raised the car back up to the first floor level, that damned Swede stepped out like nothing happened and said, 'Boys, other than bouncing up and down a few times, she worked like a charm.'"

Izz laughed and said, "Jock, I was standin' right there when Charlie got off the elevator and I bet Honnie Janousky a fiver that Charlie went back to his office and changed his underwear!"

After a couple more drinks and a story or two, Jock said, "Izz, I remember with fondness those picnic Sundays on Belle Isle. Did you and that pretty little black-haired nurse ever get serious? The last I heard, she volunteered for overseas duty during the war."

Izz told Jock all he knew about Esmeralda and Marguerite being lost in action in the battle of the Argonne Forest just before the war ended.

"I'm truly sorry, Izz. Those were two fine young ladies. I often think of those carefree Sundays on the Detroit River. Anyway, what brings you to my office today? Is there something I can do for you?"

Izz leaned forward and said, "Jock, there sure as hell is. I got a mechanical problem that's gonna need your special experience and skill. First, though, I gotta tell you up front that I and my nephew, Monk Harpinski, is workin' for Al Capone. If that makes a difference we can just shake hands and leave our friendship like it's always been."

Jock frowned, "Izz, you know I can't get involved in something illegal, but I don't need to know any details about what you've got in mind. Lay out your problem and I'll be happy to help, friend to friend, in any way I can."

Izz told Jock what he needed. He sketched a design of a spring-loaded device that could propel a hardened, pointed steel rod through a one-inch reinforced metal skin. He suggested that a six-inch diameter, twelve or fourteen-inch long heavy cadmium spring might be loaded into a steel cylinder slightly larger than the spring. A smaller cylinder, a little larger than the rod projectile, could be welded on the front of the spring holder to act as a kind of gun barrel. At this point, Izzy reassured Jock that the device would not be used in any way to cause personal injury. It was to be used one time and then discarded. Izz continued, "I can fabricate the thing so far, but I don't know the size of the spring needed, how to compress the spring in the cylinder or how to make a release mechanism. My first idea was to use one of them elevator pit springs cut down to size."

Jock sipped his whiskey, looked down in thought for a few moments and said slowly, "The pit spring would be much too heavy, Izz, but the size and resiliency of the spring would pose no problem. We deal with the Cook Spring Company in Ann Arbor, Michigan and Chet Boling would supply us with what we needed within days. Whatever we design, there's no way the device could penetrate a bank vault, so I'm guessing you need to break open a door of some sort, and you need to do it with a minimum of noise."

Izzy grinned and said, "Jock, you hit the nail right on the head and I can tell you that the device would be used only against a cheatin' crook."

Jock took a pad from his desk and began making a sketch. "I could cut two horizontal ten-inch slots on either side of a four-inch diameter, eighteen-inch long iron steam pipe. A steam pipe would give us the strength we need. A grooved ratchet gear over each slot and a pawl with a vertical lever could ride on a moveable deck. Pumping the lever back and forth against a back plate welded on the spring would cause the spring to compress against an end cap. I'll need to work on a release mechanism, but that shouldn't be too difficult. I've got a couple of tool and die men who need only an idea and a sketch to come up with an unbelievable finished prototype. This is roughly what I have in mind." Jock showed Izz his hastily drawn concept.

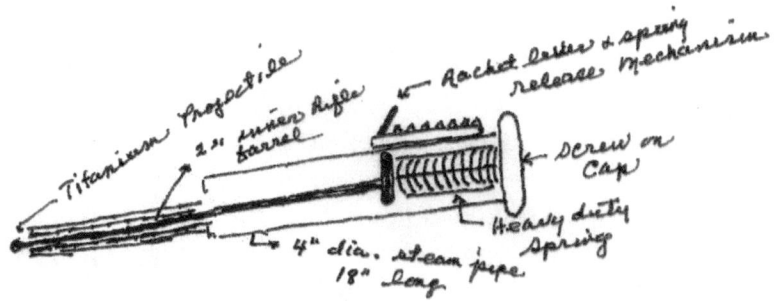

Izz grinned and said, "Now, why the hell didn't I think of that?"

"There's one caution, Izz. The loaded spring, upon release, will probably generate a forward pressure of maybe four-hundred pounds per square inch or more. That means the device would have to be securely anchored."

"Thanks for the warnin', Jock. I plan to mount the contraption using steel straps on the bed of a one-and-a-half-ton truck, with the straps bolted to I-beams on the undercarriage. I'll need five of the units, one each for four trucks and one to practice on. The cost ain't no factor, but I'd like to have the first unit in two or three weeks, if possible."

"That's plenty of time for development of the prototype and the finished units, Izz. The only expense will be for the springs, titanium projectile rods, and overtime for my two men. Any other material needed can come from our scrap bin." Jock ushered Izzy to the door and said, "It's been great seeing you again, Izz. I'll leave word at Colosimo's when the 'proto' is ready."

As Izz left Jock's office he couldn't help but feel a surge of appreciation for Jock's friendship.

The boys continued to work at the breweries, Monk at Manhattan and Izz at Sieben. The routine was the same. Every Thursday in the late afternoon, thirty kegs were loaded on each of the twelve trucks lined up inside the breweries. The deadbolt lock mechanism was set on the inside of the exit doors; there was no way to open the doors from the outside.

By 11 p.m. each Thursday, the twenty-four drivers assembled at two nearby speakeasies, twelve at Hogan's Rod 'n Reel on Foster Ave. and twelve at the Racehorse on Clark Street. Hymie Weiss watched his drivers at Hogan's and Bugs Moran kept an eye on his boys at the Racehorse. The time of departure was changed each week and only the lead driver was given that information. After a couple of hours the drivers left each bar in two's and three's and were taken to the breweries' general offices in armed Buick sedans.

Monk and Izz had successfully bribed the two lead drivers, Joey Sincola at Manhattan and Pugsy Lummin at Sieben, with five century notes each. When the lead driver finished his last drink, he was to leave his change on the bar as a tip – in a special code thought up by Izzy. A fifty-cent piece represented the center of an imaginary clock face. A quarter with heads-up was left in the position of the hour hand, and a dime heads-up represented minutes. Other coins were scattered on the bar in a haphazard manner, tails up. Monk and Izz joined in with the guys and positioned themselves to see at a glance how the coins were arranged. After a couple dry runs, the code worked perfectly.

Two weeks later Jock left word at Colosimo's for Izz to meet him at the Otis machine shop at 10:00 on Friday night. Jock had a smile on his face when Izz entered the side door and said, "Izz, I got something that will knock your socks off. Take a look at what my boys came up with." In a large vice was the prototype Jock had promised, but taken one step further. On the gleaming eighteen-inch spring barrel was welded a two-inch diameter, twenty-two-inch pipe. Jock ratcheted the heavy spring back into position and inserted a one and seven-eighths-inch titanium steel, spear-like rod. The rod was pushed up against a half-inch thick steel plate welded on the front of the spring. Jock had installed Zerk grease fittings on both the spring barrel and rod assembly for lubrication. When the ingenious release mechanism was activated, there was a swooshing sound and the sharpened rod thrust forward and penetrated a 5-inch concrete block.

Izzy just stood there dumbfounded and finally said, "Jock, it's beautiful. I ain't never seen anythin' like it. You are a god-damned genius."

Jock smiled, "I think it'll do the job you want it to do, Izz, but I'm already thinking of a few refinements and maybe applying for a patent. It might be useful in the building trades, to be used by electricians or plumbers to punch holes for wires and pipes. If it's successful you'll be an equal partner because it was your original idea. Oh, I also made it a little easier for you to install by welding four brackets on the spring barrel. The entire mechanism could be mounted on a steel plate and that way you could use shims to adjust its position up or down, or from side to side, before bolting it to the truck bed."

Izzy said, "I sure appreciate what you done, Jock. I wonder if I could take the prototype with me?"

Jock replied, "I don't see why not, Izz. The first one took some time and study, but you can pick up four more identical units by next Friday. You mentioned using the devices only once. If you don't mind, I'd like at least the prototype back for further experimentation."

"I'll bring all five back, Jock, and you can tell your tool makers that they'll be well took care of too."

Izzy spent the next few days installing Big Bertha (a name he coined after the huge railroad flatcar cannon the Germans used in World War I) on the back of the truck bed. He even made an improvement that would hide the weapon from prying eyes and give it more stability. First, he added a second cap that screwed on the front of the spring barrel. He drilled and tapped the cap and screwed a two-inch diameter rod barrel into the cap. Now the long rod barrel could be mounted and dismounted quickly using only a pipe wrench. Two parallel braces ten-inches apart gave the rod barrel stability without any vertical or horizontal play. With the rod barrel removed, the entire spring barrel assembly was moved further back from the end of the truck bed. With the rod barrel attached, the driver could maneuver the "gun" to within an inch of the brewery door lock. Jock assured Izz the four units under construction would include his modifications. On Friday Izz made the pickup, left $500 for each of Jock's craftsmen, and paid Jock for the supplies.

Saturday and Sunday found Izzy positioning and attaching the Big Berthas on the four truck beds. Monday was practice day. Izzy had mock-up steel doors installed that rolled up on rails. They were exact replicas of the brewery companies' doors. An inclined ramp, two trucks wide, sloped down to the doors. The position of the locks stood out as silhouetted black squares exactly four feet six inches up from the ramp and three inches in from the outer sides. Twelve men climbed into the back of each truck and screwed the gun barrels in place while the drivers backed the trucks into position with the Big Berthas aimed at the center of each lock. After the command to fire was given and the makeshift locks had been penetrated, the two truck drivers jumped out of their cabs, placed two twelve-inch suction discs on the doors, and swung them up. The twenty-four drivers then ran to the location of the companies' beer trucks. They had thirty seconds to start and move their trucks toward the exit door. The drivers of the "gun" trucks carrying the Big Berthas, meanwhile, exited the ramps and parked nearby. When the last beer truck passed, Izzy and Monk rolled smoke bombs into the breweries and then followed in the "gun" trucks. Izzy had the men practice this routine until they could do it in their sleep.

By the fifth or sixth dry run, the entire simulated operation, from penetrating the locks until the last truck cleared the building, took two minutes and nine seconds. The plan was for the Bugs Moran's trucks to take Western Ave. to 43rd Street and deliver their load at the Union Stockyard icehouse at Peoria and Exchange Streets. Hymie Weiss' Sieben trucks would take Ashland to Exchange Street and unload at the same icehouse. Nitti had arranged with precinct captain Ardis Riley to have two police squad cars available for escort duty as soon as the trucks passed Madison Street.

On the night of the heist Monk and Izzy were to call Nitti with the exact time that the trucks were scheduled to leave the breweries. Two of the four "gun" trucks were assigned to pick up Monk and Izzy, and they were to be met later by the other two trucks at twenty minutes before countdown.

O n Thursday night, Monk and Izzy were at the Northside speaks drinking and telling stories with Weiss, Moran and their drivers. At 1 a.m., the drivers began moving out under escort. By 1:30, Joey Sincola and Pugsy Lummin left their "tips" on the bars. With a glance, Monk and Izzy read the code: 3:20 a.m. A call to Frank Nitti started the ball rolling. Twenty-four drivers jumped into the back of the closed delivery vans in Cicero. Monk and Izzy were picked up and the vans moved within a few blocks of the two breweries. At 2:45 a.m. the "gun" barrels were screwed in place and the titanium projectile rods pushed in against the spring plates. The springs were then compressed. At precisely 2:55 a.m. the four vans backed down the ramps and positioned the "guns" within inches of the locks on the brewery doors. Izz and Monk checked their watches. At exactly 3 a.m. the Big Berthas were fired. With a swoosh, the rods penetrated the steel doors and shattered the locks.

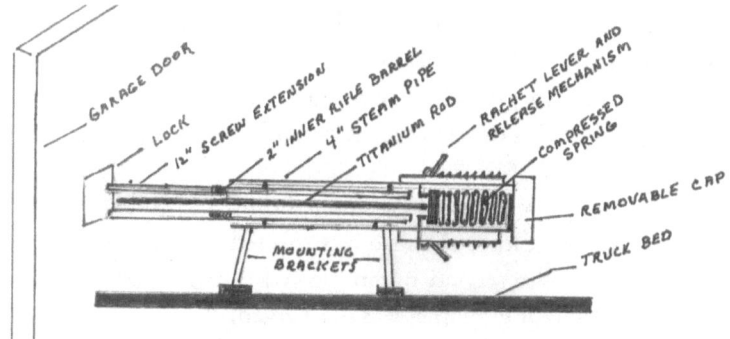

The four vans backed down the ramps and positioned the "guns" within inches of the locks on the brewery doors.

As planned, four men slammed rubber suction discs on the heavy doors and raised them up. At each brewery, twelve drivers then ran in, started the motors of the fully loaded trucks and were in motion within seconds.

Izz was greatly pleased with the elapsed time of two minutes and fifteen seconds for the Sieben heist. Best of all, the only sound produced was the penetration of the locks. He hoped things were going as smoothly for Monk over at the Manhattan brewery.

Izzy threw his smoke bombs in the Sieben brewery, and jumped quickly into the cab of his "gun" truck. He watched the beer trucks racing down Ashland toward the safety of Madison Street en route to their planned drop-off point, the Union Stockyards. Just minutes later Weiss' men ran frantically into the smoke-filled brewery staging area with guns drawn. As the smoke began to clear, Hymie Weiss slammed his hat on the floor and screamed, "That dago prick, Capone, has gotta be behind this. If he wants war, that's what the son-of-a-bitch is gonna get!"

Izz made his way to the Stockyards. All the beer trucks had arrived safely. The seven-hundred and twenty barrels of beer from the two breweries were unloaded at the icehouse by 4:15 a.m. Each driver was instructed to conceal his truck in a predetermined location and report to Frank Nitti at 9:00 that night at the Hawthorne Inn.

Izzy was satisfied. Although the heist was a straightforward one, it had depended upon both men and machinery working according to plan. The whole thing had gone off without a hitch! What he wouldn't find out until later, though, is that things hadn't gone as smoothly for Monk at the other brewery.

At the Manhattan brewery, as the last beer truck cleared the building, Monk made a hasty decision. He yelled to the driver of one of the "gun" trucks, Sid, to jump in a beer truck as it went by. Monk would detain Bugs Moran's boys as long as possible and then take the "gun" truck himself.

Monk lit the fuse on his first smoke bomb and rolled it down the ramp. No reaction! Either the fuse was snuffed out or the bomb was a dud. The fuse on the second bomb glowed a bright red, but when it detonated only a light gray mist was discharged.

Angry shouts grew louder and when random tommy gun slugs tattooed the ceiling and walls, Monk dashed for his idling truck. He jammed down the clutch pedal and engaged the accelerator lever. The truck leaped forward, but he knew Bugs Moran's powerful Buick sedan could easily overtake him. His only chance of survival depended upon what transpired in the next few minutes. He could play a deadly cat and mouse game and gain a little time by driving down and across narrow side streets, but he knew he would eventually be caught and gunned down. Monk desperately realized his best bet would be to hide in a darkened alley until he could think more clearly.

As he sat nervously in the idling truck, a possible plan began to formulate in his mind. During the summer when he was nineteen, he, Paddy, and a group of their idle friends would meet at 1 a.m. on Friday on the outskirts of Cicero and drag-race on Austin Avenue. The cops rarely intervened and, if they did, the guys scattered in all directions and were never caught. At first, the drag was about four city blocks long in a two-car elimination race, with the winner gaining only bragging rights. Later the race developed into a timed event restricted to cars five years or older and 6-cylinders, max. Individual cars raced five blocks down Austin, then had to turn around at 31st Street and dash back to the starting point on 26th Street. This kind of race required real driving skill, plus an entry fee. A guy could win twenty-five bucks or more by copping the top prize along with some friendly side bets.

Monk had asked his Uncle Izzy to soup up his 4-cylinder Ford runabout so he could compete with the larger cars. Izz performed his usual magic with motors, replacing the adequate but under-performing electrical system with a Bosch-Ford kit, the choice of professional racing drivers. A Brad-Kent carburetor replaced the original Kingston, and expensive, double-insulated Red Head Big Boy spark plugs were installed. When completed, the old engine turned out eight more horse power and twelve extra miles per hour. As a little tough-guy addition, he added a cluster of four Sparton trumpet horns under the hood. At the touch of a button the horns blasted out "sweet-ad-o-line."

Monk remembered how delighted he was with Izzy's mechanical wizardry but knew he would have to pick up a few more seconds to beat the big boys. He developed and practiced a maneuver that he thought just might give him an edge.

The night of the summer-ending wing-ding, Monk was cheered by Paddy and the usual bevy of fetching drag chicks. At the crack of the starter's gun, Monk's spritely little Ford, with newly installed transmission bands, leaped forward and quickly gained speed. Monk was the last racer, and he knew that some very fast times had been achieved in the previous races by his competition. He also knew the bigger cars squandered precious seconds backing to and fro at the intersection while making their turns. The turn would be the best place for him to gain time against the bigger cars. So when the little Ford was within twenty feet of the intersection, Monk simultaneously jammed in the brake and reverse pedals and pulled back the emergency brake, locking the rear wheels. He turned the steering wheel a quarter turn to the right, and then jerked it violently left. With the tires screeching and the rear axle gears groaning, the car spun a complete 180 degrees. The beer-happy crowd yelled and applauded the ballet-like pirouette as Monk quickly accelerated and broke for the finish line. A tap of the horn button activated the loud trumpet horns, delighting the raucous crowd as the starter dramatically swooped the checkered flag to the ground. Monk had shattered the record by three seconds.

Sitting in the truck in the darkened alley off Montrose Street, Monk fondly remembered that the prize money he had received that night was not as rewarding as the young firm bodies that had been offered up to the newly crowned "King of the Road!"

His reminiscing was brought abruptly to a halt when he noticed a silhouette of the sinister black Buick passing by, slowly heading north. Monk knew his life now hung by a slender thread. There was perhaps one last chance. He pulled out of the alley, eased the Ford truck to the middle of Montrose, and blinked the lights on and off. Then he provocatively rocked the truck back and forth, and sounded the loud Claxton horn. The dreaded Black Maria hesitated, then began a slow, wide u-turn. It was almost as though the Buick's driver saw a red toreador cape waving before him, taunting him, as he accelerated forward.

Bugs' men were taking the bait! All action now seemed to Monk to be occurring in slow motion, but he knew he could be overtaken in a matter of seconds. In his mind's eye he could visualize the huge monster bearing down on him, a hit man standing on the running board with a machine gun at the ready. Timing now had to be absolutely perfect. With the Western Ave. intersection looming ahead and his heart pounding, Monk began his life or death maneuver. The truck brake, reverse pedal and emergency lever responded even more violently in the truck than they had in his little runabout in high school. A quarter turn to the right, and a harsh turn to the left of the steering wheel swung the truck to a grinding halt perpendicular to the roadway. The top-heavy vehicle immediately began to lurch over. Panicking, Monk leaped free, sprawling on the oil-soaked pavement and sliding under a parked car. An instant later the heavy Buick smashed into the truck, careened off two parked vehicles and burst into flame. Cartridges began to explode, with lead ricocheting off buildings and cars.

With hands over his head, eyes tightly closed and face pressed into the filthy gutter, Monk could imagine the brilliant incendiary droplets of burning gasoline raining down like spent fireworks on the Fourth of July. When he dared to look, he saw and heard a screaming man engulfed in flame running toward him, still clutching a machine gun. The grotesque figure fell not two feet from Monk, scratching and clawing at the pavement. As the flames flickered and turned into a greasy black smoke, Monk knew he would never forget the smell of burning flesh or the pleading of desperate eyes that he had just witnessed.

Monk limped into an alley and slumped in the garbage and debris until he collected his senses. Police cars and fire engines shrieked in the distance as he stumbled into an all-nighter. Monk asked a cashier wearing a green eye shade for the washroom, and without raising his eyes from the *Sporting News* he pointed a jerking thumb in the direction of a curtained hallway. In the john, Monk gulped the cool water while splashing it on his face and skinned arms. He wiped the grease and filth from his clothing as best he could and returned to the counter. He ordered a cup of steaming black coffee and drank it down before venturing back out to the street.

Partly invigorated by the early morning air, he boarded a southbound Damen Ave. trolley, transferred at 23rd Street and reached Cicero about 6:30 a.m. As Monk knocked and entered Izzy's one-room flat, his uncle looked up from his morning *Trib* and said, "For crissakes, Monk, what took ya so long?"

Izzy poured Monk a double shot of Old Log Cabin with just a splash of water as he learned of his nephew's early morning ordeal. The shot seemed to do the trick, and Monk began to feel somewhat better. He was still worried, though. Worried about facing his mother in his filthy clothes, and worried about Nitti's wrecked equipment. He knew his mother wouldn't have been concerned about his not coming home because he had told her that he and Paddy were double-dating and he would be staying over at Paddy's. But how was he to explain the clothes? And how would Nitti react to losing a truck and the Big Bertha gun?

Izzy said not to worry. The truck was stolen property and the Big Bertha would be small potatoes to a man like Nitti. Nitti couldn't care less about such small details. He conceded that his sister, though, was another kettle of fish! He thought about it for a while, and came up with a workable plan. Monk confirmed that his mother didn't get home from the night shift at the packing plant until 8:30 each morning. So Izzy told Monk to get his ass on home and take a bath. Then he was to put on clean clothes, taking care to put on a long-sleeved shirt to hide the scrapes and bruises, bury his stinking clothes in the backyard, and make his mother a nice hot breakfast. Izz said that although Nitti expected them at the Hawthorne by 11 a.m., he would cover for Monk if he wanted to catch some shut-eye at the flat. But since they still had a job to do on the three panel trucks, Monk should meet him at the icehouse at two that afternoon.

All went smoothly at home, just as Uncle Izzy had predicted. In the afternoon Monk and Izz removed the Big Berthas from the three remaining trucks and delivered them as promised to Jock Adamson. Izz talked Nitti into leaving the stolen vans in an empty lot so the police would find them and return them to their owners. The job was done! Monk and Izz were off the hook and back in the good graces of Big Al.

The following day Nitti contacted Hymie Weiss and offered him a "deal" on twenty-four surplus trucks. Frankie had to hold the telephone earpiece a foot away as Weiss shouted, "You dirty son-of-a-bitchin' dago, Nitti. First you break into my business and steal my product, and then you insult me by tryin' to sell me back my own god-damned trucks."

"Now, now Hymie, calm down. That's not a nice way to talk to a friend," Nitti said as he winked at Izz and Ciro Cataldo. "I don't know nuthin' 'bout somebody stealin' your damn product. What was it, a load of cabbages? As far as the trucks is concerned, they're just a bunch of surplus wheels we acquired over time. If you ain't interested, the Genna brothers already said they'd take 'em."

Hymie knew he was licked and agreed to pay $1,500 a truck, but said in parting, "I ain't gonna forget this, Nitti, and if I ever catch any a' your damn goons in the Northside, they're dead meat."

Frankie told Hymie when the thirty-six grand was delivered to the Hawthorne Smoke Shop, he would tell him where the trucks could be picked up. Frankie planned to park the trucks in a field at the end of the streetcar line at Indianapolis Boulevard and 101st Street.

After expenses, Frank Nitti said Al's net was about eighty grand, a pretty tidy sum even for Mr. Capone, but that Al had gotten the most satisfaction out of sticking a needle into the asses of Weiss and Moran. Monk and Izzy had now paid off their Detroit debt to Al, but remained on the payroll at the much larger sum of $150 a week. Nitti gave each of the boys an envelope containing $300 and one of Al's diamond-studded belt buckles. Al said to tell them they had done a good job, and to take a week off and have some fun.

CHAPTER FOURTEEN

Monk hadn't heard from Izz for several days, and his $300 was burning a hole in his pocket. He went over to Izzy's room on Kostner Ave., but his landlady hadn't seen him. "Of course," she said, "that ain't unusual. He comes an' goes like the wind, but it don't matter none to me as long as I get my rent money on time."

Izzy finally called towards the end of their week off. Monk's mother answered the ring and in a contemptuous voice demanded to know where her brother had been. She said, "As usual, you've shown no concern for Monk's feelings. He's been worried sick about you." Izz mumbled an apology and waited for Monk to get on the phone.

"Monk, Izz here. Sorry you been worried. I've got somethin' important for both of us. Meet me at the Green Mill at four this afternoon and I'll fill you in."

The afternoon regulars whistled and poked good-natured fun at Izzy's appearance when he entered the Green Mill watering hole. He actually looked embarrassed as Inez curtsied and in a coquettish voice asked, "What is Mr. Astor drinking today?" Monk folded Inez's bar rag neatly over his left forearm, bowed, and elegantly directed Izz to his seat. Pretending irritation, Izz tugged at his collar and with chin extended said, "What the shit, can't a guy wear his best Sunday go-to-meetin' clothes without gettin' ragged by a bunch of jealous drunks!" Inez hurried over two doubles with alky chasers and life in the Mill returned to normal.

Monk took a sip and asked, "What in the hell happened to you, Izz? I was about to send out the National Guard."

"I wish now I had taken you with me, Monk. I hopped the *Wolverine* for Detroit City and spent what may be a very profitable few days for us with my old friend, Gar Wood. Remember a few months back when I told you about me and Gar bein' best pals when I first come to Detroit?"

"Hell yes, Izz. You said he built a speedboat that could do seventy or eighty miles per." "That's right. You is smarter than I sometimes give you credit for." Monk winced, but knew his unk was just joshing him.

Izz began to reminisce. "Gar showed up in Detroit City about 1914 or '15 from a little river town in Iowa. His dad was a ferryboat operator so I guess that's where he first got interested in boats. We was both workin' in Henry Ford's Hamtramck T-model plant and become buddies. It was kinda strange because I was a hell raiser and Gar was a quiet guy, maybe ten or fifteen years older than me and mostly interested in motors.

"Jake Bronson, the line boss, knew Gar was smart so he fixed it so the two of us could tinker in the machine shop on our time off. Jake probably figured we might come up with a more efficient motor or somethin' so he could claim the credit. Gar had a whole nuther idea, though. He had a little 6-horse outboard motor mounted on a rowboat tied to a tree in the Detroit River off East Jefferson. He kept workin' on that little motor, shavin' the cylinder head, playin' with the ratio on the intake and exhaust valves, and improvin' the carburetion.

"One Sunday mornin' we went out on the river and Gar said, 'Grab the gunnels, Izz, and hang on!' Well, Gar opened the throttle and the bow of that little bastard rose up and we was doin' fifteen or twenty miles an hour before you could say squat. We pulled up to the Belle Isle dock where a couple good lookin' girls was sunnin' themselfs. Of course, I introduced myself and was makin' some headway, but Gar couldn't of cared less. He was bent over the damn motor makin' adjustments like the girls didn't even exist. The reason I'm tellin' you this, Monk, is the black-haired girl I was interested in was Esmeralda Sweeney.

"Anyways, to get back to how Gar Wood fits in. He kept makin' improvements and bigger motors. By the time I come back to Chi-Town in '19, Gar had already put a Curtiss '12' airplane motor in a boat he called *Miss Detroit* that could do over 70 miles an hour. By then he was on his way to becomin' a millionaire."

Monk's eyes were starting to glass over. He said, "Izz, I hope this story's got a good ending because I'm gonna either need a couple more drinks or some violin music."

Izz got his back up and growled, "You little prick, if you wasn't my sister's kid I wouldn't even be here drinkin' with you. I'm just now comin' to the good part that could make us both State Street mongrels."

Monk smiled and perked up a little with a fresh drink as Izzy went on. "As I was sayin', I forgot all about Gar for a few years. We both kinda took different paths. One Sunday in '23 or '24 I seen a picture of Gar in the Rotogravure section of the *Trib*. He's racin' in a sleek lookin' boat called a hydroplane on the Detroit River. The paper says the new hydroplane is the fastest thing on water and can easily do 80 or 90 miles an hour. I put the whole thing out of my mind until after our little fallin' out with Nitti and Capone. While we was workin' off our obligation to Al I got this brilliant cogitation of how we might get back in the business of supplyin' Al with booze."

Monk coughed on a piece of ice and asked, "What the hell is a cogitation, Izz? You must be looking at the picture books in the Christian Science reading room again."

Izz ignored the remark, took a gulp of his boilermaker, and said, "Monk, sometimes I think you screwed up your entire education by goin' to school. A cogitation is the same damn thing as a great idea. Anyways, when Al give us the time off, I hopped the *Wolverine* to Detroit City. The next day I called up Gar Wood Industries expectin' to get a cold shoulder, but when the secretary asked who's callin' I said, 'Tell Mr. Gar Wood it's the Belle Isle rowboat gigolo.' Well, in less than three seconds Gar grabs the phone and says, 'Izzy, you damned old fart, how the hell are you? Where are you calling from?'

"We jaw for a time about this and that and Gar says he'll pick me up at the Embassy at 5:30 and we'll go to his house for supper and drinks. I go down to the lobby of the Embassy about an hour early and play three or four hands of stud with old Fred. By the way, Fred still remembers you and sends his regards. He says he's got a sure thing at the Detroit Race Track and there's a new girl in room 321 – next time you're in town. At 5:30 sharp, my eyes just about jump outta my head. A big maroon Hudson pulls up in front of the Embassy and a colored fellow in a uniform hops out and asks if I'm Mr. Izzy. He says his name is Gerald and that Mr. Wood was detained at the factory and will meet us at his home. There's three or four stumblebums tossin' dimes at the sidewalk crack in front of the Embassy and I can't help but give them a little wave as we pull away.

"I wish you could see Gar's place. Two big iron gates was opened up by a guy in a little house next to the driveway. Gerald drives about two or three hundred yards past flowers and trees and stops in front of a two-story stone and white wood house. Before I can even get out, Gar is runnin' out the front door still buttonin' up his shirt. He puts a big bear hug on me and says, 'Izz, you are a sight for sore eyes. Why haven't you contacted me in all these years?' Gerald has already took my cardboard suitcase and disappeared inside so Gar walks me into what he calls the den, and in comes a tall beautiful lady with slightly gray hair. Gar introduces me to his wife and she takes both of my hands and says, 'Isadore Brodsky, welcome to our home. You were once an important part of Gar's life, and I'm delighted that you have returned.'

"Well, Monk, I can tell you I felt a little edgy and out of place at first, but Gar and his wife made me feel like I was really somebody. After what they called a 'cocktail hour' and a wonderful supper, Mrs. Wood said, 'I know you friends have a great deal of catching up to do, so Gar, take Isadore into the den. I'll have Gerald bring brandy to go with your cigars. Isadore, your things are upstairs in the second room on the left. I must excuse myself; I have an important meeting with the Detroit Parks Commission this evening. Please make yourself comfortable and I'll look in on you old friends when I return. If you need anything, just call Gerald. I'm so happy you and Gar are together again.' I never had nobody treat me like that, and you'd have to been there and heard Mrs. Wood's voice to know she really meant everythin' she said."

Inez came back over to their table at the Green Mill carrying a near-full tray, and with a stiff back, but bending at the knees a little, picked up the empty glasses. There wasn't a drinker in the house who didn't appreciate Inez. She said, "Couple more of the same, Monk? If you wasn't so damn busy listenin' to Izzy, you mighta asked me what time I got done tonight."

Monk said, "I know what time you get off, Inez. I'll be waiting for you out back, as usual, and take you to a joint that's got better-tempered bar maids, and don't serve watered-down booze." Monk swatted Inez on her well-formed backside as she playfully pretended to be offended.

"Izz, I sure wish I'd been with you. Gar and his missus sound like great people, but I don't think you went all the way to Detroit City just to gab about the good old days. I got a feeling you and Gar talked some business."

"What the hell you doin,' Monk, readin' my mind?" Izz squeezed his eyes shut as he tossed down a double shot. A cold alky chaser helped put out the fire. Izz went on, "Gerald come in and took two big glasses he called snifters outta the fancy cupboard. He carefully measured about two fingers' worth of brandy in each one. I said, 'Gerald, if you need help fillin' them glasses, I'm your man.' Gerald looked questioningly at Gar and, seeing a nod and an upward hand signal, filled both glasses to the brim. I said, 'Let me first take a gulp of mine, Gerald, and then you can slip in a chunk of that ice.' Gar then said to an amazed Gerald, 'I'll have a little ice in mine, too, if you don't mind.'

"After Gar and me pretty well used up our past memories, I mentioned I was in need of a fast speedboat that could carry a couple thousand pound payload. Gar never even asked me what kind of business I was in. He said, 'Izz, I'm sorry, I haven't anything available at the yard right now. We are in the process of designing a new craft for the upcoming Harmsworth Trophy Race in England next year. I have it on good authority that Kaye Don, my British nemesis, is putting two Rolls Royce engines in a craft that might approach 100 miles per hour.' I finished the last of my brandy and said, 'Gar, it don't seem possible to go that fast on water – or on land, neither. Are you still drivin' your own boats?'

"Gar said, 'Oh yes, Izz, along with my brother George. I wouldn't want this to be general knowledge, but sometime in the near future we plan to install four 1,800-horse, 12-cylinder Packard engines in a hydroplane design that should do over two miles a minute.' It took me a little time to figure that meant 120 miles per hour!

"'Getting back to what you are seeking, Izz, there's a company just south of Mt. Clemens that buys all our outdated craft. They refurbish and sell them to wealthy amateur racers – mostly in Australia and New Zealand. I know they still have my old *Gar Jr.* in dry dock. She's a V-bottomed 50-footer with an 11-foot beam. She could easily do fifty or sixty miles per hour with a 2,500-pound payload, depending on the weight distribution.' Gar was pleased when I said, 'I remember that boat, Gar. You set a couple of records with her, didn't you?' He nodded modestly and said, 'You remember well, Izz.'

"Gar then passed an ivory-inlaid humidor and said, 'Take a handful, Izz. I get a box of fifty Havanas every week from a Cuban friend in Pinar del Rio.' I was about to bite the end off of my cigar when Gar leaned forward and deftly snipped off a perfect circle of tobacco with a silver cutter. He then touched a flame to my cigar using a gold lighter with a detailed, raised miniature of a speedboat crafted on one side. I don't mind admitting I was overcome with emotion when Gar pressed both the cutter and the lighter in my hand and said, 'I'd be honored, Izz, if you would accept these as a token of my admiration for you.' I struggled to find the words to convey my deep-felt sentiment. As we both leaned back in the brown Moroccan leather chairs puffing contentedly, Gar gently broke the silence. 'In 1921, the *Gar Jr.* was the world's fastest express cruiser. I had the honor that year of racing the *Havana Special* train up the Atlantic coast from Miami to New York. People found it hard to believe, but we beat the train by twelve minutes. Just last year we beat the *20th Century Limited* up the Hudson River from New York to Albany by twenty-two minutes. We put the old cruiser out to pasture a few years later, but I'm quite sure Huron Marine in St. Clair Shores would listen to any reasonable offer. If you are interested, I'll call John Rodgers tomorrow and Gerald will drive you out to the marina.' I leaned back, blew a perfect smoke ring, and said, 'Gar, I can't think of nuthin' I'd rather do. This is a perfect endin' to a great day.'"

Over the next two-and-a-half hours, and with appropriate liquid fortification, Izzy told Monk about what had transpired during the rest of his days in Detroit. The next morning, after a hearty breakfast, Gar called John Rodgers at Huron Marine to set up an appointment for 11:30 that morning. He then approached Izzy with a very delicate matter. Izzy's wardrobe left a great deal to be desired so Gar, speaking as a true friend, pointed out the value of first impressions in the business world. Since Izzy and Gerald were very similar in stature, Gar suggested, and Izzy accepted with no offense or embarrassment, the offer of Gerald's best suit, shirt, tie, socks and shoes. Gar also insisted on loaning Izzy his half-carat diamond tie stud, which Izzy said would be returned with Gerald after the Rodgers meetings were finished.

The big Hudson pulled away from the Wood residence with Izzy lounging in the back seat, looking indeed like a prosperous businessman. Izzy joked with his good-natured chauffeur and said, "Gerald, what would really be funny is if you jumped outta this here big car and opened the door for me dressed in *my* old duds!" Gerald chuckled and told Izz he would wait for him and then take him back to his hotel after the meeting.

John Rodgers, sensing something a little odd about Izzy but not daring to do or say anything to alienate Gar Wood, greeted him warmly. He said, "Mr. Brodsky, it's a pleasure to meet you. Mr. Wood mentioned his long friendship with you and indicated your possible interest in his old craft, the *Gar Jr.*"

Izzy said, "That's correct, Mr. Rodgers – if the 'craft' is suitable for my needs and the price is agreeable to my partners."

After a few benign inquiries which Izz skillfully side-stepped, Mr. Rodgers said, "Well, Mr. Brodsky, let's give the old warrior a look and see if she meets your particular requirements." (Izzy wondered how the *Gar Jr.* could be a "she," but followed Rodgers out to the yard.)

The *Gar Jr.* was in dry dock and pretty much stripped of all dignity, but the sleek form remained, and it was impressive. Rodgers said the two V-12 Packard engines were in top shape and could still easily do 70 or 80 miles an hour. Izzy checked the *Gar Jr.* over carefully and said, "The old craft is a beauty, John, but there are a few changes and additions I would need."

John Rodgers, with pencil and pad at the ready, said, "Shoot, Mr. Brodsky; we have experienced boatwrights, carpenters, and electricians on our staff."

"First," Izzy said, "we would need an oval openin' cut into the cowling just forward a' the cab and engine compartment large enough to seat twelve to fifteen people, an easy-to-remove watertight canvas for the openin', and life preservers. Reinforced flooring should be put in the seating compartment as well as the forward hold. The seats must be locked in place, but easily took out. Second and third – a windshield in front of the seating compartment and two strong searchlights on both sides of the engine cab. If your estimate is acceptable to my partners, I'll give you a firm commitment and a cashier's check for half the purchase price in a few days."

Rodgers said, "Mr. Brodsky, it seems you plan to use the *Gar Jr.* as a sightseeing boat. What a wonderful idea." Izzy made no comments that would dissuade Mr. Rodgers of this notion. "The modifications are well within our expertise. Let me meet with our marine designers and craftsmen. I can have a total cost estimate for you by 3 p.m. tomorrow."

"One more thing," Izz said, "I would like the craft completed and delivered to a dock in Lake St. Clair by August 7th. Of course a sizable amount will be advanced before your work begins and a final payment made at the time of title transfer."

John Rodgers thought for a few moments and replied, "That would give us about six weeks. I feel confident we can meet that deadline. Thank you for coming, Mr. Brodsky. Please give my regards to Mr. Wood. We'll look forward to seeing you tomorrow, mid-afternoon."

Gerald drove Izzy back to the Embassy Hotel, retrieved Izz's cardboard suitcase from the trunk of the Hudson and said, "Mr. Izzy, have a pleasant evening. I'll pick you up tomorrow at 2:30 p.m. sharp."

Izzy did, indeed, have a pleasant evening. He'd given some thought to the 9 o'clock review of "Girls, Girls, Girls" at the Avenue, but being dressed in his new clothes, he caught the eye of the new girl in 321 and didn't have to leave the Embassy.

I n the morning Izz went to the Early Bird Cafe and had a leisurely breakfast. Pete Consani was glad to see Izz, and asked him to tell Monk that Betty Lou had regained her health and was engaged to a young mining engineer. She would, thanks to the money he and Monk made available, receive her high school diploma after summer school on the day before her wedding in mid-August. As far as Victor Ciambi was concerned, he was either dead or had left town.

Izz killed a couple hours by picking up a few dollars playing a new game called 9-ball at Sharky's pool hall. He was careful to have only a drink or two so as not to jeopardize his afternoon meeting with John Rodgers.

At 2:30 p.m., the big Hudson pulled up in front of the Embassy. Two winos loitering outside the hotel were greatly impressed with the expensive Havana cigars Izz pressed into their frayed breast pockets. They gave him a sharp military salute as Gerald escorted him into the back seat of the limousine. All this was not lost on the dark-eyed Valencia as she watched from the third-floor east window. The night before she had thought Izzy was feeding her the line she had heard a hundred times before, but now she was looking forward to his return.

At the marina Izzy was immediately ushered into John Rodgers' office by a matronly woman who Izz noticed still had interesting possibilities. Rodgers grasped Izzy's hand warmly and said, "Mr. Brodsky, good to see you again. I hope you had a pleasant evening in our fair city. This Volstead silliness certainly makes it difficult for a man to spread his wings. Would you care to join me in a little adult beverage while we discuss our business?"

Rodgers chuckled when Izz said, "Why yes, John, but only because my doctor insists I bolster my 'condition' with the lawful 'one pint every ten days' rule. And by the way, my friends and my local sheriff call me Izzy."

"All right Izzy, I'm not a lawman but I'm honored to be one of your friends."

After Rodgers poured the drinks Izzy offered him a Havana, casually clipped the ends off the two cigars with a silver cutter, touched a flame to both with a gold lighter and sipped the tumbler of Canadian Club. (John Rodgers was not unaware of the elegant tooling of the miniature *Gar Jr.* on the side of the lighter.) Rodgers' opinion of Isadore Brodsky was being carefully reassessed: the chauffeur-driven Hudson, the silver cigar cutter, the gold embossed lighter, obviously a gift from Gar Wood, and the large diamond tie pin. These were certainly the accouterments of a successful businessman. Not only that, but the nationally acclaimed Gar Wood was his personal friend, but still… oh, what the hell. A cashier's check would be as good as gold and it wasn't in his best interest to question Mr. Wood. John Rodgers dismissed his doubts and got down to business. "I have some figures I think you are going to like, Izzy. My people assure me that all your modifications are doable and the August 7th date can be easily met. Most important though, the entire package, delivered at dockside, comes in at the attractive total of $28,750."

Izzy was floored by this high price, but he kept his poker face. He knew Capone could come up with the dough. With perfect control, he said, "John, I appreciate the attention you have given my project on such short notice. I'll meet with my investors in Chicago and give you our final answer within the week. Let me say that I'm impressed and feel sure my people will be as pleased as I is." What Izzy didn't know at the time and would never know was that Mr. Wood had informed John Rodgers that the final price for the *Gar Jr.* was to be under $30,000, and that this was a mere fraction of its true worth.

Luxuriating for the last time in the back seat of the limousine, Izzy reluctantly removed Gar Wood's diamond tie stud and asked Gerald to return it to Mr. Wood with his thanks. In front of the Embassy, with the motor running and three or four winos staring at them blankly, Izzy retrieved his cardboard suitcase from the trunk and said it would only take him a jiffy to change and return Gerald's duds.

Gerald said warmly, "Mister Izzy, I'd be honored if you kept my clothes. Besides, they look better on you than they do on me." A warm smile and a firm handshake expressed Izzy's feelings for his new friend.

Before leaving Detroit City, Izz hopped the Gratiot interurban trolley and rode twenty-five miles north to the small town of Mt. Clemens. A five-mile cab ride brought him to Anchor Bay where he found several isolated lakeside homes. One in particular caught his eye. Its boathouse, surrounded by overhanging trees, fronted on a short canal that fed directly into Lake St. Clair. The owner was pleased with Izzy's offer of $150 per week to rent space to warehouse his product – no questions asked. With a handshake and a $50 deposit the deal was closed. Rental was to begin on September 1st with $100 being prepaid before occupation of the property. Izzy had accomplished everything he had set out to do and looked forward to bringing Monk up to speed on his plans.

By the time Izzy finished his story at 6:30 p.m., the afternoon drinkers in the Green Mlll had made their way precariously home. Saucy, irreverent Inez brought Monk and Izzy steak and eggs, hard rolls and garden salads. She threatened to stand over them until their plates were clean. With mind and body reinvigorated, Monk offered Izzy a Camel. Izz leaned over, flipped open his gold lighter and touched a flame to both cigarettes.

Monk said, "I'm glad you went to Detroit and saw your old friend, but I know you didn't buy a boat and rent a warehouse without some kinda plan in mind. And you are talkin' a lot of money for that boat."

"That's just it, Monk. Gar has paved the way for us to buy his old speedboat from the Huron Marine Company includin' all the modifications I asked for. Once I got back to Chi-Town I did a little research. The boat has to be worth at least fifty grand and we can get her for $28,750!"

Monk was still doubtful. He said, "the price might just as well be $28 million, 750 thousand dollars, and what in hell are we gonna do with a damn speedboat? I have about $115 dollars left of that $300 Capone gave us, and knowing your ways, I bet you don't even have half of that much left."

Izz patted Monk on the arm and said, "You're right about my cash on hand. I got about eighteen dollars left, but you gotta learn to believe and trust your old unk. I've figured out a plan that'll put us on easy street. I guarantee by All Saint's Day you'll be drivin' that Stutz Bearcat you been dreamin' about."

Monk rolled his eyes and Izzy continued. "We'll be meetin' Frankie Nitti at Colosimo's tomorrow night, but just so's you feel a little better, here's a general idea of my plan. Oh, by the way, go down to Max Fishburne's on Kostner Ave. tomorrow and buy some new duds. You got to look almost as good as me when we meet Frankie."

Inez brought two more doubles and alky chasers. Monk told her something had come up and he probably couldn't meet her after work. Inez had a naughty look in her eye and said, "Damn, Monk, I was hopin' somethin' would come up tonight. Oh well, as they say, good things come to those who wait."

Izz said, "Inez, you're a bad little girl through and through. I bet you drove them Roosevelt High School boys out of their minds. Now skedaddle. Me and Monk has some business to talk over. Monk might be a little late, but I'll see he picks you up by two o'clock or so."

Izz turned to Monk and said, "You're right about our finances. Together we're probably runnin' on close ta empty, but it won't be for long. Let me lay some figures on you. To begin with, we're gonna be legit sight-seein' boat owners. That's why I told John Rodgers to cut in twelve or fifteen seats up front in the *Gar Jr.* Everybody in Detroit City and Windsor knows about Gar Wood and his speedboats. If we set up business in Windsor and put ads in the *Detroit Times* and the *Windsor Star* we'd get more customers than we could handle. We could start a daily schedule pickin' up customers in Windsor and then zippin' across the whiskey river pickin' up Detroit people. We could make three or four runs a day, and maybe a moonlight cruise on Friday night."

Monk looked at Izz in total shock and said, "Izz, what the hell have you been smoking? How are we going to pay $28,750 dollars for a boat by running gawkers up and down the river?"

"Now hold on a damn minute, Monk, you ain't give me a chance to enlarge on my plan." Izz called to Inez to bring a pad and pencil. She took her own sweet time and said, "Izz, if you're gonna write me some sweet love poems, I ain't interested."

Izz ignored her and started writing down some numbers. "First off, we ain't just gonna be carryin' sightseers. The whole reason for runnin' up and down the river is to throw the bluecoats and revenuers off base. When we start haulin' Johnnie Walker again for Big Al, the law won't even give us a notice. The tourist trade is just gravy – just sumpthin' to do durin' the daytime."

Monk looked a little sheepish and said, "I'm sorry Izz, I should have known you had a master plan. What kind of numbers are you coming up with?"

Izz was deep in thought and seemed to be talking to himself as he wrote some figures on the notepad. "I figure we could carry twelve passengers, easy, at $5 a head. Three trips a day would be $180 times five days a week equals $900. Add in the Friday night moonlight cruise at $8 a head for twelve passengers and that's another $96 a week. The moonlight cruise is mostly for gettin' the law used to us runnin' at night. We'd have at least eight weeks of good weather from the time we pick up the boat. That comes to 7,968 bucks. Now comes the good part. The *Gar Jr.*, with the seats removed, can carry thirty-five cases of Johnnie Walker in one run. That's four-hunnert-twenty fifths at a profit to us of $6 a fifth, or $2,520 a run. We could make three runs a week, easy, so in maybe ten weeks of good weather that would come to $75,600 plus the $7,968 from the cruise runs, or a grand total of $83,568, with three weeks to go before Christmas. How do you like them apples!"

Monk sat in a daze. He finally caught Inez's eye and held up two fingers. When she delivered the drinks he put his arm around her waist and said, "Baby, you better start treating Uncle Izz and me with a little more respect. By the time the snow falls we'll be able to buy this joint ten times over and set you up in a dive of your own."

Inez laughingly twirled away and said sarcastically over her shoulder, "Oh sure, big spender, by the time the first snow falls you're both just gonna need a bigger pot to piss in."

Izzy groused, "I don't know what the hell you see in that damn broad, Monk."

Monk replied, "She's all right, all show when she's working – a real Diamond Lille – but underneath, a pretty good kid."

"I'll just have to take your word for it," Izz said, reaching for a cigarette.

After Deke the bartender settled a baseball argument at a corner table with his fists, Monk asked, "So I guess that warehouse you rented is where you plan for us to stash the booze?"

"That's right, Monk. I got the key to the boathouse on Lake St. Clair right here in my pocket. It's only three or four miles north of Mt. Clemens, so it's not too far from the Detroit River but well secluded. The owner won't be no problem cuz I slipped him a $50 'retainer bonus' and give him a gentleman's handshake. The guy was as happy as a cat playin' with a live mouse and didn't even ask what I was plannin' to stash."

CHAPTER FIFTEEN

I zzy put in a call to Frank Nitti at the Metropole and said he had a "can't miss" proposition regarding several hundred cases of Johnnie Walker Black. Nitti, never one to turn down a sweet deal, said he'd give a listen and to meet him at Colosimo's Tuesday night.

Colosimo's wasn't quite the grand place it was before Big Jim got whacked and spilled his blood on the porcelain tiles of the vestibule floor. Mike "the Greek" Potzin took over after Dale Winter gave up and went back to New York. It still drew crooked politicians, top entertainers, cops on the take, businessmen, gangsters and wanna-be's. Al Capone and Frank Nitti said having a drink in Colosimo's was safer than sitting in the Cook County Jail. The chorus girls still showed just as much flesh, but the free lunch wasn't quite as good and during the harsh daylight hours the club had begun to look a little frayed around the edges. Izz and Monk had time for a drink before Frank Nitti arrived. Izz wished he still got the first drink free, but what the hell, times change.

Nitti came in about 9:30 flanked by his goon, Rocco "the Shark" Fischetti. Frankie told Rocco to sit at the bar with his eyes open and motioned Izz and Monk over to his table. The barmaid, an ex-high school English teacher, sweetly asked, "What do you gentlemen desire?" Frankie laughed and said, "These 'gentlemen' will have double shots of Old Log Cabin with alky chasers. And don't ever get caught in a narrow passageway with these 'gentlemen.'" The teacher laughed nervously as she wiped the table with her bar rag and hurriedly left.

"Now," Frankie said, "what kind of a nut case do you boys have in mind?" Izzy laid out the plan in detail. He told Frankie about the *Gar Jr.* being four times as fast as anything J. Edgar Hoover or the Coast Guard had. Nitti began to lean forward when Izz talked about the sightseeing ruse to hoodwink the Detroit police and revenuers into thinking they were a legit business. Izz assured Frankie they could run up and down the Canadian side of the river without suspicion. Nitti really got interested when Izz told him he could deliver 105 cases of Johnnie Walker a week, at $144 gross a case, until maybe the second week of December. Izz didn't think it wise to add "or until the river freezes over." Frankie particularly liked the idea of the secluded boathouse on Lake St. Clair twenty-five miles away from the prying eyes of the feds and saw no problem sending a truck each week for the pickup.

Frankie sat back, swirled the amber liquid in his glass and said, "I always liked you boys an' I'm not blamin' ya for embarrassin' Al last winter with your harebrained scheme. It actually could a' worked, but Al don't forget easy an' I heard him say more'n once that if there was any possible way to screw things up, you two dummies would find it."

With an uneasy laugh, Izz said, "Frankie, after last time, do you think we'd take on anything that'd give Al a reason to whack us? This is a iron-clad deal. There ain't nuthin' that could go wrong. I'll tell you what. Monk an' me will give up our profit on the first thirty-five cases just to prove we can pull it off." Monk gulped hard but didn't say anything.

That sweetened the deal enough for Nitti. "All right Izz, I'll go ta bat for you guys one more time. How much do you need?"

Izz replied with a straight face, "We gotta have $28,750 for the fastest boat you ever seen, $7,560 for 105 cases of Johnnie Walker up front, plus maybe a grand for start-up expenses. But remember, we'd be givin' up our $2,520 profit on the first thirty-five cases and we'll sign the bill of sale on the *Gar Jr.* over to you to hold for Al. Even if sumpthin' went wrong, which it sure as hell won't, Al will own the most famous boat in America worth over fifty grand. Frankie, I ain't pushin' but I gotta know in two days or I'll be closed down."

"If I'm hearin' ya right Izz, you'll be able to pay Al back in five or six weeks. Is that what yer sayin'?"

"That's right, Frankie. Al will be paid back in full and make almost forty grand on the booze, to boot."

Frankie stirred his drink with his index finger, took a gulp and growled, "Izz, don't you never say or even guess what Al might or might not do. That's his business, and don't ya never forget it. I'll talk to him an' see you guys here in a coupla days."

Frankie motioned to Rocco and left Colosimo's in his new '26 Buick touring car. Izz finished off Frankie's drink, leaned back with fingers clasped behind his head and said, "Monk, baby, I think we got ourselfs a deal!"

Two nights later Colosimo's was bulging at the seams. The New York Yankees were playing a three-game series with the White Sox at Comiskey Park, always a big draw for the local club. Babe Ruth had hit two homers in the second game and fans were beginning to think he might top his record fifty-nine round-trippers set in 1921. Big Bill Thompson planned to run for mayor again so was hanging on the Babe's coattails. He had staged an "all you can eat" steak dinner and Ruth was on his third porterhouse. Monk and Izz held on to a standing-room only spot at the bar until Frank Nitti came in with his bodyguard. Fischetti's eyes were nervously searching the crowd when Nitti waved the boys over to his table. Frankie ordered his usual and a couple of fresh ones for Monk and Izzy. He pointed to Ruth and said, "That damn showboater. He'll probably eat five of them steaks, drink a gallon of booze and then hit two more homers tomorrow."

After his temper had cooled, Frankie loosened up. He said, "Boys, don't look so damn glum. I got good news for you. Al is impressed with your plan an' is willin' to back you for five or six weeks. If you deliver the goods an' pay off your debt, he'll take all the Johnnie Walker you can get. Oh, one more thing. Al sez if you screw up this time you might as well get a' audience with Father Antonio for your last rites."

After the chorus girls sang and wiggled through *Ma, He's Making Eyes at Me* and *I Wish I Could Shimmy Like My Sister Kate*, Frankie passed a fat envelope to Izzy under the table.

The next morning Izz deposited $28,750 in the Continental Illinois National Bank on LaSalle Street. He directed the manager to cable $14,375 to the Guardian Bank in Detroit, to be deposited in the account of the Huron Marine Company. Izzy held out $1,000 expense money and $7,560 for 105 cases of Johnnie Walker. He then called John Rodgers, informed him that half the total price of the *Gar Jr.* had been forwarded to his account and asked if one of his mechanics could give him and Monk a crash course on the operation and maintenance of the *Gar Jr.*

by August 7. John Rodgers said he could do better than that. The *Gar Jr.* would be modified to Izzy's specifications and ready for pick up with title change on August 5th or 6th. Bill Pequoit would be assigned a full day to school them on every aspect of the boat any day they chose.

Monk called Gussie and filled him in on the master plan. Gussie was satisfied with 10% of the operation, but said there could be a problem with Reggie McKenzie. Reggie and his men were still hopping mad about getting stiffed on the last job. Monk said, "Gussie, we won't need Reggie's guys on this job. It's only a matter of getting the Johnnie Walker to the boat and loaded. You and Reggie could do it easy. Offer Reggie half percent of the net profit per load. That would come to about $125 a run. Three runs a week would make the son-of-a-bitch king of the hill in Windsor. He'll get his money after we get paid. See if Reggie's guys will be happy with $80 bucks each on what we promised them from the last job. We'll pay them the rest when our charter business gets going."

"O.K., Monk, I think Reggie an' his guys will go for that deal. Call me as soon as you and Izzy get to Detroit City."

A few weeks later, Monk and Izz, with their new wardrobes and a wad of folding money, got seats in the parlor car of the *Wolverine*. The porter, for a price, was happy to furnish them with a fifth of Old Grandad, ice, and several bottles of Vernor's ginger ale. They played stud poker with a brand new deck and used fifty-cent pieces as chips. They ate chicken sandwiches from the galley and Izz tipped the porter four bits for getting a *Detroit Times* when the train stopped in Battle Creek. When they reached the Michigan Central Depot in Detroit at 4:45 p.m. they called Vito D'Amato. Vito said, "Glad to see you boys back. Where to, the Embassy?"

Izz said, "Hell no, Vito, the Book Cadillac on Washington Street – and don't spare the horses." Izz tipped Vito a buck and told him they'd be needing him for the next few days. As they lounged on their backs on clean, soft beds, Izz said, "Monk, this is just the beginnin.' In a couple weeks we is gonna have the world by the ass!"

The following morning, while Monk slept in, Izzy caught a cab to Huron Marine in St. Clair Shores. Margo French, John Rodger's secretary, seemed unusually warm and friendly and insisted he join her for coffee and a danish while her boss consulted with a client. Izzy remembered his initial perception of Miss French in June, and didn't have reason to change his mind. He delighted in watching Margo work, especially when she returned documents to the top drawer of the office file. Izzy was brought back to reality by the pleasant voice of John Rodgers.

"Good morning, Izz. Good to see you. I hope you haven't had a long wait. Come into my office, I have your bill of sale and title transfer ready. All we need is your final payment for $14,375 and a couple signatures. I've talked to Bill Pequoit and he's looking forward to meeting you and your nephew on August 7th at the marina. He's an excellent man and will acquaint you with the operation of the *Gar Jr.*"

His immediate business completed, Izzy returned to the Book Cadillac and awaited the results of Monk and Gussie's negotiations with Reggie McKenzie later that afternoon. Monk reported that Vito D'Amato had driven the boys to 2nd Ave. and West Jefferson in plenty of time to board the *Golden Star* ferry to Windsor. He was instructed to pick them up at midnight after the last ferry arrived in Detroit.

After a couple drinks in the King's Arms bar, Reggie said he and his boys hadn't really thought they'd been left out to dry, and that he would look forward to working with them again. He readily agreed to their terms of paying for each of the 35 cases of Johnnie Walker as they were delivered to the river garage. He was more than pleased with the offer of a half percent of the net profit on all future runs. As a gesture of friendship, Reggie insisted Monk and Gussie join him as his guests at the Fox and Hounds at 7 p.m. and later share his box at the 9 o'clock girlie show at Buckingham Palace.

The boys spent the remainder of the afternoon at city hall and the Maritime Commission mired in Canadian bureaucracy, but were successful in starting the ball rolling on the issuance of a dock permit and a license to carry passengers in Canadian waters. The authorities assured them the papers would be available within ten days.

Monk and Gussie arrived early at the Fox and Hounds and were thankful they had fortified themselves with several drinks before joining Reggie in his favorite meal of haggis followed by clotted cream over lemon curd. Monk wasn't sure he would enjoy himself at the Buckingham Palace burlesque when he learned his supper of heart, lungs and liver had been boiled in the stomach of a sheep, but the charms of several young French-Canadian strippers not only purged his mind of the god-awful supper, but made the evening pleasurable and, as he would say later with a wink, rather uplifting. Vito D'Amato met the midnight ferry in his cab and a half hour later Monk walked into the luxurious lobby of the Book Cadillac.

Izzy mixed two nightcaps while listening intently to Monk's favorable report of his day in Windsor. He laughed at Monk's description of the haggis supper and said, "I heard somewhere you are what you eat – that's why I stick to good old American food." He then became serious and said, "I hate to mention this, but we is livin' pretty close to the edge again. We gotta give Reggie's guys $480 on what we owe them and we're at least a week or two from any profit from our sightseein' business. If you're agreeable, I think we'd better hole up again in that stinkin' Embassy Hotel. Monk reluctantly agreed, and the next day an astonished Vito transferred their belongings to the Embassy.

Augus 7th was a beautiful summer day. The smooth emerald green water of Lake St. Clair shimmered in the warm sunlight. Bill Piquoit met Izz and Monk at the Huron Marine dock at 9:30 where the sleek *Gar Jr.* was bobbing quietly in the cool water. Bill was a muscular man about 5'10", in his mid-forties, with graying hair and a quick smile. He had been a master mechanic for Huron Marine and a part-time speedboat racer for Gar and George Wood for over a dozen years. Bill took his time discussing the operation of the craft as well as some important do's and don'ts. He stressed the danger of over-steering at high speeds and the need to keep the rpm ratio in the green zone. Bill soon realized from Izzy's questions and comments that he was well versed in the mechanics of precision engines.

He said, "O.K. boys, let's take her out for a spin." The *Gar Jr.*'s powerful Packard engines idled at the dock with a deep throaty pulsation, then burst into an ear-shattering roar as Bill brought the joy stick quickly back. Within seconds the *Gar Jr.* was exceeding 40, 50, and then 60 miles an hour. Monk and Izz gasped for breath and hung on to the gunnels for dear life. Twenty minutes later Bill eased off of the stick and expertly approached the dock. The graceful bow slowly returned to horizontal and the craft gently settled in the bubbles of its own wake.

After lunch, Monk and Izz took turns putting the *Gar Jr.* through its paces. By 4 o'clock Bill said, "You gents look like you've been doing this for years. Brush up on the maritime rules and regulations and you'll pass any tests the Canadians can throw at you." The boys thanked Bill for his detailed instruction and patience and made arrangements for John Rodgers to deliver the *Gar Jr.* to their Windsor dock facility as soon as dockage became available.

The next few days were spent boning up on maritime regulations. Izz studied manuals on large engine maintenance while Monk concentrated on the rules governing small craft operation, safety, and commercial passenger service. With Reggie's men satisfied with their settlement, the major worry was the possibility of any wiseguys from last winter's job holding a grudge. Angie Zambelli got whacked by the Kraut, the Kraut blew town, and Victor Ciambi was either dead meat or so crippled up he couldn't cause trouble. That left Pero Gaglanti and Pauli Osanti – two guys who had moonlighted some for the Purple Gang – and of course Gino Evola. Since Johnny Milberg, Anson Neuman, and Bennie Fleisher were regulars of the Bernstein brothers' Purple Gang, they wouldn't be a threat.

Monk called Roy Bernstein and told him he had a special problem. Roy said to come out the next day and he'd give it a listen. Vito D'Amato drove Monk to the Sugar Gang's digs in Hamtramck on Wednesday and was greeted warmly by Roy and Isadore Bernstein. They both asked about Big Al and what he and Izz were up to. When Monk gave them the story, they said not to worry. Roy said his boys told him what had happened on the river and why he and Izz had to blow town so fast. Isadore said Milberg, Neuman and Fleisher were on the Purple Gang payroll at the time so didn't suffer any lost wages. Roy said as far as the bums who got stiffed was concerned, he'd put the word out on the street that Monk and Izzy's latest gig was being backed by the Purple Gang. As Monk prepared to leave, Roy yelled to Jacob Levy in the warehouse to put a case of Old Log Cabin in Monk's cab. He winked and said this latest batch was better than the last and was at least two weeks old. Both brothers said to give Izzy, Frank Nitti and Mr. Capone their regards. If he and Izz needed anything, the gang was ready and willing to help.

Monk and Izzy knew they had to keep expenses down until the charter business became profitable. They spent most days at the Huron Marine dock tinkering with the Packard motors and taking the *Gar Jr.* on test runs. One day they cruised up to the Mt. Clemens boathouse and practiced backing into the narrow canal. At night they played stud poker with matches, or took in a show at the Avenue burlesque. Scurvy Miller always introduced them as his buddies from the Windy City, and Valencia, the Embassy girl in room 321, did her part to entertain at modest prices.

At the end of the week they heard from Windsor confirming their dock permit and charter license. Monk guessed correctly that a call from a Bernstein brother had probably greased the process. Their ads in the

Detroit Times and the *Windsor Star* brought hundreds of people to the Windsor dock. Most just wanted to see the *Gar Jr.*, but ticket sales for the cruises were sold out for weeks. They quickly decided to add a fourth run each day and two more on Saturday. Gussie and Reggie volunteered to take over the extra runs. The additional money would help pay off their huge debt to Capone much sooner.

G ussie surprised Izz late one afternoon when he drove up to the Windsor dock in the '21 Hupmobile. Gussie said since he was spending so much time in Windsor, he'd had a friend who owned a coal barge bring the Hupp over one dark night. Reggie had agreed to have the car registered in his name while Gussie was in Canada. A "specialist" forged a Canadian title in Reggie's name for the reasonable sum of $50. Reggie lifted license plates off a car in a junkyard on Route 3 a few miles east of Essex.

During the following days Izz and Monk had as much fun as their passengers. The *Gar Jr.* didn't exceed 15 miles an hour on the Detroit River, but when Belle Isle was cleared, gasps were heard as the craft accelerated to 60 miles an hour in Lake St. Clair. By the third week in August, the daily runs were commonplace and the crews of Detroit police boats and revenue cutters smiled and waved at the laughing sightseers. Izz and Monk made it a habit to cross into U. S. waters on the return trip and slowly pass the Mt. Clemens boathouse. After the excursion money started rolling in, the boys moved to the swanky Detroit Leland Hotel. One night in their three-room suite Monk said, "Izz, I've been thinking. Things are going so great, what would you say we stay in the legit cruise business and ask Al for a loan extension?"

Izz sputtered and said, "Kid, you gotta be out of your damn mind if you think Capone would let us off the hook. The only reason he give us the cash was so we could supply him with booze. What do you think Al would do if I said, 'Mr. Capone, Monk and me has decided to go straight. If it's all right with you, we'd like to skip the booze haulin' and pay off our loan in installments over five years.' I'll tell you what he'd do, he'd send Jack McGurn or maybe Rocco Fischetti over and we'd be feedin' the fishes in the Detroit River by this time next week. I got to admit, it feels good to be a respectable citizen, but we got no choice, we're in this until the season ends."

"I know you're right, Izz. It's just that it would be nice to have a regular job like most people and not have to think of doin' time in the

Big House. Want to play a few hands of stud before we go down to eat?"

Izzy eagerly broke the seal on a new deck of bicycles and cut an ace. After four or five hands, he leaned back and said, "I've been meaning to ask you, Monk. Have you ever heard anythin' about how Betty Lou is doin'?"

"Yes, I talked to Pete Consani a week or so back. He got a letter from her and she said things weren't going as well as she had hoped. The fella she married got a promotion and it must have gone to his head. He's been drinking pretty heavy and Betty Lou found out he's overly friendly with a young secretary in the Cleveland-Cliffs office. Pete said he knew how much Betty Lou meant to me and was sure we would keep whatever he said to ourselves."

Izzy stroked his chin, gazed off into space for a few moments and said, "There ain't no way we could ever pay Betty Lou back for what she done for us last winter, but I got a thought. Now that the charter runs are beginning to pay off, supposin' we skim five or six hundred bucks and send it to Pete. Betty Lou don't need to know where it come from. I know we got to put aside as much as we can to pay back Big Al, but what the hell, what he don't know won't hurt him, and besides, if things get tight we can always go back ta livin' at the Embassy for a while. Maybe a few bucks would give Betty Lou a little independence."

Monk said he told Izz he was one hell of a guy – no matter what his Ma said.

The Leland was headquarters for the visiting American League baseball teams, so Monk and Izz got to know many of the players. Some late evenings they even got to jaw in the lobby with guys like Goose Goslin and "The Big Train" Walter Johnson of the Washington Senators. Johnson's career was almost over, but he loved to tell stories about his duels with Ty Cobb. He said Cobb was raggin' him pretty bad one day so he pitched him high and tight and caught him on the left ear with a fast ball. The next time Cobb came up he hit the first pitch over the right field fence. As Cobb rounded second base he yelled, "Walter, I can't hear outta my left ear, but I can still see pretty good!"

One night, when Connie Mack, the owner and manager of the Philadelphia Athletics, was sitting alone they introduced themselves, and Mr. Mack invited them to join him. Monk later said it was an education just to listen to the great manager talk about his early days in baseball.

Izz, balancing three mugs of coffee, pulled up a chair and said, "Mr. Mack, I read somewhere, I think maybe in the *Sporting News*, that your birth name was McGillicuddy. Is that a fact?" Mr. Mack smiled and said, "That's not even the half of it, Mr. Brodsky. My birth certificate lists me as Cornelius Alexander McGillicuddy. I began my Big League career as a catcher before you gents were born. At that time the catcher positioned himself several feet back of the batter and caught the ball on the first bounce. I knew I wouldn't get any positive recognition by the sports writers with a moniker like mine, so had it legally changed in 1900. Then at least it could fit into the box scores."

Mr. Mack drained his cup and said, "That was excellent coffee, Mr. Brodsky. Yours seemed to be a lot lighter in color. Was it a different brand?" Izz winked slyly at Monk and said, "No, Mr. Mack, I guess I must've just added more cream to mine." Mr. Mack declined a second cup but seemed to be in a reflective mood. "Here's a little story you boys might find interesting. Back in 1909 in the second game of the Tigers-Pittsburgh World Series, the great Pirates shortstop Honus Wagner was a few paces off the keystone bag. The hated Ty Cobb had singled to right and had taken a huge lead off first. Honus was a bowlegged, barrel-chested giant of a man who would fight you tooth and nail in a game, but was very mild-mannered off the field. Cobb, with his spikes sharpened and glistening, yelled, 'You damn Krauthead, I'm comin' down on the next pitch.' The hurler threw a perfect pitch-out and the catcher hung a rope to Wagner. Honus met Cobb three feet from the bag, side stepped his vicious slide and jammed the ball into his mouth. The great 'Georgia Peach' required several stitches and showed great respect for the 'Krauthead' from then on."

Monk laughed and said, "That's a great story, Mr. Mack, with a perfect outcome. I was wondering, who do you think is the greatest modern day player?" Mr. Mack looked at Izz and said, "Mr. Brodsky, I think I will have that second cup of coffee, but make mine the same as yours." Izz was off to the coffee bar, but knowing Mr. Mack was a teetotaler, turned and gave Monk a palms-up gesture and a guestioning look. Mr. Mack took a sip, waited a moment and said, "Mr. Brodsky, this is an exceptionally good cup of coffee – it has a nice little bite to it." The boys breathed a sigh of relief as Mr. Mack went on.

"There's no doubt in my mind, and I've seen them all – Mathewson, Johnson, Wagner, Cobb, Sisler, Hornsby and Speaker. The greatest player in the game today, and very probably in the future of baseball, is Mr.

Ruth, and he hasn't yet reached his full potential. You probably know he was a great young pitcher with Boston and a twenty-plus game winner several times. He turned the baseball world on its ear hitting twenty-nine round-trippers in 1919. During the 1920 season, playing full time in the outfield for the New York Yankees, he hit an astounding fifty-four homeruns. Mr. Ruth has a strong arm, never throws to the wrong base, is a great base runner, is always near the top in runs batted in, and can hit a baseball farther than any other human being. I also credit Mr. Ruth with restoring baseball's reputation after the 1919 Black Sox Scandal. In other words, Mr. Ruth is a manager's dream player."

"Mr. Mack," Monk asked, "with the Babe's on-base stats and a home run every five or six at bats, how do you pitch to him?"

"An excellent question, Monk." Then with a twinkle in his eye, Mr. Mack said, "I have my third-base coach follow Mr. Ruth from early morning until the first pitch. If he eats a half-dozen hot dogs, drinks seven or eight bottles of Nehi orange pop, and smokes four or five cigars after breakfast, we throw him a fast ball low and outside. Then we all watch the ball sail high into the right field stands."

"Wow," Monk said, "how do you pitch him if he behaves himself and comes to the game hungry?"

"That's an easy decision, Monk. If Mr. Ruth only has his pre-game snack of a quart of chocolate ice cream and a plate of eels, we pitch him a fast one low and inside – and watch the ball sail into the left field stands. Well boys, I thank you for your companionship and listening to an old man's musings. I'd like to catch a little nap before our team train leaves for St. Louis at midnight. We play the Browns three games and then move on to Chicago for a four-game series. We'll be back in Detroit the following week on our swing east. I'll leave box seat passes for you at the ticket office."

Early the next morning (about 4 a.m.) a soft knock on the door grew louder. When Izz opened the door, who should be hanging on the knob but the great Babe Ruth himself, snockered to the gills. Monk and Izz helped carry him, with his massive arms draped over their shoulders, into the bedroom. While sitting on the edge of the bed he put his finger to his lips and said not to tell that little shit Miller Huggins what time he came in. Monk and Izz took off his sport coat, pants and shoes, and poured him into Monk's bed. Within seconds the room reverberated with loud, even snores. Monk grabbed a blanket and spent the remainder of the night in a large comfortable Morris chair with an adjustable back. By 9 a.m., a bushy-tailed Babe Ruth was splashing in the shower and yelling for a couple of bath towels. For weeks afterward Izz would tell anyone who'd listen about having breakfast with the great Babe Ruth. Izz ordered one egg, toast and coffee. The Babe started with a pint of bourbon and ginger ale, followed by a porterhouse steak that hung over the edges of the plate, four fried eggs, fried potatoes, and a pot of black coffee. That afternoon he hit two singles, a double, and a mammoth shot over the right field bleachers. The Yankees beat the Tigers 7-2.

CHAPTER SIXTEEN

As October neared, Frank Nitti called every day and said Capone was getting restless and wanted some action, so Monk contacted Gussie at the Milner Hotel. Gussie said, "Damn, Monk, I'd jus' about give up on you guys. Sure, I can have a load ready by Saturday night. Reggie's droolin' over his half percent."

The time to meet and load the Gar was set. Monk and Izz would cruise down the river at midnight and dock at Amhurstburg, the little Canadian city on Lake Erie at the mouth of the Detroit River. The sight and sound of the *Gar Jr.* would hardly be noticed.

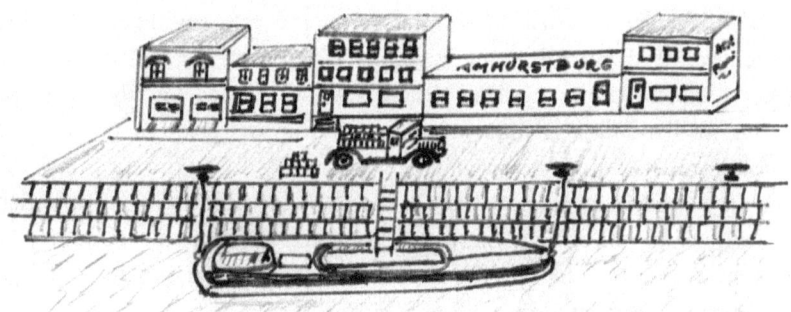

Monk and Izz would cruise down the river at midnight and dock at Amhurstburg, the little Canadian city on Lake Erie at the mouth of the Detroit River.

As the boat pulled away from the Windsor dock, Izz said, "Keep her at about fifteen miles an hour, Monk, just like we done on our moonlight cruises." By 1 a.m., the *Gar Jr.* was docked and Monk and Izzy had begun removing the passenger seats. Within thirty minutes the lights of Reggie's lorry picked up the *Gar Jr.* Monk, Izzy, Gussie and Reggie stowed thirty-five cases of Johnnie Walker Black in the forward compartment and installed the waterproof canvas tarp over the opening. The fifteen passenger seats were then loaded in the lorry. Izzy told the boys not to wait up for their return. He and Monk would dock in Windsor, catch a few snoozes at the Prince Edward and contact them around noon. There would be plenty of time to replace the seats in the *Gar Jr.*

The trip up the river was uneventful. Monk kept watch while Izz maintained a speed of ten to fifteen miles per hour.

As they entered Lake St. Clair, Izzy directed their course to the safe area of Canadian jurisdiction. The increased speed of thirty miles per hour carried the Gar due north and in exactly forty-five minutes the beacon of Mitchell Bay, Canada, came into view. Izz continued north for five more minutes, then steered the craft north by northwest directly toward the American shore and the boathouse. Within minutes the left side-by-side Packard engine began to accelerate wildly. Izzy quickly switched off the ignition, and the right engine, now bearing the entire load, became over-burdened. The rpm gauge dropped from 2500 to 1000.

Monk swung his observation seat around and shouted over the laboring engine, "What the hell happened, Izz?"

Izzy yelled at the top of his voice, "As near as I can figger, Monk, the god-damned left universal joint give out. We got only one propeller turnin'. We can make it, though, if the load don't bust the right universal."

Minutes later, with a sickening shudder, the right engine began racing violently out of control. Izzy once again switched off the ignition and the *Gar Jr.*, now without power to either propeller, drifted silently to a stop.

A brilliant flash of lightning and the almost simultaneous clap of thunder put Monk in near panic. It was about 2:30 in the morning, the Gar Jr. was loaded with 420 fifths of illegal booze, and they were stranded at least eight miles from the boathouse. Add to that, the temperature was dropping, they had no food, and come daylight, the drifting *Gar Jr.* could easily be spotted by a revenue cutter.

Pelting rain, driven eastward by mounting wind, became rivulets on the polished mahogany cowling, forcing Monk and Izzy into the cramped quarters of the engine compartment. Izzy wrapped a dirty engine cover around their shivering bodies, pulled a slightly curved pint of whiskey from his hip pocket and advised Monk to take three deep breaths and two long snorts of Old Log Cabin. Izz wiped the bottle top with his dirty shirt sleeve and said, "Monk, I can unnerstan' how scared you is, but I've been in a lot worse fixes and I guarantee we're gonna get out a' this one alive. I already got two or three plans perkin' in my head and I'll run 'em past you when this damn storm lets up."

Izzy's quiet reassurance and the warm Old Log Cabin helped put Monk somewhat at ease. By 4:30 a.m. the storm had passed and to keep Monk's mind occupied, Izz instructed him to steer with the current and watch for floating logs. They both agreed that catching the attention of a fishing boat at daybreak was unlikely. The night's storm would have riled the water and kept sensible fishermen close to the shoreline.

Izzy said his second plan would probably work, but could have serious side effects. They could deep-six the Johnnie Walker and not have to worry about being searched by a revenue agent. Izz had told Frank Nitti they would deliver the first run free, so their profit wasn't an issue. Al Capone controlled the "serious side effects." If they dumped the booze, Big Al would lose his initial investment of $2,520 and about $10,000 profit on his watered-down drinks. Izz said Al would probably send Machine Gun Jack McGurn or Pauli Del Bono and they'd both be dead meat in a week. Monk said he thought he'd like to hear plan number three.

Izz said his final idea was maybe a ten-to-one shot, but the worst that could happen was two or three years in a federal prison. He knew the Coast Guard was headquartered in Detroit and patrolled the water from Lake Huron to Lake Erie. They were supposed to help any boat on the water that got into trouble. Their chances with the Coast Guard would be a lot better than with the eager revenue guys.

Izz decided Monk should take the first watch and awaken him immediately if he saw an oncoming ship. If it was a dark revenue cutter, they'd just have to sit tight and take their chances. Big Al might let them work off their debt like last time, when they got out of the slammer. If the ship was a big white one, it'd be the Coast Guard and he wanted a chance to talk with the Captain. Izzy finished the last of the Old Log Cabin, deftly arched the empty bottle over the stern of the *Gar Jr.* and crawled into the engine compartment.

Monk was amazed that Izz could drop off so fast in the rolling and pitching boat. He had just made it to the rail several times and now had the dry heaves. Monk forced himself to stay alert through the remainder of darkness and into the early morning hours. About 8 a.m. Monk caught a glimpse of a fast-closing vessel approaching from the south. He shook Izz awake, and as the ship emerged from a fog bank they both saw a white bow plowing through the waves. It was a Coast Guard cutter!

As the welcome vessel pulled within fifty feet of the *Gar Jr.* and hove to, a voice boomed from a bullhorn. "Ahoy there. This is the Coast Guard. Are you in trouble?"

Izz cupped his hands and shouted, "Yes. We're dead in the water. Can you come aboard?"

Monk was stunned and complained, "For crissakes, Izz, that's the last thing we need."

"Now, hold your damn horses, Monk. This is where the pedal hits the metal. You let me do all the talkin'."

A dinghy was lowered and a seaman rowed a crisp white-uniformed officer to the side of the *Gar Jr.* Izzy took the officer's brown briefcase, helped him aboard and said, "Captain, we're sure glad to see you. The *Gar Jr.* here's been adrift since early last evening. I'm Isadore Brodsky – my adorin' fans call me Izzy, and this here young man in his Sunday best is my nephew, Monk Harpinski."

The officer smiled and said, "Thanks for the promotion, Mr. Brodsky – er, Izzy. I'm Lieutenant Commander Otto Metzger, and I'm glad to meet you both. I'm very familiar with the *Gar Jr.* My wife and I presented our parents, two grandparents, and several of their friends tickets to your moonlight cruise. They all said they couldn't remember having a better outing. What's your present situation?"

Izzy said they were on a high-speed test run when both universal joints of the two Packard engines shattered, and he wondered if it was possible to be towed to port.

Commander Metzger glanced at the covering over the passenger compartment and said, "You boys must have had a rough night during the squall. It's a good thing you had the protection of that canvas tarp over your heads."

Monk turned his head and grimaced.

Officer Metzger went on. "Izzy, I am authorized to assist all disabled craft on the Great Lakes and, if necessary, provide a tow line to the nearest available port. In your case, that would be, let's see, yes, St. Clair Shores. Would that meet with your approval?"

Izzy looked disappointed and said, "We're startin' a' eastern terminal on property about three or four miles north a' Mt. Clemens, Commander. That's where I've built up a supply of tools and spare parts. I know I could repair the *Gar Jr.* 'longside our new dock. Do you think it would be possible to bend the rules just a little?"

Officer Metzger pondered the question a moment and said, "I can't bend the rules, Izzy, but since we're headed north to Port Huron we'd have to backtrack to St. Clair Shores. That would cost me time and the government money. I can justify Mt. Clemens as the port of preference. When the *Neptune* approaches the latitude of your dock, disengage the tow rope and Seaman Rickleman will be dispatched in a motorized skiff to guide the Gar to your dockside.

"Izz, government regulations require me to examine several documents – your bill of sale, date of last safety inspection, and your public transportation license. Finally, I will need your signature on a form requesting aid at sea, and releasing the government from liability during the towing process. It's just a formality, nothing to be concerned about. Since we're not at dockside and the wave action is still rather energetic, I won't need to inspect the forward compartment."

Monk and Izzy breathed an unnoticed sigh of relief as Lieutenant Commander Metzger returned to the *Neptune*, smiled, and acknowledged Izzy's snappy salute.

M onk handed the last case of Johnnie Walker up to Izzy, wiped the perspiration from his brow, and said, "Izz, you are one in a million. I do believe if you had asked Commander Metzger to help us unload the Gar, he probably would have done it. But I was just wonderin', what if he had decided to check the booze compartment while we were still on the lake?"

Izzy grinned and said he didn't worry about "what ifs" and "might have beens." It was like the great colored baseball pitcher Satchel Paige always said, "Don't never look back, cause somethin' might be gainin' on you."

By mid-morning Monk and Izzy hitched a ride to the edge of Mt. Clemens in a Dean's Milk Company truck. The driver, Milt Dodds, recommended Frazer's Pier as the best fresh fish restaurant on the lake. Monk and Izzy devoured two orders of fried perch, blue gill, and lake trout, then made plans to meet in the city park by early afternoon.

Monk found a J.C. Penney store on Front Street and purchased two sets of work clothes. The clerk ringing up the sale told Monk to be sure and stop at the entrance door and shake hands with the middle-aged man enthusiastically greeting customers. That would be Mr. Penney, himself. The clerk said Mr. Penney drops in on his hundred or more stores twice a year, and they never know when he's coming. Monk changed into his new clothes, bagged his filthy old ones, and said he was honored to talk and shake hands with Mr. J.C. Penney. On the way to the park, Monk wisely stopped by the Downtown Deli and bought a roll of hard salami, a loaf of Italian bread and two boxes of Cracker Jacks. He found a shady spot in the park and shared the Cracker Jacks with three squirrels and a flock of pigeons.

Izzy stopped at the Salvation Army building on Monroe Street and was warmly greeted by Major Phillip Rudik. He briefly described his ordeal on Lake St. Clair the previous night and was not only offered the use of the shower facilities, but was provided with a razor and a complete change of nearly new clothes. Moved by the unselfish kindness shown him, Izzy left a small donation at the desk and stepped refreshed into the warming sunshine.

Izzy bought two universal joint kits at the Lake St. Clair Packard Automobile dealership on Main Street and a set of tools at the nearby Western Auto store. He was immediately attracted to the comely forty-something-year-old clerk at Western Auto, and since business seemed slow, struck up a slightly suggestive conversation. Izzy introduced himself, and with a sly wink said that after the movie heartthrob Rudolph Valentino left Chicago for Tinsel Town, he was one of the last of the red hot lovers in Windy City.

Ruby Alvarado laughed and said she was pleased to meet such a modest gent, but wondered why he hadn't followed Valentino to Hollywood.

When Izzy asked what a vigorous grown man did to entertain himself in her fair city, especially during the middle of the day, Ruby said she was amazed that he hadn't heard of the famous Mt. Clemens Mineral Spring Baths. She enjoyed Madame DuBois' Spa on Baden Street twice weekly and found the baths not only relaxing but most stimulating. In fact, she coyly mentioned that she planned to occupy private bath 2-B during her lunch break between 1 and 2 p.m. that very afternoon.

Izzy showed up at the city park an hour late, squeaky clean and in a new set of clothes. Monk knew better than to ask, and Izz didn't offer any explanations.

They pooled the last of their money, hired a Checker cab and returned to the boathouse. By 8 p.m. Izzy had completed replacing both universal joints, and had made a test run. Before leaving for Windsor he said Mr. Capone would never miss one bottle of Johnnie Walker Black.

The cruise back to Windsor was pure pleasure with Monk captaining and Izz sipping the confiscated Johnnie Walker and nibbling on the salami and Italian bread. After docking and securing the *Gar Jr.* they made their way to the King Edward Hotel. Izzy mixed nightcaps and was now sure that barring any improbable mechanical problems, their plan was flawless. The next run would guarantee them a profit of $5,040. Monk, slowly nursing his drink, had some lingering doubts, but kept them to himself.

Izzy called Frank Nitti at the Metropole Hotel in Chi-Town between charter runs the next afternoon and told him he could have a hundred and five cases of Johnnie Walker at the boathouse by early the next Sunday morning. He gave Frankie the directions, which would be pretty simple for the men to follow: pick up Route 12 at La Porte, Indiana and follow it 200 miles to downtown Detroit City. Take Gratiot north through Mt. Clemens to Hall Road, a right to East Jefferson, then left about 3½ miles to a telephone pole on the right with three red reflectors. He and Monk would meet the truck and help load. Frankie sent his congratulations and said Rico Profacini and Ciro Cataldo would be driving a big International. Frankie reminded Izzy that the first thirty-five cases was less the boys' profit, as previously agreed upon. Rico would have a brown envelope for him containing $5,040. Frankie asked, "When you gonna start payin' off yer loan from Al?"

Izzy said, "Ask Al to start deductin' five grand startin' with the second pick-up of a hunnert and five cases. We is just gettin' on our feet with the charter business. I figure we can send Al two or three grand from our charter profit back with Rico and Ciro this Sunday."

"O.K., I'll tell Al. The run from Chicago will probably take about six or seven hours, so plan to meet the boys at the boathouse Sunday mornin' at 1 a.m. sharp."

"All right Frankie, but I'm a little worried about us all bein' able to meet at exactly 1 o'clock. Suppose you have Rico and Ciro stop at the Country Inn on Maple Road and Gratiot – a couple miles south of Mt. Clemens. The joint stays open until 2 a.m. so the guys can get somethin' to eat and a drink in the back room. It's exactly eight and three-quarter miles from the Country Inn to the boathouse, so if they left the Inn at 12:40, the truck could back up to the boathouse within a minute or two of 1 a.m. We'll be bringin' another thirty-five cases that night and can lay off shore and make the 1 a.m. meetin' right on the dot. Monk and me will help the boys load the truck and they'll be on their way in twenty-five minutes. Then we can go unload the Gar in the boathouse and be on our way about a half-hour later. I'd feel better if we wasn't hangin' around any longer than necessary."

Frankie said, "That's a good plan, Izz. I'll fill the boys in on the details."

Monk and Izz could not make the charter runs the next day, Tuesday, because of strong winds and rain. Tuesday night, with the rain still pelting the sidewalk, Vito D'Amato picked up Monk and Izz at the Leland in his Checker and dropped them off at Lefty O'Doul's about 8 o'clock. Lefty's face was getting purple like it always does when he is losing an argument with a customer. Monk and Izz settled in with a couple doubles of Old Log Cabin and alky chasers, just enjoying the fun. Lefty had a chance to cool off when a copper came in and they both disappeared in the back room. After a few more drinks, Monk and Izz took on a couple of would-be hustlers at 25-point straight pool for ten bucks a game and drinks. Izz was a master at leaving a side cut just past the pocket so his opponent would take a foolish chance and leave Monk a clear shot and possible run. Before he was done, Monk would miss a cinch and leave the hustler a shot or two. The boys were so skillful at keeping the game close, the hustlers insisted on doubling and tripling the bet as the night wore on.

About 11:30, a blind man came into Lefty's and showed a printed card to anyone who would give it a look. The card read, "I was blinded in France during the Big War. If you could find it in your heart to help me, I and my family would be everlastingly grateful." Feeling flush, Monk and Izz each dropped a couple bills into the wicker basket, even though Izz was pretty sure that after making the rounds of the mostly uninterested patrons, the "blind" man would go outside, flip up his dark glasses and check the denominations of the folding money.

Toward the end of the last game a fly swooped down from the hot, green-hooded light over the table and landed on the cue ball near Monk. It sat there enjoying the cool ivory when Monk's left hand flashed out with the speed of a welterweight in his first club fight. Monk held up a closed fist and Izz said, "Good catch, Monk, you got the little bugger." Hustler number one said, "Good catch, my ass. Ain't nobody kin catch a fly like that."

"A fiver says he got it," Izz boasted.

"Make it ten," the hustler growled.

Monk opened his fist and dumped the dazed fly on the green felt. The hustler mumbled something uncomplimentary, peeled off a ten spot and said, "Let's finish the damn game." When Izz allowed that Monk had the fastest hand east of the Mississippi, the hustler said they'd find a damn fly and double the bet after the game. "There ain't nobody kin do that twice in a row." Izzy double-banked the 9 ball in the side pocket for the final win.

While the would-be hustlers and Izzy approached the bar for the pay-off drink, Monk walked down the narrow dark hallway to the men's room. Once inside he swatted the half-dozen flies congregating around the warm dirty light bulb with a soiled hand towel. Flushing all but one down the toilet, he carefully nestled the pay-off fly in his left hand. Returning to the dimly lit bar, Monk moved to a place between the gamblers and Izzy and awaited the inevitable fly. Two twenties were tucked in a beer glass in front of the mirror. Before their drinks were half gone, a potential victim settled down on the sticky surface of the bar. Monk's hand lashed out faster than the eyes of the gamblers could follow, snatched at the fly, continued up and around in a graceful arch, and with palm down, dropped the bogus pay-off fly in the drink of the closest hustler. Enraged, and somehow feeling out-snookered, the pair faced Monk and Izzy with switchblades at the ready. Izzy, in a low, controlled voice, said, "Boys, you know a couple toad stabbers ain't no match for a .38 snub. Now, get your dirty asses outta here before I spend about ten cents on a coupla ounces of lead."

As soon as the punks hurriedly left and Monk collected the twenties, Izz went for a piss. Monk was nursing his drink when he squinted through the smoky haze and saw none other than Gino Evola sitting on a high stool by the wall staring back at him. When Izz returned, Geno was gone. Izz said, "Forget it Monk. Geno's so damn dumb he can't find his ass with both hands, and after what happened to his pal Victor Ciambi he ain't gonna cause no trouble. Besides, if he ratted on us, he knows the Bernstein brothers would hunt him down and hang him on a meat hook in one a' their coolers."

T he boys completed two more booze runs on Wednesday and Friday and had one-hundred and five cases stockpiled in the boathouse for the early Sunday morning pick up. They planned another run on Saturday night before they met Nitti's men.

Monk and Izz made three charter runs on Friday. Gussie and Reggie covered the fourth from 3:30 to 5:30 p.m. as well as the moonlight cruise. After the second charter on Saturday, Gussie turned the *Gar Jr.* over to Izzy for refueling and minor maintenance. Gussie and Reggie planned to have the Johnnie Walker at the Amhurstburg dock by 10:00 that night, so Monk and Izz could make the pick-up and be in the boathouse in Mt. Clemens at 1 a.m. Sunday morning.

Everything went according to plan Saturday night. Monk and Izz reached Amhurstburg with time to spare and began removing the seats. By 10 o'clock Reggie's lorry arrived and backed up to the dock. As the cases were being stowed in the *Gar Jr.* and the seats carried to the lorry, Monk thought Reggie was in especially high spirits. Later Izz said the boys had probably stopped for a couple in Amhurstburg, and besides, this was going to be a big night for all of them.

With a smart salute to the boys on the dock, Monk pulled the *Gar Jr.* into the rip current and headed upstream at a steady fifteen miles an hour. After passing Fighting Island the estuary narrowed into the Detroit River so Monk slackened his speed to ten miles an hour until they cleared Belle Isle and entered Lake St. Clair. They now had twenty-five miles of open water and forty-five minutes to reach the boathouse.

Rico and Ciro pulled into the Country Inn parking lot at 11 p.m. After over seven hours on the road they were tired, hungry, and ready for a little relaxation. Rico asked for steak and eggs. Ciro ordered his favorite, liver and onions with a dab of sour cream. Rico wrinkled his nose when Ciro cut into the liver and said, "Good god, Ciro, any guy who would bite into that would eat the ass out of a skunk."

Ciro smacked his lips and said, "A skunk's ass ain't all that bad either, Rico." After a couple of gin and tonics, Rico looked at his watch and said, "12:40 – we is right on the mark."

Out on the open water of the lake, Izz took over the controls and kept the *Gar Jr.* at about forty miles an hour. At 12:50 they eased near shore and glided silently toward the canal. Izz backed the *Gar Jr.* into the mouth and Monk hopped up on the long footpath and pulled the boat backward to the boathouse. At two minutes past one, the big International backed into the driveway and the four men greeted one another in whispered tones.

1:07 a.m. – With the tailgate down, the one-hundred and five cases of Johnnie Walker were handed from one man to the next and the job was completed in twenty-seven minutes. Rico pressed a brown envelope into Izzy's hands. The two drivers climbed up into the cab and were on their way.

1:37 a.m. – Monk jumped into the hold of the *Gar Jr.* and began lifting their night's run of thirty-five cases up to Izz on the dock.

1:42 a.m. – The International slowed to five miles an hour and Rico made the sharp right turn from East Jefferson to Hall Road. The truck picked up speed. Suddenly, headlights flicked on and off. Two spotlights silhouetted a large black sedan in the middle of the road, blinding Rico. Ciro yelled, "Holy shit, Rico, pull up, pull up, the bastards got tommy guns on us!"
"United States Marshals!" a voice shouted. "This is Agent Purvis. Cut your motor, climb down and put your hands on your head." Rico and Ciro surrendered meekly. Their truck was impounded and the two drivers whisked away in the Buick squad car.

1:55 a.m. – Monk pulled the *Gar Jr.* to the mouth of the canal, secured it, and returned to help Izzy carry the Johnnie Walker from the dock to the storeroom.

2:15 a.m. – Izz locked the door and they both started back to the *Gar Jr.* Halfway along the path they were profiled in a flood of white light.
"Halt!" a voice commanded. "U.S. Marshals. Down on your knees with your hands on your heads." Izzy complied immediately, but Monk panicked and made a dash for the *Gar Jr.* Two shots penetrated the night air and Monk went down, face forward, with blood seeping from the wounds in his back. Agent Purvis leaped in front of Corporal Hennessy and shouted, "For crissakes, Hennessy, you don't blast a guy for running booze. Hold your fire!" Izzy ran to Monk, and partially lifting his body, sat on the stained earth and cradled Monk's head and shoulders to his chest. Monk's pale blue eyes seemed to be staring past Izzy. Rocking slowly back and forth, Izz began to softly sing the World War I song that Monk loved so well:

"Nights are long since you went away;
How I think about you all through the day,
    My Buddy, My Buddy
    No buddy quite as true.
I miss your voice and the touch of your hand,
I long to know that you understand
    My Buddy, My Buddy
    Your Buddy misses you."

2:22 a.m. October 8, 1926 – Monk was dead.

PADDY
1926

CHAPTER SEVENTEEN

I was devastated when I learned of Monk's death. I knew that he and Izzy were walking a fine line, dealing with known mobsters and low-life thugs. But to be killed by a federal agent over a violation of the Volstead Act was inexcusable. The penalty, at most, should have been a one- or two-year sentence, and for a first offender, perhaps just a fine and probation.

I was on the road while all of this was happening, but Izzy was able to get a message to me through the Gold Bond Company. I made it to Detroit in time to accompany my old friend on his final journey home to Chicago.

The funeral was held a few days later at St. Francis of Assisi on Ogden and 28th Street. Father Gambarelli performed a Requiem Mass, and I couldn't help but think of my old pal Monk in his altar boy robes, a five-dollar bill stuck to the bottom of his shoe with a wad of Black Jack chewing gum. When I went up to say my final farewell, I noticed a baseball signed by Ty Cobb, the one Izzy had given him all those years ago, resting in my friend's right hand. With Mrs. Harpinski's approval, I pinned my *Chicago Tribune* "Athlete of the Year" award on Monk's lapel.

Surrounded by several bouquets of flowers and live plants was a huge unsigned wreath. Gussie said it had been delivered by the notorious Schofield Flower Shop on State Street. After the service, when I was offering Mrs. Harpinski my condolences, she told me that all of the funeral expenses, including the bronze casket, were paid for by Frank Nitti. That showed me an entirely different side of the cruel and self-centered mobster.

For the burial, I helped Mrs. Harpinski choose a site in the Mt. Olivet Cemetery on a slight rise shaded by a stately red oak tree. The coffin was lowered into the ground and I said a final silent goodbye. As the mourners slowly walked away, I noticed a beautiful arrangement of American Beauty roses. I glanced at the message on the small white card:

> "My love will be with you always,
> Betty Lou."

The small horizontal granite headstone was not set in place for several weeks, but after that I visited as often as I could on my trips through Chicago. I would spruce up the site, pulling weeds in the spring and summer, sweeping dead leaves in the autumn, and clearing snow when it fell. I read the headstone so often that its inscription is etched into my mind.

KELSEN THEODORE HARPINSKI
JUNE 21, 1904 - OCTOBER 8, 1926

"He had yet to reach his
destined potential"

I sent Betty Lou a note through Pete Consani thanking her for the roses. I had never met her, but it felt like I had because of Monk's stories – and I told her as much. We wrote back and forth for a while after that. On December 27, 1929, her philandering husband died in a Cleveland-Cliffs mine accident. She had been secretly saving the money Izz and Monk sent her in 1926 out of the tour boat profits, and it enabled her to enroll in Harper Hospital Nursing School in Detroit. We met a few times while she was there, and it was nice to have someone to talk to about Monk. But after she completed her nursing degree in 1933, she returned to Nauganee, Michigan to work as Dr. Lahti's assistant. We still wrote occasionally, but I felt like my connections to my old pal Monk were slipping away.

As for Izzy, I visited him many times during his three-and-a-half-year incarceration in the federal prison at Milan, Michigan. The first time I saw him in stripes was during a business trip to Detroit, January of '27. I drove the twenty-five miles to Milan and identified myself to the authorities as Patrick O'Brian, a close friend of Isadore Brodsky. The assistant warden said to come back at 3:00 p.m. and I could have twenty minutes with Mr. Brodsky.

Upon my return I was patted down and instructed to sit in front of a thick glass partition. The guard demonstrated how I was to use the buttons on the two-way phone and cautioned me that our conversation would be monitored.

Izzy seemed rather morose and withdrawn at first, but when my time was up he thanked me for coming and said he hoped I would return soon.

During my second or third visit, as I was waiting for Izzy, the guard casually mentioned that the warden, Earl Thrift, was a golf enthusiast. He shook his head and said, "Can you believe it, the nut heard the temperature was going up to 35 degrees this afternoon, so he and Lt. Carruthers headed to the course about an hour ago."

On my way back to East Chicago, I picked up Route 50 just south of Milan and followed it about 150 miles to Grand Rapids. There I visited with my old friend Walter "the Haig" Hagen, at his golf equipment factory. I had met Walter in Colosimos just after he had won his third or fourth P.G.A. championship. He was the first head professional at the prestigious Oakland Hills Country Club in Detroit and upon retirement was awarded unrestricted golf privileges for life.

I was the Haig's golfing partner often over the years and many a night turned into dawn over a premium bottle or two of scotch. Walter was a born bon vivant with a go-to-hell attitude and upset the blue-bloods in England no end when he played in his first British Open. Professional golfers were looked down upon at that time and weren't permitted to use the front entrance of the hallowed golf clubs. Walter parked his pink Rolls Royce directly across from the front door of St. Andrews and sat on the running board while a gorgeous flapper helped him change into his spikes. He further outraged the citizenry when he reportedly said the only difference between the Prince of Wales and himself was that he could hit a 2-iron. I had had the honor of teaming with Walter when we won the club tournament at Oakland Hills.

After we relived old memories with the help of a fella by the name of Jack Daniels, I told my friend about Izzy's unfortunate predicament and the warden's passion for golf. I said I thought Izzy's stay in prison might be made more bearable if I could discreetly present the warden with a set of Walter Hagen golf clubs, a bag, balls and an autographed photograph.

Walter said he remembered meeting Izzy with Al Capone in Colosimos and would be delighted to help. I accompanied him to the sales display room where he picked out a set of Haig clubs, an enormous leather bag and two sleeves of balls.

In late May Walter staged his yearly "Send a Kid to Camp" celebrity golf tournament at Oakland Hills. Our foursome included Walter, Michigan Governor Fred Green – and Warden Thrift. From then until his release, Izzy and I had unlimited use of a private conference room, with our favorite beverage and assorted snacks delivered by a trustee.

More than a year after Monk's death, Izz finally unburdened himself to me. This is his story as I remember it: Agent Melvin Purvis placed him under arrest at the boathouse on Lake St. Clair on October 8, 1926. He was charged with violation of the 1920 Volstead Act and possession of a .38 caliber Smith & Wesson revolver – a felony under the 1911 Sullivan Law. He was processed and temporarily remanded in the Detroit House of Correction awaiting trial. A young lawyer, Adolph Seigler, was assigned by the court as his attorney after Judge Francis Murphy declared Izzy indigent. The *Gar Jr.* and the brown envelope containing $5,040 had been impounded as prima facie evidence. Bail was denied when Izzy gave his address as 118 Kostner Avenue, Chicago, Illinois. Izzy's trial was scheduled for November 3, 1926 in the Federal Court Building, Detroit, Michigan.

When Frank Nitti's lawyer, Clarence Darrow, replaced Seigler as Izzy's counsel, a plea bargain was offered and agreed upon. Izzy pleaded guilty to the Volstead Act violation. The felony weapons charge was dropped. Sentence was set at 3½ years. Good behavior time could be accrued. The government's counsel had offered a 2-year sentence if the modus operandi and the identity of the receiving party or parties of the contraband were revealed. Izzy rejected the offer. After sentencing, the Honorable Judge Murphy permitted Izz a few minutes with the arresting officer, Melvin Purvis.

Izz said, "Inspector Purvis, I know you was just doin' your job and I ain't holdin' you nor Agent Hennessy responsible for Monk's death. He was a young guy and lost his head. But if you could, I'd sure like to know who tipped you off to our operation. It wasn't just by chance you was at the boathouse at 1 o'clock in the mornin'."

Purvis said, "Mr. Brodsky, you are correct; we weren't there just by chance. Ordinarily I wouldn't reveal my source, but the informer is dead and I feel no empathy for him. I received a call at approximately 11 p.m. Saturday night, October 7. The voice at the other end of the line wanted to know if the government was still paying an informer 10% of the value of all confiscated contraband. When I replied in the affirmative, I was given the names, location and exact time of your operation. The caller then identified himself as one Reginald C. McKenzie."

Izzy let out a low whistle and said, "Damn, I never thought it would be Reggie. I guess it's true, there ain't no honor among thieves. Well, thanks, Mr. Purvis. I'll rest a little easier knowin' who was responsible for Monk losing his life and knowing the son-of-a-bitch has already met his maker, or worse."

Izzy was transferred to the Federal Correctional Institution in Milan, Michigan, and after processing settled in to a life of monotony. Early rising, marching silently to and from meals, monitored free time in the "yard," work assignments in the laundry and long, lonely hours in his cell comprised Izzy's day.

At the beginning of the third week Izzy said he was suddenly pulled from the hot work in the laundry and assigned to the library. One mid-afternoon Izz recognized hit man Rudolph Zonetti returning books to the stack shelves. When Izzy pushed his book cart to the end of an aisle, Zonetti sidled up to him and whispered, "Hi, Izzy, welcome to the Ritz Carleton West. I seen ya last week in the yard. I just wanted ya ta know I been circulatin' the word you was one a' Big Al's boys so ya don't have ta worry none 'bout bein' hit on and made a pet by one a' the lifers. When ya make out yer Christmas card list, make sure ta include Frank Nitti 'cause he's a regular contributor to this here library – if ya get my meanin'." Izz thanked Zonetti and thought to himself that it sure didn't hurt to have friends in high places when you're in the joint.

Izzy did what was expected of him every day and made friends with old Ned Granger, a lifer who had worked the library for fifteen or twenty years. One afternoon while putting magazines and newspapers back in order, Izz asked, "Ned, what are you in for?"

Ned, with those sad eyes of his, said, "They say I murdered a guy in cold blood over a damn poker game squabble, but that ain't the way it was at all. I caught the son-a-bitch double dealin' in five-card stud. I called him on it an' when I started to get outta my chair he sucker punched me. I remember fallin' backward and hittin' my head, an' him comin' at me with a switchblade. I reached up an' grabbed a Steel City beer bottle from the table and smashed the bottom outta it on the floor. By the time my head cleared an' we started swipin' at each other, the bar maid called the coppers. All the players scurried outta the room like cockroaches when a light is turned on, so I had no witnesses. When the cops showed I'd already rammed that broken bottle inta the bastard's neck an' he was layin' on the floor spoutin' blood and starin' at the ceilin'. It was either him or me. The lawyer they give me was a dumb-assed drunk who tol' me if I pleaded guilty the state would probably be lenient an' give me maybe fifteen minus good time, but if I went to trial I'd get the limit – life without parole. I believed the damn lawyer, pleaded guilty – and here I am, a lifer without no hope."

Izz said, "You sure got a bum rap, Ned," and after they both had a smoke, Izz asked, "By the way, how long do you keep this readin' material?"

Ned said, "The magazines a coupla months an' the big city papers four or five weeks. A professor from Michigan University comes over ever' Thursday night an' teaches a writin' class ta them which is interested. He likes ta use the mags an' papers ta show how the pros does it."

The next day Izz looked back in the *Detroit Times* and *Detroit Free Press* from about October 10 to October 25 – there it was – a story in the October 15th *Detroit Times* on page 13 describing Reggie McKenzie's murder. Izz eagerly read:

Windsor, Canada, October 15, 1926

The Royal Canadian Mounted Police early Wednesday morning, October 14, observed an abandoned passenger car in a grove of trees on Route 3, four miles north of the village of Essex. Upon examination, a body was found slumped over the steering wheel with a bullet wound in the back of the head. Sgt. Rupert Granholm said death was instantaneous and the shooting had the M.O. of a gangland murder.

Authorities reported the black 1921 Hupmobile was equipped with stolen license plates, but information in the vehicle led them to the deceased's identity: Reginald C. McKenzie of 3723 Chatham East, Windsor, Canada. It was determined by coroner Wiley H. Forneau that a scar on the left temple and bold maple leaf tattoo on the right forearm of the deceased were consistent with police records of McKenzie. Dr.

Forneau stressed, however, that a positive identification of the body by a relative or close friend would be useful in a final determination.

Izzy anxiously spread the October 16th and 17th issues of the *Times* on the table. Scanning the Monday paper drew a blank, but a short article in the Tuesday paper jumped out at him. Izzy's eyes followed his finger down the lines:

A positive identification of Reginald C. McKenzie's body has been made by a dear and close friend of the deceased. An affidavit required by the coroner's office was signed by one Gustave Peter Montrono.

Izzy smiled with satisfaction and was content knowing that Monk's lifelong friend, Gussie Montrono, could never be connected with Reggie's murder.

With accrued good-behavior time, Izzy was released from federal prison on January 18, 1930. He returned to Cicero a changed man. I think partly because he felt responsible for Monk's death and, of course, because losing one's freedom was bound to have a sobering effect. Times had changed. The go-to-hell days of the Roaring '20s were over. The '29 crash had not only closed factories and small businesses, but the supper clubs and speaks were hurting, too. People just didn't have the money or inclination to party as much. Even silent screen actress Clara Bow, the "It" girl, had fallen on hard times.

I began to see Izz less and less. The past was so hurtful there was no joy in reminiscing. I'd heard he'd taken a job in the City of Chicago Maintenance Department and was living with a woman on the South Side. In mid-February of 1934 I had a drink with Izz in the Deuces and he seemed more at ease and even spoke of a possible promotion. The news of his death in early March was totally unexpected and a terrible blow. I had lost a wonderful friend and my last link with Monk.

With the country in a deepening depression, I had to cut back on my night-time activities, but still had more than enough money scattered about in lock boxes to cover Uncle Izzy's funeral expenses, and to pay for a site next to Monk's grave in the Mt. Olivet Cemetery.

At the end of the funeral service a heavily veiled, middle-aged woman slowly hobbled on a cane to a waiting car. She did not sign the guest attendance book but scribbled, "I had a dream, dear, you had one too."

Izzy's plain granite stone bore the inscription:

ISADORE JOSEPH BRODSKY
FEBRUARY 16, 1890 - MARCH 3, 1934
"Loyalty marks the true
measure of mortal man"

As I left the familiar knoll in the cemetery, I couldn't help but think that Monk and Uncle Izzy were, at that moment, planning a way to help St. Peter get drinks and food wholesale for a party they were throwing for recent arrivals.

EPILOGUE

On October 20, 1975, Timothy O'Brian received a call that his uncle Paddy had died. The 71-year-old had been healthy most of his life, having been retired only five years before emphysema and viral pneumonia claimed his life. Timothy was an experienced C.P.A. and acted as executor for his beloved uncle's obligations and wishes, following his written instructions exactly.

Paddy had never married and had continued living in his Cicero childhood home until his passing. A small inheritance was distributed to each of six family members, including Timothy himself. Paddy had prepaid the Caldwell Funeral Home for all arrangements including a simple oak casket. Father Connolly of St. Anthony's conducted the service attended by immediate family members and a few friends.

Paddy also pre-purchased the lot directly behind the graves of Monk and Izzy in the Mt. Olivet Cemetery. Per his instructions, his simple granite stone was inscribed:

PATRICK THOMAS O'BRIAN
AUGUST 10, 1904 – OCTOBER 20, 1975
"If in need of a friend, I will
always be ready to serve"

During the months that followed, Timothy categorized Paddy's personal belongings and reviewed his finances. It was easy to put aside clothing, shoes, appliances and furniture for St. Anthony's, but what was he to do with the multitude of photographs and personal papers? Since many of the snapshots were a part of his own heritage, Timothy set aside those that he would eventually include in a family album.

Several pictures taken in 1933 evoked pleasant memories. On May 27, the opening day of the Chicago World's Fair, a kind stranger had snapped a picture of Grandmother O'Brian, Uncle Paddy and himself standing in front of the 23rd Street entrance. The thrill of being a part of the Century of Progress – and skipping a full day of third grade – had been overwhelming.

Timothy recalled being reminded by Grandmother O'Brian to use his Kodak Brownie camera judiciously because there were over one-hundred exhibits and a huge midway area – far too many attractions for one roll of film. A few of the pictures taken that day included the Hall of Science, the Golden Temple of Jehol from China, Abraham Lincoln's Boyhood Home, the 218-foot Havoline Thermometer, as well as shots of the Lindy Loop, Whirl-O-Plane and the gigantic Towering Sky-Ride.

Lunch at the Fair's Walgreen's drug store had begun to wear off when Uncle Paddy seemed to know instinctively how much a nine-year-old boy craved a crispy Downy Flake doughnut and a cold bottle of Nehi orange soda. Later that afternoon Grandmother O'Brian gently guided him over to the trained Flea Circus while he watched over his shoulder as Uncle Paddy followed a pretty lady dancing behind a large fan into a darkened tent. The ride home to Cicero on the 25th Street trolley was an anticlimax to a memorable day some forty-two years past.

Timothy decided to include three snapshots in the family album that weren't strictly family, but showed Uncle Paddy so happy and contented. In the first picture, a beautiful blonde lady snuggled close to Uncle Paddy next to a 1933 Ford sedan. The World's Fair buildings appear in the background. On the back, "World's Fair, 8-14-'33. Polly Hamilton." The second snapshot – "World's Fair, 8-14-'33. Polly Hamilton – The Egyptian Pavilion." The third snapshot – "East Chicago roller rink, 9-22-'33" showed Uncle Paddy standing behind the mystery lady, Polly Hamilton, with his arms around her waist – looking very happy!

Timothy, for the first time in his life, appreciated the miracle of photography. Here on faded paper, a 25th of a second exposure had preserved moments in the lives of his loved ones so many years ago.

A bundle of letters next drew Timothy's interest. He flipped through and noticed that several were war-time letters signed by a Betty Lou Olsen. For a moment, Timothy wondered if Uncle Paddy had a sweetheart he hadn't known about. But once he started reading the letters, he realized they were not romantic. Betty Lou, it seems, was a flight evacuation nurse in the U.S. Army Air Corps. Her letters to Paddy were heavily censored, containing only vague details of the fifteen mercy missions she flew during the Battle of the Solomon Islands in the spring and summer of 1942. For the most part, however, her letters were full of stories and reminiscences about Monk Harpinksi, whom Timothy knew had been Paddy's childhood friend.

At the bottom of the stack of letters was a newspaper clipping about a C-47 ambulance plane lost over the Coral Sea, en route from Guadalcanal to Australia, on August 10, 1942. Paddy had circled a paragraph memorializing one of the passengers, Nurse Betty Lou Olsen, whom hundreds of injured servicemen would remember as the angel with the gold watch pinned to her army blouse. The article said that Betty Lou's Air Medal and Bronze Star were presented to her mother by Secretary of War Henry Stimson on October 8, 1942.

As he dug deeper into his late uncle's possessions, Timothy found another letter, this one creased and faded from many hundreds of readings.

Paddy O'Brian
to the gold bond tool company
east Chicago indiana

August 1938

>   *dear paddy*
>   *the misses an I want to thank you fer what you done a wile back. a wile after you left sum bums come at night an smashed my dodge motor an filter an said if I bilt another I would really be sorry. they beet me pretty bad but I had the misses run over to a naibor so she is ok. we have fixed the house with new windows, new well an coal furnice. the misses now has what she calls a sowing room an a new room for the gran kids when they come. we planted 50 apple an 50 peech trees. I got a good used fordson tracter*
>   *paddy I ain't gonna ask how you come by so much money just thank*

you fer what you done as a friend. I never seen the misses so happy an me to. we put what was left in a bank fer the little kids schoolin when they get big an some fer a sick old friend. I can only say thank you agin paddy an no the lord is on yer side

yer friend opie
an the missus cantrill

if you can come down sometime the gran kids room has a cot in it

Timothy was happy with his uncle's success, but unlike Opie, he was compelled to learn where Paddy had gotten the money. He didn't remember his uncle ever being particularly well-off. Intrigued, he began going through Paddy's meticulous financial records (watching his uncle keep these records had been one of the factors that inspired Timothy to become a C.P.A.).

In one notebook, his uncle had recorded his income from the Gold Bond Tool and Hydraulic Lift Company and his every expenditure from 1926 to 1966. Total income was $167,200. There was not one month that expenditures exceeded income. No surprise here – these notebooks fit the financial picture that Timothy, as an accountant, expected to see.

Further searching uncovered four small, red, leather-bound notebooks covering the same years, 1926 to 1966, but broken down into months. As Timothy examined each book he became more incredulous. There was a column for income, and some months listed as many as five entries, but there were only ever dollar amounts. The source of the money received was never revealed.

The reasons for money paid out were mystifying. Most beneficiaries were small homeowners, and over the years 78 mortgages totaling $218,000 were paid in full; $28,520 was paid for hospital services and $55,880 for coal, water and artificial gas. Smaller amounts covered food, clothing, school supplies and toys amounting to $40,201. When totaled, the amount paid out was $341,481 – and Uncle Paddy's lifetime income was $167,200! Clearly, Opie Cantrill had not been alone as a beneficiary of Paddy O'Brian's kindness.

Timothy continued to search through his uncle's possessions, and finally found a badly worn black leather case the size of a woman's vanity. The contents included slender steel picks, 25 keys with different configurations, small wrenches, screwdrivers, talcum powder, rubber gloves, and a medical stethoscope. Wrapped in heavy velvet beneath the tools lay a blue steel .38 caliber snub-nose Smith & Wesson revolver. Timothy sat bolt upright in his chair. "My god," he thought, "Uncle Paddy was an accomplished thief!" As he reflected, he remembered the many times Paddy had talked of his extreme hatred for high-interest, money-grabbing loan sharks and shady companies. The pattern was unmistakable; Uncle Paddy robbed mercenaries and provided poor families with financial relief. How bad could that be? But still –

Timothy knew what had to be done. He placed the notebooks in the black case containing Uncle Paddy's tools and revolver. The following day he drove to the U. S. Steel Corporation in Gary, Indiana and found his childhood friend, Mark Wing, now a shift foreman, finishing lunch. Mark had been a pallbearer at Paddy's funeral and held him in high esteem. After Timothy told the story of Paddy's secret forty years of helping those in need, without a hint of personal gain, Mark readily agreed to help destroy the evidence that might dishonor Paddy's life.

Mark said he was about to charge Bessemer furnace #3 with vanadium and titanium alloys. He instructed Timothy to position himself on the third floor observation deck. Timothy watched anxiously as Mark expertly swung the huge bucket over the seething caldron. At the proper instant, the bucket was upended, pouring the alloys into the flaming inferno. Mark gave a thumbs-up sign indicating Paddy's black case had been part of the charge and was now just an ingredient in a routine batch of high-grade steel.

On his drive home, Timothy was at odds over his responsibility to authorities and his moral obligation to Uncle Paddy. He found justification and peace within himself in a verse he had admired so many years ago in a college literature class. James Henry Leigh Hunt's poem *Abou Ben Adhem* seemed now to perfectly sum up Uncle Paddy's convictions and faith. The words flowed effortlessly as Timothy unburdened his heart:

Abou Ben Adhem (may his tribe increase)
Awoke one night from a deep dream of peace,
And saw, within the moonlight in his room,
Making it rich, and like a lily in bloom,
An angel writing in a book of gold:

Exceeding peace had made Ben Adhem bold;
And to the Presence in the room he said,

"What writest Thou?" The Vision raised its head,
And with a look made of all sweet accord
Answered, "The names of those who love the Lord."

"And is mine one?" said Abou. "Nay, not so,"
Replied the angel. Abou spoke more low,
But cheerly still; and said, "I pray thee, then,
Write me as one that loves his fellow men."

The angel wrote, and vanished. The next night
It came again, with a great wakening light,
And showed the names whom love of God had blessed;
And lo! (Timothy altered the last line)
Patrick Thomas O'Brian's name led all the rest.

He was now content that Paddy would forever be judged, not by his sins, but by his love and devotion to his fellow man.

AUTHOR'S NOTE

"History is bunk." This startling pronouncement is attributed to Henry Ford, but who could spend a day at Greenfield Village and the Ford Museum in Dearborn, Michigan and believe those words were his true conception of our past? Mr. Ford spent the last third of his life meticulously collecting, categorizing, and displaying American artifacts, both large-scale and small.

I had the privilege of spending many delightful evenings with Fred Black, Mr. Ford's close associate and confidant, listening to his descriptive narration of the early development of the Dearborn facilities. Fred Black later became a University of Michigan Business School Professor.

Professor Black assured me that Henry Ford uttered those astonishing words, perhaps injudiciously, but said that they truly reflected Ford's life-long distrust of intellectuals. Mr. Ford believed that the manner in which American history was presented might well lead to inaccuracies due to faulty source information based upon hearsay, questionable research, or distortions due to the writer's agenda. Mr. Ford did believe strongly, however, in the power of visual history, as evidenced by his remarkable collections in Dearborn.

Historical fiction – and that genre accurately describes *Monk and Me* – is meant to be a pleasant diversion into the make-believe. The book is an invention of my imagination, intermixed with personal experiences and factual information.

Paddy O'Brian, Kelsen (Monk) Harpinski, Isadore (Uncle Izzy) Brodsky, Betty Lou Olsen, Mrs. Hrbec, and a host of others are fictional, but seem so close to me I almost feel they should be included on my birthday and Christmas card lists.

I hope my family members and close friends will be pleased, or at least amused, with their character parts.

Paddy's story about John Dillinger is mostly true, and Al Capone, Frank Nitti, and Mayor "Big Bill" Thompson, among others, did play prominent roles in Chicago crime and politics in the 1920s. Celebrities of the period appear in imaginary roles consistent with their public personas.

Bootleggers did smuggle alcohol across the river from Windsor to Detroit, but to my knowledge, no one ever attempted the methods employed by the characters in this book.

Edmund L. Palmer
Ann Arbor, Michigan

HISTORICAL NOTE

Alphonse Capone spent his formative years in Manhattan's Lower East Side exposed to thievery, extortion, and brutality. As a Five Points gang member his compatriot and eventual life-long friend was Lucky Luciano. By age 20 in 1919, suspected of two murders and the possible indictment for a third, Capone and his young Irish wife, Mae, and son fled to Chicago. Under the tutelage of John Torrio, his rise in the underworld was spectacular and by the mid-twenties he was the undisputed crime boss of Chicago.

Under surveillance for years by federal agents, Capone was finally indicted in 1931 for income tax evasion. He was found guilty as charged and sentenced to serve 11 years in federal prison. He was released from the notorious Alcatraz penitentiary in November 1939. His health broken and his brain diseased by neurosyphilis, Al Capone died in his Miami Beach mansion in 1947 at the age of 48.

Frank Nitti, a native of Italy, accompanied his immigrant parents to New York City as a young child; little is known of his adolescent years. As a young man he opened a barbershop in Chicago, but soon found fencing stolen jewelry much more lucrative. In the early 1920's he caught the eye of an ascending Al Capone and became the trustworthy confidant of the mobster. Known as "the enforcer," Nitti was widely feared by the underlings in Capone's mob as well as most of Chicago's gangland. It was soon recognized that his orders came directly from the big man himself.

After serving 18 months in prison during the late '20s for income tax evasion, Nitti vowed he would never again be confined in a cage. When Capone was in prison, Nitti assumed control of his empire. In 1943, facing a ten-year conviction for extortion and the threat of a mob "hit," Frank Nitti donned his finest clothes, walked along the Illinois Central railroad tracks and calmly fired a bullet into his brain.

Prohibition in the United States began with the passage of the National Prohibition Act, sponsored by Minnesota Senator Andrew Volstead, in 1919, and lasted until the Act was repealed in 1933. The Prohibition Act, known widely as the Volstead Act, contributed directly to the underworld fortune of Al Capone and indirectly to hundreds of deaths in Chicago alone. It is ironic that Senator Volstead died five days before the death of Al Capone in 1947.

ABOUT THE AUTHOR

E dmund L. Palmer grew up in Ann Arbor, Michigan, where he developed his many interests in, among other things, snakes, vintage cars, baseball, American history and photography.

During World War II, he served in the China-Burma-India Theater of war and was attached to the 14th Army Air Force, Flying Tiger Division, as a military policeman and motorcycle dispatch rider during the Japanese invasion of northern India. He received the Asiatic-Pacific Theater ribbon with three bronze stars.

His interest in American history led to a thirty-year career as a public school teacher. He earned a B.A. from Eastern Michigan University and an M.A. from the University of Michigan.

Mr. Palmer resides in Ann Arbor, Michigan with his wife, Elaine, and their adoring and adorable cocker spaniel, Teddy Bear.